I RAN AWAY
TO EVIL

BOOK 3

I RAN AWAY AWAY TO EVIL

BOOK 3

Mystic Neptune

Podium

Published in 2025 by Podium Publishing
www.podiumentertainment.com

Podium

To Megan Hood, who continues to inspire the Cozy Fantasy

community as an icon of kindness.

And to everyone in Poncho's Cafe who teased me for bursting into tears

while I was sitting there writing the ending.

Thanks. You're lucky you make delicious nerdy themed

tea lattes that sustain me.

The
Empire of Sands
Hollow
Nilhe
Peldeep
Gren's
Keep
D

The Untamed Ice Fields
Depths of Despair
North Sumbria
Thistlecrick
Servalt
Loria
Kith Bog
Sumbria

I RAN AWAY TO EVIL

BOOK 3

PROLOGUE

Madame Potts

The notification tab showed that the second game was almost finished.

[Quest: Survive Season Two of Dungeon Delves and Debutantes]
[Welcome to the World of Valaria, an Open-World Battle Otome RPG for the ages.]
[In Season One, our Heroine Henrietta has worked hard to kill the Dark Overlord, King Monfort, and defeat his minions.]
Error: **In Season One, our Heroine Henrietta has worked hard to win the heart of the Dark Lord King Keith, and his minions.**
[After overcoming her traumatic past with the help of her love interests, she finally picked a partner for Grand Duchess Calisto's Spring Ball . . . but is she ready to take the next step?]
Error: **After overcoming her traumatic past with the help of her newfound family and friends, she chose to go to the Spring Ball with the Dark Lord.**
[Season Two features three new ikemen love interests, new dungeons, access to Servalt and Sumbria, and new crafting materials. But beware the threat of revenge from the Dark Enchanted Forest!]
Error: **But beware the threats of revenge, for a new power rises in corruption and cruelty. And our Heroine will have even more at stake than she bargained for.**

90% Scenarios Completed
96% Map Explored
87% Hidden Treasures Found
91% Characters Found

[Come back to your favorite characters with even more Dungeons, Dragons, and Debutantes!]

Of course, all of the meddling had steered the storylines wildly off path from the traumatic, emotional train wreck that was the Heroine of Justice's original journey.

The fact that the Dark Lord had married the Heroine of Justice, the necromancer was about to marry the paladin, and the commander general of the Dark Horde was currently walking hand in hand with the bard through the gates of the capital city of North Sumbria was proof of that.

Almost everyone who could be shipped had been shipped. And every **Error** was a hard-won victory.

It had taken a lot of work to survive this far . . . but as long as everyone got their much-deserved Happily Ever After, then it would all be worth it.

Sigh.

My companions came through the checkpoint behind me.

"Hey, Gerda, wait up!"

CHAPTER 1

Previously on Dungeon Delves and Debutantes

Gerda

Of all the places I'd visited in Valaria, North Sumbria felt the most like *home*.

Living in a video game set in a mythical blend of eastern and western medieval fantasy meant I'd spent a lot of time searching for the creature comforts of my old world . . . and this was about as close as I was going to get.

Courtesy of Grand Duchess Calisto, North Sumbria had paved roads, magical streetlamps, elevators, and public transportation. Mana-fueled construct carriages worked much the same as cars, and magic did wonders on the suspension.

I heard my name, and I turned to my travel companions.

Rufus was the former commander general of the Dark Enchanted Forest, a canine beastman who looked like a blend of wolf and golden retriever. He was sitting on the wagon beside his fiancée, Minstrel Bronwynn Lyriel. Brownie was a half giantess who had fiery-red-tipped brown hair and dark eyes with a glint of red.

They were both much taller than I.

As a troll, I was sturdy, curvy, and on the taller side of a human, but nowhere near a giantess. My light-green skin and dark-green hair were also uniquely *troll*. I currently had mine in thirteen braids bound back at the nape of my neck. On top of being green, I also had long, sharp lower canines that stuck up and out. Surprisingly, they didn't get in the way much or affect the way I spoke.

The only resemblance to my former human self were my eyes, the same honey brown they'd always been.

I enjoyed the physique of a female bodybuilder, but the thing I loved most about my new appearance was the smattering of white fawnlike freckles on the bridge of my nose.

They were hardcore cottagecore.

"Are you both heading straight for the Coral Palace?" I asked.

Rufus jumped down and offered Donna the horse an enchanted carrot. The mare happily accepted the treat.

To me, he answered, "We are, and you?"

I held up my invitation. It was a pass through the city gate and my ticket to the wedding ceremony of Calisto's daughter, Countess Julia von Slyke, the Paladin of Light, and Necromancer Chloe Watercress—the original villainess of this season.

There was nothing on this godsforsaken world that was going to stop me from seeing those two women get married, since it'd been *my* hard work that had set them up in the first place.

Not that *they* knew that.

"I'm also staying at the palace," I informed them, waving the invite once before shoving it back into my storage space. "But I'm going to visit the market first."

"We could walk around together?" Brownie asked, hopeful. She sat in the driver's seat, pretending to drive the wagon. Her horse chuffed, and the minstrel added, "*After* we settle in Donna first, of course."

"Alright. I'll stay close to the fountain."

Brownie nodded. "We should be back in an hour."

Rufus eyed the wagon. "Do we want to store everything first?"

We were standing in an open courtyard full of other wagons and travelers being let into the city. It was crowded.

Due to the Summer Solstice Festival, shops that would've otherwise been getting ready to close were instead preparing for the night market. The city wouldn't be asleep until long after midnight.

"Good idea." Brownie fixed her lyre harp's shoulder strap then grabbed her fashionable red bag before climbing down to join us.

Donna *shrugged*, and suddenly, all of the ropes and straps and hitches fell loose until the horse was free of her wagon. The joys of a magical world. Brownie waved a hand, and everything disappeared into the bard's storage ring.

"Why do you load the wagon with things if you have a storage ring?" I asked, my curiosity getting the better of me.

Brownie shrugged. "If they're busy stealing the decoy wagon, then I can run away."

"I see." Made sense with her history. After I'd found out the bard would run into three encounters every trip, I'd started making sure *I* was one of them. A bridge troll riddle was much safer than a flock of griffins or a bandit camp . . .

"Alright." Rufus took Brownie's hand and nodded my way. "We will see you later, Miss Gerda."

Brownie waved. "Fair weather."

I finished the saying, "And fine luck."

After they were out of sight, I headed for the nearest inn. I'd need a room; somewhere I could review my new notifications in peace.

I quickly found one off the beaten path. The Morbid Mule wasn't the name of an inn I'd otherwise frequent, but it was cheap and serviceable for a few minutes of quiet.

There were updates to my quest and a few notifications in my log.

I had to open each tab to see their full information, but otherwise, I could scroll through three notifications at a time in the preview window.

[Perk Quest: Previously on Dungeon Delves and Debutantes . . .]

[Passive Perk: **Sense Fate** has activated. Duke Julian von Slyke will lose his locket at the Coral Palace West Fountain tonight . . .]

[Passive Perk: **Sense Fate** has activated. General Visha Hemsworth will be poisoned at the Fardew tavern tomorrow . . .]

I opened my Season Two quest and grinned at all the changes that were happening.

Every *Error* was a victory. Five years spent preparing to subvert the tragedies of the first season. It'd made Season Two harder in some ways because the story had gone so wildly off base, but I'd made it work.

Because listen to me when I say that an orphanage burning down was a simple plot device until you walked past said orphanage every time you visited your favorite bakery in Servalt. And who said the Heroine of Justice had to slaughter the entire Dark Enchanted Forest and then finish off the Dark Lord with a well-timed punch to the face? No one. Not on my watch!

I'd had plenty of time to level up to boss monster status and carefully curate a character build that would let me change the storyline. Every ten levels came with a title, and every title came with one skill selection. For example, at level forty, I'd chosen the Oracle title and the [Foretelling] skill, which allowed me to pick anyone and see where they would be right now in any of the original storylines. Every two levels gave one skill point, and every two skill points gave one perk. With [Foretelling 4], I'd chosen the perks [Sooth] and [Sense Fate].

[Sooth] showed me where key events were going to happen on my mini map, and [Sense Fate] notified me if I could change someone's fate as long as they got close enough to me to enter my area of effect: Level 65 x Perception 43 x Foretelling 4 = 11,180 sq/ft. A perfect size for anyone crossing my troll bridge.

I sucked at math, and so spent an unreasonable amount of time double-checking or guessing where the limits of my area of effect were . . . but I managed.

While we'd been standing around talking about our plans at the gate, one of the main love interests had entered the city and passed us by, activating my passive perks.

It would've been nice to relax and walk around the market before getting straight into it, but an NPC's work was never done.

I summoned the Master Crystal from my storage.

The future wasn't going to tell itself.

CHAPTER 2

Dragging Him Back By One Pointy Ear

Julian

Julian von Slyke took his sweet time riding up to the Coral Palace.

He was accompanied by his five trusted party members, all of whom had invites to the Summer Masquerade Ball.

He wasn't actually *needed* here this early, but his mother had insisted. It would be three more days until his younger sister's wedding, and honestly, he would've held off arriving until the day *of* if he'd thought he could get away with it.

His mother would *never* let him get away with it. Grand Duchess Calisto of North Sumbria was a legend. He shuddered to think of her storming off to the Northern Fortress and dragging him back by one pointy ear—just as she'd done to get him to Julia's debutante at the Spring Ball earlier this year.

His sister had managed to escape her coming of age ceremony until she'd reached twenty-three by gallivanting off to become a famous adventurer and the Paladin of Light. He'd been thinking about not going to the Spring Ball . . . but then, his mother had stormed the Northern Fortress and dragged him back home without a by-your-leave. At least he'd managed to dodge the afternoon tea party.

As her older brother, Julian had escorted Julia and their mother into the ballroom, danced the first dance, and then promptly escaped back to the North.

Where he belonged. Monster surges from the Northern Ice Fields' hidden dungeon could happen at any time, and he was in charge of defending the border to prevent the monsters from escaping into the rest of Valaria.

Creatures spawned in dungeons were born with monster madness, and when left unchecked, they overcrowded the dungeon and spilled out into the real world. If left unchecked too long, a dungeon could grow powerful enough to escape the confines of its pocket dimension and claim the land around it. His goal was to *find* the dungeon and defeat it before the unthinkable happened.

"Your Grace!" his childhood friend, Jeffry, called out. He was the only other half elf besides himself in Julian's regular raiding party.

Usually, if an elf and a human had a child, the system would choose one or the other to pass along to that child, and they would be born an elf *or* a human. But on the rare occasion, like with Julian's own elf father and human mother, a half elf could be born.

Suddenly, the light of the Crystal Cast Network flashed just above the roofline. The crystals were installed in every populated locale across the continent and usually reserved for use by the local high nobility exclusively.

That had all changed five years ago, however, when an unsanctioned voice had echoed across every single Crystal Cast in the known world.

The same voice that spoke today.

Hello, everyone, it's Madame Potts!
I know it's only been a few days since my last Cast, but I
couldn't help myself.
I hope you enjoyed the fireworks in Peldeep last week
because we're about to see them again in North Sumbria!
Hopefully, nothing lights on fire this time.
Visha, darling, don't drink anything except your own
waterskin until after the wedding. I'm sorry I can't say more
but just trust me on this one.
Anyone who wants to swing by the Depths of Despair
Dungeon next week will be pleased to know the boss monster
on level three isn't spawning properly. Half of its abilities
won't come back from cooldown, and it's easy experience
points.
The summer solstice marks the longest day of the year.
Anyone who offers a prayer to the goddess of Light at her
altar will be granted a month-long +1 Fire Resistance buff.
Highly recommend.
Congratulations are in order for Prince Lucial, who is
now engaged to Prince Basil of Peldeep, the third son of
Their Royal Highness Rowen of Peldeep.
Everyone will be happy to note that the molten ash vane
poisoner has been caught. Some bottles are still floating
around, and the Continental Council asks for any and all to

turn in their illegal potions. Thank you.
See you all at the Summer Solstice Celebration,
Madame Potts.

Julian turned with the rest of his party to stare at General Visha Hemsworth, who looked shocked at having been personally addressed by *the* Madame Potts. The elf was usually the color of a redwood, but at this moment, she was pale as a birch tree.

"Visha." Julian didn't think twice and pulled a midgrade antidote from his storage ring, throwing it at her. His general already had one, but better safe than sorry.

Visha caught the potion and stuffed it into the satchel storage bag she used. "Thank you, Your Grace."

"Stay cautious, even of your own waterskin," he warned, "John, send a shadow with her."

Lord Johnathon Thomas nodded and did as instructed. Unlike the other human in their party, John rarely spoke.

"You hear that, General?" Sir Tully Grey teased. "No celebratory wine means none of Colwood's famous gladevine for you."

Visha muttered a curse under her breath and turned on the paladin. "Is that you volunteering to train the knights every afternoon for a month, Sir Tully? I'll adjust the schedule."

"Wait—" The human blanched.

Julian pitied the man. Even in the North, the afternoon summer sun was unbearable. As soon as the solstice passed, it was three months of sweltering heat.

"But isn't Pram a better fit? If we switch, who's going to go out hunting?" Sir Tully pointed at the mage in their party, a pale-blue selkie with a braid of aquamarine hair hanging down to his left ear, the right side of his head clean-shaven.

"I can hunt just fine." Sir Pram smiled, pointy teeth flashing. "Just make sure you have plenty of water on hand to stave off the heatstroke and it won't be too bad."

"Says the *ice mage!*" Tully dragged a hand through his short black hair, ruffling the inch-long, top-heavy frizz.

Jeffry smirked at the crestfallen human. "You did this to yourself."

"I know." Tully resumed his usual good-natured smile. He cupped a hand and leaned toward the half-elf Jeffry, knowing that everyone could hear him even as he whispered, "But it was worth it."

CHAPTER 3

A Troll in Valaria

Gerda

I was three stalls down in the market when Brownie ran up to me, Henrietta on her heels.

"Gerda!" The queen of the Dark Enchanted Forest gave me a quick hug. Henrietta was wearing a soft-pink apron dress over her white underdress. The pink only came down to just below her knees and showed off starhart-skin boots. The starhart were a magical breed of deer whose pelt gave the wearer a speed bonus.

Henrietta, who could run faster than a sports car, really didn't need the boost, but they were very cute.

"It's lovely to see you again, Your Majesty." I smiled down at the human with affection and resisted the urge to ruffle the queen's poofy brown hair, but only because Henrietta had styled it into two braids woven with pink flowers.

"None of that." Henrietta poked my bare arm. I was in a shoulderless purple dress with white straps that dangled around my biceps. Despite my rippling muscles and thirty-one Strength, I could feel the pressure from that one tiny finger.

Henrietta's stats were monstrous.

Granted, with the average person in Valaria being no higher than level fifteen and with less than twenty points in any attribute, I shouldn't be one to talk.

Name:	Gerda Vara Jones
Occupation:	Bridge Troll
Level:	65

Experience Points:	8759/15750		
Hit Points:	777/777		
Mana Points:	1161/1161		
Class:	World Player		
Titles:			
[Troll], [Protector], [World Player], [Bridge Troll], [Oracle], [Adventurer], [Bridge Master]			
Attributes:			
Strength:	31	Intelligence:	27
Dexterity:	28	Perception:	43
Constitution:	20	Charisma:	21
Skills:			
Stubborn:	2	+Troll Magic [Dimension]:	2
Domain:	6	Foretelling:	4
System:	6	Dungeoneering:	2
Mastery:	2		
Perks:			
Mental Resistance, Sense Danger, Force, Stronghold, Appraise, Map, Quest, Troll Riddle, Pocket Dimension, Bridge Barrier, Bridge Repair, Bridge Sense, Dimension Rift, Sense Fate, Sooth, Dungeon Lore, World Bridge.			

"Is it just the two of you?" I asked. An obvious question, since they were alone, but an easy conversation starter.

"Yep." Henrietta nodded vigorously, her brown hair bouncing. "Keith dragged Rufus off to go help Chloe, so I'm free."

Brownie laughed. "If by *free* you mean you grabbed me and ran when Chloe was distracted giving Rufus the schedule, then sure."

"It was a tactical retreat! I'm not even *in* the wedding party—Keith is," Henrietta defended herself. "Besides, if I hadn't grabbed you, Chloe would've kept you locked up in the ballroom practicing your song set until you fell over."

"I'm sure it's not that bad—"

"They're giving away free pastries to everyone in the city on the day of the wedding because she went through over a hundred mini cupcake batches before she found the right cake taste mix." Henrietta's eyes glazed over at the memory. "The buttercream alone . . . Anyway."

Note to self, I thought, *prepare for a day of eating sweets.*

"Well, I'm happy to perform for Chloe all day if it'll help." Brownie shrugged. "In the meantime, let's enjoy the festivities!"

The town square night market surrounded a beautiful water fountain of four mermaids pouring out jugs of water. Merchants lucky enough to secure a spot had built pop-up stalls around the square, while the permanent shops lining the outside of the market were full of magical trinkets made popular by the grand duchess.

The Pixie Prim had their usual small shop in the town square, but today, they'd set up two pavilions outside full of potions, poisons, and magical ingredients.

I was captivated by a shelf of tiny baskets for spices, each with tiny crystals cut into the shape of a type of spice. They had glass potion bottles of every size, with beautiful swirls in the glass or engravings carved into a circle.

They also had hanging baskets, baskets with lids, baskets that held other baskets . . .

The only thing preventing me from going all out was the size of my pocket dimension. I was powerful enough to enlarge my space . . . but did I want to open an entirely new room in my troll house just to buy more baskets?

"Do you need more hens-teeth jelly?" Henrietta asked, peering at the bottle I'd been holding while contemplating my current living situation. "Because we have a crate at home. Keith uses the jelly for inking construct enchantments and he's always running out, panicking, and then ordering so much you'd think he would have enough . . .until he runs out again."

"No. I'm good." I put the glass back on the shelf and turned away. I didn't need another room in my house; I wasn't planning on living there much longer. I also didn't need more items taking up space in my Hero's Spatial Ring treasure storage.

The beautiful spiral mithril ring on my right-hand ring finger was my secret shame.

I *might* have gone overboard when I got my hands on it—and I *might* have harvested, bought, and hoarded every single item I'd come across afterwards until the thousand space storage ring was almost full.

There were *so many* random, useless things in there, like Nova's spirit grass or thistledown or Oakley melon leaves. Not to mention two hundred random spell scrolls, ninety-nine high-level health potions, thirty low-level antidotes, ten high-level antidotes, and an assortment of random specialized antidotes for poisons . . . and the poisons themselves. I even had a bottle of molten ash vane.

Maybe I had a bit of a hoarding problem, but I swear, I was just saving them for when I *really* needed them most!

"Then I think I'll buy it." Henrietta reached up to grab the bottle of hens-teeth jelly, hugging it to her chest. She had a loving smile on her face when she added, "It'll be a nice surprise for when he runs out next time."

The feeling it gave me to see her so happy was indescribable. It made the entire five years of fighting and exploring worth it.

Sure, there had been some bad times, but in a magical world of unicorns and pixies and there were just as many things to love. I knew people in my old world who would pay *anything* to be me.

A troll in Valaria.

Sure beat being a troll on the internet.

"Oh, look what I've found," I said, gently pushing the queen of the Dark Enchanted Forest toward a shelf full of the one thing I loved most about being in this world.

CHAPTER 4

There's Never a Wrong Time to Fall in Love

Julian

"Julian! My son!" Grand Duchess Calisto swept down the palace stairs to greet him.

Julian dismounted and accepted the welcome hug. "It's good to see you, Mother."

One of the attendants, an elf named Bensen, took charge of everyone's horses as Calisto looked them over with an approving nod. "It is good to see all of you made it safely."

His party members gave polite bows, though Tully started with a friendly wave before Visha elbowed him.

Calisto's eyes found Julian's again. "You came at the perfect time. We're about to go over the ceremonial schedule with Their Royal Highness."

"Do I not get to wash up first?" Julian raised an eyebrow.

"[Cleanse]," his mother replied, casting the spell on him to get rid of the dirt from the road. He could still use a proper bath, but it would have to do. She offered her arm. "No escaping."

Julian accepted and escorted his mother inside; the rest of his party followed at a distance. Cowards. "Is Rowen officiating?"

"Yes. Rowen's been marrying people left, right, and center this year, and I think they like it."

"Married by a fox." Julian shook his head. They entered through the main doors into the entrance hall, which shimmered like they were walking underwater as the sun shone on the coral motif of the walls. "They could've chosen someone more serious."

His mother squeezed his arm. "Like who? I'll make a note for when you get married."

Julian stiffened. His mother's well-timed comments always made him stumble, but now that his Dexterity was over twenty, it was easier for him to keep his balance around her. He didn't outright trip, though he needed a moment to figure out the perfect response. "I'll think of that when I find the right lady to marry."

"I have a list," Calisto replied, succinct. "Some you saw at the Spring Ball, and some you will have the opportunity to meet at the Summer Masquerade."

"Mother, I don't think it's the right time—"

"Nonsense." Grand Duchess Calisto squeezed his arm again, reassuringly, even as she cut him off. "There's never a wrong time to fall in love."

Behind them, Tully coughed to hide a laugh. Julian glanced over his shoulder at the paladin.

Visha was glaring at Tully, while Jeffry just shook his head. Pram remained stoic, and John remained silent, the pair ignoring Tully's outburst as they were wont to do.

"If there was ever a wrong time to fall in love," Julian stated, "it would be when I need to leave for the Northern Ice Fields in three days."

"*Four days*," Calisto corrected.

"Three—"

"You are *not* sneaking out of the Masquerade like you did the Spring Ball," his mother stated, her voice firm. She led the pair of them into her newest contraption—an elevator—and left his party members behind. They would have leave to settle in, while he was going to be dragged around for the rest of the day.

He resisted a sigh even as his mother said, "You've already missed the first few days of the celebration. You *will* stay until the closing ceremonies the morning after the ball, do I make myself clear?"

He hesitated, unconsciously pressing the locket he kept under his shirt. Inside was a picture of his family and a broken piece of staff that was all he had left from his father. He was itching to get back to the North . . . but it was true he hadn't been there for his family as much as he should.

"Alright." He even managed a polite nod. This was where the passive ability of his [Natural Poise] perk came in handy.

> [**Natural Poise**, passive effects: perfect posture and an air of confidence. Effects can be identified by anyone with an equal or higher Charisma. When activated, +1 Charisma for minutes equal to Charisma.]

The elevator was semitransparent, and the pair looked out over the city and the countryside as they flew higher and higher. The elevator took them to the top of one of the outer towers. It wasn't the tallest, but it let them gaze out over

North Sumbria as far as the eye could see. Julian loved the pockets of forests and winding roads over rolling hills.

"I'm glad you've seen the error of your ways." His mother smiled and pulled a piece of paper out of thin air. "Now, here's a list of marriage candidates with their family history and features. Memorize it."

It was so long that it trailed down to Julian's knees. He took it with trepidation and started rolling it back up, but his mother wasn't done, pulling out a second parchment scroll—this one longer than the last. "And *here's* a list of duties you're required to perform while you're here."

"But—"

"There is a family dinner after the meeting tonight. Tomorrow, you will be judging the finalists of the fighting tourney and announcing the winner. The day after morrow will be the wedding, and don't forget the afternoon tea with all of the eligibles before the Summer Masquerade, and then the final day's closing ceremonies."

Julian felt his heart sink with each list his mother handed him.

He tried to scan them all with his [Quick Read] perk before the elevator deposited them on the top floor, but there was *so* much more to do than the few things she'd chosen to actually mention. He gave up and put everything in his storage ring so he could greet the five people sitting around a table waiting for them in the meeting hall.

"Good, you're here. We were just going over the proceedings." Their Royal Highness Rowen of Peldeep nodded, greeting them from a seat at the other side of the round table. The shifter had taken the appearance of a stately green-skinned elf gentleman wearing an arachne-silk black tunic and trousers. King Keith and Commander General Rufus Triever of the Dark Enchanted Forest of Nilheim sat to the left of Rowen. To the right sat his sister, Countess Julia von Slyke, and her intended, Necromancer Chloe Watercress.

His sister smiled at him warmly, and he tried to return it. He hadn't been there for her as much as he would have liked, and now Julia was all grown up and starting a family of her own.

All of the letters they'd exchanged over the last twenty years far outnumbered the few times they'd sat down at the same table.

He took a seat beside his mother as Their Royal Highness continued. "The first to enter will be the commander general—Ah, my apologies, are you going by just Rufus now?"

Julian hadn't heard that Rufus had been deposed of his title, and made a note to catch up on current affairs before the Masquerade.

"As you say, Your Highness." Rufus brought his hands together on the table and leaned forward. "I'm using my class title Protector for now."

"Good, good," the fox approved. "We will have you escort Gladiator Hana Lanora from Julia's adventuring party, and King Keith will follow next escorting Striker Wendy Lanora—"

"Shouldn't Keith enter first?" Julian asked. "As a *king*?"

Rowen grinned. "They're *Chloe*'s best men, so I assume the slight is on purpose?"

"Keep it the way it is," Chloe ordered, looking smug.

"I told you that you should've made her your best man," Rufus whispered to the Dark Lord, who merely crossed his arms and accepted his fate.

Julian sat and listened while Rowen laid out the wedding ceremony, the reception, and the proceedings leading up to the event. He only had a small part to play in each which came down to "stand here," "escort Julia there," and "exit over there."

It took two hours.

CHAPTER 5

My Ex-Husband

Gerda

Raspelder berry. Meadowmint. Chamomile. Dewdrop pettle. Nettle. Peldeep Breakfast Blend.

So many varieties of tea!

I opened a jar of the Peldeep Breakfast Blend and inhaled. It was a mix of tannins with a hint of malt. The leaves were dried and crushed, unlike the intact full petals of the tisanes.

"May I help you, miss?" A pixie with bright-blue skin and violently sunflower-yellow hair flew up to the ledge of the tea shelf I was examining. She was wearing pants and a floral shirt . . . as in, a shirt made out of actual flower petals.

"Yes," I said, pointing at the jars and ordering a medium-sized bag for each of my favorite teas.

Pixie Prim tea was a staple of my daily life.

"Right away, miss!" the pixie replied, taking several trips to fulfill my order.

"Maybe I should grab some too . . ." Bronwynn searched the jars. "But I'm not sure which tea Rufus would like. He prefers wine."

"I have a fine selection of reds in the back," the pixie offered, having flown back to grab the bag of chamomile.

Bronwynn followed the pixie to the main desk, where another pixie—this one with bright-yellow skin and pink hair—showed the half giantess their alcohol selection.

"Is there anything you're looking for at the market?" I asked Henrietta, who was standing beside me, eyeing the tea.

"Actually"—the queen shot me a conspiratorial look—"I'm thinking about picking up a gift for Brownie's engagement."

I raised an eyebrow.

"We barely got to talk about her plans back in the Hollow." Henrietta crossed her arms and pouted. "And she doesn't seem that . . . I don't know, serious about it?"

"Do they have to be in a rush?"

Henrietta sighed. "No, and I know my own wedding was quick—"

"You fell pretty fast for tall, dark-haired, and evil," I teased.

My queen blushed but smiled.

It'd taken a year of prep work to prevent the massacre that would've been Henrietta romping around the Dark Enchanted Forest.

First, I'd made dueling between nobles a common occurrence.

As usual, when enacting change, I'd started in North Sumbria and worked my way out from there. Anything that was popular in North Sumbria quickly caught on elsewhere, so if I got everyone to think that fighting to the death was gauche, then I'd potentially prevent the full-on bloodbath that would be Henrietta arriving at the Black Fortress.

Even I couldn't have anticipated there would be *no* bloodshed and that the guards would just politely let the girl enter to duel their king. That had been a miracle on its own, and I wished I'd been there to see how she'd accomplished it.

The second thing I'd done was organize a straight path to the castle for Henrietta. I'd kindly asked any and all magical creatures who *could* be mistaken for monsters to leave the area. Anyone who lived within sight of the Great Road heading toward Drendil had had to be convinced to vacate.

I'd only had to bonk a few dire wolves on the nose before they'd learned they should keep to the hills farther from the path. They'd still kept close to Lake Loria and would come down to drink from her waters, but otherwise, they'd known to stay clear.

I'd left the unicorns. The mushfolk would've been easy experience points for the princess, so I'd parted with enough gold to find them a nice birch meadow near the border to Servalt. I'd been worried about the phoenix birds who lived in the woods nearby, but they'd just laid eggs and weren't going to be easily moved.

After watching them closely for a month, I'd ended up saving the nest from an earth wyrm attack, and the phoenix couple had gifted me two tail feathers before moving their nest deeper into the woods.

And then, I'd made sure I was Henrietta's first *encounter*, as Bronwynn would put it.

Speaking of the bard, she was walking back over with her chosen bottle.

"What about you?" Henrietta asked, looking up at me.

"What *about* me?" I asked, confused at the turn in the conversation.

My queen's smile took on a predatory gleam as she asked, "You went to the Spring Ball. Are you sure you didn't see *anyone* who pulled at your heartstrings?"

"Wait." Bronwynn returned at the worst time. "Do you like someone, Gerda?"

I managed a tight smile. "No. I don't."

Honestly, I'd played through every route in Season One: The laid-back adventurer Trevor Malory, leader of the Lancers; the obnoxious Sir Phineas, the most powerful knight her age and most likely to become knight commander after Havork; Duke Wyldon of Servalt, the glasses-wearing prime minister's son who came to negotiate a treaty after Henrietta killed the Dark Lord; and Knight Commander Bastian of Peldeep, an ambassador for King Basil of Peldeep, who came to discuss the same.

After all of the routes had been finished, I'd even unlocked the two bonus routes.

I'd rushed through the first, a grueling story with the irredeemable Master Thomas, and then I'd played through the second bonus route six times.

I knew Julian von Slyke's storyline like the back of my hand, and he was the love interest I stanned the hardest . . . which was why I'd deliberately steered clear of the duke of the North all these years.

I couldn't trust myself in his presence. That half elf needed a hug.

"I'm sorry." Henrietta patted my arm. "I know you had a bad experience before. If you wanted to, I bet we could get you a session with Rufus. He's *brilliant.*"

"I don't—" I started, then paused. "Gerda the Bridge Troll" had had an awful ex-husband, and my own ex from *the before* wasn't much to write home about either.

Maybe *I* needed a hug.

"He really is the best," Bronwynn agreed, talking about her fiancé. She stored the wine in her storage ring. "I'm sure we could work something out."

"I'm fine," I insisted. "Now, enough about my tragic backstory—let's go enjoy the festival."

There wasn't anyone waiting for me back in my old world, and Dale—Gerda's troll ex-husband—had only ever gotten the one chance to hurt me.

On the day I'd first arrived . . .

Five Years Ago

I didn't see the truck that hit me, but I *felt* it.

While I lay there, listening to the white noise and screaming, it wasn't my life that flashed before my eyes—it was my TBR. My to-be-read, unfinished books and games and graphic novels and all of the stories I'd never get to finish. Like my current favorite: *Dungeon Delves and Debutantes*, an *otome* romance video game that I'd adored to excess and played through every route. And I'd finally bought the sequel. It lay beside me, the box broken open and the disc shattered on the pavement.

A wave of nausea struck, and I closed my eyes against the pain. I never opened my human eyes again.

It was strange, becoming Gerda. The white noise continued for some time as our memories met and melded. A long dream that felt so very, very real.

Her childhood in the Baldorin Mountains. My summers at the family lake house. Her childhood friend's cruel tricks which lead to her gaining the Protector class at age ten. My parents' divorce in middle school. Her unfortunate marriage to that same childhood friend. Me breaking up with my fiancé in college because of my future mother-in-law's constant and never-ending abuse. Gerda being forced to hold off monster attacks by herself with her abilities, all while her husband took the credit.

The long, hard days which felt suffocating.

And then, I was hit by cold water. The first thing I noticed when I opened my eyes was the flashing box at the corner of my vision.

[You have been **Revived**.]
[Warning! Your Health has dropped below 30%.
Rest recommended.]

I dragged my attention away from the notifications tab. There were more, but I had other things I needed to do.

I rolled over onto my back and heaved a deep, uneven breath.

"Get up," an angry voice snarled. "I didn't hit you that hard."

He was wrong, of course. He'd hit Gerda—us—me? He'd hit *me* hard enough to kill. These thoughts could be sorted later; for now, it was time to show our husband a lesson he was *never* going to forget.

Sorry, *ex-husband*.

CHAPTER 6

The Audacity

Julian

When Julian finally escaped, it was after dark.

He found his way to his old rooms, the ones he'd used as the heir. Everything inside still looked the same as during his childhood. While he *could* have taken over the main suite, he'd insisted that his mother keep it.

There were too many memories of his father in that place.

He felt stifled and went to open the door to the veranda off of the receiving room. His room in the main tower faced the city. The grand duke's official rooms were one floor higher and to the left.

Julian always felt restless in the palace. He might not be the level ninety-one Arcane Sorcerer his father had been, but Julian still had a decade to catch up to where Grand Duke Lysander von Slyke had been when his father fought Sumbria in the civil war.

Name:	Julian von Slyke
Occupation:	Duke
Age:	29
Level:	63
Experience Points:	6669/15250
Hit Points:	1274/1274
Mana Points:	500/500

Class:	Monster Slayer		
Titles:			
[Half Elf], [Duke], [Guardian], [Adventurer], [Commander], [Monster Hunter], [Border Master]			
Attributes:			
Strength:	49	**Intelligence:**	20
Dexterity:	22	**Perception:**	25
Constitution:	26	**Charisma:**	20
Skills:			
Stoic:	2	**Dungeoneering:**	2
Bureaucracy:	2	**Leadership:**	4
Defense:	4	**Tracking:**	4
+Shield Arts [Divine]	2		
Perks:			
Natural Poise, Quick Read, Barrier, Guard, Monster Lore, Battle Call, Personnel, Scan, Light Foot, Multi-Target Shield, Hold the Line, Crushing Blow, Silent Guard, Divine Heal, Charge.			

Unlike his father, who specialized in offense, Julian had walked the path of the shield.

Music drifted up from below. The Summer Solstice Festival was in full swing, and people were singing and dancing in the town square. The night market was lit with magical floating lights, and the smell of street food carried on the breeze.

He pulled out his locket from under his shirt and opened it, revealing a portrait of his family on the right side. Julia was smiling a gap-toothed grin, sitting on their mother's lap. Julian was standing beside his mother, looking awkward and stiff. His father, Grand Duke Lysander, stood behind with one hand on Grand Duchess Calisto's shoulder and the other on Julian's.

The other side of the locket held a shard of crystal behind a pane of glass.

"I'm sorry it's taking so long," he told his father, rubbing his thumb over the picture. Then he closed the locket and pressed it against his forehead for a moment before dropping it back to hang against his clothes.

Julian leaned on the railings, conscious of the magical barrier surrounding the tower. It prevented anyone who wasn't authorized from coming or going. When Julian was young, it would catch him from falling off the balcony.

Now that he was older, he could pass through it if he wished . . . but it would alert his mother. Granted, after Madame Potts' threatening casts, the grand duchess had set up an overwhelming amount of detection spells around the entire palace.

It was unlikely that he'd be able to leave without him knowing.

Ah, well, this was supposed to be a *party*. What was a little more excitement? He leapt.

[You have attempted to use the Perk: **Light Foot**. You have succeeded. Spend 3 mana per second to control your footwork. Every step is sure and soft. You can travel up to 63ft in a single leap. Anyone with a Perception equal to or higher than your Dexterity 22 will be able to hear you.]

Fireworks rose into the sky and exploded into colorful fire, illuminating his descent. There was a small courtyard below with a simple fountain surrounded by benches. The unassuming stone decorations were offset by the beautiful fae glade vines in full bloom under the moonlight. The large flowers were green with a pinkish hue in the center.

Julian landed gently on the stone bench then jumped to the outer wall in a single bound.

A sentry, startled from watching the fireworks, whipped around to glare at whomever had had the audacity to scale the palace wall. He stopped short when he saw the serene nod of the duke.

"As you were," Julian ordered before hopping down to the street.

It was a quick walk to the market.

A half giantess was up on a bench with her lyre harp out, playing a song that echoed out over the town square. Everyone was singing along to "Tammy's Tavern," and a few were even dancing.

Julian leaned against a lamppost to watch, breathing in the refreshing cool night air. The lanterns didn't put out as much light as the magic lights that floated around to brighten up the festivities, but they were more mana efficient and kept the city lit all year round for the same cost as the magic lights used for just this week.

He wasn't there long before he noticed it. Years of fighting monsters and dungeon delving had honed his senses—someone was watching him. A shiver crawled down his spine.

He searched the crowd until he found her, standing just a ways past the bard.

A troll.

She was dressed in a clinging purple corset dress. Her long dark-green hair fell over her shoulders in intricate braids, and flowers had been tucked into the strands. Even at this distance, he could see the gleam in her clear light-brown eyes reflecting the magical lights dancing overhead.

Her gaze bore into him.

There was something in those eyes that made him catch his breath. An understanding? A recognition. It was soft like pity but cut with intimacy.

Then the troll frowned and glanced behind him. Julian turned, but there wasn't anything to see.

When he looked back, she was gone.

CHAPTER 7

Pure Fan Service

Gerda

I shouldn't have done that.

Tonight had been going so well. I'd bought flowers for my hair, and Henrietta had enjoyed trying all of the street food—don't ask me how she ate so much for someone so tiny—and Minstrel Brownie had taken to breaking out into song every time there was a pause in the scheduled performance.

The original band hired for the town square, The Hart and Hare, took a thirty-minute break every two hours. Now was one of those breaks, and Brownie was having a blast entertaining the crowd.

I had to admit, she was *amazing*. Her music was upbeat and catchy, and she had a beautiful singing voice.

Yes, everything had been going well . . . until I spotted *him*.

Duke Julian of North Sumbria. The half elf took after his human mother, dark skinned and sharp featured. His purple hair was from his elven father's side, and he wore it long and bound in locks tied at the back of his head.

He was leaning against a magical lantern post, listening to the music.

I couldn't help staring at him; he was just that strikingly attractive. Something about the way he always looked stern—it made me want to tease him. While playing through his route, he'd only ever smiled at the end. And only if I'd made all of the right choices along the way.

Making him smile had been worth all of the effort I'd put in.

Without Henrietta going down the hidden route, there'd been no reason for Julian to leave his fortress. And I'd missed him at the Spring Ball while trying to save everyone.

Tonight, his outfit was pure fan service. He was wearing black leather traveling clothes, knee-high boots, and a belt without a pouch or dagger. He had a warrior's build, though I had to admit I was a little more toned than he was.

His silver eyes suddenly met mine from across the square.

I froze.

And I might have panicked. But only for a second. Glancing over his shoulder, I did my best to pretend that I was really looking at someone *behind* him. When Julian's eyes followed mine, I used the opportunity to step out of sight, ducking behind the nearest stall.

If he was at the market . . . The premonition from earlier flashed through my mind. He must have dropped his locket on his way out of the palace.

I hesitated for only a second. Brownie was still very much distracted with her performance, and Henrietta was nearby arm wrestling someone for a free floofpoof roast skewer. I'd had my own taste of the lightly salted roasted bird earlier. It tasted a lot like chicken . . . but then again, a lot of the monsters tasted like chicken.

"Henrietta?" I waited until the queen slammed her challenger's arm down and claimed her floofpoof prize before getting her attention.

"Gerda!" She smiled at me and pointed at the lineup of five burly individuals all ready for a turn. "Would you like me to win you a snack?"

I shook my head even as the next contestant, an ogre twice the size of Henrietta, took the seat and offered his hand. "Not if I crush you first, girlie!"

"Bring it!" Henrietta laughed then slammed the ogre's hand into the table so hard the table creaked.

"I am going to turn in for the evening," I let her know. "But I'll see you tomorrow."

"Have a good night," Henrietta replied. Then she turned back to the ogre, who was shaking out his sore hand. The Dark Lady patted her opponent on the arm reassuringly. "That was great! I'll have the soy-glaze flying pork skewer, please."

The vendor rushed to fulfill the order even as the ogre accepted defeat and paid for the food.

I left the busy town square and headed up the main road to the palace. There was no need to backtrack and follow the duke from where he'd come—[Sense Fate] had already told me where the locket had fallen.

This would have been an ideal game scenario for the Heroine of Justice and Duke Julian to come together. Instead, I was going to pick up the locket and turn it over to the palace staff.

Her Royal Viciousness, Queen Henrietta had already found her Happily Ever After. There was no heroine left to go and solve all of the quests that continued to pop up, so it was up to me to ensure things didn't go too far off the rails.

That had been my original purpose for becoming Madame Potts. If Henrietta was too busy to complete all of the important scenarios and I was tied down to my bridges, then I could just let everyone know what was going to happen, and they could solve the problems on their own. Every nation in Valaria had their own high-level elite to throw at trouble.

I arrived at the palace's outer gate and flashed my invitation. It was something I'd won from Julia months back. The woman had been on a warpath to make it to the Black Fortress as fast as possible, so I'd traded passage—and even offered her a shortcut with my bridge teleport skills—for special guest invitations to each of the major events in North Sumbria this year.

Julia was a good sort, and within the week she'd sent me passes for the Spring Ball, the Summer Masquerade, the Fall Ball, and the Winter Feast.

A palace guard checked my invitation for forgery then checked in with housekeeping to pick out a room for my stay. To make things easier, I asked for one in the western wing.

Once through, I took the nice cobblestone walkway that followed alongside the main road, heading straight for a courtyard on the western side and checking my perk to make sure I was going in the right direction.

[Passive Perk: **Sense Fate** has activated. Duke Julian von Slyke will lose his locket at the Coral Palace West Fountain tonight.]
[You have crossed paths with a fate that can be changed. Area of effect radius: Level 65 x Perception 43 x Foretelling 4 = 11,180 sq/ ft. Fate herself will guide you.]
["There falls a sacred treasure, a clue toward the crowned. Give back the lost before the mask, and see the scepter found."]

As far as Fate's riddles went, this one was surprisingly easy. Though I worried that she called it a sacred treasure . . . I didn't want to steal Julian's locket to complete my Season Two treasures quest. I'd found all of the treasures from Season One because I'd already known where they were hidden. That wasn't the case with Season Two.

So far, I'd managed to do quite well for myself, all told.

[Quest: Season One Treasures Found 10/10 Complete]

The pride of a gamer; I'd found *every* treasure from Season One:
The Ancient Gamblers Amulet, which let me convert my EXP costs to gold.
The Master Cast Crystal, which connected to all Cast Crystals.
The Coldiron Skillet, which raised the chance of success on all culinary skills.
The Badgerclaw Best Blade, which was a poison sword permanently coated in dragonsbane.

The Arcane Catspaw Gloves, which identified a target's highest-value item and stole it.

The Trickster's Scarf that let the wearer change their appearance to foxfolk, lizardkin, human, elf, dwarf, troll, ogre, selkie, or preela.

The Hero's Spatial Ring, which kept items frozen in time and had a thousand-item max capacity, with each space allowing up to ninety-nine of that item. It was currently at 899/1000 spaces used.

The Legendary Sunlight Mallet, that granted a seventy-five percent chance to repair *any item* up to Legendary grade, three times daily.

And lastly, the Veralyn's Enchanted Restraint Manacles, which prevented access to all nonpassive titles, skills, perks, bonded and equipped items, and it capped the wearer's attributes at fifteen.

But I'd played through Season One enough times that I could find the hidden treasures with my eyes closed. Season Two was a test to my actual abilities, especially when I couldn't be sure an item was actually a "treasure" until I held it.

[Quest: Season Two Treasures Found 7/10

Nova's Celestial Pendant: An opal pendant that glows near celestials and darkens near demons. +5 Charisma with Divine.

King Kraken's Heart: A ruby pendant that allows you to breathe underwater. +5 Charisma with sea creatures.

Valarian Royal Mantle: +3 to Charisma when equipped. 5/6 set pieces found.

Valarian Royal Breastplate: +3 to Strength when equipped. 5/6 set pieces found.

Valarian Royal Shield: +3 to Constitution when equipped. 5/6 set pieces found.

Valarian Royal Crown: +3 to Perception when equipped. 5/6 set pieces found.

Valarian Royal Sword: +3 to Dexterity when equipped. 5/6 set pieces found.]

I was *one item* away from finding all six pieces in the Valarian Royal Set . . . and if Fate's riddle was any hint, the Valarian Royal Scepter was linked with Julian and his locket.

Even without my [Map] perk, I knew how to find the Coral Palace west fountain. I'd combed over the entire place while playing through Julian's route and knew it well. Which was good, because I felt overanxious. Treasure hunting in public put me on edge, and I felt like Julian was right behind me, *watching me* look for his treasure.

I pushed away the thought.

It took a *little* bit of searching, but I found the pendant in the grass beside a bench.

Moonlight glinted off the broken loop of white gold that had previously kept it secure on its chain. Pulling out my Legendary Sunlight Mallet, I lightly tapped it against the locket.

[You have attempted to use the **Legendary Sunlight Mallet** to repair **Duke Julian's Cherished Locket** - Epic grade. You are unskilled. 75% chance of success. You have failed.]

I sighed as a piece of locket chipped off. That was fine; I still had two more attempts today. Worst case, I could try again when the mallet ability reset at midnight.

The mallet hit a second time as an angry voice called out behind me, "Stop!"

[You have attempted to use the **Legendary Sunlight Mallet** to repair **Duke Julian's Cherished Locket** - Epic grade. You are unskilled. 75% chance of success. You have succeeded.]

CHAPTER 8

She Had Very Cute Freckles

Julian

Julian followed the troll to the courtyard below his window.

At first, he'd lost her in the town square. She'd disappeared so suddenly that it'd startled him into searching for her . . . but no matter where he'd looked, he couldn't find the troll.

She'd well and truly vanished.

He didn't know why he'd cared; he *shouldn't* have cared. But she had left his hair on end and his senses reeling. It wasn't bloodlust or killing intent. She didn't *feel* like an assassin . . . though she could very well be one.

After a cursory look around the market, he'd forced himself to stop. The festival had suddenly lost its appeal, and he'd turned homeward, disappointed.

That was when he'd spotted the lone green figure walking out of the palace guardhouse. And despite everything *he'd just told himself* . . .

Julian had followed her.

He'd taken up watch on the palace wall as she'd made her way to just below his window—all right, six floors neath his window—and crouched to pick up something beside the bench.

It was a locket.

His locket.

His hands reached up to press against the absent weight on his chest as he activated [Light Foot] and hurried toward the troll. He was midair when she summoned a tiny, unassuming hammer.

And hit his locket.

Anger boiled in his heart as a piece of the latch broke off, panic lacing his voice as he landed behind her and shouted, "Stop!"

But it was too late; the troll hit his pendant a second time.

"*What do you think you're doing?*" There was a dark pit in his chest as he desperately lashed out, grabbing her wrist. Wordlessly, the troll stored her hammer and offered him the pendant in her free hand.

It shone like new.

Even the years of wear and tear were gone, and there was a newfound luster to the gold casing and loop. He hesitantly released her wrist.

"Take it," she said, dropping the pendant into Julian's hand and taking a step back.

"How . . ."

"Good night," she stated firmly. And as if that was the end of the conversation, she turned on her heel to leave. Julian couldn't let her escape; he followed after her.

"How did you know it was here?"

She ignored him and headed for the nearby palace steps.

"*How did you know it was here?*" he repeated, moving ahead to block her path halfway up the stairs.

She stopped, but didn't look him in the eye. Drawing in a deep breath, she pointed at the pendant in Julian's hand and asked, "What's in the locket?"

He wasn't expecting her to ignore his question for one of her own. "I'll answer yours if you'll answer mine?"

She finally looked up.

Honey brown eyes met his, and it was no surprise they were the first thing he'd noticed across a crowd of people. They were just as striking and unnerving as he remembered, and he almost flinched under their intense scrutiny. His gaze fell to the freckles that bridged her green nose.

She had very cute freckles.

"I found it and was going to fix it and hand it over to the servants," she said slowly.

"You just found it," Julian stated. For some reason, he didn't believe a word.

"Yes."

"In an out-of-the-way corner of the castle, hidden in the grass."

"I saw it on my way inside." She pointed up at the spiraling coral tower above them. "I'm staying in the west wing."

The door at the top of the stairs opened into the corridor that connected the main building to the west wing. Each of the towers of the Coral Palace was connected to each other by a corridor on the ground floor and by ornate sky bridges high overhead.

He frowned. Julian didn't believe in coincidence; Lady Luck was not his patron.

"My family," he answered.

She looked confused, her brows arching slightly. "What?"

Julian pressed the latch, and the locket opened, revealing the portrait of his family on one side. "It's a picture of my family."

The troll stared, but she wasn't looking at the portrait. Her eyes caught the gleam of the tiny crystal shard locked behind a panel of glass. "Ah, that makes sense," she mumbled, and *then* looked at the portrait. She smiled. "You were so young."

This entire conversation was strange. Julian snapped the pendant shut. The troll—No, he should stop calling her that. "What is your name?"

"Gerda Jones, Your Grace, but you can call me Gerda." She crossed her arms.

The name sounded familiar, but he couldn't place it.

"Gerda." He said it softly, trying to remember where he'd heard it before—From his "Elites of the Dark Forest" papers. There'd been a recent addition. "The Bridge Troll?"

She shot him a smile, flashing white teeth. The lower canines were the only teeth longer than the rest, impressively so. "The very same. Now, it's late, and we have a big day ahead of us tomorrow, so . . . if you'll excuse me?"

He hesitated, but he knew; wanting to talk to her wasn't reason enough to trap her here any longer.

Julian stepped aside, and Gerda marched up the rest of the stairs with purpose. The pendant weighed heavy in his hand, and he rubbed a thumb over its smooth casing. She'd reached the door when he added, "Good night, Miss Gerda . . . And thank you."

"You're welcome," she replied, not looking back. Then she was gone.

Julian stood on the stairs for a long time. He felt like he'd made a mistake somehow, but he didn't know what, replaying their conversation over and over in his head. Eventually, he unlatched his necklace and slid it through the repaired golden ring. He had no idea how it'd broken. If he hadn't watched Gerda pick it up, he would've thought the only way it could've left his person was if it'd been stolen by some master thief.

The item was epic grade. It didn't just *break*.

Perhaps it *was* Luck.

But why?

He put it on and headed into bed, the troll still on his mind.

CHAPTER 9

Why Did He Have to Be So Pretty?

Gerda

The second the door closed behind me, I *ran*.

It was a short distance to the west wing elevator, but I ignored it, choosing the stairs instead. I didn't *want* to be trapped in an elevator right now—not while adrenaline was still coursing through me. I took the stairs two at a time, and by the time I reached the sixth floor, my heart had settled enough that I could focus on anything *other* than escaping the duke of the North.

Despite my fake calm, I'd been in a constant state of panic from the moment I'd heard his voice.

It had been a wonder I'd been able to say anything to him at all with the myriad of emotions that had accompanied his presence, from excitement to nervousness to fear—not at the anger or accusation that had flashed in his silver eyes. No. I was afraid because I'd *really* liked the Julian I'd met while playing Henrietta. But I wasn't Henrietta, and this wasn't a game.

The sixth floor of the tower held three guest rooms. I went inside mine, kicked off my shoes, and promptly fell on the bed, screaming into my pillow.

"Why does he have to be so pretty?" I mumbled. His gaze was so fierce that it had sent shivers down my spine. His straight eyebrows came together in a way that made it look like he was hard to please and constantly unamused, but there were laugh lines around his full lips.

The picture of him as a young boy had been so cute I'd almost melted.

Alright, time to pull myself together and figure out a plan.

The sixth piece of my treasure quest was in the locket; likely the shard of crystal. I didn't think I wanted to complete the set if it meant stealing the locket.

Most of the treasures I'd found up until this point had been in secret vaults or hidden dungeon rooms. I'd picked up the Royal Valarian Mantle in the rubble of the Annual Spellscript Collegium in Servalt last winter. Other exceptions were the King Kraken's Heart, which I'd stolen from an elf, and the Master Cast Crystal, which had come from a *long* fetch quest.

It had all started with an ogre named Morga, who lived in the Dark Enchanted Forest. She had a habit of eating people who annoyed her, but her favorite food was fruit. I'd just needed to get past the dire wolves and unicorns to pick a Moondew apple and bring it to her, and then she'd granted me leave to take one item out of her treasure chest.

Of course, the treasures in the chest were just things she'd collected over the years from all of her victims. Instead of seeing the items as a pop-up list to choose from like in the game, I'd actually gotten to rifle through the whole pile. There'd been the knife I was looking for, but also a nice pair of white spider-silk knee-high socks.

I'd paid her for the socks.

After that, I'd brought the knife to an old widow who lived in Servalt and let her know about her husband's sorry fate. She'd thanked me and offered me a tattered old map as a reward. The map had led to a hidden cave in the mountains behind Thistlecrick, deep in the Dark Enchanted Forest.

Even if I *had* played the video game before, I *never* would have found my way without the map. It had taken three hours to trek up the mountain and even longer to find the cave. I'd also needed the enchantment on the map to magically open the barrier around the entrance.

Inside, I'd found a letter from the Archwizard Jeffrey, creator of the Crystal-Cast Crystals, congratulating his successor on figuring out the map. The cave had held the Master Crystal and the theoretical notes on the Crystal-Cast system.

I still had the papers in my storage ring and intended to pass them along to Grand Duchess Calisto when I had the opportunity. She was the only person skilled enough to use the knowledge effectively.

I rolled onto my back and sighed, my mind wandering once again to Calisto's son.

And his locket.

And the treasure *inside* his locket.

There was an obvious route in the game. I bet that if Henrietta raised Julian's favorability to a certain level, he'd just *give* her the locket as a token of his love.

But I wasn't Henrietta; I was Gerda. The Bridge Troll.

Did I even *need* to complete the second season scenario and find all of the set pieces?

Henrietta had probably needed them to fight Necromancer Chloe and the army of undead from the Dark Enchanted Forest . . . but I didn't need to fight Chloe. My goal was to level up [World Bridge] until it was powerful enough to maybe send me home.

Simple and easy.

> [Perk: **World Bridge**. Establish a permanent link to any bridge you
> cross, even those not under your control. You may travel to that
> bridge as if it were under your control. All previous **+Troll Magic
> [Dimension]** bridges under your control are included in **World
> Bridge.**
> Bonus Abilities Available:
> 1: If you control all bridges in a Domain, gain double experience
> for bridges in that Domain. Current Domains Unlocked: Dark
> Enchanted Forest.
> 2: If you control a bridge in all Domains, mana cost to travel
> between Domains is halved. Current Domains Unlocked: Dark
> Enchanted Forest, Drendil, Peldeep, Servalt, North Sumbria,
> Sumbria.
> 3: If you control the furthest bridges at the four corners of Valaria,
> unlock the ability to travel between any bridge you have ever
> crossed, even before obtaining **World Bridge**. This power can pass
> through the Void into alternate and subspaces for additional mana
> cost. Current Bridges: South: Faren's Arch in Sumbria; West: Daf-
> folyn Bridge in Peldeep; East: Sea-to-Sky Bridge in Servalt.
> 4: If you control all bridges in Valaria, unlock Hidden Domain:
> Valarian Royal Palace. **World Bridge** Perk upgrade: Empress of All
> Bridges. Unlock Title: Empress of Valaria.]

[World Bridge] had different abilities I could unlock, and one would let
me travel to *any* bridge I'd ever crossed. And since I was Gerda, and Gerda was
me . . . I was hoping that meant I could go to a bridge from *the before*.

I only had one bridge left to find, but it was going to be the hardest one yet.
The Northern Ice Fields were a treacherous frozen land crawling with high-level
monsters, storms, and a dangerous mountain ridge between here and the area I
needed to reach.

Would I even make it there without the completed set?

A plus-three boost was great and all, but when the set was completed, each of
my abilities would get a plus-five bonus. Times six items, that was a plus-thirty
buff to my stats . . . and since leveling up gave me two points to attributes per
level, the set was the equivalent to going up *fifteen levels*.

That was hard to pass up . . .

But Duke Julian wasn't a bunch of pixels on a screen reading predetermined
lines . . . Even if he did walk into encounters, he was still a *person*.

And that locket *meant* something to him.

Duke Julian's backstory had played a huge role in his hidden route during Season One. He'd lost his father at such a young age and felt helpless. All this time, he'd thrown himself into guarding North Sumbria . . . but he was isolating himself, away from the people he cared about the most, grieving alone.

He loved his family, but he didn't feel worthy of their love until he could stand in his father's place. And he didn't feel like he could love anyone else for fear of losing them.

Stupid Sumbria, if only I'd been reincarnated into the story twenty years ago, then maybe I could've done more to help everyone.

Instead, I was here.

And still undecided about everything.

CHAPTER 10

Preferably Unalive

Julian

Breakfast was his mother reminding him, again, about his tasks for the day.

". . . there are three categories of finalists. There's the junior division, with Rocco the fire mage against Sandy Moor the summoner. Then, in the newcomer tourney, we have Candace Stannard, the giantess, against Cimor the Monk. A bad matchup, but that just means if Cimor wins, anyone who bet on her is walking away with a heavy purse—"

Julian cut her off. "You bet on her, didn't you."

"Of course." Grand Duchess Calisto smirked. "Now, the finalists for the main Summer Solstice Tourney were both unexpected rising stars: We have a mouse named Vance Underwood, and Kenji Toriyama from Peldeep, both high-level sword arts users."

"Is Vance a mousekin or a beastman who can shift into a mouse?" Julian questioned idly. Mouse was small for a shifter, but he didn't want to automatically assume they were the unchanging mousekin. There were many different kinds of kin, from ratkin to lizardkin to catkin and everything in between. They always kept the same form, unlike beastfolk, who could shift from everyday folk to full-on beast.

"Neither," his mother surprised him. "Vance is a *knowing mouse* who immigrated here from the Dark Enchanted Forest. He's *very* reputable and known for guarding merchant caravans."

"Huh." Julian stabbed a bit of scrambled egg. They were sitting at the breakfast table, the summer sunrise not an hour gone and already the world was bright and ready for the day. Birds were chirping in the trees, and the city was just starting to wake up.

Julian was used to getting up early, but he wasn't used to tossing and turning all night thinking about a mysterious troll.

And there he was, thinking about her *again*.

He shoved her out of his mind and refocused on the conversation at hand.

". . . and *that* is why you'll be overseeing the bout. We don't want any *interference*." There was steel in Calisto's voice, which instantly made Julian glance up and regret that he'd missed the first part while his thoughts had wandered.

"Interferences?" he broached.

"The Blackfog spies." His mother's hand tapped with irritation. One finger at a time fell with a soft *tik* as her sharp, manicured nails, painted purple, hit the breakfast table. "We haven't found any yet, but that just makes me all the more nervous."

Julian tilted his head. "Madame Potts didn't say that the Blackfog spies were going to attack. She just said there were going to be fireworks."

His mother's eyes shot up. "The fireworks in Peldeep were from Their Royal Highness Rowen fighting the spies during an illegal assassination attempt on their person. They burned down *half* of the Emerald Palace."

"Ah."

"And I like *both* halves of my palace, thank you very much!"

"Morning." Julia walked in, yawning, with a bright smile on her face. His sister was tall, just shy of six feet, and built like a knight. Her black skin was the color of the midnight sky, just like their mother's, though she had a red undertone that burned her cheeks whenever she was angry. Or embarrassed.

Neither had their mother's dark-red hair, but they'd both been born with the duchess's gray eyes. Julia's eyes even shone silver when she used her powers as the Paladin of Light. And where Julian's locks were the same color as their father's—a rich purple—Julia's hair was the same straight black as their maternal grandmother. She kept it cut shoulder length.

"Still no word on the spies, then?" Julia asked, spooning some scrambled eggs and two slices of fried flying pig meat onto her plate. She grabbed a freshly baked bun and lathered markleberry spread on top.

"No," Calisto sighed. "Which you would have known if you'd come to breakfast on time. Now that you're finally here, I have something to show you both." Calisto waved her hand, and a piece of paper materialized in the air in front of her. She caught it and handed it to Julian first.

MADAME POTTS
Their Royal Highness Rowen of Peldeep
Earl Oakley of Sumbria
Countess Oakley of Sumbria
Lord Geoffrey of Oakley
Commander Carsen Jules
Nera of Servalt

Joseph of Servalt
Princess Contessa la Rouche of Ildsfeld
Knight Commander Havork of Drendil
Grand Duchess Calisto von Slyke
Countess Julia von Slyke
Necromancer Chloe Watercress
Commander General Rufus Triever
General Knolith of Nilheim
Gerda the Bridge Troll
Chikli of Nilheim
Sithli of Nilheim
Milith of Nilheim
Tulith of Nilheim
Lilith of Nilheim

. . .

The list continued with over fifty names jotted down. The first one, Madame Potts, was the only one in all capital letters. Julian frowned when he saw his mother and sister on the list, and his eyes lingered on Gerda's name before he handed it over to Julia.

"What is this?" he asked.

"In the last few altercations," Calisto explained, "the leaders of the spies carried a list of targets. Different operatives carried different names, and these are all of the names that have been collected so far."

"Targets?" Julia demanded, slamming the list onto the table. "For what purpose?"

Calisto tapped her fingers on the table again. "We've only begun to piece it together. The leaders were told only as much as they needed to know, but people talk. Some of them had lists ordering permadeath, with my name included. So was Rowen's and Havork's, and everyone from Nilheim—" Julia sucked in a breath, but Calisto added, "*except* Chloe."

His sister frowned. "What about the other names?"

"They were to be *secured*," Calisto said. "Preferably unalive."

At least that was reversible with a Revive or Resurrect potion. Permanent death was just that, *permanent*.

"What else did we learn?" Julian did his best to memorize the list of names.

"That the group has been around for *decades*, if not longer, but they've only started getting seriously involved in international affairs now. The Spring Ball was the turning point, and the lists were distributed right after." His mother looked each of them in the eye. "A lot of Blackfog members were simple information brokers before that, and the rest are recent hires."

"What changed?"

"Duke Lector made a contract with the leader of the Blackfog spies. He seemed to think he was in control of them, and they would come to his rescue when we took him into custody." Calisto leaned back in her chair and folded her hands in front of her on the table. "No such help ever came."

"Why?" Julian asked, knowing there might not be an answer.

"If I could guess . . ." His mother frowned. "Any contract he had with them might have ended upon his death. Or they decided he was too much of a liability and didn't have a use for him any longer."

"Who are 'they'?" And why did it feel like he wouldn't be getting any of this information if he didn't ask for it?

Calisto shrugged. "So far, there are two lead suspects. A woman with blonde hair and pink teleportation magic—"

"The one who keeps messing with Madame Potts?" Julia cut in.

"The same," Calisto affirmed. "And the other suspect is currently unalive in our dungeon."

"Ah, I suppose that narrows the list, then," Julia said brightly.

There was a moment's pause, then Julian spoke quietly. "If the Blackfog think they can get away with harming either of you . . . then they're in for a surprise."

Calisto nodded, approving his anger. His mother looked ready to burn something down herself.

"And if they think they can mess up *my* wedding"—Julia crossed her arms as her eyes shone with a silver light—"then they'd better have made peace with their patrons. How is security?"

Their mother smiled. "Excellent."

Between his mother's inventions, their trained guards, and Julian's own team, they should have enough on their side to overcome anything thrown at them.

Julian asked, "Who else knows?"

"Rowen handed over the list to the ruler or representative of each nation last night. They didn't want to wait for the official Continental Council meeting, as you can imagine," Calisto said. The meeting wasn't scheduled until the end of the festival, and by then, it would be too late. "So I need you to keep your eyes open at the tourney today. Which, need I remind you, starts in less than an hour?"

Julian sighed but rose to go and perform his duty.

CHAPTER 11

I Loved the Tea in Valaria

Gerda

The sun rose early, but *I* did not.

I was *usually* a morning person. My day started by enjoying a nice long bath with the sunrise, after which I'd make breakfast and a cup of tea. Then, I'd pop out to a few bridges before coming in for lunch. My [Oracle] abilities were brutal and taxing, so *if* I checked in on anyone, it was after noon. That way, I could have an hour-long nap to recover from the headache.

I spent my days defending bridges, exploring the Dark Enchanted Forest for loot, looking for more bridges, or just relaxing at home. After dinner, I'd turn in for the night and read a few chapters of my book before going to sleep early.

Yesterday, I had *not* gone to sleep early. Instead, I'd stayed up for hours replaying my meeting with Julian over and over again in my mind.

Now, it was roughly the time I was *supposed* to be meeting Henrietta and Brownie for breakfast, so I rolled out of bed and threw on a sundress before heading down. I tied back my braids while I was in the elevator and promised myself that I would properly wash and rebraid my hair before the Masquerade.

"Gerda!" Lady Amaryllis, Saintess of Lithnilheim, was sitting at the table with a cup of mint tea and a buttered huckleberry scone. Lithnilheim was the name of the spirit of the Dark Enchanted Forest ruled by King Keith and Queen Henrietta, and shortened to Nilheim by everyone but the Hollow elves.

The elves had lived in the forest for as long as the forest had existed. They barely acknowledged the Dark Lord and mostly stuck to their city. The fact that Lady Amy was here *at all* was nothing short of a miracle—one brought about by the black grimalcat sitting on the elf's lap.

"Good morning." Slake Drakeford, Adventurer Extraordinaire and legendary grimalcat, blinked at me slowly. He was black all over, from his tiny beanie cat paws to his bat wings, with the exception of two green horns on his head and matching green eyes.

"It's good to see you both." I smiled warmly at the pair. Amy was as green as I was, but her hair was brown and done up in intricate elven braids as befitting her station. Both of our ears were long and pointed, though hers pointed outward while mine hugged closer to my hair.

"I'm sure it is," Slake replied. He hopped down and wandered toward the door. When he arrived at the entrance, he sat just out of sight for anyone coming inside and waited.

I wasn't one to bother a grimalcat—they had a habit of swift and brutal vengeance to all who annoyed them—so I nodded politely and turned back to Lady Amy. "What are your plans for the day?"

"I have *no idea*," she said excitedly. "I thought I was going to be trapped in the palace all week waiting for the Continental Council, but they had an emergency meeting yesterday and decided to slip me in too, so now I'm free for the rest of the festival!"

"What was the verdict?" I asked.

I'd been there when the molten ash vane poisoner from the Hollow had been caught red-handed, a young girl who'd just taken over the business from her grandmother and had had no idea she was breaking international law by making banned poisons that melted people from the inside out. The recipe had been in her family's notebook, so she'd happily made and added it to her regular shipments.

The other countries weren't like the Dark Enchanted Forest. Where *I* lived, if I needed an invisibility potion, I could just stumble around the woods until I came upon a Juliper flower or an old woman handing out quests with an invisibility potion as the reward.

For the rest of the continent, black-market dealers received batches of potions and poisons—illegal or otherwise—and handled their sale and distribution.

"Slake spoke on Mia's behalf, and as soon as they found out she wasn't working with the Blackfog spies, the council pretty much lost interest." Amy forked off a piece of her scone and ate it, humming happily. "King Keith is dealing with the aftermath, and I'll be visiting the Black Fortress when this is all done to talk about reparations."

I shuddered almost imperceptibly, remembering the last time *I'd* been summoned to the Black Fortress. My discomfort must've shown on my face, because Amy eyed me nervously.

"What?" she asked.

"It's nothing." I waved off her concern. "Just remembering the time I got audited . . . twice."

Lady Amy nodded knowingly. "Because of your bridges?"

"Because of my bridges." I put a few pieces of flying pork bacon and a cheese roll on a plate, then poured myself a cup of black tea with a splash of milk. Joining her at the table, I took a sip of tea first, relishing in the hot beverage. It was an earthy blend, with slightly oversteeped leaves. There was a nice hint of citrus in the brew as well.

A standard Pixie Prim blend.

Unlike where I came from, there were a lot more varieties of tea here. Of course, they weren't distinguished by Ceylon or Assam or Darjeeling or Keemun, like the flavors I was used to back home. The tea here was unique to the region it was grown in. I missed a nice orange pekoe, but this was a close substitute.

I *loved* the tea in Valaria.

There were still the same harvesting times; the first flush of the season happened in March and April, the second in May to June, the third in July to August, and the last in September to October. A few magical variants bloomed only once, over the winter, in a fifth flush. Winter tea was delicious, though it quickly lost its potency after the frosts melted, and any serious tea lover would have to wait until the snow fell again to drink it.

Behind me, I could hear Rufus and Brownie coming down the hallway. They were busy planning their day. "I think you're right and we can slip away for the tourney," Rufus spoke, appearing in the doorway. "When is your cousin competing?"

"Meow."

Before Brownie could reply, Slake interrupted, rubbing himself between the bard's legs. Brownie dipped down and picked up the grimalcat, affectionately rubbing the beast behind his ears.

"Slake," Rufus greeted, and I detected a hint of frustration. "Good morning."

"It is, isn't it," the grimalcat replied, swishing his tail.

"To answer your question"—Brownie smiled across at her intended—"Candace is competing in the second match."

"Hm." Rufus tapped his chin, considering. "How about I join you?"

"Really?!" Brownie asked, concerned. "Are you sure?"

"I'm sure. Worst case, I'll just step out."

Lady Amy smiled, "Can I tag along?"

"Count me in, too," I added before finishing off my roll.

"Slake?" Brownie asked, but the grimalcat hopped out of her arms and landed on the floor.

He rubbed his paw against his cheek and said, "I'm busy."

"Alright everyone," Brownie dragged Rufus to the breakfast table. "Give us ten minutes to eat, and then we can all head out."

CHAPTER 12

Contestants, Are You Rrready?

Julian

"In the west corner, we have the fiery, the furry, the ever-ferocious *ROCCO THE RACCOON*!"

The announcer's voice boomed loudly over the crowds as a large gate opened on the left side of the arena and a raccoon beastfolk entered. He ran on all fours, in half-transformed beastman form, loping up the steps and arriving on the magical platform. Rocco clasped his hands into a fist and pumped it over his head once, twice, and thrice.

And then, he burst into flames.

It was a great show. Julian nodded in approval. He was sitting in the highest alcove seats above the arena, sipping on a glass of crushed ice tea infused with elderberries and slices of cucumber. It was refreshing under the hot sun.

The crowd's volume only increased as the eastern gate rose and the announcer's voice introduced Rocco's opponent.

"And in the opposite corner . . . *SANDY MOOR!* Graceful as a swan, voice of a nightingale, and beauty beyond compare. Folks, her summoner's dance will leave you wanting to follow orders right beside her summons!"

A human woman with long black hair and clear blue eyes walked into the arena. Sandy obviously had well over twenty Charisma, probably closer to thirty, and a high-enough Dexterity to walk with unnatural grace. Her smile made members of the audience swoon. She was wearing a dancer's flowing skirt, black tights, and a long-sleeve, skintight shirt that showed off her belly button.

When she stopped across from Rocco, who was still on fire and bristling with a fierce glare on his face, Sandy lifted both arms above her head and then dipped into a beautiful bow, turned in a circle, and then sank into a fighting stance. Her skirts settled elegantly about her, her hair falling perfectly into place.

She motioned with one outstretched hand for Rocco to come at her. The crowd went wild.

"Contestants, are you *rrready*?" The announcer, a selkie man named Rish, stood on a stand just below Julian's box seats.

Rocco and Sandy both nodded, not taking their eyes off of each other.

"Then the final match of the youth tournament shall . . ." There was a deliberate pause before a loud gong sounded and Rish shouted, "BEGIN!"

A split second later, Rocco spat a chantless [Fireball] at Sandy's face. Sandy dodged to the left and spun, her voice a delicate song that Julian could hear clear as day over the crowd.

"As one with the earth,
a strength from the arm,
defender, my friend
protect me from harm.
[Summon: Carl]."

A few members of the crowd were influenced by her charm-laced voice, walking toward the stage until roused by their neighbors. Julian had a high-enough level that he didn't need to worry about the natural charm in her words. He leaned back and took another sip.

Rocco leapt to attack her directly, but he was blocked as a stoneskin wombat emerged from the summoning circle on the ground. The monster swatted Rocco like a fly, sending him rolling. He flipped end over end twice before popping back up to his feet.

"Carl." Sandy pointed at her opponent. "Charge."

Rocco dove to the side as Carl the Stoneskin Wombat curled up into a ball and rolled toward him. The big beasties were known for their hard-plated butt. If Carl managed to sit on Rocco, the raccoon would take considerable damage, and his fire would struggle to get through Carl's thick hide.

Meanwhile, the announcer had kept up a steady explanation. "And Rocco leaps over the stoneskin, shooting out a stream of fire at Sandy—but she dances to the side! What a move, folks! And what's this? He's running circles around them? Is he hoping to tire the wombat out? I hope not! Wait! No! AMAZING! He's trapped them in a circle of flames! What will Sandy do now?!"

Julian finished his drink and leaned forward in his chair. These tourneys were a fun part of the festival, but they were also a great place for contestants to showcase their talent and receive job offers going forward. From royals to famous adventuring parties, everyone who was anyone would be interested in prospective combatants skilled enough to make it to the final rounds of a big tournament like this.

The match wouldn't last much longer. While the stoneskin was still in good form, Sandy was overheating, and Rocco was running out of stamina. Additionally, Sandy's build was designed to cast [Debuff] on her opponents while her summons attacked. She'd missed hitting the wily raccoon two out of three times, and her mana was running out.

Suddenly, in a surprising move, Rocco stopped short in the middle of the arena. Carl rolled straight through a wall of fire and finally managed to hit the raccoon. It seemed like the beastman had given up . . . but then, something spectacular happened.

Rocco took the hit—but he'd set himself up to get launched across the arena *straight* into Sandy. The calm look on the woman's face finally broke when Rocco burst through the flames and headbutted her in the stomach. She was pushed back and landed with one heel slightly out of the ring.

It was time for Julian to fulfill his role as overseer for the tournament.

Standing up, he walked forward and pulled a small lever. A flag descended from the side of his platform, pointing toward the western gate. At the same time, he pulled the other lever and dropped the flag that pointed toward the eastern gate.

A tie.

Rocco had fallen unconscious from the headbutt, and Sandy had been pushed out of the ring.

There was a dull roar from the crowd, and calls for a rematch started to shake the arena itself.

"You saw it here, folks!" Rish was eating it up. "A TIE! What do we want? A rematch! When will it happen? The judges will decide! What a battle! What a show! Who could have bet on this?!"

A lone audience member jumped to their feet, screaming in joy. One person, clearly, *had* bet on this.

The referees quickly administered potions to Rocco and Sandy before ushering them to stand before the royal box. Julian then spoke into the arena's sound amplification enchantment. "An impressive feat. You're both worthy of reaching the finals."

The pair stood up straighter.

"But there can be only *one* champion," he said. "As such, a rematch will be held on the last morning of the festival, before the closing ceremonies. Go, and prepare yourselves!" Before Julian could finish, the crowd was yelling again. People chanted the names of the two contestants while Rocco and Sandy shook hands, much to the delight of the spectators, and then walked back through their gates.

Julian retook his seat and ordered another drink. He needed something to hold and distract himself with. After a thought, he also ordered something called a charcuterie, a wooden platter with bread and cheese, cured meats, pickles and nuts, and various jams and butter. It had been introduced last summer, and this was his first opportunity to try it. This one came with honey butter, chive jam, sausages, pickled cabbage, and salted liliput flower seeds.

It was only a short break—a quarter hour—before the newcomer tourney finalists' match. A few people came and left, and some were still finding their seats when the announcer started in on the next round of combatants.

Julian missed the announcements. There was someone directly across the arena from him who was trying to find a seat. Julian was so distracted staring at the troll that he nearly jumped when the gong signaled the start of the battle below.

Frustrated with himself, Julian dragged his eyes away from Gerda the Bridge Troll and back to the task at hand—watching a storm giantess utterly destroy a preela monk in the ring.

CHAPTER 13

I Can Just Debuff Myself

Gerda

"Candace is about to start!" Brownie hurried us into our seats.

We were running a bit late because a *certain* Dark Lady had shown up later than Brownie or myself. The announcer was already introducing the contestants when we arrived, and all of us piled into seats right beside the doors. I was in the aisle, followed by Henrietta, Brownie, Rufus, and Amy.

"I brought snacks!" Henrietta pulled out bags of candied nuts and started passing them around.

"This is amazing, Brownie!" The elf saintess laughed. "I can't believe your cousin made it into the finals!"

The two combatants were already facing each other, ready to start. Cimor the Monk was holding a long staff at the ready. She was a preela, one of the long-limbed people from the Empire of Sands. She had black fur all down the back of her body, and tan skin in the front. Her long tapered ears each had a tuft at the end, and her thin wings were tucked away for the fight.

Candace, Brownie's cousin, was a giantess who stood almost twice the height of the preela, with pale skin and long silver hair. She was large and in charge, and was holding a shadow dagger in each hand.

"Are you sure you want to do this?" Brownie asked Rufus. The beastman was bristling a bit at the edges, but otherwise looked fine.

"It's not so bad. Slake gave me the idea."

"What idea?"

Rufus pulled out an empty poison bottle. "I can just debuff myself."

The announcer's voice rang clear over the crowd. "Now, it's time for the battle you've all been waiting for! Contestants, on your honor—*BEGIN!*"

Brownie immediately jumped up to cheer for Candace. Rufus was smiling at his bard, and Lady Amy was on the edge of her seat, eyes gleaming. Henrietta was eating.

I sat back and pretended not to notice a very obvious distraction.

Someone was watching me.

As a boss-level monster, my claim to fame was my forty-three Perception. If I didn't notice the eyes of one Duke Julian staring at me from across the arena, then it was time to hang up my Cast Crystal and go back to being a nameless NPC. I tried to ignore him by watching the battle.

Cimor deflected a thrown shadow dagger then ran up her staff to kick Candace in the face.

Silver eyes bore into me.

Candace stumbled but reached up in time to block the staff before it also hit her in the face.

I could *feel* his unwavering gaze.

All right, if the battle couldn't distract me from the handsome duke staring holes into me from across the arena, I had a notification tab full of updates.

The first was an oracle.

[**Oracle:** You are witness to the strings of Fate and her weave. The
story unfolds, and the Chosen of each deity mark the way.
You have found 8/12 Chosen.
Impending Scenarios: 5/12 Chosen.
Arbiter of Shadow - The Guild Engagement
Steward of Life - The Burning Bridge
Harbinger of Dream - The Soul Quest
Paladin of Light - The Wedding Jitters
Heroine of Justice - The Great Chase
Timeline access restricted.
Available Scenarios: All Scenarios within current Domain boundaries available. All Scenarios impending within 6.5 days available.
Oracle timeline: 4 mins 30 seconds.
Please select Chosen.]

That was *a lot* of scenarios. The thought made me sick. [Oracle] wasn't a fun ability, and activating it left me powerless and trapped for the full four and a half minutes. I was going to need to slip out after the match and find somewhere safe to check in on things. I really hoped the discomfort would be worth it . . . The other notifications I had were from my bridges.

[Martha's Bridge: 14 Travelers. Current cost: 91 EXP. Ancient
Gamblers Amulet in effect. 91 EXP converted into 91 Copper
Pieces.]
[Black Fortress Bridge: 39 Travelers. Current cost: 253 EXP.
Ancient Gamblers Amulet in effect. 253 EXP converted into 2
Silver 53 Copper Pieces.]

The list went on.

As a bridge troll, I was magically obligated to watch over and toll any bridge under my control.

[Bridge Troll]

[A Bridge Troll is connected to their bridge and must defend it. Let
no one pass lest they solve your riddle, pay the toll, or defeat you!
Riddle: Issue a Riddle. If a traveler succeeds in guessing the riddle,
grant them safe passage across the bridge. If a traveler who has
answered the riddle is injured while crossing the bridge, you suffer
[Debuff: Deal-Breaker] for 24 hours.
Toll: Charge a Toll. A traveler may choose to pay a toll to cross the
bridge. The toll is equal to one-tenth the traveler's level rounded
down. If a traveler who has paid the toll is injured while crossing
the bridge, you suffer [Debuff: Deal-Breaker] for 24 hours.
Defeat: Defend the Bridge. If you are defeated in battle or the traveler crosses your bridge without solving a riddle or paying a toll,
you are defeated. You forfeit Experience Points equal to one-tenth
your level rounded down.]

The penalties kept any *normal* troll from taking over every bridge in sight, but I wasn't any *normal* troll. My Ancient Gamblers Amulet converted EXP cost into a gold cost—and I was richer than most dragons, so I could afford it.

The crowd roared, and I looked up.

Candace had hit Cimor in the stomach, sending the monk flying. The preela was almost out of the ring when Cimor activated an ability and kicked the air, changing her direction and launching herself high into the sky overhead. Her wings opened just long enough to slow her fall, and then Cimor tucked them away safely out of the way again—a preela's wings were thin and delicate and not meant to withstand battle. "What a move! Cimor managed to land in the circle! What skill! What talent! But Candace isn't letting her relax. This is why they call her *the Stormbringer!*" The announcer was ecstatic.

Dark clouds filled the sky as billowing mist formed around the hands of the giantess. Lightning sparks danced over her hair, and her eyes had gone black. Cimor, for her part, planted both feet and began to spin her staff in a circle as a makeshift shield. A bolt of lightning shot at the preela, who somehow deflected it, sending it striking the ground six feet away.

My skin prickled. It turned out, Duke Julian wasn't the *only* one staring at me.

After searching the crowd and finding nothing, I realized I would need to resort to using my advanced Perception if I was going to find the culprit, especially since my [Sense Danger] perk was suddenly *screaming* at me in warning. I didn't like to focus on things unless I *had* to; that way lay madness. But now, I actively *looked* around me.

My Perception registered from every individual grain of sand on the floor to the follicles of hair on a catgirl excitedly cheering on the other side of the arena. I kept it up even after I found the hooded figure peeking over the roof above Duke Julian's box seat and pointing at me.

A gentle whistle filled the air before I caught a sky-blue-colored arrow an inch from my nose.

The hooded figure startled, lilac eyes wide. Then she vanished.

"Gerda!" Henrietta was on her feet, yelling. "Drop it! It's kazil poison!"

I didn't need to be told twice, letting the arrow hit the floor in front of me. Kazil turned anyone it touched into a frog. Luckily, only the arrowhead seemed poisoned and I was still a troll.

"What is the meaning of this?"

I looked up.

Duke Julian was standing in the aisle *right beside me*, and the entire arena had gone dead silent.

CHAPTER 14

The Easiest Target

Julian

Julian used [Scan] to detect for poison before picking the arrow up. His [Silent Guard] allowed him to cast his abilities without saying them aloud—an important perk to have when monster hunting.

"Wait, it's poisoned!" Gerda shouted at him, grabbing his arm. She also *finally* looked him in the eye. With how much she'd managed to *avoid* doing so, the small victory made Julian's lips twitch in a small smile.

"I am not a fool," he chided. "I know how to handle a poisoned arrow."

"As you say, Your Grace." Gerda's mouth snapped into a frown, but she dropped her head into a polite bow. He resisted the strange urge to reach out and tilt her head upward again so she would be forced to look him in the eye . . . and turned to address the arena instead.

The battle had come to a complete stop. Candace and Cimor were now standing at attention in their opening placements, and the unnatural quiet of the crowd felt like it would break at the slightest provocation. Julian's voice carried over the silence. "We have secured the arena and have everything under control."

There was a murmur. Any other year, and a small assassination attempt like this wouldn't have been noteworthy—but everyone remembered the warnings from Madame Potts. Still, a single arrow was *not* the same as "fireworks," and the arrow hadn't even been *on* fire.

"There will be a ten-minute intermission before we resume," he announced. "Starting *now*."

The place erupted in conversation as Julian turned back to Gerda, who still had her head lowered. For some reason, that irritated him. "Gerda the Bridge Troll," he said. "Meet with me after the match."

"Is there a problem?" Henrietta, the queen of the Dark Enchanted Forest, leaned over and put a hand on Gerda's shoulder in support. Henrietta normally blended into the background, but she was supporting Gerda with a fierce determination that physically charged the air around them.

It was an aura laced with sword intent.

"I simply wish to speak with her and collect a statement for the incident report," Julian reassured the Dark Lady. "You may accompany her, if you wish."

"That won't be necessary," Gerda hurriedly told Henrietta. "You wanted to take Lady Amy to see the Hall of Inventions after this. I can meet you there. It won't take long."

Henrietta asked, "Are you sure? I can represent you."

"I'm just taking a statement," Julian repeated. For some reason, that made Henrietta shoot him a look full of suspicion, so he added, "And confirming her safety. She's the *victim* here, and still in possible danger."

Henrietta wavered, likely remembering the list of Blackfog targets. Sensing his win, Julian concluded, "Now, I would like to officially apologize, Miss Gerda, for the attack you've received while attending our event. You will be informed of any outcome to our investigation. I will see you after the match. Your Majesty." Julian added a nod to Queen Henrietta before leaving.

Julian's Strength stat was his highest attribute at forty-nine, and it allowed him to jump the distance with ease. To control his fall, he activated [Light Foot] and landed gently on the edge of his box seats with practiced grace. As far as Julian was concerned, for quality of life, nothing could beat fast travel skills.

A black-robed figure was awaiting him, trussed up and gagged, courtesy of John.

His rogue was very good at his job. John was silent, he was observant, and he was professional. If it weren't for his tendency to get drunk and sob uncontrollably about missing his daughter, everyone would've assumed he was as cold and standoffish as he appeared at work.

But that was exactly what it was: work. And John was good at it.

He launched straight into his report. "Twenty-three-year-old Ellanora Green. Assassin registered with the Peldeep Assassin Assembly. Five foot six, brown hair, purple eyes, pale complexion. She had a contract on Gerda the Bridge Troll."

Julian nodded.

John handed over the contract, signed and stamped and official. "I've taken her into custody for three reasons: Gerda the Bridge Troll is a citizen of Nilheim, and both North Sumbria and Nilheim hold contracts to only allow assassinations on members of the elite governing class. Her daggers are *not* Assembly standard issue pettle steel pommels, and she was in possession of this."

He passed over a second sheet of paper.

The shocked grunt from Ellanora made it obvious that John must've stolen the second note without her knowledge. The human went from silently waiting in the corner to struggling. Julian and John left her to it. John was a master of his craft, and a monster in his class.

"Gerda is technically an elite," Julian said offhandedly before glancing at the list.

MADAME POTTS
Necromancer Chloe Watercress
Commander General Rufus of Nilheim
Grand Duchess Calisto of North Sumbria
Countess Julia of North Sumbria
Gerda the Bridge Troll

Behind them, the announcer was calling people back to their seats. It was almost time to restart the fight. Julian crouched and pulled down the gag on the spy, who was shooting him a look of fear and determination. He asked, "I only have *one* question: You had several targets, so why attack the troll first?"

Whatever she was expecting, that didn't seem to be it. The assassin shrugged. "She seemed like the easiest target."

He nodded then put the gag back into place. Standing up, he waved John to deal with transporting her away for questioning. It was time to resume his own work.

Julian lifted his arm and signaled Rish to start.

"IS EVERYBODY READY TO RESTART THE ACTION?" The announcer's voice rang out over the arena as Candace and Cimor saluted each other. In the stands, Gerda the Bridge Troll was distractedly tapping her finger against her chin and staring off into space.

"BEGIN!"

CHAPTER 15

So I Can't Tell You

Gerda

Candace won the bout.

Cimor had swung her staff, the giantess had caught it at the last second, and then, Candace had activated a lightning ability that had exploded up the staff in a blast of shining electrical arcs. They'd zigged and zagged, and now, both women were suffering from outrageously frizzy hair.

It had been enough to knock out the preela.

I hadn't paid much attention to the fight until the flashy ending. Instead, I'd been ruminating over my latest prophecy.

[Passive Perk: **Sense Fate** has activated. Duke Julian von Slyke will be poisoned during his next meal . . .]

When I selected the prompt, it gave me slightly more details but also showcased why I rarely bothered to read the full description of Fate's prophecies.

[Passive Perk: **Sense Fate** has activated. Duke Julian von Slyke will be poisoned during his next meal.]
[You have crossed paths with a fate that can be changed. Area of effect radius: Level 65 x Perception 43 x Foretelling 4 = 11,180 sq/ ft. Fate herself will guide you.]
["Truly all wonders are to the Chosen of Fate, that suffer the trappings of near death, she weeps. What hour is the turn of the blessed feast, there servings only sorrow and supposed sleep."]

Ugh.

In all honesty, half of the time, even *I* couldn't make out what Fate's messages meant. And I was the riddle *master*. My best guess would be that Julian was going to get poisoned with something like Paralysis or Sleep. The "hour turning a blessed feast" was probably lunch—at noon.

Which was immediately after the next fight.

"GO CANDACE!" Brownie yelled, and I looked up in time to catch the flashy ending of the bout. Candace was pumping her fist in the air to the roar of the crowd. I stood and cheered with the rest of my companions.

"VICTORY TO STORMBRINGER CANDACE!" the voice announced, *almost* as loud as Brownie's celebratory cheering.

When Candace was done basking in her victory, she turned to meet the healers, waving off their concern for her until Cimor had been fully checked and administered a [Heal]. When Cimor opened her eyes, she found a large palm extended out to her. The giantess helped the preela to her feet, and they officially shook hands. Candace slapped Cimor on the back, almost gently, and invited the woman out for a drink.

"Let's go congratulate her!" Brownie exclaimed, grabbing Rufus by the hand. Henrietta and I stepped into the aisle to let them out.

"Not as bad as I thought it would be," Rufus said as he passed. "The debuff worked!"

There would be a fifteen-minute break to get snacks and use the facilities before the next bout. The last round was between someone named Vance Underwood and Kenji Toriyama, a human I'd fought with once before. Kenji was an excellent sword arts user, and true to the *otome* nature of this world, carried around a ridiculously oversized *odachi*.

I'd given the human a riddle.

> "What goes around the wood,
> But isn't known to roam
> And never goes inside the wood,
> Yet calls the forest home?"

And instead of answering right away, he'd challenged me to a duel. After hearing of my battle with the Drendil army, he'd sought me out to test his strength. When he realized that I far surpassed him in level, however, he'd lowered his blade and answered my riddle instead. "The bark of a tree."

Kenji positively *screamed* samurai. He came from Peldeep, which embraced a lot of Japanese culture for a nation that had *no idea* Japan even existed. The system awarded skills based on behavior and training, and functioned with a level of interdimensional cultural appropriation that I tried to ignore. I was trapped here, and just trying to survive. If anything, the familiar European and Asian world-building was a saving grace. That, and knowing the language.

Now, if only I could find chocolate, then I would go from *surviving* to *thriving*.

Markleberry didn't count. It was close, but it was a *berry*.

And on that topic, I still needed to figure out how to prevent Duke Julian from getting poisoned at lunch. Or, barring that, make sure to save him.

"Do you want to join me?" Amy asked, interrupting my thoughts. "I'm going to grab more snacks."

"You go ahead."

When we were alone, Henrietta patted my arm, her gentle eyes worried for me. "Are you *sure* you're alright, Gerda?"

"I'm okay," I assured her. And I was. No injuries at all.

Henrietta visibly hesitated before leaning forward and whispering, "We found a list of targets on the captured Blackfog spies. The council has decided not to disclose the information yet, so I'm not allowed to tell you if *your name is on the list.*"

I nodded my appreciation. "Thanks for not telling me."

"Just . . . promise you'll be careful?" Henrietta asked.

"I'll be careful," I assured her.

The fifteen minutes came and went, and everyone was back in their seats ready for Vance and Kenji's bout. Everyone except Rufus.

Brownie gave us a thumbs-up. "He's going to take a walk. We'll meet up at the Hall of Inventions after this."

Fanfare met the new arrivals, and I leaned down to let Henrietta know that I would be stepping out to meet Julian early. She tried to join me, but I told her no, and she begrudgingly accepted. When I finally stepped inside the corridor and out of sight from the stands, I was met by three knights in North Sumbrian livery.

"Miss Jones?" The youngest elf in the group stepped forward and bowed politely. "May we escort you?"

"You may."

CHAPTER 16

The Final Round

Julian

Julian was in charge of overseeing this tournament, judging any rules that were broken, and issuing the champion title. His word was the final decision for everything . . . and he could barely focus on the match. Why?

First and foremost was a certain white-freckled distraction. She was so *incredibly* suspicious. First her watching him from across the crowded market, her expert vanishing act—and then, she'd just *randomly* found his locket? And out of an entire auditorium, she just *coincidentally* sat directly opposite him and was targeted for assassination?

He wasn't a fool; she was clearly keeping tabs on him. It was almost like she was *trying* to catch his attention. But why?

He tried to refocus on the match, but his eyes kept drifting in her direction. Which meant he immediately spotted when she left early. She could've just been stepping away to use the washroom . . . but he sincerely doubted that. He was thankful that he'd dispatched a guard on the troll.

"AND VANCE LANDS A BLOW! But is it enough? No! Kenji has activated his [Wind Blade]!" the announcer called out, drawing Julian's attention back to the battle below. It was just as impressive as the previous two.

Vance was a palm-size mouse with a sword as big as a toothpick, but his Strength stat must have been in the thirties or higher since he was able to parry Kenji's blade with ease.

In order to fight Kenji properly, Vance would scurry left and right before launching himself at the human. Taking the opportunity when Kenji was a hair's breadth too slow, Vance managed to slice the knuckle on the human's left index finger. A trail of red dripped down onto his sword before Kenji stepped back and drew in a deep breath, whispering, "[Aura Blade.]"

With practiced grace, the man slowly swung his sword in a diagonal slash. Vance, sensing the danger, leapt high into the air, rolling head over tail twice. The cutting energy that burst out of the sword missed the mouse's vitals but sliced clean through his tail.

Vance landed, awkwardly tilting from the loss of balance before righting himself. He glanced at his chopped tail and squeaked a swear.

"Your Grace." John was suddenly beside Julian. "The bridge troll is in the back room."

"She's come early?" Julian didn't turn from the fight. The mouse lifted his sword straight into the air, and Kenji braced for whatever Vance was going to strike him with. Strangely, knowing Gerda was already here finally allowed him to properly concentrate on the battle. The tiny blade in Vance's paws was starting to glow with purple light.

"She said she wanted to avoid the crowd," John replied.

When the light fully engulfed the little mouse, he disappeared. It wasn't invisibility magic. Julian stood and took a step to the edge of his box so he could look closer. And then, Kenji suddenly fell backward to the ground, a tiny sword between his eyebrows and a tiny mouse sitting on his face.

The confusion turned into cheers as Vance hurriedly scurried off to the side while the healers rushed forward to help.

"Was that . . . ?" Julian muttered.

"A [Time] skill." John nodded. "He can bank a certain amount of time and then spend it to attack in an instant. Faster than I could perceive. The effectiveness of the attack is hampered by its loading time, but it's an incredible ability to possess."

The announcer was similarly explaining to the confused crowd. "And Kenji is down for the count! Vance used his famous [Delayed Strike], and what a finale! What a rare talent!"

Vance bowed to his recovering opponent. The human stood and dusted himself off, then sheathed his blade and returned the bow, low at the waist.

Julian lowered the appropriate flag and announced, "Victory in the final round to Vance Underwood! Well fought, both of you." He then turned away as Rish took over recounting the day's bouts, their winners, and the upcoming events in the arena.

"Send an invitation to Vance," Julian ordered. "With a skill like that, he's wasted as a caravan guard."

John nodded. "Yes, sir."

"Also, send the extra guards stationed here to the Hall of Inventions. The Dark Lady said they were headed there next." Too many of her companions were on the list, and it didn't sit right with him to leave them be. Julian opened the door to the back room just in time to watch the tea trolley carrying his lunch tip over and splatter all over the floor.

"Oh! *I'm* sorry." Gerda stood over the mess. Unexpectedly, the troll met his gaze. "I didn't know it was Your Grace's habit to poison his guests?"

CHAPTER 17

Too Close for Comfort

Gerda

I could hear Julian speaking through the door, and so timed the spill *just* right.

My plan was simple; either catch the person serving lunch in the act of poisoning it—or prevent Julian from eating that lunch altogether. Hearing the commotion, two guard knights checked in from the hallway, but Julian motioned for them to wait.

"Explain." The order was simple, yet paired with Julian's frown, it became cold and threatening. Now that I'd had the chance to interact with Duke Julian a few times, it was getting easier to control myself, but I chose to hold my tongue and observe.

The waiter, who'd introduced himself as Mr. Prail, was trying to regain some composure.

"I-I only—" Before he could finish, a shadow shot out from under the table. It moved like waves on a calm lake disturbed by some underwater beast until it joined the shadow under John's feet.

"Miss Gerda arrived, and Mr. Prail offered her tea," John stated. "The troll took her teacup with a smile, then stood and pushed the trolley over."

"Your Grace"—Mr. Prail bowed low—"I'm innocent. There's *no* poison in Miss Gerda's teacup!"

John reached for the offending cup, which I offered readily.

"He's right," John concluded.

Julian raised an eyebrow and crossed his arms, regarding me with expectation.

"*See!*" the waiter declared, triumphant.

In all honesty, I'd actually thought about poisoning the tea *myself* to stop lunch, but I didn't want to frame the poor waiter if Mr. Prail was *actually* innocent. There were so many other ways Julian could've gotten poisoned; one of the guards could be a traitor carrying a poisoned dagger, someone could throw a poison smoke bomb into the room, or a ninja could suddenly appear from the ceiling and shoot him with a poisoned dart.

Though with John here, the last one seemed unlikely.

Thinking I should have John check the rest of the food, *just in case,* I countered, "Did I *say* that you'd poisoned my *teacup*?"

Mr. Prail stiffened almost imperceptibly. The way his eyebrow tightened and his hand clenched ever so slightly alerted me even before my [Sense Danger], and I acted on pure instinct, whipping my hand out and grabbing his wrist.

He cried out in exaggerated pain. "Ow, stop! Help!"

At my sudden movement, John positioned himself between the duke and I, but Julian didn't even flinch. "Miss Gerda," he stated. "Kindly unhand my staff."

I *knew* my instincts were correct. "I won't hurt him; I'm just going to prove my point." Equipping one of my treasures, a pair of oversized black leather gloves appeared on my hands. I used my free hand to sweep a circular motion in front of Mr. Prail's chest.

> [You have attempted to use **Arcane Catspaw Gloves** to steal the target's most valuable item: **Storage Ring**. 98% chance of success. You have succeeded.]

I reopened my fingers with a toe ring in my hand.

Gross.

Letting go of the waiter, I tossed the ring at John, who caught it with ease. Honestly, there was a chance that my accusations wouldn't be grounds to search Mr. Prail's ring, but Mr. Prail sealed his own fate when he turned on his heel and tried to run for the door. With the duke on one side and two guards on the other, he'd taken his chances with the guards and was promptly subdued.

"Empty it," Julian ordered.

The ring's magically sealed contents appeared in front of us. John caught a half-empty bottle of a Paralysis potion, a low-grade antidote, and a piece of parchment on his palm. The rest of the ring's contents, including thirty gold coins, a change of clothes, a rope, and a sleeping roll tumbled to the floor.

He handed the parchment to Julian, who nodded. The rogue then stepped forward to take the waiter into custody, and the pair of them sank into a pool of shadows. Meanwhile, I unequipped my legendary gloves, wiping my hands together in a job well done.

I'd survived an official meeting with my favorite character and managed to prevent him from getting poisoned.

Good job, me.

"Miss Gerda." Duke Julian regarded me calmly.

"Your Grace," I replied, standing amidst the mess. The room was in chaos, with the trolley still knocked over and the ring's contents haphazardly lying about.

The duke's lips twitched, and a genuine smile pulled at the corners ever so slightly. My Perception wouldn't lie to me about something like this, and I'll admit it left me rattled.

He was *smiling?*

Then, the half elf had to go and act out of character even more. Julian walked forward until he was *much* too close for comfort. My chair was right behind me, so I fell into it to add a bit of distance between us. How had I thought I was going to be okay? I gripped my skirts to stop the tremors.

Before I could figure out another escape, Julian held up Mr. Prail's scroll. It was a signed and approved assassination order from Servalt's Assassin's Guild.

Targeting *me.*

"We took this one from the archer." A second page appeared in his hand, and it was from the Peldeep Assassin Assembly.

The duke backed off and took the seat across from me, finally giving me space to breathe. If I was Mr. Prail's target, how did Julian get poisoned?

The object of my thoughts leaned forward in his chair. "So, why don't we have that talk?"

CHAPTER 18

Interesting

Julian

The second Julian had approached her, Gerda's cheeks had flushed, highlighting the white freckles on the bridge of her nose.

He liked her freckles.

"Let's start"—Julian waved the offending papers—"with your assassination orders. Who do you think could be targeting you?"

The troll sighed, a surprisingly long-suffering sigh. "Anyone who's ever crossed one of my bridges?"

He raised an eyebrow. "How many bridges do you control?"

"Lady's secret." She smiled, showing off her long lower canines.

While he was curious to learn more about the troll, now wasn't the time. "And your statement about the first assassination attempt? For the record."

Gerda crossed her arms. "I arrived, found my seat, and someone shot at me. The end."

Julian had to stop himself from outright snorting, stifling a laugh with the back of his hand. How was she this amusing? Even John, who gave concise reports without any superfluous detail, wasn't *that* succinct.

Gerda's gaze fell to his lips, and her eyes went wide. Seeing as he'd surprised her somehow—and for that reason alone—he let himself give in to idle curiosity and smiled directly at her.

She looked away and covered her face.

Interesting.

"Do you know about *the list*?"

She regained some composure and answered, "I do."

Julian then surmised, "Which is how you were prepared for the arrow—"

"No," Gerda interrupted, shaking her head. One long dark-green braid slid over her exposed shoulder and pooled in her lap. It was a momentary distraction.

"No?"

"I found out about the list *after* I was shot at," she corrected him. "I caught the arrow because it was an easy catch."

"An easy *poisoned* catch," he reminded her.

"One you yourself have touched," she countered.

His smile got bigger. "True."

Gerda frowned. "I've given my statement, so if there's nothing else?"

He didn't *want* her to leave yet. His instincts were telling him that he needed her for something. They were missing a piece of the puzzle, and if he just pushed . . .

"The Blackfog spies are in my duchy," he said, choosing the direct approach. "They are targeting you and others. Do you know anything?"

Gerda opened her mouth, probably to say no, but closed it again. She gave him a thoughtful look. When she finally did speak, it wasn't what he'd expected. "The Spring Ball."

"What about the Spring Ball?" Julian asked.

"Do I know anything about the Blackfog spies?" she repeated, listing things off on her fingers. "Who are they? An intelligence agency that operates around the entire continent. What are they? An information broker up until recently. When did things change? After the Spring Ball, when they were suddenly hands-on, hiring mercenaries, and trying to hurt people. *Where* doesn't help us because they are targeting people everywhere except the Empire of Sands. But we're not even going to consider the empire as an enemy because . . . ?"

"The queen," Julian answered immediately. It was well known how the empire was experiencing one of its most prosperous reigns in history and had done so by disbanding half of the army back into the working class so they could keep up with supply and demand for their trade.

"And what happened at the Spring Ball that is tied to the Blackfog spies?" Gerda answered her own question. "Marquess Chadwick kidnapped a Blackfog spy—"

Julian frowned. "Marquess Chadwick was directly under Duke Lector, who was working with the Blackfog spies."

"Exactly." Gerda tapped her chin. "So why would Chadwick have kidnapped the spy?"

". . . Because he didn't know that the spies were working for the duke?" Julian said, pointing out the obvious.

"*Or*"—there was a glint in her eyes as Gerda reasoned—"because the Blackfog spies weren't working for Duke Lector."

Julian argued, "Your own kingdom was invaded by the duke with their aid."

"*After* the Spring Ball," Gerda said. "Before that, Servalt was using contract mercenaries and both assassin guilds, but no Blackfog spies."

He frowned, considering her words. "Alright."

"That's what I know," she concluded. "Look into what changed at the Spring Ball, and you'll—" She stopped short in the middle of her sentence. Julian waited; she'd obviously thought of something. "Look into what changed at the Spring Ball," Gerda repeated, slower, "and we might figure out their motive."

He waited still, expecting her to continue with her thoughts, but they remained hidden. Instead, Gerda rose to her feet, Julian only a breath behind her.

"Now, if you'll excuse me, my friends are waiting."

She was headed for the door; she was *leaving*. Julian chased after her.

"Wait," he told her. She paused at the door and looked back at him. It was the same as last night all over again, but this time, he had the upper hand. "You are being targeted," he reminded her. "Which is why I'm going to assign you a guard during your visit."

"Respectfully, Your Grace," Gerda said, "I refuse." Her eyes were fierce and fiery.

"Miss Gerda," he spoke her name softly. "Please don't take this as me laughing at your abilities. Accept my guard while you're here."

"The fact that your sister can't beat me should've already confirmed my abilities," the troll snapped, but it seemed like her mind was somewhere else. She was looking at a notification.

Julian was impressed; his sister was a battle-loving adventurer who could solo some dungeons.

"Besides"—Gerda shook her head—"you have enough problems on your hands. You can't spare the guards."

At that moment, John sent him an emergency message using his [Shadow Chat] skill. It resembled the communication interface available to parties formed while dungeon delving, but it only worked if one of John's shadow clones was attached to Julian.

[Come to the Hall of Inventions. You're going to want to see this.]

Julian read the note twice, but that was all it said.

He looked down at the troll. "How did you know?"

"Know what?" She looked up at him with big, innocent eyes, but he could see that her hands were clenched in her skirts. "If the city is full of Blackfog spies, you can't afford to have a guard following me around shopping. Isn't that obvious?"

A whistle blew off in the distance, loud and shrill.

CHAPTER 19

I'd Changed Everything

Gerda

Julian shot me an exasperated look that didn't fit his character description at all. How could he be described as tall, dark, and emotionally scarred when he looked at me like *that?*

He'd even *laughed* a few minutes ago!

"This isn't over!" he said, pulling back to make room for me to open the door. Despite my mind telling me everything would be fine, my hands still had a tremor as I hurried to let us out.

Gerda's body had *years* of trauma, and as soon as someone bigger closed in on my personal space, my blood pressure went through the roof and my hands started shaking. After five years, I'd gotten it into a manageable response.

Once in the hallway, I put some distance between us. "I would think it is."

"It's not," he stated firmly.

My perfectly planned escape wasn't so perfect when we were both going in the same direction. Julian had another notification in the corner of his vision that distracted him, and he cursed. The whistle sounded a second time, accompanied by a high-pitched scream.

"I'll see you again soon," he told me, turning to one of the open arch glassless windows that lined the wall of the hallway. It was a beautiful architectural design, and very fitting for a large fantasy arena.

Julian jumped out of the window.

I wished I could just jump out of a window this high up like some magical girl. Mechanically, I probably could . . . but I was wearing a light summer dress, and as much as fantasy undergarments were very pretty, I didn't want everyone in the streets to see *mine.* Besides, I was going to take my time clearing out.

I was not needed to field the chaos that was happening at the Hall of Inventions.

This was the fun part about being close to any of the main characters—my abilities went off all day. My [Map] was overwhelmingly yellow to show me where scenarios were going to happen, and my [Sense Fate] warned me about every little thing, while [Sense Danger] was having a heyday being in the thick of it. Thanks to these abilities, I was surviving Season Two even though I'd never gotten the chance to play through it.

I knew what was *generally* supposed to happen:

Necromancer Chloe would return to the Dark Enchanted Forest to find her people dead, and since it would be too late to [Resurrect] or [Revive] everyone, she would [Raise] an army of undead instead.

Any of the already undead wouldn't be able to be reanimated, and in her wrath, Chloe would reclaim the forest and attack Drendil. Keith was even supposed to show up as a final boss, but I had no idea why he wouldn't have just resumed being king after Chloe [Raised] him.

Nowhere in the prerelease videos or news updates had the Blackfog spies been mentioned. I could *barely* recall the one time they'd come up in Season One. In the game, Duke Wyldon had visited the black market with Henrietta and ended up buying vital information from a Blackfog spy that had helped take down Duke Lector at the Spring Ball.

But what had changed about the Spring Ball?

Everything. *I'd* changed everything. The butterfly effect from my years of altering the plot had come to full fruition that night, and now, we had a spy problem.

Up until today, I'd assumed Duke Lector had taken control of the spies in his attempt to overthrow the throne and declare himself king of Servalt . . . but now, I thought he was being used by the spies as much as he'd used them.

But was this a *new* villain or someone I'd faced playing Season One?

I ran the mini villains through my mind.

A young woman named Lady Tate was the villainess in Servalt. She was engaged to Marquess Chadwick—poor soul—and had harassed Duke Wyldon on her fiancé's orders.

Lady Luise, in Drendil, had wanted to marry Henrietta for power, and had used every violent trick in the book to make the heroine submit to her. Sir Phineas, known as an arrogant and hot-blooded knight to all, had caught Lady Luise hurting Henrietta and stepped forward to save her. He was the *tsundere* route.

The other two normal routes had had an interesting twist because the male leads became the villains to each other . . .

Knight Commander Bastian of Peldeep and Adventurer Trevor Malory teamed up with Henrietta to clear a few dungeons. They developed a bond. If she chose Bastian, Trevor tried to kidnap her and run off to the Empire of Sands. If she chose Trevor, Bastian lost control of his drakin powers, turned into a dragon, and tried to kill Trevor.

There were two bonus routes, one for Duke Julian and one for Master Thomas Martin of Servalt.

Lady Cassandra Cress was the main villainess in Julian's route because she wanted to marry into the North Sumbrian royal family. She took insult with Henrietta for her relaxed mannerisms and sought to embarrass the heroine at every turn.

Master Thomas was a Master Mage, and a candidate to take over the Mages Tower. He was calculating, insulting, and insufferable to the point that I'd almost quit playing the game during his mystical meteor route. He was his own villain, and the *yandere* route.

And the dark ending was *very* dark.

I couldn't be certain if any of them had fallen for Henrietta before the Spring Ball, but since she had been romping around the Dark Enchanted Forest the entire time . . . it seemed unlikely.

The staff passed me a pamphlet as I exited the arena. The Mages Tower was going to be doing a demonstration of their latest spells and enchantments after lunch.

I turned in the direction of the chaos.

The Hall of Inventions was only two streets over, and the shouting from panicked pedestrians was accompanied by the repeated shrill from the whistles carried by the city guard. Everyone was heading in the opposite direction of the pandemonium, but I sauntered toward it at a casual pace.

The only thing louder than the screaming was the unmistakable cacophony of *croaking*.

CHAPTER 20

Damage Control

Julian

There were frogs. Everywhere.

"You could have reported *this*," Julian confronted his rogue.

John was standing at attention with an armful of confused frogs, his face impassive. "I could have."

The city knights were out in full force, corralling a swarm of civilians-turned-frogs. They were doing a surprisingly good job controlling the area, but it was the layout of the street itself that was the saving grace. The Hall of Inventions wrapped around a busy corner in a distinct L-shape. The right side continued in a row of shops, and the left side had a stone wall blocking off carriage parking and storage for the Hall.

The frogs had nowhere to hide there.

Opposite, there was a corner café nestled close together between a crepe shop and a barbershop.

Queen Henrietta was zipping around with an outrageously fast travel ability, picking up amphibians and dropping them off at the foot of the stairs leading into the Hall of Inventions. Julian had used his [Barrier] to prevent the frogs from entering the Hall. Half of the knights were managing the crowds, while the other half used his protected area to create a safe space for the captured creatures.

Minstrel Bronwynn had climbed on top of one of the dragon statues beside the Hall stairs and sat on its head. She paused from playing her lyre harp only long enough to down a mana potion before launching back into song. Julian resisted her [Siren Song] even as the skill hit him. Luckily, Brownie was a high-enough level that it worked on most of the frogs. They were drawn to her music and climbing over each other to croak at her feet.

"Move them toward the music!" Captain Auralee yelled over the noise of the crowd.

"You've got this, love!" Rufus called out from farther away. The beastman was using some sort of calming skill to slow down the frogs that were outside the bard's area of effect. As he walked, he scooped up the creatures and gently tossed them into the puddle of happy frogs at the bard's feet.

It was chaos, but it was under control.

"John, drop the frogs and go get Chloe."

She was the most powerful mage he knew who specialized in curses and poisons. He would try to heal the frogs himself, but he wanted all the help he could get.

"Yes, Your Grace." John put down the frogs inside the [Barrier] then sunk into his own shadow.

Around thirty frogs were at the bard's feet, and Julian counted another twenty hopping down the road. He downed a mana potion before activating his highest-level ability.

"[Multi-Target Shield]!" he shouted, and magical shields appeared around many of the frogs making their escape. He could have done this *without* speaking aloud, but it was better to show everyone that their duke was here, and he was doing something productive. "[Divine Heal]."

> [You have attempted to use the Perk: **Multi-Target Shield**. Shield Arts [Divine] 12 + Dexterity 22 = 34 Shields. Available Targets: 21. You have selected 21 Targets. You have partially succeeded. 18 Targets Shielded.]
> [Select Durability Type: Communal or Unique. You have selected Unique Durability. Individual Shields will each have their own Durability.]
> [Select Durability Strength: 10 Mana per Level. You have selected 1 Durability. Mana Cost: 180 Mana.]

He targeted the frogs farthest from the fray and made his selections without actually reading through the perk information. He'd done this enough times to know the drill. With one durability, the shield would break after taking]ten points of damage *or* defend against one attack up to a hundred points of damage. Any additional damage would carry over and land on the target.

He switched to his next perk.

> [You have attempted to use the Perk: **Divine Heal**. Targets equal to Shielded Targets. Available Targets: 18.

Heal: Select Health increase. Mana Cost: 2 Mana per 1 Health
Point.
Cure: Kazil detected. Exhaustion detected. Bunions detected.
Misheal detected.]

Julian selected all and mentally chose [Cure].

[You have **Cured** 18 Kazil. Advanced Poisons cost 15 Mana each.
Mana Cost: 270 Mana.]
[Warning! Your Mana has dropped below 10%]
[You have **Cured** 2 Exhaustion. Status Ailment Minor cost 5 Mana
each. Mana Cost: 10 Mana.]
[Warning! Your Mana has dropped below 10%]
[You have **Cured** 1 Bunion. Status Ailment Critical cost 20 Mana
each. Mana Cost: 20 Mana.]
[Warning! Your Mana has dropped below 5%]

He probably shouldn't have healed the other status ailments listed, but he
had five hundred mana from his combined twenty-five Perception and twenty
Intelligence. He had used a hundred and eighty mana to activate his shields, and
another two hundred and seventy to cure them, leaving him with fifty mana to
cover the rest.

The low-mana effects hit him hard, and he reeled from the headache and
nausea, but managed while he summoned another potion. Closing his eyes, he
tried not to throw up as the mana potion brought his stats back to normal. He
opened his eyes to see the shielded frogs had turned back into people. Family and
friends rushed forward to help their loved ones, but were kept back by his ability.

He cancelled the shields.

A little old catkin lady sat on the ground right beside Julian, looking around
nervously before patting herself to be sure she was there. Julian helped her stand
and handed her over to a nearby knight.

Thankfully, the kazil poison was a magical replica of the [Frog Curse] spell,
and those who suffered its effects had all of their apparel and equipped items
changed with them. Julian would have had a nightmare on his hands if twenty-
odd naked festivalgoers suddenly *poofed* into being on his city streets.

"I think we've got them all, Your Grace." Captain Auralee, leader of the
capital city's Black Brigade Knights, walked up to Julian, pressing a fist to her
heart in greeting. The last three frogs were rounded up and deposited at Bronwynn's feet.

"Good job, Captain," he said. "Make sure that everyone who was affected
stays long enough to give a report. Necromancer Chloe should be here any

second. The frogs are affected with kazil poison, and we can start using any anti-dotes on hand to try and mitigate the effects."

Rufus approached Julian and the captain. "Duke Julian, Bronwynn will only be able to hold the frogs for another fifteen minutes or so."

"Were you here when this happened?" Julian asked.

"I was," Rufus reported calmly. "I arrived early and grabbed a tea across the street. The rest of my group arrived not long after the final match. That was when a woman working in the café started handing out free samples—"

"Captain." Julian didn't bother waiting for the beastman to finish his story before pointing at the café. She was gone in a flash of fast travel.

Rufus continued. "My passive effects notified me in time, but Bronwynn turned into a frog right away. I gave her an antidote, and when she was back to normal, we started on damage control."

Julian sighed. "Thank you for your assistance."

Chloe's voice echoed through the crowd. "What in the nine rings is happening here?"

Perfect timing.

CHAPTER 21

When You Fell for Duke Julian

Gerda

The mayhem had died down by the time I made my way to the Hall of Inventions.

"Please stay seated until you're cleared to leave," a guardswoman shouted over the croaking.

"[Cure]." Countess Julia, the Paladin of Light, was systematically picking up frogs and then bopping them on the nose. She stopped to take a mana potion every other frog.

Her build was for battle, not healing.

Necromancer Chloe was handing out antidotes and checking the condition of the cured. She was the perfect example of a calm, composed, and professional paramedic. She only came up to my chin, but she was a force to be reckoned with.

"Gerda!" Henrietta waved from across the street. Bronwynn was sitting on a statue of a dragon at the base of the stairwell into the Hall of Inventions, and Rufus was counselling the newly cured. Duke Julian, who was speaking with his shadowy assistant, stopped to shoot me *a look*. It was a very intense look. Absolute Fan Service.

"Excuse me, miss," an elven guard stepped forward to waylay me. "But we have closed down the street and no one is allowed entry."

"I am with Her Majesty." I waved back at Henrietta.

"Then you may wait over here until the area is cleared," the guard instructed, pointing to the café. Lady Amy was already sitting at a table so I joined her. She was all too happy to tell me everything I'd missed.

This was another great thing about *not* being in charge: If something happened, I didn't have to clean up the mess.

It took an hour before everything was finished.

"Any news on why the Blackfog spies turned people into a bunch of frogs?" I asked Henrietta when our party reunited. Even as I spoke, my Perception let me know that people were coming up behind me.

Chloe's voice answered. "To ruin my wedding?"

"It'll be fine, love," Countess Julia tried to cheer up her angry fiancée. I stepped back to welcome them into the conversation.

"We were supposed to be reviewing the cheese plates! And our final dress fitting starts in thirty minutes." Chloe huffed. "Anyway, Rufus, I *need* you for the fitting."

"You do not." Rufus reached out and took Bronwynn's hand.

"Bring your wife, I don't care, but you *will* come try on the suit we've prepared." Chloe pointed at Rufus. "And then we have the rehearsal dinner."

"No use fighting it." Countess Julia chuckled as she turned to Lady Amy. "There is a missive from your father back at the palace."

The woman deflated. "Then I'll return with you."

Rufus sighed dramatically. "Fine."

"I guess we'll see you later." Bronwynn waved goodbye. Chloe and Julia also grabbed Julian and dragged him away, but not before he shot me another *look*. I resisted the urge to wave at him, settling for a winning smile.

Even his suspicious frown looked hot.

I turned to Henrietta and asked, "Do we still have time to tour the Hall of Inventions"—the Dark Lady's stomach chose that moment to let out an impressive rumble—"or do you want to grab lunch?"

Henrietta took my arm, careful not to break it. "I'm so hungry I could eat a horse—and I'm allergic to horses!"

"Let's go to Megan's Tea House. I'm in the mood for something sweet."

Henrietta nodded. "And you can tell me when you fell for Duke Julian."

I didn't trip. I didn't flinch. In fact, I was incredibly proud that I simply raised an eyebrow at my friend and asked, "What makes you think I like His Grace?"

"You can't see yourself." Henrietta smiled. "But the way your eyes follow him . . . you look like you want to *eat* the man."

"I don't eat elf," I deadpanned while the heroine laughed out loud.

"You can't fool me," she teased. "You can't keep your eyes off him, and you keep sending him this playful smile like you have a secret that you're not going to share with him."

I attempted to refute her claims. "He's the person in charge—of course I'm going to check back and see what he's doing. Besides, I'll have you know I'm naturally this secretive, and we all know it."

"You are a curmudgeon who delights in trolling people," Henrietta countered. "Pun intended. But it's not the same. *Do* you have a secret on the duke?"

"Ha-ha, make fun of the bridge troll," I mocked offense. "How would I know any of his secrets? I live in the Dark Enchanted Forest, and he lives in the Northern Ice Fields."

"That's not a no." Henrietta smiled slyly.

We arrived at the teahouse, and I opened the door for us.

"It's an *implied* no."

Megan's Tea House was large enough for twelve small tables and a single seat at the shop window. Climbing vines hung from the walls, and plants were happily living their best life in every corner of the establishment. Since it was past the lunch rush, there were only two others in the eatery.

A faun greeted us with a warm smile from behind her counter. "Welcome to Megan's." Her voice was kind and welcoming. "Please place your order with me, and I'll be happy to bring it to your table."

CHAPTER 22

She Flew Off

Julian

"How hard is it to walk you up the aisle, let go, and stand by the front seats?" Julian grumbled to his sister, who was gripping his hand very, *very* hard.

He ignored the notification window showing him *just* how much damage he'd taken so far.

"We will practice as many times as it takes," Duchess Calisto chastised from her spot at those same front seats.

"I think I'm going to throw up," Julia said casually.

At first glance, she looked like the calm, confident Paladin of Light renowned for her charming smile. At second glance, Julian could tell her facial muscles hadn't so much as twitched in some time, and her eyes were glazed.

"You're doing great, love!" Chloe called from the dais of the castle sanctuary.

The Sanctuary was dedicated to Light, and could hold at least two hundred people. There were long windows stretching up the hall, with colorful gold and silver sun and moon embellishments etched into the glass. It was bright and welcoming, and the banner behind the dais featured the cycles of the celestial bodies. Their Royal Highness Rowen of Peldeep stood there in the guise of a long white-haired stately court official. They even had a long thin beard that hung down to their chest, and a small red cap. Everyone else was in normal attire.

After finishing with the tailor, Julian had been brought directly to the sanctuary, where he'd listened to the detailed wedding plan, *again*, and was now doing the walk-through.

This was his fourth walk up the aisle.

His sister had managed fine the first time, but each walk had seen her getting more nervous. They were halfway up the aisle before she whispered, "I don't think I can do this."

Julian tried to calm her with a soft, "I'd rather be eating dinner myself; do you know what we are having after this?"

His sister's body went from rigid stiffness to uncontrollable shaking. Her smile broke, and she repeated, "No, I don't think I can do *this*."

And then she flew off. Literally.

Her [Wings of Light] burst out, and she kicked into the air before flying out the open sanctuary doors.

"Julia!" Chloe called out, concern and surprise in her voice. The necromancer enveloped herself in shadows and disappeared, presumably to run after her nervous bride.

There was an awkward pause before Grand Duchess Calisto turned to Julian and said, "*This changes nothing*. We will rehearse until *we* have it right, with or without the brides."

Julian wanted to go after his sister, but he knew she preferred to have some time alone when she needed to think about things—and if anyone found her, it should be Chloe. If they worked it out, then the wedding would proceed as planned. If Julia truly didn't want to marry the necromancer, then that was that. He'd support his sister in whatever path she chose. It was easy as that.

What *wasn't* easy was having to go through four more passes of the rehearsal before being set free.

Dinner that evening was goose stuffed with minced wild carrots and fennel root, seasoned with rosemary and sage and Sweet Anne's Lace root. There was a side of wild daffolyn greens tossed with creamy dillweed dressing, and twice-baked purple sweet potatoes with butter and chives.

It was delightful.

"Mother-in-law!" Chloe chose the moment that he was chewing a large bite of potato to burst through the dining room doors in a panic. "Julia is missing!"

To her credit, his mother patted her lips gently before standing up without question. "I'll send out the guard."

Julian coughed. "Are you sure?"

His sister often hid away to process her feelings as a child, and from the letters they often exchanged, she'd continued to do so. One time, she'd gone missing for three days and was found practicing the sword in an old weapons storage room in the basement of the palace. Another time, she'd holed up in the attic above the stables for a week while she came to terms with her nanny retiring.

He didn't think he was being unreasonable, and wasn't expecting the glares directed his way.

The wedding party was already packing up to help. Rufus frowned at a notification, and King Keith was whispering into a button on his open tunic. Julia's bridesmaids—Gladiator Hana Lanora and Striker Wendy Lanora—were on their feet equipping their weapons. Hana sheathed a sword at her waist while Wendy equipped holy knives, a tiny crossbow, and a golden lasso. The items glowed with faint holy light.

"The city is under constant annoyance by a group of spies who have Julia's name on a list of targets," his mother reminded him, already sending the guards quests with her [Grand Duchess] ability. "It is always better to be cautious."

"I know my darling." Chloe crossed her arms. "She isn't in the east lookout or the west fountain *or* the palace training rooms. And the guards say they didn't see her fly over the walls. She's hard to miss."

"That just proves my point then, doesn't it?" Julian stabbed a chunk of daf-folyn from his salad. "If she's still in the palace, then she isn't missing. She's probably just chosen some place we won't think to look so that she can blow off some steam."

"I know this is not my place, but even if she *is* merely hiding, we should still try and find her today," Their Royal Highness Rowen stressed, "You know, *before* the wedding."

"Rowen is right." Duchess Calisto stood, sweeping a lock of hair over her shoulder.

"I usually am." The fox grinned, then tapped their chin. "I will search the east wing, since that is where I am staying."

"I appreciate that, Rowen." The duchess nodded their way.

"We'll help search the north," Hana and Wendy said together.

"And we'll search the south." King Keith stood with Rufus and Bronwynn. "Henrietta and Gerda will search the city on their way here."

Julian sighed. "Then I'll search the west wing."

"We are not to enter private rooms without cause," Grand Duchess Calisto informed. "My personal knights have been dispatched along with the guards. If you see one of them, tell them your findings."

There were three units of North Sumbrian knights. The Grey Hawk Knights, who guarded his mother; the Black Brigade Knights, who were responsible for the safety of the towns and cities throughout the duchy; and the Coral Mare Knights, who protected the palace.

Grand Duchess Calisto walked over and placed a hand on Chloe's shoulder. "Don't worry, we'll find her."

CHAPTER 23

So You Think He's Cute

Gerda

Earlier

We decided to order lunch in two stages: savory and then dessert.

I had the floofpoof egg salad sandwich with miner's lettuce, fresh tomatoes, and a cream sauce. My soup of choice was a smooth and nutty squash base with small dumplings and bacon bits.

Henrietta picked a grilled sandwich with flying pig's belly cooked in red sauce that reminded me of smoky maple barbeque, and topped with miner's lettuce, tomatoes, scallions, and a fried goose egg. She'd paired it with miso soup loaded with tiny cut mushrooms and green onions and wild carrots.

"Delicious," Henrietta said happily, finishing her meal and sitting back. She'd tackled her food with gusto the second it had appeared, while I was still enjoying my soup.

"Hm," I made a satisfied noise around a warm spoonful.

"I think this is my new favorite teahouse in all of Valaria," Henrietta announced, taking a sip of her iced berry tisane.

"You should decide that *after* we've tried the dessert," I advised. When I was done, we picked up our dishes and returned them to a bin at the counter. The treats we'd ordered earlier were handed over, and we walked back to our seats. Before we continued, we cut each in half and split.

"Now for the moment of truth." Henrietta lifted a piece of my markleberry crescent-shaped pastry, and we both took a bite. It looked like a croissant, but it was baked with an egg wash and tasted like fluffy Japanese milk bread. The berry filling tasted like chocolate jam.

A markleberry was as large as an avocado and purple on the outside. Inside, it was a dark brown and tasted like chocolate pudding. Every berry had three seeds in the center. Sadly, it didn't have the consistency of chocolate, and was usually frozen or processed into jams, jellies, or sauces Sometimes, it was whipped with unigoat cream for a very close but not exact milk chocolate flavor. The sugar of the berry meant that it already had a natural sweetness.

And it was just another reminder that I was trapped in a fantastical world.

"Perfection," Henrietta sighed, content.

I picked up a piece of Henrietta's dessert. It was this world's equivalent to a soft matcha brioche loaf made with Valarian green tea. It didn't taste like Earth's *green tea*, but the color of the brew was green, and so that is what it was called.

People were the same in every world.

The bread was baked with dried strawberries and served warm from the oven with butter.

"New favorite teahouse," I agreed.

Henrietta smiled and shot me a side-eye. "Don't think I've forgotten that we were talking about your feelings for our half-elf friend." She'd done me the courtesy of not naming names now that we were inside a shop. Albeit one with only the shopkeeper and few others to overhear.

"*There is nothing to talk about*," I stated firmly. And really, there wasn't. *Sure*, I stanned Julian. He was tall, dark, and brooding. And hardworking. And—

Alright, enough of that.

The man's biggest flaw was that he wasn't considerate in the conventional way. He hid himself in the North and stayed there, and while he loved his family, he wouldn't risk change to be with them.

And he was fixated on leveling up.

All in all, not someone right for a bridge troll from the Dark Enchanted Forest.

"Does that mean you won't try for him?" Henrietta asked, sipping her berry blend tisane. "Even if it's just for fun, the festival is a great time to flirt."

I snorted. "You want me to *flirt*? With the *duke*?"

"Why not?" Henrietta pointed her teaspoon at me. "You are beautiful, witty, charming, and powerful. He should count himself lucky to hold your hand."

She was so sincere it was sweet. "I'm pretty sure he isn't interested in holding my hand. Or anyone's."

"I don't know. The way he was staring at you . . ."

I shook my head. "Just because I find someone attractive doesn't mean I should suddenly go on the offensive. Luck knows I'm already busy enough without man troubles added on. Need I remind you that I am the target of espionage and assassination? And what's with all these assassination attempts, anyway?!"

I knew the general outline for season two, and there wasn't a hint of the spies rising up and attacking world powers. The plot seemed contrived, shoe-horned in to keep things running . . . but at this point in the story, we should have had some exposition or idea of their goals. We didn't even know who the leader of the Blackfog spies was, or what they wanted.

And it couldn't just be to watch the world burn.

"I mean, these things happen all the time," Henrietta pointed out. "Maybe someone new took over and wanted to stir up trouble? And they couldn't find an easier—if more expensive—way to go about spreading chaos."

"They turned a bunch of civilians into frogs, Henrietta, *frogs*." I stuffed the last bit of bread into my mouth. It was good enough that a soft noise of pleasure escaped me.

"I'm definitely bringing Keith here after the wedding," Henrietta vowed.

I nodded, then took my last bite.

"And you can bring Julian."

I choked. "Are you done yet? I have *no* plans to speak with the duke ever again. And even if I did . . . he's heading back to the North as soon as the closing ceremonies end, so it would be a bad idea to get attached."

"You're *sure?*" She played with her empty tea cup.

I stood up. "If you are going to keep teasing me, do it while we look at Grand Duchess Calisto's Hall of Inventions."

"All right." She agreed, and we headed back the way we'd come.

"Welcome to the Hall of Inventions," a fox woman greeted us with her best customer service smile at the entry and handed us a pamphlet. "Please don't touch anything or you will burst into flames. No eating in the display area. Magic of any kind is prohibited inside the building. And please check out our catalogue at the end if you wish to order any of our inventions for yourself."

"Thank you!" Henrietta beamed, taking the slip and unfurling it so that she could read over the map. "Oh, Gerda! It says they have a new line of cold storage options in the annex. They even have an entire section just for magical kitchenwares!"

I smiled down at the woman, her excitement catching. "Lead on."

It took us two hours to wander around the building of magically engineered tools which almost all closely resembled electronics from my world. There were a few exceptions: a pair of wings that let you fly as the fae did, and a wardrobe that magically put away all of the clean laundry thrown inside it. I may have considered ordering the last.

Laundry wasn't fun in any world, and at this point, I made do with Brenda's Brownies Cleaning Service and stored my clothes in my Hero's Spatial Ring . . . But if I made a walk-in closet off of my bedroom space, I could stick a double-wide wardrobe inside and live with the luxury of a walk-in self-maintaining closet.

Truly tempting.

"I wonder if Rinrin—Oh, one second." Henrietta pulled out a string necklace from under her clothes with a small button on it that buzzed gently. She poked it three times.

"Henrietta?" Keith's voice was soft as a whisper, and I thanked my Perception that I could hear him at all.

"Yes, my love?" Henrietta also spoke quietly in response.

"Julia is missing."

CHAPTER 24

The Void Mage

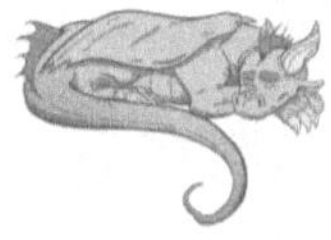

Julian

Julian looked up from the west wing garden. He was standing at the fountain below his window and absently playing with his locket.

There were guards *everywhere.*

He'd searched the west wing. Twice. And the gardens, the stables, and the path around the wall leading *back* to the gardens. He wasn't expecting to find anything, and so far, he hadn't.

"John," he said, and the man formed out of Julian's shadow.

"Yes, Your Grace?"

"How is the search?"

John reported, "Visha is making everyone do a second pass through the dungeons, Tully is flirting with a maid behind the stables, Jeffry is with the kitchen staff reading over order forms so he can track if someone requests food from an unregistered suite. And Pram is outside the palace walls asking if anyone has spotted something suspicious."

"Good, and yourself?"

"I have tried four different [Tracking] perks on items I liberated from Julia's room. Nothing has worked so far," he said calmly..

Julian didn't mind the theft. "So it *was* a kidnapping."

"Unless your sister leveled up since last we met."

Julian grabbed one of the shirts. "Tell Mother that I'm moving my search to the city."

John vanished as Julian leapt over the palace wall and found himself walking down the same streets he'd frequented the night before. His [Tracking] might not be as powerful as John's, but he could still try. He would comb the entire city thrice over by morning if he had to. *His little sister was missing.*

Julian resisted the urge to punch something and tried [Tracking] in the market.

Nothing.

The only thing keeping hold of his barely contained frustration was the fact the lists they'd confiscated all unanimously stated the same thing: No permadeath.

He moved on from the marketplace to the north end of the city, [Tracking] every three blocks. The alarms hadn't sounded, but he could see palace knights searching with the city guard. The extra security wasn't given a second look by the citizens due to Madame Potts's warnings.

What he wouldn't give for a Potts's Cast right now.

"Your Grace." One of the palace knights ran up to him. "We have news."

"Report," Julian ordered, a shred of hope filling his voice.

"Her Grace teleported to the Mercenary Guild in Servalt," the knight told him. "She found three people who had worked for Blackfog in the past and brought them back for questioning."

"Where are they?"

"In the main parlor, Your Grace."

Julian raised an eyebrow. "Not the prison interrogation rooms?"

The knight shook his head. "The parlor."

Julian ran back the way he'd come.

He was there in minutes, and didn't hold back his anticipation as he burst into the parlor. A human, an elf, and a fox he'd never met before stared up at him. Whatever conversation had been happening stopped at his entrance, and his mother frowned.

"Son. Please, join us."

Julian refused to feel like a boy being chastised, taking the seat nearest her, head held high. "What have I missed?"

"Barry was just telling us about his experience as a Blackfog." Grand Duchess Calisto waved a hand at a human swordsman sitting across from her. Their Royal Highness Rowen stood by the window, and Chloe sat pouting in a chair on the opposite side of his mother. The necromancer did *not* look happy, but she remained silent.

The three . . . *guests* were all comfortably settled in with tea and sweets.

"Ah, yes, well, we'd done odd jobs for the network before, and every time, it were by official quest." Barry scratched his head, looking surprisingly relaxed. The human had brown skin and shoulder-length dark-green hair with blond streaks. His hands were marred with calluses and knife wounds. "And while it's good money, it's also pretty dangerous work, you know?"

"What Barry is *trying* to say," an elf with soft-pink skin and brown hair dressed in wizards robes nervously cut in, "is that we joined the subjugation quest in the Dark Enchanted Forest. We both met the criteria because my father is from Nilheim and Barry was born in Gren's Keep."

"That's none of their business, Lomen." Barry shot the elf a betrayed look. "I don't go around telling everyone your dad's a male—"

"Alright, alright! I'm sorry." Lomen rushed to cut off the human. "I just wanted to explain from the beginning."

"Or we can just tell them we took a quest and they gave us a list of targets and how to defeat them." Barry said.

"That's what I got as well," the fox added. She had long orange-red hair and black eyes.

"Who gave you the list?" Grand Duchess Calisto sipped her tea.

"The Void mage." Barry shuddered. "She was very meticulous and even gave us poisons catered to each person we were supposed to fight." He stopped there, reached out for a cookie from the table, and ate it happily. Everyone waited but Barry seemed content to eat his cookie.

Julian didn't have much patience. "And the Void mage?"

The fox answered. "She's a Charisma based class—about my height, blond hair, blue eyes, pale skin, and pink magic."

"And she's *weird*," Barry added.

Lomen drew a hand down his face in frustration. "That isn't helpful, Barry."

"But it's true!"

"He's right," the fox said. "Every time she spoke, it made my skin crawl."

"Suki, Barry, and Lomen." Julian's mother set down her teacup and pushed it aside, directing her aura at the three. The entire room suddenly felt the pressure of the power released by her level. She might be a Crafting class, but she was still over level *eighty*. "We believe that this Void mage has captured my daughter. For what purpose, I do not know—but you're going to help us find her."

CHAPTER 25

Stalking the Duke

Gerda

When the message came through, Henrietta immediately went into full Heroine of Justice mode and decided to put me somewhere "safe."

"If I'm going to search the city," she reasoned, "I'll need you to stay here so I don't worry!" She pointed at the city guardhouse that she'd brought me to. Henrietta wasn't exactly happy to leave me there, but I'd refused a "ride" back to the palace.

I was *not* about to let the Dark Lady princess-carry me to the palace. Not when I could get there myself. "I'll be fine!" I reassured her. Again.

"I still think you should teleport back to your bridge."

"And have to walk back here from the forest?" I laughed.

It was a misleading statement, as I'd already walked across a sky bridge that arched between the west wing and the central palace, and could portal there with [World Bridge] at any time. Unfortunately, at this point, I'd taken too long trying to convince Henrietta, and my inhuman Perception noticed John's shadow appear and attach itself to mine.

"Just, *stay here*," my queen ordered.

"Alright," I lied.

She hesitated only another second before activating, "[Quick Step]."

Henrietta was a highly trained scout and attacker; she would grid-pattern search the entire city streets within the hour. I paid attention to the direction she was headed in so I could time my own actions going forward.

"Miss?" One of the city knights greeted me as I entered the guardhouse. "How may we help you?"

"Hello." I waved at the elf. "I'm wondering if I could wait here for my friends to come get me?"

He shot me an understanding look. "Of course. Please, make yourself comfortable."

The small guardhouse, one of many stationed around the city, consisted of a small receiving area with a chair on either side, a defensive booth with a city knight stationed behind it, and the door into an enchanted holding cell beside the booth.

I took a seat.

Since John was still attached to my shadow, I was limited in what I could immediately do without revealing too much to the rogue. I chose "[Map]."

> [You have activated the Perk: **Map**. A mini map revealing the areas you have explored is available. System assist **Zoom** unlocked. System assist **Track Troll Riddle** unlocked. System assist **Danger Area** unlocked. System assist **Quest Item Area** unlocked. System assist **Sooth Area** unlocked. System assist **Locate Bridge** unlocked.]

The ability came with a tiny mini map that popped up in my regular notification interface, but activating the map itself pulled up a larger version that took over the system window.

With my [System] skill on level six, I was able to add six different map features.

[Zoom] was obvious, allowing me to zoom in and out on the map. [Track Troll Riddle] was connected to a specific ability I had using the [Troll Riddle] perk, which allowed me to give delayed riddles. *You have three days to learn my name*, Rumpelstiltskin style. This was also designed to let someone who couldn't answer or pay leave with a timed debt. They could come back later with payment or I could hunt them down on my map. The perk itself came with a general "They went that-a-way!" feeling, but having an icon on my mini map was much more helpful.

[Danger Area] was also pretty intuitive, and it shaded out areas of the map that were dangerous with a soft transparent red. This was more hit-and-miss than it seemed because I was now so powerful that a lot of things no longer registered as dangerous on my map. I could walk around the first few floors of any dungeon and not have it go off at all.

[Quest Item Area] shaded places in green that had an item I'd accepted a quest to find. It was helpful, but if the item was in a dungeon or in someone's spatial ring, then it wouldn't show up on the map at all.

[Sooth Area] highlighted in yellow an area of the map directly related to any of the scenarios my abilities foretold. And the last, [Locate Bridge], I'd picked up just in time to start my quest for world-bridge domination! And by that, I meant I got it around the time I'd claimed all of the Dark Enchanted Forest bridges and was starting to link ones in other kingdoms.

[Sooth Area] was what I needed now.

"Gotcha."

The city lay sprawled out on the map, and two areas immediately caught my attention. There was a yellowed-out part of the map in the Coral Palace, the arena, and at the eastern city gate. There was also a green circle; someone with one of my quest items was moving around the Coral Palace and I wondered if it could be Julian.

The map wouldn't show the locket previously because the item was locked inside a subspace, but now that I *knew* it had the treasure, was the map following the locket?

I hoped not. I didn't know how I felt about my [Map] stalking the duke. Or that the marker was now leaving the palace . . . and heading in a straight line for the yellow highlighted area by the port gate.

I needed to leave now if I was going to help at all.

A group of festivalgoers were walking past the guardhouse, and I stood. "Thank you, those are my friends."

The knight waved. "Have a good night, miss."

"You too."

Then I slipped out into the night, following the crowd as they walked up the street. My shadow came with, so I waited until I'd cleared sight of the guard station and then activated my skill. "[World Bridge]."

[You have attempted to use the Perk: **World Bridge**. You have succeeded. You may travel to any bridge you have crossed or controlled since obtaining **World Bridge**.

Select bridge from the available options . . .]

CHAPTER 26

That's Right I'm Right

Julian

"The North Sumbrian Mercenary Guild is a foolish place to start looking." Barry told Julian as he led their group through the city. "Besides, that will be *just* what the spies are expecting us to do!"

Back at the palace, Suki and Barry had argued extensively about where to search. The fox wanted to go to the Mercenary Guild. She'd reasoned they could look for clues and find quests that matched previous Blackfog contracts. Hiring from the various mercenary, assassin, and adventuring guilds had been the norm for the spies up until this point. Since Julia was an elite, there could very well be a legal contract registered at the guild, making it a good place to start looking.

Barry disagreed, saying they should directly search the northeast gate as it was closest to the port. Since the Void mage wasn't able to portal in and out of the city due to Grand Duchess Calisto's new security enchantments, she would need to use one of the gates. The merchant quarters frequently had large transport caravans coming and going: an easy place to smuggle out a spy and a missing countess. There were also rentable warehouses and plenty of spots to hide Julia if she hadn't been moved out of the city yet.

Julian thought that anyone skilled enough to kidnap Julia without getting caught by his mother's overwhelming security, might be able to walk out of any city gate just fine. But he held his tongue.

Instead of wasting more time, multiple search parties had been formed.

Julian, Rufus and Bronwynn were currently following Barry and Lomen to the port city gate. Chloe, Wendy, and Hana went with Suki to the Mercenary Guild. Henrietta and Keith went to the Adventurer's Guild, and Visha, Pram, and Tully were sent to watch the other city gates just in case.

"If the Blackfog think we'll be focusing on the guilds, isn't it a good idea to send a search party there?" Bronwynn pipped up, "They can draw attention away from us."

"Well *actually*—,"

"*Here we go*," Lomen whispered under his breath.

"—The second Suki walks through those doors, it's going to tell the Blackfog two things: that you're officially looking for the countess *and* that you're with mercenaries who've worked with the Blackfog before." Barry frowned. "We'll have to hurry now that they know someone who *actually* knows what they're doing has joined the search. No offense."

"None taken," Julian answered for everyone.

Barry added, "The gate inspectors are mercantile and easier to subdue. Any merchant worth their salt could slip out a kidnapped countess."

"He's right," Lomen sighed.

"That's right I'm right!" Barry smiled.

"We've arrived," Julian said, coming to a stop when they were in view of the gate. "Now what?"

There were two wagons loading at the storage bays nearby, and at least twenty people were going about their day's work this side of the gate.

"Now we should divide and conquer." Barry made a circle with his thumb and index finger and scanned the area. He sighed. "What we *should* have done was create two teams—having one come this way and the other go out another gate to search the docks separately."

"But we didn't do that," Julian pointed out.

"Brownie and I can handle the docks." Rufus spoke for the first time. There was a sudden *pop*, and Rufus puffed into his folk form. He was still blond with gold eyes, but he was shorter and furless.

"Leave this to us." Brownie took her partner's arm and then pitched her voice *just so* as they walked away. "Do you *really* think we can find work during the festival? Who needs more guards when the city is already crawling with them?"

Rufus replied, "There's always work at the docks; you know that."

"Alright." She sighed wistfully. "But we should save up more next year. I want to celebrate the entire *week*."

"Now that's taken care of, we should hurry. So try to keep up." Barry settled one hand comfortably on his sword, bent his knees, and jumped, landing easily on the rooftop directly overhead.

Lomen cursed under his breath and started whispering a spell. Soon, he was levitating up to the second-story roof and disappearing out of sight. Julian activated his own movement ability and caught up with a quietly arguing Barry and Lomen.

"Your Grace." Barry turned and pointed at the two wagons inside the city gate. "Lomen is going to search those while you follow me."

"Where?"

Barry pointed at one particular building of storage bays. "I've done three smuggling trips through North Sumbria, and we've always used that—" The sentence ended in a muffled mumble as Lomen's hand whipped out and covered the human's mouth. The elf shouted an impressively quiet whisper. *"Don't say it!"*

A silver arch appeared on Barry's forehead with a thin black dagger painted through it. It was a sign that he had betrayed someone in the black market.

In Valaria, the Continental Council rarely punished petty criminals for contract minion work. There was no sense in sentencing someone for just doing their job. This created an interesting problem where hired workers, like assassins, would get arrested and then set free because they'd only *been doing their job.*

But that was at the hireling level. What separated them from other criminals was simple: knowledge.

Anyone who was brought into the darker side of the underworld were subject to oaths of secrecy as they planned heists, organized assassinations, and transported stolen or illegal goods.

If a government wanted to actually stop criminal activity in their realm, they were forced to address the leaders and power behind the crime, because punishments were reserved for those in the know.

And you were either *in the know* or you were not.

"Look what you've done!" Lomen sighed. He confirmed Julian's suspicions when he added, "You have the [Deal-Breaker] mark. What are your stats?"

Julian was not surprised to find out that the two were, in fact, *in the know.*

"Nothing majorly inconvenient." Barry shrugged. "I was tired of being a smuggler anyway."

"So you thought the best way to stop was to betray your confidentiality contract instead of—I don't know—*quitting like a normal person?*" Lomen scolded. "You couldn't just say, 'because it looks suspicious'? You're *impossible.*"

"Gentlemen." Julian's voice remained neutral as he interrupted. "I'm willing to put in a good word for you with the Council as long as we find my sister. Need I remind you that time is of the essence?"

"Ah, yes, sorry." Lomen waved for Barry to continue.

"As I was saying." Barry walked over to the alley closest to the storage bay and sneaked a peek to make sure there wasn't anyone below. "We need to check the bay before they move the goods. And if the bay is empty, we should head straight for the docks. You could even run ahead, Your Grace."

"Why do I have the feeling if I did, you would both turn tail and run off?" Julian asked.

"That does sound like something I would do." Barry nodded. "But I think your sister is more important to you than we are."

The swordsman was right.

"Let's go."

CHAPTER 27

The Keeper of Fate

Gerda

I walked onto the bridge connecting to the west wing tower, some twenty floors above the ground, and simply chose not to bring my erstwhile shadow with me.

The sky bridge was reinforced with magic, and there was a protective barrier just below that would catch anyone who slipped and fell off its surface. Ornate coral-pink railings came up to my hip on either side of the bridge. From this vantage point, I could make out the faint shimmer of the magically engineered barriers set up by the grand duchess. Whatever guards she had up against nefarious ne'er-do-wells portaling into the palace did not ward against bridge magic.

They were different skills entirely, but also different magics. The portal skill tree functioned without preset points, which meant that the system directly connected from where a portal user was to the place they were going to portal to. Bridge magic, on the other hand, made permanent connections to my controlled bridges. There was no portal; I was just walking across a bridge.

If portal magic was founded on traveling through space, bridge magic was built on dimensional magic—and worked outside of the realm itself. It was a cheat which let me break into dungeons, bypass certain barriers, and create permanent links in a way that portals didn't.

Making my way across the bridge, there was movement below as knights combed the palace grounds, searching for the missing Countess Julia. There was no point in hiding my presence and making myself a target, so I simply walked into the west wing and took the stairs down to my room.

"[Oracle]." Once inside, I lay down on my bed and activated my title. I wanted to see what would happen if I didn't interfere,

[**Oracle:** You are witness to the strings of Fate and her weave. The story unfolds, and the Chosen of each deity mark the way.
You have found 8/12 Chosen.
Impending Scenarios: 5/12 Chosen.
Arbiter of Shadow - The Guild Engagement
Steward of Life - The Burning Bridge
Harbinger of Dreams - The Soul Quest
Paladin of Light - The Chloe Question
Heroine of Justice - The Great Chase
Timeline access restricted.
Available Scenarios: All Scenarios within current Domain boundaries available. All Scenarios impending within 6.5 days available.
Oracle timeline: 4 mins 30 seconds.
Please select Chosen.]

[Oracle] was one of the primary reasons I could affect the story as much as I did, but it was dangerous.

I selected *Paladin of Light*. Green light engulfed my eyesight.

I was sitting in a warehouse's cold floor, hands shackled above my head with Veralyn's Enchanted Restraint Manacles. I felt weak and tired.

"You're awake, Paladin of Light," a voice spoke from the darkness.

"Who are you?" My heart beat faster in my chest. This was the worst time to be kidnapped! I needed to escape and find my way back to Chloe.

"I'm the Keeper of Fate." A figure stepped closer, and I could make out a small feminine frame. "And I'm here with a proposal. I recommend you take it."

I grinned up at the woman, hiding my unease with my winning smile. "Sorry, Keeper, but I'm already taken."

"You should listen, because I'm willing to let your lover live . . . for another's fate."

It was hard, but I kept my lighthearted disposition. Leaning back, I crossed my legs in front of me and shrugged. "I don't make deals with villains. If you so much as touch a hair on my wife's head, then no god or goddess in the nine realms will be able to save you."

My captor didn't take the threat to heart and continued. "Oh, I'm not a villain. I am a reckoning."

"Oh, really?" That didn't sound good.

"I'm tired of trying to right the weave one fate at a time," the voice grumbled. "So if I can gather enough of the fated into one place, I can get rid of them all at once!"

"I thought you said you wouldn't harm Chloe?" I accused, knowing full well that any search party would have my love front and center.

"Yes. The necromancer, the heroine, and the duke may live." The figure paced angrily. "But the Dark Lord must die, and his general."

"But . . . why?" Curiosity got the better of me. "The entire continent has been turned on its head from the Blackfog rising. Why permanent death? You've even been caught targeting civilians. It makes no sense."

"I'm like you, Paladin of Light. I have a duty, and I serve a path." The figure snapped her fingers, and a single pink light appeared, hovering over her shoulder. Her hair was blonde, and her eyes were cornflower blue. She was one of the most beautiful people I'd ever laid eyes upon. Revulsion and adoration warred within me. I was in love with Chloe, but for a single, heartbreaking moment, I almost felt something for the woman before me.

She lifted a hand, pink magical threads bound to each finger. One thread shimmered brighter than the rest, and a portal appeared.

"I am the Keeper of Fate"—she shot me a too-sweet smile as she reached out and grabbed my hair—"and I'm going to make everything right again."

Without a by-your-leave, she portaled me away.

I broke from the trance, breathing erratically. It was mentally draining to wrench my mind from the four-minute scenario, and I started dry heaving from the awful feeling.

It took a while, but I eventually crawled off the bed and left from the merchant cargo area by the port city gate. It was the only part of my map with warehouses.

A knight stopped me on the second floor. "Where are you going?"

"To look around the city."

"Have you been in the palace all day?"

"No," I deliberately told the truth so that I wouldn't set off any abilities. "I was helping search for our missing countess, since I was with Queen Henrietta when she got the news."

"If you find anything, please report immediately."

"I will."

It took two more interrogations before I was out of the palace grounds.

I was not a travel-based character type, and I hated running, so I walked to the main thoroughfare a block away and found a rickshaw willing to take me to the northeast gate for extra coin.

The wolfman shot me a toothy grin as he bit the silver coin I gave him before pocketing it and grabbing the handles of his person-pulled carriage. I fit myself comfortably on a wooden seat, and he was off.

We were two streets from the gate when I called out, "Driver! You can let me out here!"

The Western Star Needs to Crest the Tree Line

Julian

Julian followed Barry and Lomen into the alley. There were five doors: four on the left and one on the building they'd just jumped down from.

"I'll check if any are guarded." Lomen raised his staff and covered the tip with a black cloth before casting his spell. "By Shade and Light Revealed that Which is Concealed [Inspect]."

The fabric hid the burst of red light from the spell.

"This door is unlocked, and I don't detect any protection spells," the mage whispered, pointing at the door on the right. "Let me check the other doors."

The shadows on the wall beside Julian rippled. John had returned.

The human rogue wouldn't reveal himself until ordered to; they'd been on enough missions together where stealth was life and death. Once he had merged with Julian's shadow, he sent a [Shadow Chat].

[The bridge troll escaped my shadow.]

"What?" The word slipped out before he could hold it back.

[The bridge troll escaped my shadow.]

Julian furrowed his brow, replying in the chat.

[When?]
[A few minutes after you left the palace.]
[Why are you only telling me this now?]
[She used some sort of portal skill, so I'd assumed she didn't go far . . .]

John's shadow sounded sheepish. The city restricted portal use within small areas, and the rogues tracking skills were powerful enough he should've found Gerda easily.

[I was wrong. And your mother had a task for my palace shadow, so I was unable to leave from there to chase you. This is the shadow that was originally with the bridge troll.]
[What did my mother want?]
[She had me retrieve the Arc Warden from the treasury and bring it to her in the palace observatory.]

Julian cursed.

Barry raised an eyebrow at the duke, but Lomen flinched, saying, "I-I'm done."

"Good, because we just ran out of time."

He eyed the pair.

Lomen seemed like the anxious type who followed through with his orders, but Barry was in it for the amusement and the challenge. The latter wasn't a safe bet, but he was the more likely to get the job done *well*.

"Barry, I need you out of the port gates. *Now*," Julian instructed. "I'll give you a bag of gold *and* a shiny treasure from my personal stash if you inspect the docks and rescue my sister should you find her."

"Why now?" the human asked, but his eyes gleamed at the request.

"Because the entire city is about to get magically sealed."

"Alright. Later, Lomen." Barry smiled, waved at the elf, and then he was *gone*. Julian's twenty-five Perception wasn't enough to catch what happened, but he did note the scuff in the dust of the alley floor.

"Wait!" Lomen's voice was high pitched, and he turned on Julian. "You aren't expecting us to actually find and rescue your sister on this side *without* Barry?"

"Did you learn anything from your spell earlier?" Julian gestured at the doors.

"Of course." Lomen pointed his staff at the second door on the left. "That door is the only one magically guarded."

Julian nodded. "Can you get through its defense?"

The elf scoffed. "Who am I?" He raised his free hand. "By Gates between and Sight Unseen, Threads Unwind and Pass through Clean, [Undetected Interference]."

The spell took, and he picked the lock without setting off any alarms, opening the door into a long hallway that spanned the side of the building. Before Lomen could go in, Julian held him back and activated his [Barrier].

[You have attempted to use the Perk: **Multi-Target Shield**. You have succeeded . . .]

As long as Lomen had a shield on him, Julian could activate further abilities to protect the mage. "*Now* you can go."

There were no doors on the inside where he could clearly see them on the outside. It looked promising, but he wanted eyes everywhere.

[John, go check the next building and meet me in the loading bay area in ten minutes.]

The shadow slipped out before Julian closed the door behind him. Lomen had a finger pressed to his own lips while waving to catch Julian's attention. There were voices coming from one end of the hall.

The pair moved closer.

". . . and *you* promised we'd be out of here before dinner!" a man's voice grumbled. He had a slight accent that softened his *O*'s into *A*'s. It was a dialect common to seafarers on the southwest coast. "*Now* you're saying it's too soon? *What's* too soon?"

Another voice replied, this one deep and somber. "The western star needs to crest the tree line."

"We wait that long, and we might not make it out to sea!" the first voice countered, frustration clear. "I'm calling it—we ride out *now*."

"It is too late to leave now," the deep voice said sadly. "Wait until the star tomorrow."

"*Tomorrow?!* The depths with your nonsense, Wayfaring Vashid. If you aren't on the carriage in five minutes, then we're leaving you behind."

"My friend—" the deeper voice called out as a door opened and then loudly closed. There was a sigh, and the man spoke into the silence. "There is no use if the way is already barred."

CHAPTER 29

Any Fool Who'd Read an *Isekai* Should Know the Drill by Now

Gerda

The after effects from using [Oracle] were still annoying me.

The nausea was worse than the headache, but the hardest part was trying to wrench myself out of the mindset of the person I'd become for those four minutes. At least Julia was a good person; some chosen of the gods made my flesh crawl. My [Oracle] abilities could only link me to a god's chosen that I'd actually met—which was why I'd had no idea until *this moment* that the Keeper of Fate was walking around in a plot panic trying to undo my expertly crafted story deviations.

Parts of her plan made no sense to me, like turning people into frogs. Or how she was going to attack everyone at the wedding if the wedding was cancelled due to an *absent Julia*? The craziest part was how close we'd come to each other but never actually met, like the time she'd destroyed the bridge my house was connected to. I'd been sitting at my table, happily folding pastry dough around spiced apple slices and shaping them into a galette *when my entire house had started shaking*. Pink magic had warred with my teal one, and then a notification had told me that my bridge link had been severed.

It'd taken *all* of my effort to move my dimensional home to another bridge and catch my dishes at the same time.

Now, I was finally going to get to meet the woman . . . *after* I took the time to down two advanced mana potions.

This entire area was highlighted yellow on my map. The green dot was moving through a building to my left, so I decided to search the storage bays on my right. How? I did what any decent video game player would do in my situation.

I cheated.

I'd been living in this world for *five* years . . . and more specifically, I'd been living in the Dark Enchanted Forest. Any fool who'd read an *isekai* should know the drill by now!

[Appraise] and Hero's Spatial Ring was a broken combination and I'd gathered hundreds of random useful items.

I pulled out a Juliper petal and slipped it under my tongue.

[You are under the effects of **Juliper Petal** and will remain Invisible until it is removed or the petal dissolves. The duration of **Juliper Petal** is equal to lifespan before harvest. Time remaining: 00:13:46. One-time use item.]

I walked straight down the road, moving as quietly as I could. Inhuman Dexterity for the win.

Suddenly, a swordsman raced by me, going so fast I felt my hair rustle from their passing. No one else on the street seemed to notice the figure rush through the port gates.

"Hurry it up!" an elf with gray skin and black hair called out to the four hired hands packing the last wagon. "Alice is on her way back from the guild, and we need to be ready to head out as soon as she gets here."

"Two more trips," a panther beastman called out, having just dropped his crate onto the back of the wagon. "One for the rest of our cargo and another for the decoy."

"Who's staying behind to deliver the letters?" a second panther beastman asked. The pair looked like siblings, though the second was shorter by a hand length.

"No one you know." The elf frowned. "Now silence. We aren't the only ones using the port gate today."

"Evan's crew says they might be delayed until tomorrow," the taller beastman said.

I slipped through the open storage gate while they were talking. I was going to just assume *the decoy* was about Julia, and that anyone sent down to the docks to find her was going to get ambushed. Something to worry about if I didn't find the countess in time to call off the search.

Once inside, I searched the main bay for any larger crates. I found nothing, but the back wall had three doors. One was open, and a lizardkin was loading up sacks into a cart. Figuring the other two were also smaller storage rooms, I moved to the middle door and pressed my ear to it.

My forty-three Perception detected no one inside. I would have heard their breathing; I could hear the blood running through veins if I concentrated hard enough. It was unpleasant, so I usually chose not to.

Moving to the last door, I was with Luck; there was heavy breathing beyond.

My Rogue skills were nonexistent, but I could potentially use acid slime, or maybe just break the door off its hinges with my Strength. There was the chance it was guarded with magic . . . but at this point, I took a gamble and just tried the handle.

It was unlocked.

The only thing in the room was Julia, unconscious and chained to a wall with Veralyn's Enchanted Restraint Manacles. She didn't have on her usual armor, instead wearing a thin-strapped shirt showing off her muscular frame and heavy leather pants with pockets sewn just above the outer knee. Her midnight-black skin had a sickly sheen to it, but she looked otherwise uninjured.

I checked the inner handle of the door before I closed it behind me and shook my head when the storage room was unlocked from the inside as well. Not the most secure for keeping a highly skilled prisoner.

Someone trusted in Fate a little *too* much.

"Julia?" I knelt down and touched her on the arm. The half elf was sitting, legs sprawled out, back against the wall, and hands up as the manacles attached to a ring overhead.

She didn't wake up, the countdown on her status debuff still in effect.

"Alright, I guess I'll have to do this the hard way." I cracked my fingers in front of me then pulled out the jar of aforementioned acid slime. It wouldn't burn through the manacles themselves, but it did a number on the ring.

"Time to get out of here," I said, picking her up in a princess carry. I needed to walk to properly activate my skill. "[World Bridge]."

[You have attempted to use the Perk: **World Bridge**. You have succeeded. You may travel to any bridge you have crossed or con-trolled since obtaining **World Bridge**.
Select bridge from the available options:
Alora Troll Bridge
Alkor Troll Bridge
Ander's Widow Bridge
Baltor Toll Bridge
Castimal Pass Bridge
Coral Palace West Bridge . . .]

I mentally selected Coral Palace West Bridge and selected Julia and myself.

That was when the door of the storage room opened, and the Keeper of Fate walked through. I knew, based on my notification tab, that I had *at least* a minute left until I became visible again. I knew that, but the blonde woman did not.

"You!" she yelled, looking me directly in the eye and pointing a finger. Pink magic erupted from her hand, but it was too late.

I took a step and vanished.

CHAPTER 30

The Arc Warden

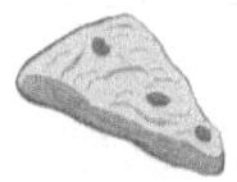

Julian

Julian and Lomen found nothing of interest and returned to search the room at the end of the hall.

They did so by throwing open the door—mage staff and sword blazing—ready to ambush anyone inside. There was no one. The room was an empty storage bay, large doors shut, with a window and a smaller entry door also closed.

Julian made his way to the window.

Everyone in the street was running for their wagons like their life depended on it. Others hollered directions as the caravan of carriages all raced for the port gate.

"Well, I feel foolish." Lomen blushed, lowering his flaming staff.

"Don't," Julian told him. "It's better to be safe."

"*GREYSON!*" a musical voice screeched outside. A woman was trying to block a carriage from leaving through the port gate. "You can't leave!"

"If *she's* been found that means *we've* been found," a gruff-looking elf shouted back. "And you even let her escape!"

Julian immediately guessed whom they were speaking of, and anger warred with relief. Someone had found his sister. She was safe.

The elf held out his palm facing forward and said, "[Clear Road]."

It was a perk favored by travelers which let the caster move without hitting others in traffic. The wagons practically bent reality around the young blonde woman, and Greyson led his charge through the port gate.

Julian wouldn't let even *one* of those who'd kidnapped his sister escape. Ripping off the door from its hinges, he stepped out into the street and pointed at the caravan. "[Tracking]."

[You have attempted to use the Skill: **Tracking**. You may track Targets equal to your Tracking 4 x Perception 25 = 100. You will know the direction of each Target tracked.
Skill Bonus effect: **Border Master** removes distance limiter.
Warning! Targets who enter dungeons or alternate spaces will not be tracked, but will reappear after they have returned to this realm. You have selected 17 Targets. You have partially succeeded. One Target has resisted **Tracking**.]

Sixteen faint red arrows appeared at his feet, overlapping as they all pointed in the same direction, following everyone *except* the blonde woman.

She turned to stare at Julian, her eyes narrowing when she saw who had attempted to use an ability on her.

"The duke of North Sumbria?" she spoke softly, and then smiled a charming, beautiful smile. Pink threads of magic appeared on her fingertips. "Perfect. *Come here.*"

It sent a shiver down his spine, and he found himself taking a step in her direction, unbidden. With a bit of effort, he shook off the compulsion to obey her.

Julian equipped his actual shield just in time to deflect a pink thread and shout, "Fireball!"

She retreated her magic and ducked to the side, then stopped when no fire erupted from his shield. It wasn't a spell or ability Julian possessed, but then, Lomen's spell whirled over his shoulder, the heat brushing uncomfortably close to his pulled-back dreads.

"You dare—[Watcher of Fate]!"

At the same time, Julian activated [Charge]. Her skill hit him right before he reached her, freezing him in place. It bypassed his shield, completely ignoring his Master-level protection.

[You have been affected by the Skill: **Watcher of Fate**. Your fate has been sealed for sixty-three seconds or until you are no longer being watched. Character Sheet sealed. Abilities sealed. Movement sealed. Health Points sealed. Mana Points sealed. Immune to all Damage.]
[You have been affected by the Skill: **Watcher of Fate**. Time until effect wears off 00:00:52]
[You have been affected by the Skill: **Watcher of Fate**. Time until effect wears off 00:00:51]

The woman glared at him. Her beautiful cornflower blue eyes were as clear as the sky and captivating. Her hair looked so smooth that he could run his hands through it. And her frown made him hurt.

He felt *disgusting*.

When someone put so many points into Charisma, it affected the world around them. This woman had min-maxed her attributes so much so that she was far beyond what any *normal* person could achieve.

"Well, you're as good as your sister, I suppose." She tapped her chin, eyeing Julian up and down. She glanced over his shoulder. "Why do I know you?"

Lomen replied, obviously trapped in her Charisma, "We have met before, beautiful—"

"No matter," she cut him off, lifting her hands. "I'll take you both."

[You have been affected by the Skill: **Watcher of Fate**. Time until effect wears off 00:00:41]

Pink threads glowed, tied to each digit. She wiggled her left hand once, and the thread on her index finger came into focus. It formed a long pink thread that created a circle large enough to walk through, and with a flash of light, a portal appeared.

She reached out to touch Julian when a wave of magical energy washed over the entire area in a forceful shimmer. The portal collapsed, the pink threads dissolving into nothingness. Another dome of magic encircled the entire city.

[You have been affected by the Skill: **Watcher of Fate**. Time until effect wears off 00:00:32]

The woman stomped her foot cutely. "*Why is Fate doing this to me?!*"

The last of the caravan behind her was caught on this side of the port gate, watching their companions ride off down the road. Not that they would get away.

If Julian could've smiled, he would have.

His mother had activated the Arc Warden. The magical artifact took an incredible amount of mana to maintain, so much so that she couldn't have done it alone. While in effect, certain powers couldn't be used within the sphere. Fast travel, portals, dimensionals, spatial . . . even spell scrolls were void under its enchantment.

Everyone was left to their own power to walk, run, swim, or fly. It was meant to hold a city under siege or protect it during a siege from the outside.

[You have been affected by the Skill: **Watcher of Fate**. Time until effect wears off 00:00:19]

"I guess we have to do this the hard way." The woman pulled out a poison vial from her pocket and uncorked the lid.

Julian wasn't the biggest fan of dying, but he was used to it. Over the years, he'd needed to be resurrected countless times by his party members while exploring the North. And his mother didn't hold to Sumbrian inheritance laws, so dying here wouldn't affect his title.

The only real problem he had with her poisoning him was the *type* of poison she held in her hand. If it was what it looked like . . .

"Now, hold still." She smiled at her own joke and dumped the bottle onto Julian's head.

[You have been affected by the Skill: **Watcher of Fate**. Time until effect wears off 00:00:11]

She smiled and tossed aside the bottle—then spun around to catch a knife before it stabbed her in the back. She promptly dodged two more and ducked a flying axe. The weapon sailed past Julian's cheek, barely missing him.

John had arrived, but it was too late.

The moment the blonde woman looked away, [Watcher of Fate] had ended early, and he was hit by a new notification.

[You have been poisoned by **Kazil**. You are now a Frog. Health 10/10. Mana 1/1. Skill: **Hopping**.]

Julian shrank.

"Someone catch that frog!" a voice that sounded remarkably like Chloe shouted from afar.

The frog looked up.

There was a beautiful woman standing right in front of him. Her blonde hair was like the sun, and her blue eyes were like the calmest water in a very welcoming pond.

He hopped toward her.

She reached for him, but a strange dirt wall shot up between them. He protested as loud as he could and tried to jump over it, but it stretched up into the sky. High overhead, the woman was flying on white feathered wings. Like an angel.

Strong hands wrapped around him. "Got you!"

He struggled to get away as water suddenly got poured onto his back. As fast as Julian had become a frog, the antidote turned him back into a half elf. He landed on the ground.

It took a second to steady himself.

Overhead, attacks followed after the woman. The *celestial.*

"[Soul Bind]."

"[Holy Arrow]."

"[Wind Blade]."

Only [Wind Blade] managed to hit her, but it barely slowed her down. She flew west and then dropped out of sight. Hana ran past Julian, Wendy on her heels.

"*DON'T LET HER GET AWAY!*" Chloe arrived last, her own physical abilities limited without a fast-travel skill.

The necromancer's eyes turned into pools of black, and she dropped to one knee. Inky tendrils of darkness that burst out of her and spread in all directions, searching the carriages and stretching into the buildings nearby.

"Please be here," she whispered, her eyes unseeing. "Please, please, please—"

At this rate, she was going to give herself mana burn, so Julian dragged himself to his feet.

"Chloe. Chloe, it's all right." He put a hand on her shoulder. "Julia's escaped—"

"She did?" The necromancer's spell broke, and she looked up at him with regular eyes full of tears. "She's alright?"

Julian hesitated to say as much when he himself didn't know, but then, John interrupted. "Julia was just found at the palace. She's fine."

"I have to go to her." Chloe dragged herself to her feet, rubbing her eyes.

"At least take a mana potion first—"

She waved him off and started running. Julian turned to his rogue. "Did your shadow catch the celestial?"

John shook his head.

"Then I guess we're going hunting."

Julian would [Track] every single person who'd tried to hurt his family.

He would search for them all night if he had to.

And with the Arc Warden, they had nowhere left to run.

CHAPTER 31

A Toll on a Troll

Gerda

I stepped out onto the bridge for the second time that evening.

Julia was still asleep, so I carefully put her down and straightened her into a comfortable position. The railings would prevent her from rolling off the sides, and someone would find her soon.

[Warning! Your Mana has dropped below 10%]

I immediately popped a mana potion and downed it. No sense in messing with fate and getting caught unprepared. Once that was done, I dropped the empty bottle back into my storage ring and crouched down to do a quick check on Julia.

She didn't *appear* to have any obvious injuries, though her wrists were rubbed red from the manacles. King Keith was the master crafter who'd created most of the Veralyn's Enchanted Restraint Manacles on the continent . . . so I was sure he'd have a way to free the Paladin of Light from hers.

Her foot twitched as I debated pouring a health potion on her—just in case—and I jumped back in surprise. She was stirring, and that meant I had two choices: escape before anyone realized I'd saved her, or stay and claim the glory of rescuing the damsel in distress.

I ran away.

Listen, I knew there were guards stationed about the palace; some of them were even patrolling the larger sky bridges that stretched above and below me. And there were three ravens flitting about the grounds that could be anyone's familiars.

I knew that, but I took my chances.

Instead of bolting, I walked calmly to the tower, opened the door, and let myself in.

My timing was perfect; I had barely closed the door behind me when I heard Julia draw a sharp breath and try to sit up. My hands were shaking.

Holding my skirts, I fast walked down the stairs to my room.

My Perception was on high alert, and I could hear things behind the walls around me. A shallow breath, a music box, and the faint sounds of someone enjoying company all came through to me as I made my descent. There was the sound of pounding feet on the stairs above and below me, but I knew I was going to make it.

I was safe in my room before anyone crossed my path.

Leaning my back against my door, I slid to the floor and tried to rub my hands together to calm myself down. I waited there for a very, very long time.

No one came.

Honestly, if they *did* come for me, I might even let them take me in for questioning. There wasn't much left for me to do except see the wedding and then be off. I only had one bridge left until I could get out of this dumb video game world. Maybe.

Still, no one came.

"Alright, Gerda," I reassured myself. "You've done it again. Good job."

Talking to myself helped. There was no one else to talk to about this kind of thing, and living alone was starting to take a toll on me.

The thought made me smile. A toll on a troll.

I stood up and walked over to flop face-first onto the bed. And then I heard it. Soldiers coming back down the west tower.

I tensed.

"At least she's come out in time for the wedding," a cheerful voice said, accompanied by the subtle clink of plate mail.

"You don't actually think she was just cooling off some steam?" a woman's voice said, incredulous. A third voice demanded. "Tully, you can't be serious. They activated the *Arc Warden*."

Ah, Sir Tully was one of Julian's party members. I could only assume his two companions were the same.

"What?" Tully asked. "A bunch of mercenaries tell us Julia's in the port district and then the entire palace raids the place to find nothing—"

"They didn't find *nothing*. They were attacked," the woman interrupted. "Besides, of course they didn't find Julia. She was back by then."

"Proving my point. No one can portal anywhere within the Arc Warden," Tully grumbled. "I'm at half the speed with my Heavy Armor class right now."

The woman sounded exasperated when she explained, "She portaled in *before* the Arc Warden, Tully."

"I still can't believe we missed whoever's been portaling onto that bridge, *again*," the third voice said sharply.

"You were the one who said it was probably just someone out for a walk returning to their rooms, Jeffry," Tully reminded the third voice.

A fourth voice suggested, "Maybe it was Countess Julia both times?"

"You can only portal into the palace if you're already *in* the palace," the woman reminded them. "And we searched *everywhere*."

"Obviously *not* everywhere, if Julia showed up . . ." Tully's voice trailed off. The voices had come and gone, and anything else they said was too hard to hear. I rolled over onto my back and covered my eyes.

Of course the palace noticed my comings and goings.

I had no idea what the Arc Warden was, and I didn't care. After everything, I was so exhausted and sore that I couldn't even be bothered to change my clothes . . .

I fell asleep like that, lying on top of the covers.

CHAPTER 32

A Game

Julian

It took over an hour to round up the mercenaries and meet back at the port gate.

Julian oversaw tracking each individual that'd been trapped on this side of the Arc Warden, and without abilities to boost their base speed, his higher stats gave him plenty of advantage. Unfortunately, Wendy and Hana arrived with no news of the celestial or her whereabouts.

Grand Duchess Calisto and Their Royal Highness Rowen of Peldeep had started the Arc Warden, summoning Dark Magician King Keith of Nilheim, Witch Agatha of Winter's End, and Master Thomas of Servalt to take turns powering it until their search came to a close. Julian had to be the one to report through John's shadow that they'd found everyone *but* the celestial. There had been a heated debate, but since Julia was home safe, his mother had stopped the Arc Warden and released the city.

No one was happy.

Before meeting in person with his mother, Julian brought John to his office to hear the full report and poured them both a stiff drink.

"While the Arc Warden was in effect, Protector Rufus and Minstrel Bronwynn helped the Black Brigade Knights detain the merchants outside the city and have retired to an inn half an hour down the road. They will return in the morning in time for the wedding."

Julian nodded, glad to know they were safe.

John continued. "Julia was found on the bridge to the west wing with no memory of how she got there. She informed us that she was ambushed with a [Sleep] spell shortly after she flew off from the wedding rehearsal."

"*This* side of the palace wall?" Julian's voice was stone cold.

"Yes."

His fists were clenched at his side as he thought. Turning to his friend, he asked John, "What would you do?"

John shrugged. "I would interrogate your prisoners, discover they are simple hired hands who know nothing of importance, maybe learn where they were headed, their schedule, and any useful passwords . . . but nothing much else."

Julian cursed.

"Then," John added, "considering the fact that the mercenary and assassin guilds have played a major part in this operation, I would send over a ruthless auditor to make me feel better"—that had Julian fighting a small smile—"and *then* prepare for the worst tomorrow," he concluded.

Julian sighed. "How?" There wasn't anyone more qualified to ask than his own rogue.

John was silent for a moment, deep in thought. Finally, he said, "A game."

That was not at all what Julian thought he was going to say. "A game?"

"Yes." John, his otherwise stalwart and emotionless shadow, suddenly gave Julian a vicious smile. His teeth flashed white in a rare show of amusement. "A game. You have almost every high-level elite on the continent attending this wedding?"

"Almost two hundred guests," he confirmed. An outrageous amount. Julian couldn't imagine more than twenty at his own ceremony. Not that he planned to get married any time soon.

"Well," John reasoned, "thanks to Madame Potts, the entire continent knows that Blackfog spies are going to be stirring up trouble during the festival. Why not start the day off with an invitation to the entire wedding guest list that who-ever catches a Blackfog spy will get a prize. Maybe the person who assists the most can have one of your esteemed mother's inventions."

"John." Julian lifted a hand and placed it firmly on his rogue's shoulder. "You're a genius."

"True."

It was Julian's turn to smile at his friend. "Let's finish up and go tell my mother."

"Duke Julian has arrived," the attendant informed everyone before he could burst into the same parlor unannounced twice in one day.

His mother was standing with Their Royal Highness. She knew instantly that John was attached to his shadow and acknowledged the rogue with a simple nod at Julian's feet before addressing her son. "Welcome back."

"We've finished our investigation," Julian said. "The caravan leader, Grey-son, admitted to knowing about Julia's kidnapping and will be brought before the council."

"I can't believe they managed to get me all the way to the city gate," his sister said, frowning. Seeing her here, safe, was a welcome relief.

"I can't believe I almost lost you," said the tiny blonde woman sitting on Julia's lap, arms wrapped around her neck.

"I'm fine, love," Julia reassured Chloe, patting the necromancer's back. Chloe's eyes were still puffy from her earlier upset.

"I've also learned that the Void mage is named Alice," Julian continued.

"Do you know why they kidnapped Julia in the first place?" his mother asked. She looked better than could be expected from having most of her mana drained by a legendary-grade enchanted device.

"We'll have to ask Alice when we catch her," Julian said.

Chloe huffed. "You had a chance to catch her, and you let her escape!"

"I was *a frog*, what's *your* excuse?" Julian shot back. It sounded defensive even to his own ears, and he took a deep breath to calm himself. Chloe was a pricklebush sometimes, but she loved his sister, and that was what mattered. He continued, "Still, we *did* capture everyone else, and there's more."

"More?" his mother prompted.

"Barry, the swordsman spy, found a warehouse down by the docks and released six more people who'd been captured."

"*Six?*" Grand Duchess Calisto said sharply.

"Who?" Their Highness Rowen inquired. The fox was still in their guise from the wedding rehearsal, and stroked their beard, curious.

"Lily Montgomery," Julian replied, "Duke—"

"Lily?" Julia interrupted. "I passed her when I left the church!"

"Did she get kidnapped because she saw the kidnapping?" His mother frowned. "Have you asked?

Julian shook his head. "She was taken *two days ago*."

His mother frowned at that before looking up and to the left at her character sheet.

There was a knock on the door, and Knight Commander Lex Toring of the Grey Hawk Knights walked into the room. The ogre filled the door, equipped with silver plate armor engraved with a hawk. He was the leader of Calisto's personal knight squadron.

"You summoned, Your Grace?" Sir Lex bowed perfectly, the serious and loyal knight. Julian remembered climbing onto the ogre as a young boy and riding on his shoulders. Back when his father was still alive.

"Find the financial deputy, Lily Montgomery," she ordered. "She is a suspected spy who can change her shape. Send one of your knights to each of the servants' wings to accompany the heads of house while they review everyone's quality of work. Say it's in preparation for the wedding, but if anyone isn't competent in a field they were previously, approach with caution."

"The Grey Hawk Knights, Your Grace?" Sir Lex asked, hesitant. His soldiers were *supposed* to be guarding *her*. It was the Coral Mare Knights who should've been responsible for securing the palace.

"Yes, I want the best on the search," his mother replied, which didn't seem to satisfy the knight, but he bowed and did as he was told.

"Is that all?" Chloe demanded. "You find out that the person who kidnapped Julia could be walking around the palace as we speak, and you quietly check in on the staff? You should drag out *everyone in the palace* and inspect them!"

"Dear"—his sister poked Chloe's cheek—"we can't just—"

"Why not?!" The necromancer wasn't deterred.

"The staff have rights," Julian stated. "They are people, and they deserve security and protection, not harassment and suspicion. And our guests are our *guests*."

"Is it suspicion," Their Royal Highness asked, cocking their head, "if we *know* at least one of them is a spy?"

"Things are different here; you *know* that, Rowen. We will inspect the staff in our own way," Duchess Calisto chided the fox.

"I'm just saying." The fox shrugged but let it go, leaning back in their chair.

"If I may continue?" Julian asked. Chloe looked unhappy, but she didn't interrupt. "We also found Duke Wyldon of Servalt, Sir Phineas of Drendil, Lady Cassandra Cress of North Sumbria, Trevor Malory of Drendil, and Prince Malakai."

That got Rowen's attention, a dark aura filling the room even as their face remained impassive. "*My* son, Prince Malakai?"

Julian nodded. "Yes. The prince is currently en route to greet you, though he requested a stop by the kitchens first."

"I see." Rowen's power settled slightly, and they turned to Grand Duchess Calisto with a too bright smile. "It's a good thing everyone was rescued, then."

The implied threat was understandable.

"We will have to ask for a report from each captive for the council." His mother looked Rowen in the eye. There was a split second before the fox ruler agreed. It wasn't going to be torture; it was just going to be questioning and paperwork. "As you say."

Julian coughed. "Everyone found was verified before they were brought to the palace. Anyone who wished to go home has been told to wait for their respective countries' embassies to process travel documents to leave the city."

That would also give them time for the members of the council to question the freed captives.

Julian brought out a piece of paper and handed it to his mother. "Now, about tomorrow . . ."

CHAPTER 33

A Fabulous Fairy-Tale Look

Gerda

Someone slipped an envelope under the door to my room.

It was past midnight, and after a few hours of rest, I was feeling marginally better; enough to roll off the bed and read the letter. [Appraise] let me know it was official, and when I cracked it open, nothing exploded, so that was nice.

It was a greeting from the North Sumbrian royals, with a clear schedule laid out for the wedding ceremony and an invitation to participate in a special game unique to the festivities. The grand prize for the most Blackfog spies foiled over the course of the day was a custom-built magical elevator—to be delivered and installed at a destination of choice—with smaller prizes for capturing *anyone* out to ruin the wedding. That included but was not limited to assassins, ceremonial disruptions, or anyone otherwise making themselves a nuisance.

"Let's do this," I whispered to myself, gripping the letter.

The pep talk helped, and I made myself comfortable on the bed before opening my character sheet.

[**Oracle:** You are witness to the strings of Fate and her weave. The story unfolds, and the Chosen of each deity mark the way.

You have found 9/12 Chosen.

Impending Scenarios: 5/12 Chosen.

Keeper of Fate - The Royal Wedding

Paladin of Light - The Love Lost

Bringer of Chaos - The Shoals Battle

Guardian of Death - The Final Elite

Heroine of Justice - The Void Duel

Timeline access restricted.

Available Scenarios: All Scenarios within current Domain boundar-
ies available. All Scenarios impending within 6.5 days available.
Oracle timeline: 4 mins 30 seconds.
Please select Chosen.]

Seeing the Keeper of Fate on my list, I put my head in my hands and thanked Luck for yesterday. Getting caught with Julia had been the best possible outcome. I selected her option.

Rage bristled under my skin as another one of my plans fell through, leaving me back at square one. Everything I'd fought for; everything I'd set up—all of it, discovered and destroyed. I would've suspected a spy among my spies if it weren't for that meddling Madame Potts and her abilities to read the future.

She'd ruined everything.

The heroine had been deprived of her fate; she was supposed to slaughter the Dark Enchanted Forest, not marry into it! The Dark Lord should've perished before the Spring Ball, and the necromancer by the Masquerade.

Even the Bridge Troll had survived to ruin my plans.

It'd been luck, kidnapping Julia. Anyone permitted entry into the sanctuary would've sufficed, but using the Paladin of Light to kill the necromancer would've returned their weave to its rightful fate.

Until that, too, had failed.

But I wasn't going to give up. I could never give up Fate. I would return things to the way they were supposed to be, starting with this wedding.

"Princess Contessa la Rouche of Ildsfeld, your seat." The servant waved me into a pew. Even if it restricted my abilities, [Take Fate] let me steal a captured target's character sheet to use as my own, and the princess was safely stored out of the way for now. I'd come to witness my efforts in action and ensure there wasn't any more meddling.

One of my spies, the baron of Tour on Marsh, caught my eye and nodded. At least the paladin going missing had drawn attention away long enough to set more traps. I smiled. Even if they discovered all of my traps before the ceremony, that would only lull them into a false sense of security while my secret weapon planted more from the inside.

Even one life returned to the weave would be worth it.

The fireworks in Peldeep were nothing to the magical surprise I had planted now . . .

Coming out of the oracle left me shaking uncontrollably, I curled up into a ball and tried to claw the new person out of my head.

The rage. The bloodthirst that coursed through me and made me want to burn everything in my path. Information warred and blended. Hatred for Madame Potts—for *myself*—made me want to tear at my own flesh. [Mental

Resistance] saved me. The feelings surged and settled, though the headache remained. Putting myself in a new mind was always taxing.

I knew I needed to check in on the others if I was going to try and save everyone . . . but I still hesitated activating my skill again so soon. At least with Henrietta or Julia I would become someone I could stomach.

After taking a mana potion to replenish my reserves, I selected another Chosen.

"Chloe! No!" I cried out.

A trap enchantment had activated on the dais, opening a pitch-black hole under Chloe as she was consumed by the Void. I reached to grab her, but my hand met a pink shield instead. The adorable tendrils of my love's shadow magic reached up to meet my hand, pressing from inside as both of us took damage from the touch.

"I love you." Chloe smiled at me as her legs sank into the darkness. "Always."

I screamed and activated [Solar Fist], striking the shield. It shuddered under the weight of my attack. I tried to strike a second time, but the Void had taken most of my hand.

"Stand back, Julia." Mother was engulfed in fire, but ignored the flames as she directed her magic toward the dome. The pink bubble shattered—but it was too late.

Chloe was gone, consumed by the Void, never to be resurrected.

A burst of light erupted from me, my senses reeling from the sheer pressure that built in my chest and exploded outward. Screams. The sound of running. A window shattered overhead, showering the hall in broken glass that cut flesh, but no pain reached me.

"Julia!" Through the glare, I saw Julian yelling my name. He was sword to sword with an elven dignitary. Mother was no longer on fire, as Sir Pram had cast ice magic to frost the terrain. One wall of the sanctuary was covered in vines.

Their Royal Highness walked out of a billowing cloud of wolfsbane, unharmed, in time to catch an arrow from the direction of the oath registry table. Rowen stumbled, white foam at their mouth from the poison . . .

It took me a while to get to sleep through the sobbing.

"Gerda!" Henrietta found me at breakfast still ruminating over my own plans to save the day. The Dark Lady sat down beside me in the palace dining hall, still in her regular attire despite the wedding only a few hours away. I'd only just watched her scenario an hour before, so seeing her in person made for a strange sense of settling reality—especially since her scenario was just as awful and heart-wrenching as the other two.

"Good morning, Your Majesty." I stuffed a small summer tomato into my mouth and bit down. I'd chosen a classic breakfast with scrambled floofpoof eggs, thick-cut flying pork bacon, a slice of golden sourdough, and some fresh baby tomatoes.

"Enough of that! I heard you broke your promise and left the guardhouse early . . ." Henrietta's eyes were full of worry. "What if something had happened to you?"

"Something *did* happen to me," I told her. "A shadow user tried to attach to me right under the guards' noses! I didn't know what else to do, so I took your advice and portaled to my bridge. It took a bit, but I *did* make it back to my rooms safely."

The best falsehoods weren't falsehoods at all.

Henrietta grabbed my green arm and squeezed gently. "I'm happy you're safe, even *if* you had to walk back and wait outside for the Arc. Maybe *try* to lie low today?"

I showed her the piece of paper I'd been perusing. "Then how am I supposed to win myself an elevator?"

"Ha!" Henrietta let go and picked up a fork to tackle her own breakfast. She had a stack of waffles with markleberry jam in the first layer, strawberries and whipped unigoat cream in the second, and the top had more whipped cream and a light drizzle of strawberry syrup. "You could surprise people by rising up from below the bridge in style! It would be *spectacular*."

"And slow," I argued, taking a bite of my eggs and enjoying the fluffy soft taste. "They'd be long gone by the time I exited onto the bridge."

"True." Henrietta's nose crinkled in thought.

"*If* I won . . ." I paused for effect. "I could give *you* the elevator."

Henrietta laughed. "Keith would be beside himself with excitement to take it apart and find out how it works, and see if he could make one."

"He would," I said, then changed the subject. "What are your plans for today?"

"I'll help Keith get ready and run any errands that need running before the ceremony." She sighed. "I wish Chloe and Julia didn't have all this added stress for their special day."

I nodded; it was unfortunate.

"How about you?" Henrietta turned her eyes my way.

"I'm probably going to go straight to the hall, search for traps, and wait around with the rest of the party guests. Mingle a bit. And then use the ladies' room before the rush," I told her.

Again, technically *not* lying.

"Good idea," my queen approved, nodding her head happily. "If you need anything, just shout. This whole place is under guard, and Chloe made enough Revive potions to bring back the entire hall if need be."

"Impressive." I wasn't a potion maker, but she must have burned through a lot of time, money, and mana to whip out two hundred Revives. I couldn't imagine where she'd found the time—possibly a reserve stash.

"Right?" Henrietta got a bit of whipped cream on her hand and quickly licked it clean. She never changed.

"That won't help anyone from a kingdom who disinherits on death," I pointed out. "But I guess if they chanced coming to this particular wedding even after Madame Potts's warning, that's their problem."

After we finished breakfast, Henrietta left to go change and get ready with Keith.

My own dress was a more elaborate bright-purple version of my usual style, with white flowers over the bust. The overdress cinched at the underbust line, opening at the front to reveal a soft white underdress. It fell in waves, with more flowers embroidered at the edges.

The only thing I wasn't happy with was my hair. My braids were pulled back into a half updo, with one each left down to frame my face as makeshift bangs. Unfortunately, I *hadn't* gotten the time to properly wash and redo my braids, so they were seriously fraying. To hide the chaos, I'd stuck small white and purple phoebe flowers here and there.

I also wore my silver Ancient Gamblers Amulet, which was unassumingly plain but matched the white highlights in my outfit.

A fabulous fairy-tale look, if I did say so myself.

There were guards *everywhere*, and I joined a lineup of guests who'd arrived early to go over the sanctuary and try for the grand prize.

A few members of the Continental Council were there as well, including an unamused Witch Agatha arguing with Master Thomas. Behind them, the Grand Pontiff of Sumbria stood alone, looking high and mighty. His nose was in the air, and his long ears twitched in annoyance whenever Witch Agatha said something particularly curt.

This year was the first in two decades that Grand Duchess Calisto had allowed the noble elite from Sumbria to attend her events. Prior to this, she'd only granted *specifically vetted ambassadors* access to cross the border, and only for the Continental Council meeting the day *after* any ball or feast.

She was making an attempt at peace.

It was especially telling that she'd welcomed the Grand Pontiff to the wedding . . . as it was his predecessor who had killed Grand Duke Lysander in the civil war.

In anticipation of the crush, the Grey Hawk Knights were out in force, checking invitations and securing the area. I resisted the urge to face-palm as I joined the end of the line. This just gave any ne'er-do-well the perfect opportunity to set traps under the guise of *searching* for them.

It was rare, thankfully, but sometimes, a prediction telling everyone to *stop* a thing actually helped that thing happen. A great case in point was Sumbria— they outright ignored any and all warnings I gave them, which meant that evil could thrive when I reported it.

For example, tell everyone to send guards to an unlucky coastal town about to get hit by one pirate ship? An entire *fleet of pirates* will show up because they'll know the elven elders will *deliberately* turn a blind eye because *I* made the announcement. It was infuriating, and I was still stumped on what to do about it.

A few minutes later, a scribe arrived with a tablet for guests to join a waitlist. I put myself down in the last available time slot, just behind Duchess Calisto herself, because I was a genius.

Now, I had two hours to myself. Plenty of time to get other important things settled.

CHAPTER 34

How Much You Are Willing to Pay

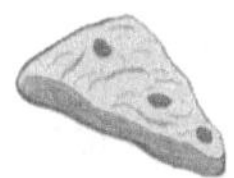

Julian

"So let me get this straight." Julian slipped on his vest and slowly did up each button. "You have been working with the Blackfog spies for over thirty years?"

"Yes." Greyson sat on a chair, hands in his lap and eyes unwavering.

John was standing to the side, holding Julian's outfit for the wedding. He'd sent the rogue to fetch it as soon as it was obvious that Julian would be running late. This was the final interview he had to do after an entire morning of gaining very little information from the regular caravan hires.

He'd saved the best for last.

The three of them were in a room in the dungeons. It was an hour before the ceremony, and he was supposed to be checking in at Julia's dressing room any second now. After last night, any fears his sister had of going through with the wedding were gone. She'd had a good conversation with Chloe, and Julian had pretended not to notice his sister returning to her rooms only an hour before sunrise.

He finished doing up his buttons before confronting his prisoner. "And your loyalty made you break the law?"

"No," Greyson replied.

"No?" Julian was at least expecting an excuse. He raised a hand, and John helped him slip into the dark-purple coat. It hung down to his thigh and was embroidered with decorative diamonds around the hem and cuffs and neckline. He was wearing a white undertunic and white pants with silver and purple embroidery that matched the coat.

"The guild mistress is not someone I can refuse." Greyson leaned back in his chair. "I'd rather take the mines or pay a fee than go against *that* woman."

"What can you tell me about her?"

"That depends." Greyson kept a neutral face, eyeing Julian.

"On what?"

Greyson held out a hand and rubbed his thumb and index together. "How much you're willing to pay."

"My lord, I could just—" John's face was impassive as he casually dropped a threat, but Julian shook his head.

"They're information dealers." He waved away his friend's concern and asked Greyson, "How much?"

Greyson held up two fingers and his thumb.

"Three hundred gold?" Julian summoned a pouch and started dropping gold coins from his storage ring into the opening.

"Thirty *platinum*," Greyson countered. "And that's a discount because I'm currently . . . *upset* with our leader at the moment."

Julian didn't react as he added a *quarter* of the budget for the Northern Fortress to the pouch before tossing it at the shark. "You know that I'm going to levy enough fines on your company for what you did to my sister that this money is going to be useless, yes?"

Greyson caught the bag and hefted it once before setting it on the floor beside his chair. He had no access to his rings while bound with the enchanted manacles. When the spy straightened, he was smiling, and the silver crest of the [Deal-Breaker] debuff shone on his forehead.

"Guild Mistress Alice Smith, five feet tall, a hundred and forty pounds, blue-eyed, blonde-haired celestial. As gorgeous as she is intelligent, and a complete psychopath. She contacted me a week ago, but she's been on a warpath for months. My *buddy* in Peldeep let me know that she was the real deal after she caused a stir at the Apple Blossom Festival."

Julian raised an eyebrow when he realized that was all he was going to get out of the man. Greyson held up one finger, and Julian sighed.

A second pouch dropped down beside the first.

Greyson continued. "She infiltrated seven spies into the Emerald Palace and used them to try and perma-kill Their Royal Highness of Peldeep. The attempt was thwarted. The spies were all caught, but not before a section of the palace burned down. The guild mistress abandoned them and escaped alone using her portal abilities."

Julian frowned. "What made you break the law for someone like that?"

The man stiffened. There was a strange tension in his body as he countered Julian's question with his own. "We are an information guild . . . Have you ever faced someone who knew your *every* secret? Your darkest fear?" His eyes were reliving whatever horror the celestial had put him through. Greyson managed a chuckle and added, "Whose Charisma warped your will and made you question your entire life as she manipulated you into turning against yourself? I won't tell you what *I'm* most afraid of for any gold—but I will tell you that Alice is just as terrifying."

That was all the time he had. Julian nodded. "Thank you for your time. John, lock our helpful informant up separately from the others."

Greyson hesitated. "At least tell me where you're sending my people?"

"I'm not sending them anywhere." Julian smiled darkly. "If you leave now, you'll be safe from whatever Guild Mistress Alice unleashes on *my family's home.* You should stick around to see how it ends."

"Wait." Greyson jumped to his feet, his jaw set. "Just my crew. They know nothing of importance."

"They knew about my sister." That meant they knew enough to be tried.

Greyson hesitated, "I'll tell you something to help you in exchange for their safety—"

"Done." Julian didn't think twice. "*I swear to Justice that I will send your men for menial labor in a reputable reform mine for no more than one year's time.*"

Divine mana played over Julian's senses as the god heard his vow and accepted it.

And in return, Greyson let them know exactly *how* Alice was able to accomplish all of her deeds. All it took was one *specific* perk.

CHAPTER 35

Spitting Fire to It and Watching It Burn

Gerda

"Katie, you're a *genius*." Chef Andrew Grosser held up a leaf of paper with my latest recipe on it and smiled brightly. The lizardkin was one of the minions from the Dark Enchanted Forest who'd passed a trades test and emigrated to North Sumbria.

The Trickster's Scarf did its job well, even if wearing it was brutal in this hot weather. My fox tail flicked twice in amusement. "Thank you, Andrew. It takes one to know one."

He waved off my compliment and read the paper one more time before spitting fire to it and watching it burn. He looked up at me with a teasing smile. "Same terms?"

I nodded. "Three months to the date. Please and thank you."

"Of course." The lizardkin caught my hand and bowed, kissing the air above it gently. "Any chance you're sticking around until after the festival? I'd *love* to buy you a drink."

"Sorry, darling." I withdrew my hand and waved. "You know I'm too busy for any fun."

"A lizardman can dream," he sighed but didn't let my repeated rejections get him down. "See you next time."

I bid the lizardman farewell, and he slipped back into the palace kitchen.

He was one of the few people I'd approached with recipes from my world. It had started with a craving for cinnamon buns. I'd made myself a batch then packaged one up and left it and the recipe at a bakery I loved in Servalt. I'd added a note that said they could sell cinnamon buns if they waited one month to do so. When they followed my request, I'd come back and offered other recipes as well. Now they sold galettes, donuts and fritters. I'd approached others with ramen and soft serve ice cream and medallion-cut ratatouille.

When I sent out recipes, I always required a delay. If someone I approached revealed the letter or tried to release the item early, then I never contacted them again. I wasn't too upset by it: I wasn't claiming these were my recipes. They were just my favorite foods, and I was determined to taste them in the wild . . . even if I had to introduce them into the wild myself.

The recipe I'd brought today was something I'd been working on for a while: pizza.

I couldn't wait to see how it developed.

The second place I stopped by was the third floor of the east wing, a location that perfectly overlooked the dais in the sanctuary, and where I estimated a very excitable assassin would be standing when they leapt through the beautiful stained glass window below.

Still in disguise, I took a deep breath and pulled out a flowerpot from my Hero's Spatial Ring. With care, I placed the somnia vale blossoms on the ledge and then walked out as quickly as possible. The hallway had a door to either side, and anyone who walked in wouldn't be leaving.

They could be retrieved later, asleep in the hallway.

At that point, I ducked into a washroom and took off my scarf, changing back into Gerda the Bridge Troll, then I headed for the garden that circled the sanctuary on three sides to search for traps.

"Excuse me!" I called out to the closest knight, who immediately came over to see what I'd found.

My voice drew the attention of other trap finders in the garden: a pink pixie, an elder fae with antlers, and a mouse wearing squire attire. The first two were chatting among themselves, while the mouse was off on his own, searching in hard-to-reach places.

"Yes, miss?" The knight was a very tall, red-bearded human. I was thankful that he'd stopped a respectful distance away.

"I think I found something." I waved at the place that *should* have some form of vine trap. In my foretelling, magical vines had sprouted from this area on the outside of the building, blocking the windows and trapping people inside.

"One moment, please." The knight pulled out a crystal. "Captain, I think we've found something. East side."

A minute later, a shadow slipped out of the bushes, and John rose out to greet them.

"Miss Gerda?" The rogue raised one eyebrow at me, and I returned the look with a smile.

"Lord Johnathon," I greeted back, waving my hand in the general area of where the trap *should* be. I had zero trap-finding skills, and Perception could only get me so far.

John carefully pulled aside some mulberry bushes growing close to the walls. The man's eyes suddenly turned black, pools of mist leaking out the sides in some horror-film, anime-power-of-darkness vibe, and I waited patiently for his abilities to scan the area.

Not at the bushes we were standing in front of but about two feet to the left, he pointed. "Found it." Black tendrils shot out of John's finger and encircled something on the wall. He yanked, and a small sack landed in his palm.

"What is it?" the knight asked, curiosity getting the better of him.

In a bold move, John upended the sack's contents onto his palm. Three bramblebriar seeds tumbled out. They would grow into a magical vine immune to magic which could only be cut by a fae blade. There *were* fae at the wedding, so it wasn't foolproof, but it would've definitely slowed down everyone's escape.

"Well done, Miss Gerda," John said, considering the seeds. "We will add one trap to your tally."

"Just one? Stick around," I half joked. "It's almost my turn inside."

"I think I will." There was *a hint* of amusement in his voice as John followed me to the front of the sanctuary. Their Royal Highness let Master Thomas of Servalt out, then waved at me.

"Miss Gerda." Their Royal Highness raised an eyebrow at my companion. "Lord Johnathon. *You* aren't on the list."

The rogue monotoned, "I'm just here to watch."

That sparked a light in Rowen's eyes. "Then come in. You have until Her Grace arrives to search."

The sanctuary was just as it appeared in my vision. I walked up to the third pew on the left and pointed at the back leg. "Here." Then I pointed at a triangular stone in the pew on the fifth row on the right. "Here." Walking over, I pointed at the tassel tie holding the curtains for a stained glass window covered in stars. "Here." Then I pointed at the swirl of an armrest at the end of a bench two rows up from the curtain. "Here."

From one end of the hall to the next, I pointed at every place I could remotely recall having *some* form of pit trap, firewall, wolfsbane, mystery poison, plant attack, paralyzing smoke, electrical shock, magical cage, more wolfsbane, and another bramblebriar sack—this one tucked in a crack of the western wall.

Not all of the traps were still there . . . and there was a moment when Their Royal Highness turned a sharp smile toward me and asked how I could've known about the dais pit trap, since they'd already discovered it moments before I arrived. I'd been sweating as I said, "My ability lets me see traces of traps, but I can't guarantee they're still there."

The half-truth had satisfied the fox, and they'd accepted my words. It was John who did all of the actual work of identifying and disarming each of the traps I pointed out, and for that, I was grateful.

I arrived at the front of the hall with eighteen traps total for my tally. But I wasn't finished. Standing in front of the dais where Julia was supposed to stand, I closed my eyes, remembering the feel of my hand Voiding and the sound of outraged screams in my ears. At last, I opened my eyes and pulled a dagger from my storage, throwing it across the room.

Cold mithril touched my throat as John reacted to me drawing a weapon in the sanctuary.

My blade sliced through a candlestick on the small table that was set aside for the signing of the marriage license. A poof of smoke erupted from the candle, and a ninja appeared, bow and arrow drawn.

Their Royal Highness reacted the fastest, turning into a giant multitailed fox spirit and eating the archer while John caught the arrow with his free hand.

"I'm done," I told the rogue, pretending like panic wasn't building inside me from how *close* his knife was to my neck. How close *he* was. John wasn't taller than me, like my ex had been, but combined with the threat, It sent me over the edge.

"Apologies." John lowered the blade pressed against my green skin and took a step back on his own. "And well done."

I hid my shaking hands by gripping my skirt.

"Well, Miss Gerda!" Rowen turned back into their disguise and rejoined us. "I feel like I can safely say you've won this contest—"

"Oh?" Grand Duchess Calisto stood in the sanctuary door, her escort knights in tow. "Don't cut me short *too* early, Rowen."

I curtsied politely to the woman, who smiled at me. "I will summon you if I don't best your count, Miss Gerda. Thank you for joining in the contest." It was a clear dismissal. I hesitated.

"Your Grace—" I broached. She raised an eyebrow but let me continue. "I understand that the leader of the Blackfog spies is a portal user?"

Calisto frowned. "Yes?"

"I'm something of a portal user myself—and if *I* were going to trap me, here is how I'd do it . . ."

I offered up my suggestions, and John, a shadow portal user, confirmed the idea. Her Grace immediately sent her knight to retrieve an arcane enchantment from her workshop while she got to trap searching.

I'd done all that I could.

CHAPTER 36

Anyone Intent on Murder, Do So Now or Hold Your Peace

Julian

"You look beautiful," Julian whispered to his sister.

And she did.

Her long black hair was woven with tiny glittering gems like stars in the night sky. Her dress was cream white, with sleeves that fell off the shoulders. A single black fabric flower was pinned above her heart. She wore a plain gold locket similar to the silver one he had around his own neck. Each contained a portrait of their family and a gift from their late father behind an enchanted pane of glass.

"I'm ready." Julia smiled up at him. Gone was the nervousness from the rehearsal.

She *looked* ready . . . but more than that, she looked *happy*.

"I'm proud of you." He leaned forward and kissed her on the forehead. "Congratulations, little sister."

She swatted him with the hand that wasn't holding her violet and lily bouquet. A soft lyre-harp played among the other members of the wedding party. Once they were all in place, Their Royal Highness would give a speech, and then Julian would escort his sister inside.

Julian hesitated before touching his own locket through his shirt. "Julia, don't hesitate to use our father's gift if you need it."

Her eyes fell, and her voice caught as she replied, "I-I've already used mine."

"What?" He frowned. "When?"

"It was at the Spell Script Collegium—where I met Chloe." His little sister sounded like a child who had been caught sneaking into the armory when she wasn't supposed to. "There was an accident, and we got trapped in a burning building. A part of the roof collapsed on us, and I wasn't going to be able to hold it up for much longer . . ."

He waited for her to continue. She shot him a guilty look. "I wouldn't have used it even then, but Chloe . . . she broke the seal."

"And why did *Chloe* have to break the seal?" Julian tried to hide the frustration in his voice, but he obviously failed when his sister flinched.

"I'm sorry." Her voice was soft, and Julian resisted the urge to shake her. She was his confident, little sister, who was acting like he would be upset with her—like she'd somehow *failed* him.

"Julia. The locket's there *to protect you,*" he stressed, trying to make her understand. "*Of course* you should use it. I owe your wife a thank you."

"You're not angry?" she asked carefully.

"Never," he assured her. It must have been weighing on her all this time, because she hugged him. When they broke apart, he poked her on the shoulder. "But you're going to have to tell me *everything* later."

She shot him a grin. "You'll have to wait until we get back from the honeymoon because I'm surprising Chloe with a getaway."

"Fine."

Inside the sanctuary, Their Royal Highness Rowen of Peldeep was finishing their welcome speech with a simple, "Anyone intent on murder, do so now or hold your peace until *after* the ceremony." A pause. "Excellent."

Then, the sound of Minstrel Bronwynn's lyre harp playing the opening notes to Julia's favorite song signaled it was time, and they walked together through the open doors of the sanctuary. With the sheer number of assassination attempts foiled already, Julian was on high alert. He'd even cast [Guard] on Julia, which would transfer any damage she received onto himself.

His eyes swept over the guests standing for the entry of the bride. He noted with amusement that Gerda stood in a place of honor beside his mother. How *that* had come to pass was a story he was interested in hearing.

They arrived at the front of the hall much too quickly, where he squeezed Julia's hand once before letting go and taking his place beside his mother, opposite the troll.

Chloe wore a formfitting black dress also bedecked in gemstones, a white fabric belt made out of the same material as Julia's dress winding around her waist. She reached forward and took Julia's hands. His sister beamed down at Chloe, only looking away for a moment to pass her bouquet off to Hana.

Their Royal Highness addressed the guests. "You may be seated."

The wedding party at the front of the hall all placed a hand on their hearts and nodded to the couple before walking to their seats on the outside of the front rows. On Chloe's side, Rufus and King Keith joined Henrietta, and on Julia's side, Hana and Wendy sat beside Gerda.

Julia and Chloe would make their vows before the gods on their own. This was a North Sumbrian tradition which ensured anyone who stood before the gods did so of their own free will. Their family and friends could walk with them to the front, but they would stand alone when they offered their oath.

"We welcome all before Light to witness the marriage of these two: Countess Julia von Slyke, Paladin of Light, and Necromancer Chloe Watercress of Nilheim." Their Royal Highness swept out their arms. "Marriage. That beloved arrangement is why we are here today. To celebrate the love, true love, that brought these two before us.

"Whether Fate tied your souls together or Luck gave you a chance to fall in love, your heart is your own to give. And it is by your own free will that you have come here today. Julia and Chloe, you have decided to embark on this extraordinary adventure together. A journey filled with laughter, love, and a shared dream.

"Marriage is not defeating a boss monster or conquering a dungeon or leveling up. It is the shared experience points you earn along the way, the decisions you make every day, and the battles you fight side by side.

"In your darkest hour. In your greatest triumph. This is the person you have chosen to join your party for life."

Julia was next to tears as Chloe squeezed her hands in reassurance.

"Chloe," Their Royal Highness asked, "do you take Julia to be your wife?"

CHAPTER 37

Ladies, You May Kiss Your Bride

Gerda

I sat beside Grand Duchess Calisto with a front-row seat to the wedding. It was an honor I'd received for finding the most traps.

While I was frustrated that I wouldn't be able to deliberately sit close to the Void mage assassin and foil her plans with a violent Sleep potion to the face . . . I was *beyond* happy that I got to watch one of my favorite ships up close as they tied the knot.

"I do," Chloe said firmly. The necromancer reached up to wipe a tear from Julia's cheek and the taller woman leaned into Chloe's touch.

I wasn't crying.

Yet.

Chloe's loving voice traveled over the hall. "Julia, I have waited patiently for this day."

There was a cough from the audience, and I looked in time to see Henrietta elbow King Keith in the side. RIP Keith. The Dark Lord almost expired on the spot but managed to gather himself long enough to palm a health potion.

Ignoring the audience, Chloe lowered her hand back down and laced Julia's fingers with her own.

"My love, you are the beat of my heart, the breath on my lips. Though I'm a caster who holds life and death in my palms, I didn't know what it was like to be alive until I met you." The necromancer drew their interlaced fingers to her lips and placed a soft kiss on the back of Julia's hand.

"I pledge to be your partner. Your resting place. To welcome you home from every journey. I pledge to love you, unconditionally, through laughter and light, through darkness and pain. Beyond death. I vow to Light, before friend and foe, that I will protect, honor, and defend you. And anyone who would come between us *will fertilize our flowers*."

Chloe flashed a vicious smile. I already knew that the woman had a propensity for possessive love. That was one of the reasons everyone shipped her with Julia; the prickly mage with the boisterous Paladin of Light.

The necromancer summoned a mithril band from her storage and placed it on Julia's ring finger, her eyes glowing softly with her vow. "Let this day be the day all know that I am yours, and *you are mine*."

Beside me, Grand Duchess Calisto sniffled. The woman was crying happy tears.

"So it is said, so it is done." Their Royal Highness nodded, and then they turned to Julia and asked, "Julia, do you take Chloe to be your wife?"

"I do." Julia smiled through her tears and took a steadying breath. "Chloe, I cannot imagine a world without you. Since the first day I met you, I've found a home that I *want* to return to. I cherish every day we are together, through the good and the bad.

"My heart is committed to be with you for as long as blood runs through my veins. My soul is yours, in this life and the next. I am a passionate woman, and until you, I'd never met anyone whom I felt like I could share myself with. My thoughts, my hopes, my dreams. You are more than my partner. You are my best friend. My lodestone. *My wife*." Julia pulled out her own wedding band and slipped it onto Chloe's finger. The paladin's hands shone with a faint glow as she said, "I swear by Light to be ever faithful and true. I vow to choose you, every day, because *you* are my Happily Ever After."

"So it is said, so it is done." Their Royal Highness grinned, showing off their fox fangs. "Then it is with great pleasure that I pronounce you two *wed*. Ladies, you may kiss your bride."

Chloe reached out and wound one arm around the paladin's waist, the other hooking Julia's leg, spinning and dipping her wife into a passionate kiss.

I bolted to my feet, cheering with the crowd. Someone activated an enchantment on the sanctuary's stained glass windows, and each pane of glass lit up the hall in a stunning array of colors. Bronwynn plucked a short refrain of music. And after a long kiss, Julia and Chloe pulled apart, laughing.

I exchanged a look with Their Royal Highness, and Rowen winked. They reached out to place a hand on each of the newlyweds.

"Congratulations, both of you." Rowen's face split into a playful grin.

And then, all three disappeared in a puff of smoke.

CHAPTER 38

Before Reaching Their Untimely Demise

Julian

He didn't want to suspect the fox of treachery, but Julian had to admit his heart dropped out of his chest the instant his sister vanished.

In response, Julian immediately activated [Multi-Target Shield] on everyone in the first two rows. Just in time, too, as a [Fireball] blasted to the front of the hall and a dozen figures charged the dais. Beside him, his mother activated a powerful magical enchantment.

"Surrender," his mother's voice resounded throughout the hall, "or perish." Her calm direction reassured him, and Julian immediately jumped into action.

Almost all of the two hundred guests were important dignitaries or elite, and they moved accordingly. Many were here *for* the show and calmly stepped away from the pews and into the alcoves along the walls, leaving roughly forty people in the main aisle.

Not everyone was interested in winning a magical elevator.

When the attackers didn't *immediately* surrender, his mother summoned a six-foot-tall stone golem and sat on its shoulders as it began firing bolts of electricity. It was actually for show, he knew, since her concentration was entirely on maintaining the building enchantment.

"[Barrier]." Julian put up a single clear shield between the noncombatants and the fighting, willing four points of durability into the barrier and draining his mana considerably. It wouldn't protect them if they left the area, but it did block the plumes of poisonous smoke someone had just dropped into the fray. A few beastfolk fell to the ground and changed into their beast forms as they succumbed to the wolfsbane, including Rufus.

From his vantage point, Julian could see a number of poisoned victims miraculously heal right before reaching their untimely demise. His sister-in-law was still here, hidden but keeping everyone alive. That meant Julia was also here, probably on guard, keeping Chloe alive.

"[Light Foot]." He landed on the dais and offered direction as he saw fit with [Battle Call]. "Queen Henrietta, the green dress on your right! Pram, ice the terrain! Visha, guard the door!"

While Pram froze people to the floor, Witch Agatha used her ice powers to seal the windows. She was a known lover of art, and so set about protecting the stained glass murals with a vengeance.

"Mother, to the left!"

He was a tad late, and her golem lost a leg to an assassin's axe, slumping sideways. But Calisto wasn't deterred. His mother was one of the strongest people on the continent; she could sink this entire building into the earth or obliterate everyone in the room with one of her more powerful magically crafted weapons . . . but she didn't.

Instead, she prioritized securing the area, protecting her guests, and cleaning up the mess; it wouldn't do to accidentally scuff a dignitary's shoe and risk future trade agreements.

Even now, the noncombatants were gossiping among themselves behind Julian's [Barrier]. One fox girl, Lady Brittany from Peldeep, fanned herself while watching her husband fight the baron of Tour on Marsh. An elder fae with a pixie on her shoulder calmly leaned against a staff while the pixie summoned a floating tea set for the pair. And snacks.

King Keith was also in the noncombat area for some reason, standing beside Gerda the Bridge Troll and looking dejected. Most had their own shields up as well—but Julian didn't relax. It was his responsibility to keep the fighting to the combat area, and to make sure those who sought protection found it.

"Tully, you're in acid."

"Visha, protect Lord Brittany."

"Hana, archer to your left."

While he was talking, a stray [Fireball] hit his [Barrier], and he had to use another mana potion to restrengthen it. Otherwise, the battle itself was going well. The leader of his mother's knights was locking blades with a ratkin paladin. Three archers had been taken down when Henrietta threw a pew on top of them. The baron of Tour on Marsh was bested by General Visha, who trussed him up like a floofpoof at a feast.

Of course, that was when the baron spat a poison-tipped dagger into Visha's face. The elf clutched at her throat and collapsed forward, but Tully ran by and dumped on her an antidote specifically designed for the waurg poison.

Julian flinched; Tully was going to have a field day teasing Visha for letting her guard down, especially since the fight was practically over. Whatever the

Blackfog had attempted to do here, it wasn't anywhere *near* enough to defeat his family. It was almost laughable.

Especially after all the time and energy they'd put in preparing.

"Eeeek!" There was a crash, and a high-pitched voice cried out behind him.

Julian turned to see the unexpected.

Princess Contessa—a black-haired woman with light-brown skin from the Empire of Sands, and one of the noncombatants—was sitting on the floor with her hands up. And Gerda the Bridge Troll stood over her, axe in hand.

Julian cursed, uncertain which of the pair to subdue.

He dropped the remainder of his mana into a [Multi-Target Shield] *just* in time for Gerda to swing the blunt of her axe at the princess. The human lifted her arms daintily to defend, but his shield deflected the blow.

The recoil sent Gerda reeling back.

That one attack was enough to deal his shield two hundred points of damage and destroy it. He cursed again.

"That's enough," Julian told the pair, walking toward them as he summoned *another* mana potion. "Gerda, *stand down*. We'll take it from here."

Unfortunately, neither of them appeared cooperative.

"You again!" The princess climbed to her feet, whipping out a decorative fan—a *deadly* decorative fan tipped with poisoned spines.

"Me again," the troll agreed, lifting her axe to strike.

The princess and the troll were *both* on the Blackfog hit list, and while his gut told him that he should place all of his trust in the troll—he would rather detain them *both* for questioning.

"John, stop those two."

CHAPTER 39

Carefully Planned Foiling

Gerda

The second the battle started, I dropped everything to go after the Keeper of Fate.

I had no idea how I was going to talk my way into revealing her secret identity, but in the worst-case scenario, I could just blame [Sense Danger]. Or fall back on that well-timed Sleep potion to the face.

I finally spotted her on the opposite side of the hall. Pram had just iced the floor and was now making an ice wall to protect the noncombatants against the opposite wall of the sanctuary. To reach her, I'd need to circle around or brave the battlefield between.

The good news was, King Keith was on this side with me, safely tucked behind Julian's [Barrier], where Alice couldn't reach him. Henrietta's oracle scenario had started when the battle was at an end and the damage already done. In that future, Chloe was permanently gone, and many of the guests had died in the chaos—unfortunate for them, due to their differing inheritance laws. It was a reminder that the keeper didn't need to actually *kill* everyone to further her plan; half of her list could have their fates irrevocably altered with a simple unaliving.

Henrietta had been walking back to Keith so she could comfort her husband in his grief when the Keeper of Fate had hit the Dark Lord with a bottle of molten ash vane.

It had only gone further downhill from there.

So in *this* timeline, I'd equipped one of my two life-saving phoenix tail feathers and waited until the keeper tried to cross the room before moving to intercept her.

Now hearing that John was on his way, I switched to a distraction tactic.

"Riddle me this," I said, swinging my axe back until the smooth wooden handle rested on my exposed shoulder. "How are you going to escape now, *spy?*"

"You *brute*. Do you think they'll listen to your nonsense?" The keeper glared from behind her fan, looking down her nose at me in her best princess fashion. "*I* am no spy. You speak with the Princess Contessa la Rouche of Ildsfeld!"

The woman's disguise was exemplary, as to be expected from the leader of an international spy organization.

"*Are* you, though?" I goaded, trying to keep her attention from John's shadow. It had started ten paces back where Julian stood, arms crossed and patiently waiting.

She narrowed her eyes. "*Of course I am.*"

I smiled a challenge. "I thought you were the Keeper of Fate?"

"How do you know that name?" she started, then her eyes narrowed. "*Wait!*"

I thought she'd noticed John's shadow—but no, her eyes never left my face as she considered something.

"No . . . I don't believe it." She scoffed. "It *can't* be you."

I raised an eyebrow. "I'm the one who found all of your traps—and now, *you* are trapped."

"You think so?" She snapped her deadly fan shut and paused dramatically.

Nothing happened.

Her eyes went wide, then narrowed in pure, unadulterated hatred. "*What did you do?*"

"You won't escape while I'm still here." I smirked.

It was, in fact, Grand Duchess Calisto who'd taken my advice and used one of her enchantments to separate the sanctuary into a pocket dimension. It guaranteed that no one could escape—including the pink portal mage who had kidnapped her daughter.

But the keeper didn't know that.

At that point, my perception *felt* John's shadow touch my own. Perfect. I wanted him safely under my feet for the next part of my plan.

"Surrender, Keeper. The door is barred!" I said, *deliberately* looking away and pointing at the sanctuary's front doors. The Keeper of Fate took my bait and threw her potion bottle at me.

By the looks of it . . . it *was* molten ash vane. I calmly stepped aside and let the bottle shatter on the floor behind me.

It looked like I didn't need to use up a phoenix feather after all.

If I were John, I would've used this opportunity to capture her right away, but the master rogue waited. The Keeper of Fate stared at the bottle and then back at me. "You . . ."

"Any *other* tricks?" I asked, tapping my foot to inspire John. Why was he waiting?

"All this time," she said, her voice coming out as a hoarse laugh. "All this time, *you were a bridge troll?*"

"Yes?"

"YOU RUINED EVERYTHING!" She whipped her fan out. "*DO YOU KNOW WHAT YOU'VE DONE?!*"

"John!" I shouted, dodging two poisoned air blades that narrowly missed my ear. "Now would be—"

The man was already on it, appearing from the floor and clamping a set of manacles onto the keeper's wrists. Princess Contessa la Rouche of Ildsfeld changed from a tall black-haired human into a familiar blonde-haired, blue-eyed woman with enough charm to knock out a troll.

I should know; I could feel it in my gut.

"*I'M GOING TO END YOU—Let me go!*" The woman screamed her frustration and tried to break free of John's hold on her manacles. It was useless with all of her stats reduced, but I took a step back anyway, bumping into Duke Julian's firm chest.

It was a very nice chest.

"Miss Gerda." Julian lifted one finger to push the blade of my axe away from his face. I hurriedly stored the weapon in my ring and stepped to the side.

Visha was with him, the elf immediately stepping forward to help take charge of the keeper. On the other side of the hall, Julia, Chloe, and Their Royal Highness had reappeared, and Grand Duchess Calisto was thanking everyone for coming, and reminding them that there would be a reception lunch in the dining hall in one hour's time.

"I can't *wait* to hear how you will explain this. But first—" Julian turned dark eyes on the keeper. "It is so good to see you again, Guild Mistress Alice. *We have much to discuss*, you and I."

Alice stopped struggling against her bonds and turned my way. She didn't spare the duke a glance, instead yelling at me, "You think you've won? These bonds won't keep me, and I *will* come for you—"

"I see we'll have to do this elsewhere." Julian cut off Alice by bending down to block her view. "You are under arrest by warrant of the Continental Council." His voice dropped to an angry timber. "And you *will* go quietly or we will be forced to take drastic action. Visha, check with mother where she wants our *special guest.*"

The celestial glared but kept her mouth shut as she was dragged away.

"Now, Miss Gerda." Julian turned back to me, a pair of manacles dangling from the half elf's hands. It was like something straight out of fanfiction art. I *almost* fought it, but Henrietta had spotted me and was on her way over. Besides, thanks to my own intervention, I couldn't portal out even if I wanted to.

"I think you already *know* why I'm detaining you," he said as he clasped the manacles around my wrists.

[**Veralyn's Enchanted Restraint Manacles:** A modified version of the restraints designed for St. George's Trials. Prevents access to all nonpassive Titles, Skills, Perks, Bonded, and Equipped Items. All Attribute stats capped at 15.]

I raised an eyebrow. "Because I'm brilliant and figured out who the mastermind was?"

"Among other things," he stated.

"You didn't need to manacle me to bring me in for questioning," I told him.

"Are you *sure*?" Julian countered. "When *someone* easily escaped my level fifty-four rogue yesterday?"

"Okay, that's fair."

"*What is the meaning of this?*" The Dark Lady had arrived.

"I'm just taking her in for questioning—"

"Questioning? *Again*?" Henrietta crossed her arms.

"You can release the bridge troll; she's innocent." Grand Duchess Calisto also walked up to join us. She looked like she'd been through all seven hells and back again, and was using Their Royal Highness as a crutch. Visha held Alice nearby.

Behind her, all that remained was the wedding party. Sir Tully and Pram stood by the exits. Hana and Wendy were picking up the scattered remnants of the brides' bouquets that littered the floor. Chloe was seated, with Julia supporting her wife by handing her mana potion after mana potion.

"Ha, *innocent*?" Alice barked a laugh that drew everyone's attention. Her face twisted in some secret, malicious smile before her eyes met mine, and she said, "You have all been deceived. That's not Gerda the Bridge Troll—*that's Madame Potts.*"

CHAPTER 40

The Elusive, Beautiful, Charming, and Brilliant Madame Potts

Julian

Julian turned and faced the troll, who stared wide-eyed at Guild Mistress Alice.

"Wait, really?!" Queen Henrietta's frown turned into a wide smile as she immediately accepted the word as fact and literally clapped with joy. "*You're Madame Potts?*"

Julian considered the revelation. It would certainly explain how she'd known where his locket was, and how she'd caught an arrow midflight. And how she'd known about the kazil poison frogs in advance.

And how she'd helped them capture Alice.

The bridge troll tried to wave off the accusation. "Me?"

"*Yes, you!*" Guild Mistress Alice shot back. "It's so obvious now. You mentioned me in a Cast after I destroyed your bridge escaping the Emerald Palace. All this time, I thought you lived in the part I burned down!"

Their Royal Highness whispered softly to Julian's mother, "After *you* are done with Alice, it's *my* turn."

Calisto nodded her agreement.

Alice continued. "It explains how you found my traps. And why some random bridge troll found Julia before everyone else!"

"*You* saved Julia?" Julian asked, interrupting.

"Ah. Well . . ." Gerda shot Julian a look he couldn't read before addressing the room. "That is pretty incriminating evidence . . . but so what?"

"Wait!" Sir Tully exclaimed at the same time. "*You* won the trap prize? Not fair if Madame Potts was competing!"

"Even *if* it were true"—the troll looked down on Alice—"Madame Potts has saved every person in this hall, *except you.*"

"Or me," Julian added.

"*Technically,*" she stressed the word, "you might have eaten that poison lunch if I weren't there."

He didn't point out they were supposed to be talking about a time when *Madame Potts* had saved him.

"My *point*"—Gerda was already turning back to Alice—"is whether I'm the elusive, beautiful, charming, and brilliant Madame Potts or just some *random bridge troll*, it doesn't matter, does it? *I still beat you.*"

"You cheated!" Alice yelled. "I wouldn't even have to *be* here if I weren't cleaning up *your mess!* You say you saved people, but you've ruined *everything!* Look at what you did to the Heroine of Justice!"

Gerda shot back. "Fate is not predetermined—Madame Potts *proved that.* And Henrietta has every right to be with whomever she wants."

"The Dark Lord is *not* one of her fated mates!" Alice declared.

"Don't listen." King Keith reached out and covered his wife's ears, knowing it wouldn't do much.

"It's alright." Queen Henrietta reached up with one hand and placed it on his. She looked up at him with a reassuring gaze. "I'm very happy with my choice."

"*You married a demon!*" Alice spat. "He's a monster! With horns!"

"A demi," Keith corrected. "I'm not even half demon. And you're one to talk, *celestial.*"

"I like your horn," Henrietta said, then blushed.

"And I'm lucky you do," Keith replied, also blushing.

"See? Everyone's getting their Happily Ever After." Gerda smirked. "Besides, Fate's plan was *dreadful.* Is her storyline even *worth* fighting for?"

"*You dare!*" Alice fought Visha's hold, trying to physically attack the troll but unable to do so with her lowered stats.

"*If I have to live in this world, then I have to dare,*" said Gerda, her voice darker and resolute.

Julian felt the weight of her words hit him.

"You lost because you thought it was okay to force people down a path not of their choosing. But people *always* have a choice, even when it seems hopeless." Gerda lifted her manacles. "Even trapped, I could try to run or fight, or walk out of here with my head held high. That is how the world works. Fate and Luck walk hand in hand, and *nothing is certain.*"

Alice narrowed her eyes at the bridge troll. "Is that who put you up to this? Luck is the only one who has as much control over the story as my goddess. Are you her champion?"

"Why can't I be working with Fate?" Gerda countered. "Perhaps she's grown tired of her own plot?"

"Ridiculous!" Alice snarled. "Utterly ridiculous!"

"Is it, though?" Sir Tully added from the side.

"Shh." Visha elbowed the paladin.

"I think I've heard enough," Grand Duchess Calisto stated. "Visha, you may take Guild Mistress Alice to the Elkhorn Hall."

His mother was sending Alice to her personal dungeon.

"I hope you enjoy your *Happily Ever After*," the Keeper of Fate told them as she was escorted out, "because Fate isn't going to just sit back and watch."

And with that threat, she left the hall.

Gerda looked up at Julian, lifting her manacles. "Do I have to go to the dungeon too?"

"No need for that, Miss Gerda . . . Or should I say, *Madame Potts*?" Julian pulled out the key to her manacles. But she surprised him.

"You have no real proof that I'm Madame Potts." She lifted her hands away from Julian and chastised him. "Don't unlock my manacles based on what *that* psychopathic murderer said! You should unlock these because you think that I'm innocent and you were wrong to ever doubt me."

Julian couldn't hide the amusement on his face as he reached out and easily caught the troll's bound hands. He dragged them back to unlock the binds, feeling the slight tremor in her fingers.

"Thank you for saving my sister," he said sincerely. "And I'm sorry for doubting you."

"I'm not," Tully told Pram. "She's right; we *should* detain anyone suspicious." Pram just shrugged as Julian offhandedly planned further punishment for Tully when they returned north.

Gerda rubbed her wrists, glaring up at Julian. "Only Alice thinks I saved Julia—I'm just your average, overpowered bridge troll."

She didn't sound convincing, and Julian opened his mouth to tease her.

"I have proof." Except his mother cut in, matter of fact.

At the troll's raised eyebrows, his mother gave her a gentle, pitying stare. "You honestly thought I didn't have enchanted golems spying on every part of my castle during the festival?"

"Ah," Gerda accepted readily, looking sheepish. "Sensible of you."

"Especially when *somebody* foretold trouble?" Calisto teased.

Gerda looked around at everyone who was left and sighed. "All right, I give up. Let me explain—"

"Before you do," King Keith cut her off, pointedly looking around the room. "I say we move this elsewhere; maybe over lunch?"

CHAPTER 41

Spill the Tea

Gerda

I was sitting on a couch, sandwiched between Henrietta and King Keith, while most everyone who had previously been in the sanctuary found a spot in the parlor.

Grand Duchess Calisto and Duke Julian sat across from me, Her Grace downing a second mana potion. Their Royal Highness hovered behind them instead of taking one of the available chairs. The fox was obviously impatient to be elsewhere, exacting revenge on a suspecting spy, but couldn't resist their curiosity.

The newlyweds and their party members were absent, playing host at the official luncheon. Sir Tully was running laps outside, and Visha was on guard duty for Alice in the dungeon. That left Pram and John, the latter of which was in Julian's shadow.

Pram was handling a tray of snacks, and pouring drinks. The selkie was a deft hand, and I happily sipped from a cup of caruleal tea, a blend from southern Peldeep that was pink and hinted of grapefruit.

"Alright, spill the tea!" Henrietta couldn't contain her excitement and stared up at me with bright, shining eyes. "Are you actually Madame Potts?"

I considered my response.

"It's pronounced *Madame*," I joked, knowing it didn't matter because no one here spoke French except for me. I took another sip from my handleless teacup to calm my racing heart.

The room reacted differently all at once.

"Of course," King Keith muttered under his breath. The Dark Lord was still hurt that I'd taken over all of his bridges, and it showed.

Silver eyes narrowed as Duke Julian regarded me. Whatever he thought, he said nothing.

Because at that point, Their Royal Highness changed shape.

The guise of a stately gentleman with long white facial hair and bushy eyebrows wearing heavy court robes faded into a huge fox towering overhead. Their many tails were half hidden in a red-and-white fog. Rowen's usually playful slit eyes were open, staring at me intently. I felt their aura, and some skill hit me as they confirmed, "*You* are Madame Potts?"

I didn't flinch under the weight. "Yes."

It was the truth, and Rowen *saw* it. The pressure from their aura subsided, and the fox nodded once. Suddenly, they shifted again, this time into a middle-aged androgynous adventurer wearing a thin circlet, with long black hair tied at the nape of their neck.

"Then I owe you a great debt." Rowen walked around the couch and took a seat in the armchair next to Duchess Calisto. Bracing both elbows on their knees, the fox said with utmost sincerity, "*Thank you.*"

"You're welcome. I'm glad I could help," I replied, resisting the urge to tell them it was nothing or otherwise downplay my part in saving their life. I had a feeling they would take that as an insult.

"I would *also* like to thank you," Grand Duchess Calisto spoke, drawing everyone's attention, "since I assume today would have gone *a lot* differently if you had not been there."

"Ah, yes." It was time to get back to the matter at hand. "The skill I use to see the future is random, and it only shows me *one* of many future outcomes. I just pointed out where the traps were going to go off, and John found them for me."

My particular set of abilities were actually overpowered, but I wasn't here to show off. I was here to survive. Even if no one here seemed like the type to lock me away in a tower for my future-telling skills, why chance it?

"So, your knight was right." King Keith eyed Julian. "Miss Gerda *was* cheating."

"Everyone had a chance to inspect the hall, love, and there were no limits on which skill could be used to search," Henrietta chastised. "Besides, it's a point of pride that *our* bridge troll is the winner."

"Gods." The Dark Lord reached up and pinched the bridge of his nose. "After today, everyone is going to find out that Madame Potts lives in *our* kingdom. We already get enough attention . . ."

He sounded preemptively exhausted, and Henrietta tried to cheer him up. "It'll be fine. Between the two of us, I'm sure we can protect Miss Gerda."

"That's not . . ." Keith began, then changed tactics. "Thank you, love."

"He's right." Their Royal Highness leaned back and crossed their legs, regarding me with curiosity. "Now that it's known, I can't imagine the secret being safe for long. Especially when the leader of the largest information guild on the continent is the one who figured it out. What do you plan to do now?"

"I haven't decided," I lied. By the look on Rowen's face, they could tell. Instead of prying, they simply nodded and offered, "Peldeep will always welcome you."

"Rowen!" Henrietta turned on the fox, eyes blazing. "No poaching our elite!"

Keith physically bit his lip and remained silent.

Grand Duchess Calisto said, "Just make sure that whatever you decide is ready for after the Masquerade, Miss Gerda, because you will have to explain yourself at the next Continental Council meeting."

It was expected after everything I'd done, but I wasn't looking forward to it. "Of course, Your Grace."

"We'll be there for you." Henrietta put a hand on mine. "Just like you've been there for us."

It wasn't just the Dark Lady. Everyone in the room felt like they gave some tell of support from a nod or smile.

"Thank you." I smiled at my queen.

"Do you want to tell us?" Henrietta's eyes shone. "About being Madame Potts?"

"Alright," I hesitated, wondering what I should say.

"Here." Henrietta immediately passed me my cup of tea and grabbed a snack for herself. "When you're ready."

It was exactly how we talked around the table in my kitchen, as if we weren't surrounded by a room of people watching me. I took a sip of my caruleal tea and then spoke.

"I guess I'll start at the beginning?"

CHAPTER 42

A Distractable Legend

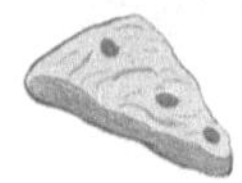

Julian

"It all started the day my ex-husband beat me to death," Gerda the Bridge Troll explained, delivering that bone-chilling statement with a casual smile.

Julian tensed, grateful he wasn't holding anything as he felt his nails bite into the flesh of his palm. Henrietta was less fortunate; the Dark Lady was holding a huckleberry biscuit from the snack tray. She turned the pastry into powder.

"*He did what?*"

"[Cleanse]." Keith waved a hand to help tidy up the mess before asking, "I'm assuming you were not living in the Dark Enchanted Forest at that time?"

"The Baldorin Mountains," she explained, reaching out a comforting hand and placing it on Henrietta's arm. "I *told* you I was divorced."

"You didn't tell me what happened *before* you were divorced!" Henrietta laid her own hand on top of the troll's. "But don't mind me, go on."

The Dark Lady said so, but the second Gerda turned away to continue her story, Henrietta shared a look with Keith. Julian felt no pity for whatever she'd do to the fool who had harmed the bridge troll. At this point, he should have reminded Gerda that she was meant to be answering security questions and not the details of her love life, but he *wanted* to hear Gerda's backstory. He was invested, as was everyone else.

Madame Potts was a legend. A distractible legend.

"We'd wed *until death do us part*." Gerda took a sip of her tea. "And when he tried to protest the separation, I threw him off a mountain. That's when I left for the Dark Enchanted Forest."

"Good riddance," Henrietta stated. The Dark Lady picked up a new biscuit and stuffed it in her mouth.

"Larry the Bridge Troll was retiring, and I was looking for a home." Gerda's face softened. "He taught me everything I needed to know to open up the [Bridge Troll] skill tree. My foresight came later."

Their Royal Highness asked, "Was that around the time you made your first Crystal Cast?"

"Yes." She scrunched her nose, drawing Julian's attention to her white freckles. "While I was questing in the Dark Enchanted Forest, I found the Master Cast Crystal and used that to start forewarning everyone about important upcoming events—such as Your Highness's death."

"And my guild leader's death," the royal added. "And the dungeon breaks."

"What about the helpful tips?" Henrietta asked. "Like the broken respawn points or where to get buffs?"

"I overhear a lot of things on my bridge," she replied. "And I have some dungeoneering knowledge."

Rowen's lips tightened into a line, and Julian wondered if she wasn't telling the whole truth. The fox didn't interrupt her, though, simply grabbing a scone for themselves.

Gerda was already moving on to the next part of her story. "Anyway, anything I discover that might be helpful I try to work into my podcast—Madame Potts Cast, I mean. The problem is that today, there was no way I could've fixed everything with a simple Cast." She stopped talking, and her silence spoke for itself.

Gerda had only been caught because she'd chosen to save them.

Julian broke the quiet. "Miss Gerda. You said you found the traps because you saw them go off?"

"Yes?"

"Then did you also see the traitor who put them there?" He tried to keep the anger from his voice.

"I did not."

His mother spoke then. "Julian, I'm sure Miss Gerda would have told us already if she knew who it was . . ."

The bridge troll visibly flinched. "Your Grace," Gerda said to his mother, "the reason I haven't brought up my suspicions is because they are just that: suspicions."

Calisto nodded. "You mean Master Thomas?"

"You knew?" Gerda looked shocked and then contrite. "Of course you knew."

"The boy is an all-powerful mage who was the last to enter the sanctuary before you." Calisto sipped her tea, finishing off the last of it and placing it down firmly. "He might be strong . . . but he's terrible at overestimating his own brilliance."

Their Royal Highness started leaking pressure back over the room. "*Thomas* is a Blackfog spy?"

"No," Gerda said firmly enough to draw everyone's attention back to the troll. "He's not a spy."

"Is that Madame Potts speaking?" Rowen demanded, "Or another suspicion?"

"As Madame Potts," she stressed, "I can promise you that Master Thomas is *not* a Blackfog spy . . . and—"

"And?"

The troll fought with herself, like she wanted to say something but couldn't, then let out an aggravated sigh.

"There are grounds enough to arrest him," Julian offered. "I can do it now—"

"Wait!" The troll finally gave in. "I'm trying to find the words to convince you to leave Thomas alone because his future *must* stay the same!"

Julian couldn't agree. "If he hurt my family, then I don't care what his future *should* be. He will answer for his past *now*."

Gerda stood up from her seat, looking over every single person in the room. When she spoke, she pitched her voice *just* enough that it sounded like he was listening to a real Madame Potts's Cast.

"*If anything happens to Master Thomas during the Masquerade, then North Sumbria will fall to chaos.*" Gerda turned to Julian. "*And* you *will die.*"

Their Royal Highness frowned. "She speaks the truth."

"I do."

His mother lifted a hand to Julian, who instinctively took it. She braced to stand, and he realized just how exhausted she really was. He stood with her to act as a crutch.

"I cannot promise the future, Miss Gerda," Grand Duchess Calisto told the troll, "but for now, North Sumbria will listen to your advice."

Julian knew what that meant—the master mage was free to walk around as if nothing had happened. It didn't sit right with him, but there wasn't anything he could do once his mother had made her will known.

"Thank you, Your Grace." The troll bowed her head, her braid slipping delicately over her shoulder. It hung to her thighs, so she wrapped both hands around it to keep it close.

"And Miss Gerda?"

She straightened at her name.

"I'll send someone to check on that bridge after the festival. In the meantime, I hope you have a good stay in the Coral Palace."

Gerda's white freckles blushed a soft and surprisingly endearing shade of pink.

"Now, if you will excuse me, everyone, I am going to congratulate my daughter and her wife." The duchess allowed Julian to escort her out, leaning heavily on his arm for support. "To the dining hall," she ordered; he didn't argue. The luncheon wasn't the official reception, it was simply a gathering after the ceremony to offer Julia and Chloe well wishes. The ball tomorrow evening would act as the *official* reception and toast for the newlyweds.

He quietly passed his mother his last advanced mana potion, and she downed it before walking into the dining hall. She was a stubborn woman, smiling through a mana burn headache.

She came, she greeted, and she even managed a piece of cheese.

After ten minutes, Julian put his foot down and made an excuse to get his mother off to her rooms and straight into bed. He didn't want Chloe to have to revive her new mother-in-law on her first day in the family.

Despite her grumbling, Julian summoned a healer to check over Calisto's health, then plied her with another mana potion before leaving her to rest.

And then, he went for a walk.

CHAPTER 43

Physics Played Little Part When Stat Sheets Were Involved

Gerda

The Dark Lord and Lady were the last to leave, everyone else having left shortly after Julian and Calisto. Their Royal Highness had even extended an invite for tea in the Emerald Palace the next time I was in Peldeep, a reminder I was going to have to get used to the new VIP treatment as Madame Potts.

"Do *you* want to be the one to tell Brownie and Lady Amaryllis, or can I?" Henrietta asked while on the way to the dining hall. She held my arm in a tight hug as we walked. I survived.

"I'm sure the whole palace knows by now, but do what you want." I sighed. "Honestly, I wasn't expecting to keep it a secret as long as I did."

"You could have remained elusive," King Keith said, raising a single eyebrow at me, "if you hadn't gotten involved yourself."

"Yes," I acknowledged, "but where's the fun in that?"

"Safer," he countered.

I shook my head. "Sometimes I need to act myself. I can't be Casting every ten minutes—it would get obnoxious, and it would let the people I'm trying to stop know that *I* know their plans."

"How much *do* you see?" King Keith asked. He was trying to be subtle—and failing. The Dark Lord was obviously uncomfortable with my powers.

"Enough to be helpful."

I didn't need to share everything, and it was best to keep the Dark Lord on his toes.

"Gerda?" Henrietta said, letting go of my arm. "I'm glad you're here. And I'm glad I met you. And I want you to know that I am very, very happy with my *current* fate."

With that, she reached for her husband, who immediately locked hands with Henrietta.

What Alice said must have hurt them.

"I'm happy to have helped," I replied. There was a warmth in my chest looking at them. Some of the changes I'd made hadn't turned out as nice, so I needed a little self-confidence boost now and then. And watching Henrietta and Keith provided ample.

"We're almost there." King Keith shot me a look. "Last chance to run."

All of my fears were founded when the knights on duty outside the dining hall saw me and exchanged knowing looks. They didn't outright *say* anything, but they were having conversations with their eyes that would put anime characters to shame.

Henrietta jumped in to say, "You don't want to run away—they have an *entire buffet* of specialty import dishes from the Empire of Sands."

The door to the dining hall was open, and I could already smell the rich, heady smells of curry and coriander and turmeric. Even the unpleasant business of making a first public appearance wasn't going to stop me from trying whatever was making that smell.

"It's alright," I told them. "I'm ready."

As it was a casual affair, we were welcomed inside by a palace attendant without being announced. It didn't matter; everyone near the door noticed us and started speaking quietly to each other.

My perception, of course, heard everything loud and clear.

"Is she *really* Madame Potts?"

"My uncle was caught in that capybara stampede. We all told him to listen to the Cast—"

"I'm not saying it's completely unbelievable, but a *bridge troll?*"

It was nice walking into the dining hall with the rulers of the Dark Enchanted Forest. People talked, but no one was brave enough to approach. *No one* interrupted the Dark Lord and Lady of Nilheim, especially when Her Viciousness was talking adamantly on very important matters.

"The black-and-white grain is wild rice from the Empire." Henrietta positively vibrated with her excitement. "They mix it with river fish and form it into medallions that are then seared in aramu nut oil. The seasoning, Chloe told me, is a combination of crushed sami seeds, dill weed, and powdered purple lotus petals. And they have a nut curry simmered in *three* types of dried fruits, and overnight roasted unigoat!"

King Keith followed his wife and listened intently to her detailed accounting of lunch. The Dark Lord was a known lover of food, and he looked as excited as Henrietta. Despite the scone earlier, I was surprisingly ravenous, and filled my plate from the buffet table running down the center of the room.

People were standing in groups nearby or seated at the tables on the far side. The patio doors were open, and the soft sounds of music and conversation could be heard drifting in from the garden.

"You're finally here!" Minstrel Bronwynn greeted Henrietta with a wide grin, the half giantess clad in a silk red dress that draped over one shoulder and was cinched at the waist with a black velvet belt. She wore black slippers covered in tiny rubies that matched her earrings and necklace set.

Rufus was close behind her, sporting a long black tunic with ruby buttons, calf-length pants, and a red belt to match. In beastman form, he didn't require shoes.

"We had a lot to discuss." The Dark Lady shot me a teasing side-eye.

"It's all everyone's talking about," Brownie told me. "Chloe is annoyed, but Julia is using the opportunity to downplay the battle at the sanctuary. Instead of people complaining about how short and anticlimactic the wedding battle was, they're talking about the big reveal." She leaned in conspiratorially and hid her words behind a hand. "And between you and the guild mistress, I'm not sure who's the bigger reveal."

"The Blackfog aren't as well known," King Keith mused. "Their leader being captured is interesting, but *not*, I think, as interesting as finding out that Madame Potts is a common bridge troll."

"Not so common!" Henrietta defended me. "She held off the Drendil army all by herself, and she rescued *you* from the Void mage."

"The Void mage," King Keith pointed out, "whom we just captured?"

"I'm surprised," Rufus cut in, "at *how* little Void magic she hit us with."

I coughed, remembering Chloe getting consumed by a Void trap. It wasn't a fun way to go. Aloud, I said, "Alice isn't able to use her abilities while in disguise; it would be different if we'd faced off against her as her *real* self."

Brownie frowned. "Why did that sound like foreshadowing?"

That made me laugh. "Because *everything* I say sounds like foreshadowing? *I'm Madame Potts.*"

As we were speaking, others in the hall were inconspicuously and not-so-inconspicuously listening in; on this side of the dining hall, at least, conversation had fallen to a dull whisper. One young lady from North Sumbria was actually tilting on an angle toward us and looked past the point she should have already keeled over.

Physics, of course, played little part when stat sheets were involved.

When I declared for everyone to hear that I *was*, in fact, *the* Madame Potts, it was like some tenuous barrier between us and the other guests broke.

"Minstrel Bronwynn! It's so good to see you here. Won't you introduce me to your companions?"

The first of a wave of interested guests descended . . .

And I was beset.

CHAPTER 44

Intimately Sure of Him and His Ways

Julian

The western garden fountain bubbled happily under the hot sun.

He didn't know why, but every time Julian had gone for a walk by himself, he'd found his way back to this fountain. In the North, Julian rarely had time to himself; he was either defending the border or exploring the Ice Fields. Any spare time he *did* have, he spent writing letters to his mother and little sister. Julia's replies were scattered at best, absent for months at worst.

When she *did* write to him, her letters were full of her adventures, the most recent being that time she'd saved a mushfolk village from an angry griffin in the Dark Enchanted Forest, a dungeon delve in Peldeep where she'd found a treasure chest full of enchanted socks, and notably, Chloe's proposal.

His mother, on the other hand, wrote routinely, with subtle and not-so-subtle hints that she would like him to come home.

Julian had a goal in the North, more so than simply preventing the Ice Fields' dungeon monsters from storming across the border; he wanted to find and conquer the dungeon *itself* and stop the threat altogether. And until that happened, being home made him feel restless. He needed to leave soon, before he got too comfortable . . . Before he started having second thoughts about leaving.

A soft *click* drew his attention. Gerda ducked through a door before quickly closing it behind her. She was breathing deeply, as if she'd been running.

"Miss Gerda?"

She spun to face him. "Your Grace?"

"Going on a walk?" he asked.

She glanced back over her shoulder before joining him at the bottom of the short stairs. "I'm going anywhere that isn't full of people," she admitted. "I enjoy gatherings as much as the next troll, but not when I'm the center of attention."

"That bad?" he inquired.

"No one came to physical blows. It was just a lot of fake niceties from people who were too polite to ask me to tell them their future." Her shoulders slumped. "I told Henrietta I'd be back, so this is only a short reprieve."

A cool breeze ruffled her hair, and the troll turned her face into the wind. She was lovely.

"I should be going." He took a step back, suddenly feeling a different *kind* of restlessness.

"Wait." She turned back his way and then joined him. Suddenly, they were both walking on the path together.

"Yes?"

She smiled. "You live at the northern border?"

"I do."

"What's it like?"

"Beautiful and harsh," he answered immediately. "The Northern Fortress isn't so bad, but the further you head into the Ice Fields, the more dangerous it gets—from monsters *and* the cold."

"I see . . ." She tapped her chin, deep in thought as they arrived at the bench where she'd found his locket. "Are you going back early? Or are you staying till the end of the ball?"

"The day after the ball, actually . . ." Though he didn't tell her he was still hoping to sneak away early if the opportunity arose. He asked, "Why?"

Gerda gathered herself. "I was going to ask you for a favor—"

"Alright," he accepted. "What's the favor?"

She eyed him, concerned. "Shouldn't you hear what the favor is *before* you agree?"

"You expect me to deny you? After today?" Julian sat down on the bench, staring up at Gerda. Honestly, he felt no small amount of guilt that helping his family had revealed the troll's hidden identity . . . And about the manacles, too.

"Yes. Well, I *did...*" she replied. "Now, I need time to think."

"You were just about to ask, so what is there to think about?" Julian crossed his arms.

The sun reflected in her soft brown eyes, and she had to move slightly to escape the glare. "That was before I knew you'd say yes to *whatever* I asked for!"

"What *were* you going to ask for?" He was genuinely curious.

"An escort," she replied offhandedly.

That startled him. Julian's eyes swept once over the troll.

Her long hair reminded him of dark malachite as it caught the summer sun. She had strong, well-toned muscles that could rival any Martial class, and a warm, playful smile that made him feel like she was hiding a secret. And she was wearing a shade of purple that *almost* matched his own, though hers was lighter.

After seeing Henrietta and Keith in coordinated, matching outfits, he couldn't unsee the similarities. He didn't have a partner for the Summer Masquerade; he'd never stayed long enough to warrant needing one. And if it were anyone else, he'd have politely refused.

But not now. Oddly enough, the idea excited him. He enjoyed her company.

"I would be happy to escort you, Miss Gerda." He nodded. "When and where should I pick you up?"

Previous Masquerades had started with an hour social where everyone was afforded the opportunity to mingle in costume and enjoy the illusion of anonymity. Because this year's event was going to act as Julia's reception, there was also going to be a welcome speech, a toast, dancing, and the unmasking later.

Gerda stopped tapping her chin and smiled down at him. "I can be ready any time. Are you *sure* you won't regret this? After today, there's probably going to be a target on my head."

"That's the role of an escort, is it not?" he teased. "To see you safely there and back again?"

"True." She nodded.

He would need time to prepare. After this morning, the number of potions in his storage ring were running low. He'd restock extra mana and health potions for the ball, and maybe a few antidotes as well. And he could keep one of the resting rooms locked for her to escape to if she needed it.

"I guess there are *some* nice things about being Madame Potts," Gerda commented.

He shook his head. "I would have said yes even if you *weren't* Madame Potts." Realizing how that could be implied, Julian hurried to explain, "Since *you* were the one who saved my sister, not some voice on a Cast. Thank you."

"You're welcome." Gerda nodded at Julian's shadow. "I couldn't have done it without John."

"He's actually off right now," Julian told her. He couldn't imagine having this same conversation with John listening in.

"I thought he was *always* with you?" She scrunched her nose, once more speaking about him with certainty.

Just like the first night they'd met.

She had thrown him off because it'd felt strange talking to someone who sounded so intimately sure of him and his ways . . . now, he knew why. If his bridge troll could see into his future, then she probably knew a great deal about Julian.

"John's at home with his family; he left after our meeting." Almost all of the man's shadows were gone too, leaving only one behind to hang around the celestial in case of an emergency.

"I see." Gerda glanced back the way she'd come. "I should probably get back to Henrietta before she worries."

Julian resisted the urge to try and keep her here. He wanted to spend the entire afternoon talking. She was interesting company.

Instead, he stood to leave as well. "Then, why don't we meet here thirty minutes before the Masquerade?"

"*Before* the Masquerade?" The troll whipped around to face him. Gerda looked confused.

Julian was standing about an arm's length away and staring straight into her uncertain eyes.

"Ah." He realized his mistake. "Did you want to go to the tea party together?"

CHAPTER 45

My Favorite Invited Me to the Ball on a Logistical Whim

Gerda

I couldn't believe my luck.

I'd gone outside to get a moment of fresh air and found the one person I actually wanted to talk to. And he'd even agreed to escort me north. Seeing Julian sitting on a garden bench staring up at me with his piercing silver eyes, I'd felt the need to fan myself from the heat.

I hadn't.

I was a grown woman who could remain professional. No matter that the half elf had shoulder-length purple dreadlocks pulled back into a ponytail and a face that I could get lost in. Seriously, why had they made him exactly my type?

I reminded myself that I'd seen plenty of muscled warrior men since my arrival; I could calm down. Especially if I was going to be spending a week or more in his company, traveling to the border.

I could *probably* make it without the escort, but Julian and his team had spent years exploring the Ice Fields. They would know which monsters I was going to face and their average levels. I was sure I could get information from his teammates. Sir Tully was an open book in the *otome*—always willing to share helpful tips about surviving in the North.

But then, it sounded like Julian was going to slip away from the ball and head north early. While I wouldn't usually mind . . . this might be the last time I saw Henrietta or Brownie or Amy and I wanted more time to say goodbye . . .

Then he hit me with something unexpected.

"Ah. Did you want to go to the tea party together?"

"Wait, what?" I asked, raising a hand between us.

He clarified for me. "Did you want me to escort you to the tea party or the ball? Or both?"

"*Oh no.*" It was like being hit by a bucket of cold and hot water at the same time. *He'd thought I was asking him to escort me to the ball!*

And he'd said *yes!*

But he'd only said yes as a favor for saving his sister's life. Which, if it were coming from anyone else, I would've found incredibly insulting.

With Julian, it was both flattering *and* insulting.

"No?" Julian asked.

"I didn't mean *no*. I meant *no*," I tried to explain and failed, and tried again. "I was asking you for an escort to the Northern Ice Fields."

Julian's complexion darkened in a blush—then his eyes narrowed with concern. "This isn't because everyone found out that you're Madame Potts, is it? The North might be isolated, but it's not a safe place to live. I'm sure any number of countries would offer you protection—North Sumbria included."

"No," I said. Again. "I have a quest in the North. I'd already planned to go there after the festival."

Julian asked, "So the favor was to leave with my party members and travel north together?"

"Yes," I replied, and his face fell. Something goaded me and I teased, "Why? Did you *want* to take me to the ball?"

The duke considered that. *Actually* considered it. "Yes. I think I do."

I was shocked. In the *otome*, in order for Henrietta to win over Julian, she'd had to do *a lot* of cat-and-mouse tactics. One of the reasons I'd enjoyed his route so much was that I'd found the options so intuitive. The duke was aloof but lonely. He enjoyed conversation but felt awkward when he was enjoying himself. Short and meaningful interactions came naturally, and it was so satisfying when he'd finally come right out and said what he actually wanted.

But that was that and this was this. I narrowed my eyes at the half elf. "It's because I'm Madame Potts, isn't it?"

"I thought I already said it's not that." He shook his head. "I was thinking it would give us time to talk about logistics. For your trip."

I couldn't argue that, though I wanted to. As much as I was annoyed that my favorite invited me to the ball on a logistical whim, I would still get to go to the ball with Duke Julian von Slyke.

"Alright," I said, resting a hand on my hip and looking him up and down. "You can take me to the afternoon tea party *and* the ball. And you can pick me up here thirty minutes before the tea party."

He grinned, his white teeth flashing in a heart-stopping smile that made me rethink my decision to spend an entire day with him tomorrow. "*It would be my pleasure*, Miss Gerda."

"Then, if that's all, I have to leave," I stated, deciding it was time for a tactical retreat. I gave a quick nod before marching off into the palace, leaving the duke behind in the western gardens.

I didn't look back.

Against my better judgment, I returned to the luncheon. Henrietta and Keith were there, as was Lady Amy and Minstrel Bronwynn and everyone else. I didn't go inside right away, standing by the door against the wall, enjoying a last moment of quiet.

It was amazing, really.

Everything I'd accomplished since entering this world. There was still more—I knew there was. The story wasn't over until the dragon Feliwyn awoke. She was supposed to be the actual final boss, and she was still fast asleep. But aside from Sumbria being an absolute mess, everyone else was sorted . . . and I didn't need to stay and fix Sumbria. All of the people I'd cared about finding happiness were right here. Happy.

"Madame Potts?"

I turned to see two young women, relatives of Grand Duchess Calisto by the looks of them, standing a polite distance away.

"We just wanted to say it's an honor to meet you." The one on the left wore a red silhouette dress commonly found in the Empire of Sands. It started with an embroidered circular collar around the throat and left the shoulders bare. The front panel was just wide enough to cover the collarbone, wrap over the breasts, and meet the back panel under the arms. Silver vines were embroidered on the dress to look like pinstripes, giving it a slimming look on the statuesque human. She had thick, sun-kissed brown hair that fell to her elbows.

"I'm Gail, and this is Tabitha."

The one on the right waved, shyly. She wore a blue silhouette dress with similar silver embroidery, and a silver scarf belt around her hips. Her hair was black and decorated with silver rings.

"It's nice to meet you both." I returned their eager smiles. "How are you enjoying the festival?"

"It's brilliant," Tabitha answered.

Gail nodded enthusiastically. "This is our second ball. Aunt Calisto made us wait until our debutante before we were allowed to attend."

"Even though Cousin Julia was going as early as age ten," Tabitha added.

"And I've heard His Grace started at six!" Gail played with a lock of hair separated by silver rings. It was a beautiful hairstyle that I decided I might try next time I went somewhere fancy.

Of course, if I went north immediately after this, I might be gone by the fall or winter celebrations.

"I'm just imagining Duke Julian running around as a young boy." I laughed. "I feel like he was more well behaved than his sister."

"You're right about that." Tabitha leaned in. "But then Julian left when Uncle Lysander died."

"He was a great man," I told them, knowing the backstory. Lysander had fought in the civil war and fallen in the final battle—but not before he'd cut a canyon down the center of Sumbria in a wizard's duel with the Sage of Aegis.

"Ladies"—I pushed off from the wall and waved toward a pair of empty seats nearby—"would you like to sit?"

They shared an excited look between them and joined me. Henrietta saw me come in and nodded from across the room, staying where she was. Keith was in an animated conversation with Witch Agatha and it didn't look like they were going to be finished anytime soon.

That left me plenty of time to get to talk with Gail and Tabitha. The two were a fountain of knowledge about Duke Julian's childhood . . . and I was planning on coaxing out *every* family story I could.

CHAPTER 46

Have You Come to Kill Me So Soon?

Julian

Julian had a problem.

He couldn't stop thinking about the bridge troll.

It was long after she'd left, and he had *work* to do.

He wanted to blame the fact that Gerda was Madame Potts . . . but he'd already had this same problem multiple times before that discovery. She just got under his skin. The way she was always one step ahead kept him on his toes, but more so the way she came at things intrigued him.

He wished she were here now because he wanted to hear her thoughts on the interrogation.

"This isn't going to hold me for long." Guild Mistress Alice indicated the prison around her. "So you might as well ask your questions now—I'll even answer them."

"Why?" Julian dragged his mind back to the matter at hand. Namely, questioning the celestial who'd been making a mess of Valaria.

Alice was sitting on a wooden chair, a table between them. Her manacled wrists were resting on it, and she would intermittently cast a look at the magical wall as if she knew *exactly* what it was. Visha stood in the corner, on guard.

Their Royal Highness was lounging in a room beyond, watching everything with magic. Witch Agatha had joined the fox, as had Master Thomas of Servalt and the recently arrived Wizard Lorthar. The wizard of Hemlock Hill had been summoned as soon as they'd taken Alice into custody, as he had the highest-level interrogation spells on the continent. Julian wondered if Lorthar heard the news about Madame Potts since he'd rushed over so quickly.

Focus.

"Because despite this minor setback, I've finally gotten *my* answers. So, I'm feeling generous." She smiled at him, her bright blue eyes catching the light of the magical glowing orbs that illuminated the room. His chest tightened.

The urge to do *anything* to make her smile was there, but he could ignore it. The manacles lowered her charisma down to fifteen, so she must also have a passive persuasive perk. He felt his skin crawl.

"I'm not sure you understand what's going to happen next."

"Of course I do." She rolled her eyes. "I'm going to answer all of your questions, and depending on how long it takes me to escape, I'll just be answering those same questions again and again in front of the other Continental Council members. This isn't the first time I've been captured, you know?"

"But it *is* the first time *Guild Mistress Alice* has been captured," Julian pointed out.

"True," she conceded. "So, what did you want to know?"

He thought for a second. ". . . Why don't we start by confirming what I already assumed: that you are the champion of Fate, and you are in charge of keeping everything according to Fate's plan?"

"As you say." She leaned on her elbow, placing a delicate cheek onto the palm of one hand. The manacle looked uncomfortable, and it would be better for everyone if he took it off.

Julian recognized the need to let her go was as false as her smile. It was nothing like the gentle feeling he'd had earlier, when he'd grabbed Gerda's hands and freed her. The sight of the bridge troll teasing him was night and day to the sickening influence of Alice's ability.

"Are the Blackfog going to continue targeting members of this list while you are imprisoned?" Julian summoned the paper from his inventory and placed it on the table between them.

Alice scanned the list. "No."

Julian gave into a moment of curiosity and turned the questions to the hypothetical. He tapped the list. "Let's say that fate continues in the wrong direction, and everyone on this list gets a second chance to live—"

"That cannot happen," she interrupted him.

"Why?"

Alice practically rolled her eyes. "Because."

Julian waited for her to continue.

"*Because*," she repeated, emphasizing her words. "Fate weaves the future based on the champions of each god—making sure they don't interfere with each other's storylines. Each champion has different choices they can make, but the scenarios are *specifically* catered to keep the world on track, and *right now*, our timeline isn't following *any* fate."

"So what?" Julian asked. "Why can't we make new choices and live our own lives? Isn't that why we have Fate *and* Luck?"

Alice answered vehemently. "No. Luck is the reason we have multiple paths to choose."

"And Madame Potts chose her path," he goaded the celestial. "Why is that any different?"

Alice thumped her fists on the table, her manacles clanking. "Madame Potts isn't even supposed to be here! She's not a part of *any* timeline. Her interference is a burden on the system itself!"

"But she is here," Julian said, even more impressed with Gerda, knowing how much the world was against her and yet still finding her own place in it. "Whether by Fate or Luck or any other god you haven't suspected."

"She won't be for long." Alice's face flashed with something dark. "Now that I know who she is, I can deal with this farce and get everything back on track before the next World Scenario."

Julian ignored the anger that surged when she outright threatened Gerda, hiding it behind his already showing look of displeasure. "What happens if you *don't* revert everything by the next World Scenario? When *is* the next World Scenario?"

"When the first leaf falls in autumn," Alice ground out. "When Fate rewrites a new storyline, *or she doesn't.*"

"What does that mean?"

"It *means*"—Alice looked at him with equal parts frustration and pity—"that the gods might decide our realm isn't working properly and they should start over. Wouldn't *you* undo it all and start again if your pattern failed?"

They fell into silence as he stared at the celestial. At that time, the door opened behind him.

"You're early," Julian remarked.

Their Royal Highness swept in, looking like a tall red-haired woman. A black mermaid dress with a slit to the knee hugged their frame, and a black crown rested on their hair.

Alice smiled up at the fox. "Afternoon, Rowen. Have you come to kill me so soon?"

Their Royal Highness smiled a vicious fox grin, showing too many sharp teeth. "Guild Mistress Alice. I thought I would fix your misguided thoughts before our Duke Julian started falling prey to your oh-so-incorrect words." Their Royal Highness laid a hand on Julian's shoulder and met his eyes. "Nothing is going to happen if I continue to live."

"You don't know that." Alice angrily came to her feet, her chin set.

"Unlike *your* goddess, who only speaks in rhymes and riddles, *my* patron is happy to convene with *his* chosen—when Warren bothers to ask." The last was said in an aggrieved aside.

The ruler lifted their hands, and a black orb appeared, hovering over their open palm. The voice that traveled through the magical artifact made Julian's teeth hurt from the ambient power radiating through his quiet words.

"*We have known the traveler and watched her ways.*" The message crawled like molasses through Julian's spine, building pressure on every part of his body and mind. Comfort wrapped around his spirit, even as a chill crept along his flesh. "*The path ahead is another's domain, but the weave is being woven as we walk, and I will not claim the realm to Shadow.*"

The darkness in the orb stilled.

The fox stared down at the celestial. "So you have no more need to kill me or anyone else on that list."

CHAPTER 47

The Duke Would Like Me to Escort You to the Dungeon

Gerda

It was an amazingly informative afternoon.

Gail and Tabitha were only too happy to share family stories, like the time Julian had gone missing when he was four, only to turn up eight hours later asleep in the kitchen pantry having eaten an entire basket of bimbleberries. And when he was seven and tried to use a shield that was too big for him, dropping it and breaking his toe.

Or the time he'd cut off the bottom of Grand Duchess Calisto's brand-new ball gown to fit Julia for playing dress-up when he was nine. *Or* the time that Tabitha's mother had been poisoned at a ball when he was twelve, and Julian had tried "helping" by casting a shield around her . . . a shield that *prevented* anyone from approaching the poor woman with an antidote.

It was fine, Tabitha assured me; her mother had survived.

Gail and Tabitha were too young to remember much themselves, but they'd overheard enough from their older relatives to fill the afternoon. And so far, only six people had tried to interrupt us. Very rude, to think they were more important than listening to the cute childhood shenanigans of my favorite character.

The luncheon was wrapping up when someone approached me whom I feared would need more than a simple shooing away.

"Greetings," the villainess, Lady Cassandra Cress, stood before our seated group just as Gail was regaling me with a fun story about the time Julia had accidentally split the dining room table in half, before their Aunt Calisto realized she needed to reinforce everything. The Paladin of Light wasn't as strong as Henrietta—few were—but that didn't mean she couldn't crumple a wooden table in a temper tantrum.

Lady Cassandra Cress had red hair and high eyebrows that made her look perpetually annoyed. The woman kept her ears covered by her hairstyle and a wide pearl-set headband. She did so deliberately because her father was angry that she was born human instead of an elf . . . which was a simple way of saying she had a lifetime of household trauma.

Two friends stood nervously behind her.

"Lady Cassandra," I said, succinctly. Some part of me had wanted to snub her for all of the struggles she'd put Henrietta through while I was trying to win over Duke Julian, but I held myself back. "Are you also here to tell me funny stories about the bride?"

This *was* a post-wedding luncheon.

Lady Cassandra fanned herself imperiously. "I am here to find out who I will marry."

I couldn't resist a poke. "Is it one of us?"

Gail stared up at Lady Cassandra in polite terror, while Tabitha covered her mouth with her own fan to hide a laugh.

"Hm," the woman humphed. "I have come to *you*, Madame Potts, for a fortune. Tell me, who here is worthy of my hand?"

I almost said something unkind, but I caught the slight tremor in Lady Cassandra's fan. The woman was an impressive menace to society, but she was also out here trying her best . . . or so I told myself. Besides, this was an opportunity to give another character I liked a chance at a happily ever after.

Even *if* that character had foolishly fallen for Lady Cassandra.

The woman was desperate to marry Duke Julian to appease her incredibly ornery father and was ignoring the one person who already loved her. As I was thinking, a silence fell between us. Gail and Tabitha shared a look, and Lady Cassandra held her breath. Answering her would set a terrible precedent, but maybe this was exactly what I needed to set an example.

"You know"—I cocked my head to the side—"I only foretell *disasters* . . . Are you *sure* you want me to look into your love life?"

The lady stiffened. It was more than I'd afforded anyone else who'd come up to me tonight, but the implications were enough to make the lady pause.

Then she drew herself up and stated, "I am sure."

"Okay." I turned to Gail and used her formal address. "If you apologize to Lady Mercer for the interruption, and Gail is alright with it."

"I am!" Gail nodded vigorously. I stifled a laugh and said, "You're supposed to agree *after* the apology. It's only polite."

Lady Cassandra chewed her lip in frustration but nodded at Gail. She ground out, "I'm sorry for interrupting, Lady Mercer."

That scratched my itch for revenge on the villainess who'd come between me and Julian—I meant, Henrietta and Julian. Lady Cassandra was the *worst* kind of villainess. She'd created situations where the main characters had to live through excruciatingly embarrassing moments of awkwardness.

It'd made me rage playing through each of her scenarios.

But that was then, and this was now.

"Foretell Fate," I said, making up some ability name I didn't have. Closing my eyes, I counted to ten before opening them and then glanced at my character sheet. I read over my stats like I was reading some prophecy that had popped up showing me Lady Cassandra's fate.

Oh, my experience points had gone up to 9662/15750. It was nice to see all of my hard work here was paying off.

When I gauged that enough time had passed, I focused again on Lady Cassandra. She was red in the face and unsteady, but ready for whatever terrible future awaited her.

"*If* you get engaged this year . . ." I whispered softly, and she hurriedly bent forward to hear whatever it was I had to say, along with everyone else in the room. "Then it will fail, and your house will fall to ruin. Your friends will abandon you, and your true love will sacrifice himself to save you, but it will be too late."

She recoiled, her face twisted in horror. I held firm. That was her fate in Henrietta's route in North Sumbria, and it would be her fate again if she didn't figure things out and make a change.

Now, I spoke loud enough for everyone to hear. "*But!* If you get engaged to the one who already loves you when the first flower blooms in spring, you have hope for your own Happily Ever After."

Lady Cassandra closed her mouth and stared at me, her face going through a variety of emotions: frustration, hopelessness . . . fear. She curtsied perfectly and managed a curt, "Thank you, Madame Potts." She then turned on her heels and stormed out of the luncheon.

The entire place erupted with discussion on my prophecy. People even started inching closer again, intent blazing in their eyes.

I stood for a well-timed and hasty retreat.

"Lady Gail, Lady Tabitha, it was a pleasure." I smiled at the girls. They'd remained at the edge of their chairs during my performance. Now, they leapt to their feet to curtsy farewell properly. I gave them a reassuring smile. "I look forward to seeing you both at the tea party tomorrow, and maybe hearing the end of Gail's story."

Between the tea party and the Masquerade Ball, it felt like this festival was never going to end.

I slipped from the dining hall and headed toward my room. If I started now, I might have enough time to properly do my hair . . .

"Miss Gerda!" Sir Tully jogged toward me at breakneck speed. He stopped just shy of an arm's length away, smiling. "Miss Gerda, the duke would like me to escort you to the dungeon."

I raised an eyebrow at the human, wondering if he knew how easily misunderstood something like that could be.

"Alright, lead on."

CHAPTER 48

You Have Been Warned

Julian

A Few Minutes Ago

"Your god speaks in riddles just as well as my goddess!" Alice scoffed. She leaned back in her chair, unimpressed. "But since you've so kindly shared yours, I'll read you mine."

Alice focused on a pop-up window no one else could see. Her eyes flickered, searching through her notification tab ability log until she found Fate's prophecy.

> *"What mortals toil to the coiling thread.*
> *Why weave the same when knots form in the line.*
> *The loom feeds a snag in Fate looming.*
> *So seek first those of second death.*
> *Find tears in time before time unravels.*
> *The weave undone. To walk away. To stay.*
> *Embrace death by the first fallen leaf.*
> *Tie ends or end in Void."*

Her voice didn't have the weight of a literal god, but her charisma passive perk was a good mortal comparison. Julian had to repeat the words over with a clear mind, *without* Alice's personal inflections.

"Do you see?" The guild mistress refocused, shooting Rowen a scathing look. "*You* are a tear in the weave. There was no timeline in which you were meant to survive, and you being here might destroy us all. So think about *that* while you go live your *Happily Ever After*—however long it lasts."

The fox kept a smile on their face, but their hands were clenched. "I see how you interpret this, but between the two, I would say Shadow is clearer. So I *will* think on it while I go about living my life, and I *will not* let you continue terrorizing the continent with your fears of 'what if.'"

"You know I'm right," said the celestial, her blue eyes flashing to the magical wall. "And so do they. What happens when things start to go wrong? Will they turn on you if the system fails them? Shadow just said that *Shadow* won't doom the world. He does not speak for all. What if Fate forsakes us? Everyone will know then that you chose *yourself* over the world."

"Enough," Their Royal Highness snapped, their aura fluctuating behind their fake smile.

Julian pitied Rowen, seeing the words having an effect on the old fox. The idea that his own family and friends would be put at risk did play across his mind, but Julian refused to pander to the guild mistress before a second opinion. Something about Alice just felt . . . *chaotic*. Where Gerda had all the answers and a careful plan, Alice did not.

Julian knew he wasn't being entirely fair. There were reports that the Blackfog *had* managed to accomplish many things in the past. But no matter how he saw it, Julian would trust Gerda before Alice any day. Besides, *if* Alice had her way, then his sister-in-law might not live very long. Chloe was a part of his family now, and that meant protecting her just as much as Julia.

The celestial shrugged. "You have been warned."

"Then I guess it's my turn to warn *you*." Rowen's voice dropped ominously as the smile slipped from their face. "Mine and my own are no longer going to play a role in your plans." The fox shot Julian a look and asked, "You are keeping Guild Mistress Alice until the first leaf falls?"

She cut him off before Julian could answer.

"He's keeping me until I escape." She glanced around her, scrutinizing the mithril enchanted room. "I give it three days."

"Her fate will be decided by the council," Julian told Rowen. To Alice, he raised an eyebrow in challenge. "You couldn't escape the sanctuary; do you think that Fate will help free you now?"

"Who needs a goddess to escape *this*?" Alice countered. "You know I'm the highest-level Spy class on the continent? Even *these* won't slow me down."

She lifted the Veralyn's Enchanted Restraint Manacles on her wrists. They were still secure. The keys were in Julian's storage, and he checked to make sure they were there.

His small desire to release her was *also* still there, which was why he hadn't handed over the key to anyone else. No sense tempting fate with someone less guarded.

"I've only answered your questions because I'm being *nice*." The celestial huffed. "And I was *hoping* you would see things clearly."

Rowen considered, then smiled again—a very pointy-toothed grin. "Why don't we ask Miss Gerda what *she* thinks on the prophecy, and if you will escape?"

Guild Mistress Alice sucked in a breath at the troll's name, her face twisting into an ugly fit of rage. "Let that monster *try* to stop me."

"She's bested you before," Rowen pointed out, digging into the wound.

"I can summon her," Julian agreed. He *really* wanted to hear her opinion on Fate's message.

Who better to ponder over a riddle than a bridge troll?

"While you do that"—Rowen took a seat at the table, their eyes glinting with playfulness and a hint of something darker—"I'll start my own interrogation. I'd *love* to hear more about your time in Peldeep, Guild Mistress."

Suddenly, the pressure in the room amplified. Rowen released their full aura, and it suppressed Julian so forcefully that he had to fight to breathe. "Have fun," Julian barely managed to say before nodding to Visha and exiting the room. His general appeared unphased, though Julian felt bad about leaving her to guard inside while Rowen was showing off their strength.

The pressure lifted off Julian's shoulders when he closed the door behind him, but his heartbeat still pounded against his chest.

The viewing area from the other side of the magical wall was teeming with conversation, more so than he'd anticipated. Usually, interrogations were a close study, as it wouldn't do to miss anything.

Not so today.

"I've already sent someone for Gerda," Witch Agatha said. She pointed at Master Thomas, who looked ready to light someone on fire. "Now, tell *that* one to calm down."

Julian already had reservations about Master Thomas joining the viewing room due to his potential personal connection with the celestial, but he'd invited all council members and couldn't turn one away. Julian just made sure that others were there with Master Thomas; as powerful as the young man was, he was no match for Agatha or Lorthar, let alone both.

"Is no one else worried about what that celestial just said?" Master Thomas fumed, obviously continuing a conversation that Julian had walked in on. "I'm not saying we should knife Rowen in the back, but look at Peldeep law. We could urge Rowen to step down and act as if they're dead. Or abdicate—"

"Or what?" Wizard Lorthar waved away the young mage's concerns. "You want us to go after everyone on the Blackfog list and continue where they left off?"

"If the Continental Council ordered everyone on that list to stand down until fall, we could potentially prevent whatever disaster the Keeper of Fate is foretelling," Master Thomas urged, "*without* her foolish desire for bloodshed."

"You would follow the direction of a chosen who lost their way? One so utterly untrustworthy and murderous?" Witch Agatha tsked. "Mages, bah, always overthinking things."

Wizard Lorthar chided, "Agatha, that was uncalled for. You know Thomas is speaking from a place of concern."

"He can speak at the council," she retorted. The meeting was in two days, the afternoon after the Masquerade, and perfectly timed to add her sentence to the agenda.

"I can speak whenever I please. And I *will* bring this to the council meeting," Master Thomas huffed, clearly insulted and struggling to remain respectful to the older magic users.

Julian turned back to the interrogation hall to see Rowen in the middle of their questioning. The fox slammed a fist on the table, looming over the calm, collected Alice. Their voice was a cutting whisper.

"I have let your people live in my realm, and for this? You have forsaken them."

"They are the hands and feet of Fate, and *you* know that *I* know you've hired Blackfog services in the past." The celestial turned, her eyes sweeping over every-one in the viewing room. Julian could've almost sworn she'd caught his eyes. "You *all* have."

Witch Agatha tensed while Wizard Lorthar sighed, impressed. "She's really very good at that."

There was a soft knock at the door.

CHAPTER 49

Who Do You Think I Am?

Gerda

"You summoned me?" I politely greeted everyone with a short curtsy.

Julian stood in front of three seated council members.

Wizard Lorthar wore black wizard robes open to reveal a cardigan knit sweater over black leather pants. His striking eyebrows were impressive, and he had swept-back, pointy, shoulder-length, salt-and-pepper hair revealing one ear covered in piercings with three dangling earrings.

The infamous Witch Agatha of Winter's End was relaxing in her chair and fiddling with a crystal pendant around her neck. The woman wore a blue dress with embroidery around the corset front and around the skirt hem. It was stamped with softer blue ice diamond patterns that shimmered when she moved. Her hair was piled into a tight bun on the top of her head, and she had added three small silver gemstones under each eye.

Master Thomas of Servalt was upset, the young mage frowning up at my duke. His light brown hair was long, and his green eyes were bright as the bottom of an alder's leaf in spring. I knew from experience that he usually wore reading glasses but took them off for important meetings like today. Tucked under his tunic was a magical amulet of antiscrying, and the ring on his right pinkie was a storage ring.

"Thank you for coming, Miss Gerda." Duke Julian waved at the last seat. "Would you join us?"

I wanted to make some quip reply . . . but we weren't alone. This wasn't going to be as fun as my usual back-and-forth with the duke. "Okay, but I do have some matters to attend to after this. Will you be keeping me long?"

"You may leave at any time," Duke Julian assured me.

"I've heard you say that a few times in place of an affirmative," Witch Agatha stated. "*Okay* . . . What does it actually mean?"

This wasn't the first time I'd been asked this question, though it was the first time I was going to give my carefully crafted explanation in front of anyone powerful enough to see through a lie. "The origin is still debated by my people of whether it came from *all correct* or *oh yes*."

"We didn't bring her here to discuss the etymology of troll slang," Master Thomas interrupted, his voice laced with disapproval. "Get on with it."

Witch Agatha frowned while Duke Julian waved my attention to a wall. "We've turned off scrying, but Guild Mistress Alice is being questioned in the next room. She's said something we would ask your opinion on."

My curiosity getting the better of me, I focused all of my perception on the wall between us and the next room—and heard nothing. Which was impressive. Grand Duchess Calisto should be resting off her mana burn to complete an eight-hour rest cycle before tomorrow's afternoon tea, so the room was likely a permanent pocket dimension prison. "How can I help?"

"I will share with you two riddles by two gods." Duke Julian cleared his throat. "The first was from the god of Shadow: '*We have known the traveler and watched her ways. But I will not claim the realm to Shadow, and the weave is being woven as we walk.*'"

I waited to hear more, but that was it. I tapped my chin as I considered, then asked, "What was the question?"

"Their Royal Highness wanted to know what would happen if they defied Fate and continued to live."

"As a note," Wizard Lorthar spoke from his seat, eyeing me with an air of interest, "we do not know what the *exact* question was, since they only provided us with a recording of Shadow's reply."

"Hm." I closed my eyes, drawing breath. Other's might assume that Shadow was speaking about Alice as the 'traveler'. My ego was apparently as big as Thomas's because I knew Shadow was talking about none other than myself.

A traveler between worlds.

I opened my eyes. "I have heard many riddles, and this sounds pretty clear. Shadow says that the weave is being woven as we walk, and it doesn't matter if we change things because Fate will just weave whatever choices we make into her plan."

"That was my conclusion as well," Julian said with relief.

"And it might have been *sufficient*, but we are not talking about one fate and one riddle," Master Thomas pointed out. He turned angry eyes on me and accused, "These riddles will affect more than *just* Their Royal Highness of Peldeep."

The mage held up a scroll and unrolled it with a dramatic flick of his wrist. It was a list of names, starting with Madame Potts. "All sixty-three fates that you've touched will need to be addressed—"

I cut him off with a laugh.

"Sixty-three? *Who do you think I am?*" I could see that Master Thomas had no idea about my accomplishments as Madame Potts, and so I decided to tell him. "I've saved hundreds if not *thousands*. Dungeon breaks that wiped out entire villages? I prevented. Pirate attacks that sunk whole merchant fleets? I foiled. Assassins, bandits, stampedes, kidnappings, fires, floods—this *list* is an insult."

"Well said." Julian put a hand on the back of my chair in support.

I changed my mind; I took back everything. This *was* fun.

Master Thomas made to reply, but Julian continued. "It looks like this Alice doesn't know as much as she claimed, or this would be a much longer list."

"So it would seem," Thomas ground out, magically rolling the parchment closed with a snap. "But what about the second riddle? Let us hear what *Madame Potts* has to say when faced with a riddle from Fate herself."

He looked ready to see me fail, and I rolled my eyes. If he only knew how many times I'd had to listen to Fate go off in some convoluted message . . .

"I'm ready when you are."

CHAPTER 50

Fate's Always Loved a Good Villainess Trope

Julian

"What mortals toil to the coiling thread. Why weave the same when knots form in the line. The loom feeds a snag in Fate looming. So seek first those of second death. Find tears in time before time unravels. The weave undone. To walk away. To stay. Embrace death by the first fallen leaf. Tie ends or end in Void."

Gerda flinched, and Julian wondered that she had no skill to help her obfuscate her emotions. He was impressed that she'd kept her secret identity this long with only her will and wit.

"Okay . . ." she started, but then stopped. "Before I tell you what I know of Fate, you should probably activate a truth spell."

Wizard Lorthar replied, "I already have."

The troll nodded. "Fate speaks in riddles because she isn't seeing one person or one path. She's looking at countless threads that come together across worlds and how they weave together. So, the first thing we need to do to understand her message is figure out *who* is involved and *what fate* can be changed.

"In this case, I think Alice assumed the prophecy is about: 'So seek first those of second death.' Combining it with the previous lines, Alice is focusing on those who have died and come back when they were not fated to, like myself, and anyone who was fated to die but was saved, like Their Royal Highness Rowen of Peldeep."

Wizard Lorthar nodded to say the troll was speaking the truth.

"*But*"—Gerda shook her head—"those like Rowen are not *on* a second death. They're still on their first life. And *even if they had died*, they would be on their second chance at *life*, not *death*."

Her logic was sound, and her points succinct . . . so Julian didn't know why there was a growing feeling of unease in the pit of his stomach.

Witch Agatha interrupted his thoughts to ask, "So why isn't it a warning that those 'of second death' aren't causing the problems, those who *have* lived twice and *would* have died a 'second death'?"

"Because *Fate* is looming," Gerda replied, as if it were obvious. "That's the point."

Master Thomas scoffed. "*What's* the point?"

"The prophecy was for the champion of Fate, by Fate," Gerda said, stressing her words. "Which is why we have nothing to fear. Since Fate herself is the answer."

Julian did not see how there was nothing to fear when they were discussing the unraveling of time itself, and so said, "I don't follow—"

"No one does!" Master Thomas cut him off. "The troll is speaking in circles. Is this really the *expert* you praised, Duke Julian?"

"I *thought* it was obvious." Gerda shrugged. Her voice turned too kind as she offered, "But *of course* I could dumb it down for you, Master Thomas."

Witch Agatha made a choking noise that Julian was all too familiar with. It probably wasn't the best insult because even though she *had* aimed it at the mage, everyone in the room was an unintended target, Julian included.

"If you please, Miss Gerda." Wizard Lorthar appeared unaffected by the insult, saying simply, "I would like to hear more."

Fate is talking to herself and asking why she should fight change. Why should she weave the same story when things have already snagged or changed?" Gerda explained her reasoning. "Fate isn't threatening to unravel the weave—If Fate is sending this riddle to her Chosen, then she's telling Alice to help settle the new storylines and tie up any loose ends."

She drew breath and continued. "We can even combine the two riddles and see the same answers: Shadow stresses walking *forward*, and Fate is talking about the coming autumn leaves. She wants things sorted and the new storylines stable before the end of summer, *not* reverted back to the way they were."

"An interesting take." Wizard Lorthar leaned forward in his chair and scrutinized the bridge troll. "*Not* one that Mistress Alice would agree with."

"How do we know you aren't trying to convince us to ignore Fate's warning because the other way to interpret the prophecy points at Madame Potts as a thorn in Fate's side?" Master Thomas spoke mockingly. "The ire of a goddess can destroy worlds, and you want us to do nothing?"

"It is true that I'm *obviously* one of the people Fate is talking about in her message." Gerda shrugged nonchalantly. "Since I'm one of the people changing her story. But if you listen to the riddle, it should be clear: Fate is asking *herself* about time. She talks about mortals, but from a place where she is interacting with them as a deity."

"And if you're wrong and Fate really does unravel the weave?" Thomas challenged.

Julian tried to keep the sarcasm from his voice as he replied, "I should *think* that the other gods would've said something by now, if that were the case."

The more he thought about it, the more he sided with Gerda's interpretation over Alice's. And Julian had to admit he *trusted* the troll far more than the guild mistress.

"Why don't we just ask them?" Witch Agatha suggested. "We *have* two other chosen in the palace. Queen Henrietta is the Heroine of Justice, is she not? And your own sister is the Paladin of Light."

The door into Alice's prison opened, and Their Royal Highness stormed out in a fit of red-and-white smoke. The fox slammed the door behind themselves.

"*That celestial,*" they growled, running a hand through their long hair before eyeing the room. Rowen walked over to Julian and put a hand on his shoulder. "I think you should keep her locked up until the Winter Feast. For extra precaution."

"That is for the council to decide," Master Thomas reminded. Julian felt the urge to agree with Rowen if for no other reason than he would be upsetting the mage.

"We can discuss that in the future," Julian answered politically instead. "In the meantime, Gerda has kindly let us know that the message from Fate probably isn't as foreboding as we'd first assumed."

"Technically," Wizard Lorthar countered, "we haven't heard her thoughts on the other parts of the riddle. She's said nothing about where everything ends in Void."

"And to be fair," Witch Agatha added unhelpfully, "Shadow only *implied* that He wouldn't end the world . . . The god said nothing about Void choosing to do so."

"*I* think we shouldn't even be *listening* to Madame Potts," Master Thomas griped, looking down at Gerda with contempt. "Since she is not an impartial party and already admitted that she is part of the problem."

Gerda shook her head. "I never said there was a problem; just the opposite."

Julian coughed into his hand to hide his laugh. Their Royal Highness swept around the room to stand between Wizard Lorthar and Master Thomas, facing the troll. "Then what *did* you discuss?"

"I was merely pointing out"—Gerda nodded at the royal—"that if you haven't died already, then you aren't living a second death, and even if you *had* survived the molten ash vane, you would be living your second *life*. Simple, but these things usually are."

"And the Void?" Wizard Lorthar repeated. He didn't seem too concerned, but persisted anyway.

The troll waved at the door in the wall. "Have you considered that Guild Mistress Alice is a Void mage? Why isn't it just saying that she'll need to use her Void powers to complete a task?"

"Why do you lie?" Wizard Lorthar's voice took on an edge that was not previously there.

Gerda sighed. "Because I'm self-centered, and it might also be about me. I've died already, and I'm on a quest that can unlock a Void-based skill. But if *that's* the case, I would be pleased to finish the task and 'tie ends or end in Void.'"

Wizard Lorthar didn't withdraw his intent. "One final question; *why* should we listen to a random bridge troll on the inner workings of Fate and *not* the chosen of Fate herself?"

That same bridge troll stood her ground admirably. "There is another reason Fate gave that message to her chosen—but you won't like it."

Lorthar's lips pulled into a thin smile. "Tell me."

"Because Fate doesn't care about you or me or her chosen. All she cares about is a good *story*." Gerda stood up suddenly, and Julian stepped up beside her. She met the eyes of everyone in the circle except his own. Oddly, that didn't bother him; it was as if she assumed he was on her side and felt no need to defend herself to him.

She continued. "Fate told Alice exactly what she needed to hear to put her on a path to peace *or* destruction. Either she'd continue working with the new story, or she'd become a new villain we could focus on—and Fate's always loved a good villainess trope."

Gerda lifted her hand to Julian, who instinctively took it.

"That is my final word on the matter. You may summon me if you have any more questions"—she curtsied to the room—"but I really *do* have to be on my way."

"Thank you, Miss Gerda." Wizard Lorthar nodded his approved dismissal.

"Wait." Master Thomas also stood. "You really aren't arresting her? *She's Madame Potts.*"

"I don't see how that has anything to do with anything, Thomas," Witch Agatha rebuked.

The mage turned red in the face as he declared, "She has broken *multiple* international laws: operating the Crystal Cast without a permit, inciting civil unrest, defamation of royal personage, slander against the state, cross-border oracle espionage without a license—"

"And she's saved us all," Julian cut in as the troll stared up at him in appreciation.

"Don't mind him." Wizard Lorthar waved at the pair before turning a dark eye on the mage. "You two go on while we have a word with Master Thomas. But don't leave before the council meeting—we'll have to make time for a proper trial with each of the kingdoms."

Their Royal Highness reached out and rested a not-so-friendly hand on the young mage's shoulder, forcing him back into his chair. "Sit down, Thomas. I have a few *questions* for you."

Julian nodded at the council members before leaving with Gerda still on his arm.

When they were alone in the hallway, she sighed. "If I have to stay until after the meeting . . . does this mean you can't take me north?"

"If you aren't detained indefinitely, I don't see why not." Julian didn't know why, but the idea of her traveling north alone irked him. "I can wait."

"Thank you."

Julian wondered where she was going next, at the risk of angering members of the council to leave before they dismissed her.

He asked as much.

"To my rooms—or a bathhouse, if you have one." She lifted one of her long braids. "I need to wash my hair."

CHAPTER 51

A Saintess Who Forgives Everyone Else

Gerda

The palace did, in fact, have a bathhouse. More like a magical spa.

I'd chosen the Everglade treatment, which smelled like a eucalyptus scrub, and I was currently relaxing in a decorative stone bathtub while an aesthetician massaged my scalp. The lather of soap in my hair felt light and fluffy, and my whole body soaked in a warm bubble bath that smelled like the forest.

"Miss Gerda! Your hair is *spectacular!*" An elf attendant named Lucille admired my tresses as she ran a comb through my long braid-wavy locks.

"It is a lot of work, but worth it," I spoke softly, my eyes closed. The stress of the day washed away, and I let myself relax. My jaw unclenched. I took slow and steady deep breaths, inhaling sharp pine-smelling undertones that cleared my sinuses. My shoulders dropped, my fingers straightened, and my body released the tension I had been holding in for far too long.

"If you could, I'd like about four inches off the bottom," I requested.

"Just the dead ends?" Lucille picked up a new strand and ran the comb through it. The light pull on my scalp and the teeth of the comb on my head felt wonderful. "I can do that."

Everything felt wonderful. I made a happy noise.

Lucille rinsed my hair outside of the tub. Magical water from her hands let her thoroughly clean my seemingly endless amount of thick long hair. When it was finished, she brought out rosemary oil and carefully worked it into the strands.

Even with magic, it took hours to wash, cut, and dry my hair, then rebraid it.

And after that, I had an hour-long back massage.

Dinnertime was in full force when I left the bathhouse. Instead of going down to the dining hall, I went straight back to my rooms. I had dinner in my storage ring, and I wasn't in the mood for socializing. I'd had a bit too much of people recently.

The thought of eating dinner with Julian flashed in my mind. The half elf had delivered me to the bathhouse in near shock at my request, and his momentary lack of control had been cute.

I'd stopped feeling nervous when he was in close proximity. Speaking with him was fun. Teasing him was a delight. And looking at him was a treat.

I sighed.

Tomorrow was going to be a test on my control.

Every year, four times a year, Grand Duchess Calisto held a seasonal ball. One in late spring, a masquerade in early summer, another ball in late autumn, and a winter feast on the longest night.

And before each event, there was an afternoon tea to greet debutantes and newcomers to the social sphere. Anyone worth knowing by birth or level would be invited to Calisto's tea party on their welcome into society.

I was apparently considered both now that my secret identity had been revealed.

To get ready, I'd chosen a soft gown with a thick-backed white corset on my torso covered in delicate lace. The sleeves were long, loose see-through lace that came together in a band at my wrist. I had a silk beige belt where the built-in corset ended at my waist. The dress skirt was pleated and came down to my calf, showing off tiny white heels with fairytale-like lace ribbons that wound up my legs. The ties were at the knee, and not visible beneath the skirt.

I wore drop earrings, a single point with seven thin strips of white gold bangles that dangled down halfway to my shoulders. Whenever I moved just so, they clinked together gently and drew the eye. White was a striking color against my green skin. To compliment the look, I added white gold charms to my braids and then pulled them into a half updo.

I would admit I was nervous and took longer than I thought I would. I had to rush to the meeting hall where the debutantes all met ahead of time.

"Miss Gerda." A servant came up to greet me when I arrived. "Please feel free to mingle until the duchess arrives. If you do not have a partner, do not worry. There are an even number of guests, and everyone will have a chance to pair up."

"Thank you." I nodded, taking a step off to the side of the group.

I didn't see Julian.

There were around twenty other people milling about in pairs already or joining in introductions and finding a partner to walk inside with.

Lady Amy immediately caught my attention. She was on the opposite end of the palace lobby, standing beside the entrance to the east wing. The elf was arguing quietly with a young man as he held her fast by the arm. The human had tousled finger-length brown hair. Unfortunately, he was facing the other way, so I couldn't see his face.

I knew that Lady Amy could handle herself, but I didn't like the fact that she'd tried to wrest herself free once and he'd held on. I was walking their way even before I started eavesdropping.

"If you can't, then why are we even having this conversation?" The elf looked like she was going to cry. Or punch something. Or both. "I'm not saying I'm judging you, but—"

"Isn't that *exactly* what you're saying?" The man let go of her and took a step back.

"No, I just—"

"You just want me to stop being me so that we can be together?" he demanded, pain in his voice. "So that your father will approve? But that's not how this works, Amy."

"You can be an assassin and not kill people," she countered.

The man laughed, a sharp thing. "And you can be a saintess who forgives everyone *else*, for all I care."

Someone stepped in my path.

"Madame Potts! I know I shouldn't introduce myself when we haven't formally met yet, but isn't this afternoon tea all about meeting people?" A giant was between me and my target. I stared up into dark eyes and a charming smile. "I'm Erik Stormbreaker."

He was too close.

"That's nice. But if you will excuse me—"

"Do you have a partner, Miss Gerda?" There were a few others who'd used the opportunity to join in. One, a foxman with black hair wearing long red robes with black peonies interrupted me. His ear twitched once. "Or do you prefer Madame Potts?"

"Now, Shiro, I got up the nerve to speak with her first." Erik pulled at his dark-blue vest. "The least you could do is let her reject me first before cutting in."

"I'm afraid I have to reject both of you, gentlemen," I stated, taking a step back and gripping my skirt. "I already have a date."

"Ah, of course." Erik sighed as Shiro patted him on the arm in pity.

With that, I walked around the pair to see that Lady Amy was now standing alone, looking lost.

"Amy!" I called, hurrying over to the young woman.

She turned when she heard her name and sniffed once before putting on a welcoming face. "Gerda, you're here."

"How are things?" I asked, walking right up to her and taking her arm like a close friend. She seemed to appreciate the sentiment and sniffed once more.

"I'm sorry, I've just been . . . busy . . . with things." Amy glanced toward the east wing and then sighed before drawing herself up and asking me, "What about you? I'm sorry that your secret got out; it wasn't me—I promise!"

"I know it wasn't . . ." Her sincerity made me pause. "Wait, did you already know?"

"That you were Madame Potts? Um, yeah. I figured it out that first time I came over to your house." She blushed a bit, her dark-green skin going darker in her cheeks. "You just, I don't know, sounded the same? You talked the same, I mean."

"I'm impressed. But no, the leader of the Blackfog spies outed my identity," I explained. Thinking back on it, I frowned. "Wait . . . I don't remember seeing you during the ceremony?"

How could I have missed that? I knew I'd been focused on stopping the Keeper of Fate, but I couldn't believe I'd overlooked the elf's absence. Something terrible could have happened to her, and I wouldn't have even noticed.

Amy hurriedly explained, "I, um, I was running late and missed entering before they started."

"And you wouldn't have been able to slip in," I said, feeling sorry that she'd had to wait outside, "since Grand Duchess Calisto separated the building into a pocket dimension after that."

"Exactly." The elf relaxed, thinking I'd fallen for her excuses.

"Is the man you were arguing with the reason you were late?"

Lady Amy drew in a sharp breath and argued, "No, he's—I haven't—We haven't—There isn't anything going on between us—"

I took pity on the flustered woman and squeezed her arm reassuringly. "I overheard your argument. I'm sorry it didn't work out."

"You-You heard us?" Instead of reassuring her, Lady Amy went as pale green as my own softer shades.

"Just the end," I explained, worried about her reaction. I would need to tell Henrietta to check in on Amy—and ask what Justice said about the prophecy at the same time. There were so many things to remember to do, I was worried I'd miss one.

I should poke Brownie as well. If Lady Amy was in the middle of her first love—and a forbidden romance by what little I'd caught of it—she would need all the friends she could get.

I patted the girl on the back. "It'll be okay, Amy. Why don't we talk after the tea party? You kept my secret when you could have shared, so I'll keep yours. What do you say?"

She finally calmed. "Alright."

"I haven't met very many people here, but why don't I introduce you to some that I do know?" I offered, pointing at Erik and Shiro. They were still ribbing each other, but aside from rudely approaching me without an invitation earlier, they'd earned points for taking no for an answer. "And we can see about finding you a partner by the time Duchess Calisto gets here."

CHAPTER 52

He Dropped to His Knees

Julian

Earlier That Day

"You want me to ask Justice?" Queen Henrietta looked at Julian like he'd grown a second head.

"If you could?"

"I was surprised to find out myself, but Justice doesn't commune with his chosen." King Keith wrapped an arm around his wife's waist.

"It's true." Queen Henrietta nodded. "I've spoken with him only twice; when he announced in his temple that I was his chosen, and when my parents wanted me to use my connection with him to better their personal standing . . . And both times, I had to actually go to his temple and pray. He told me that he wouldn't treat me any differently to others because it wouldn't be 'fair,' and that I had to prove myself on my own."

"But you could ask?" Julian urged.

"I can," Queen Henrietta said. "Do you have a Temple of Justice in the palace?"

"We have one in the town." Julian gave them directions and asked them to get back to him with what they found.

His sister was easier. He waited until Julia summoned breakfast to determine that she was awake, then dragged her disheveled, disgruntled form off to the sanctuary.

"I can't believe you interrupted us for this." His little sister shot daggers at him with her eyes. "See if I don't ruin *your* wedding night."

"It is almost noon, Julia," he replied.

"Hmph."

He opened the door to the sanctuary and pushed his sister inside. It was mostly repaired, the debris swept, and the broken glass panes set aside. Duchess Calisto had the highest-level repair magic of any in her castle, and they were all just waiting for her to recover her strength so she could fix the murals and stained glass windows.

"I need you to ask Light what she thinks about Fate's prophecy, and if the gods will really destroy our world if we let Madame Potts save people she isn't supposed to save," Julian said. "Please?"

"Fine." The Paladin of Light sighed, then started to glow. "Oh, great patroness, Light of the world, hear this humble servant. I—"

"*JULIA! WHAT HAVE YOU DONE TO MY* TEMPLE?" Light's voice was as overwhelming as Shadow's, more so even due to the goddess's proximity and wrath.

He dropped to his knees from the sheer weight of the goddess's intent. She was like a solar flare walking over his body. Dragon flame in his soul. Blinding white hurt his eyes as the sanctuary exploded in light all around him.

"*THOSE WERE RENBENT MURALS! AND ELIZABETTA LORE SPENT THIRTEEN YEARS MAKING THOSE GLASS WINDOWS. THE DRAPES! ARACHNE WOVEN SILK FROM THE ANCIENT CITY OF SHARN. ALL RUINED!*"

His sister tried to speak. "Forgive us, Light. Mother will repair it as soon as she can, I promise. Please, my brother is wondering if the gods are planning to end the world—"

"*THIS DISRESPECT ALONE IS ENOUGH TO MAKE ME END THE WORLD!*" Almost unbearable heat radiated in waves with her words. "*BUT DO THEY ASK ME? NO! FATE IS TOO DIVIDED AMONG HER THREADS TO HEAR A WORD, AND LUCK IS BUSY TOYING WITH JUSTICE. MY SIBLINGS NEVER ASK MY OPINION. WHY WOULD THEY? I'M JUST LIGHT. WHAT WOULD I KNOW OF THE HEAVENS? MY CELESTIAL STARS ARE ONLY THE DUST OF CREATION. MY AMBIENT MAGIC THE HOPE AGAINST THE DARK.*"

"You are my goddess. Life would die without your sun, and Shadow would have no shade without your light," Julia spoke softly, flattering her patroness. "*Of course* you are the Heavens."

"*THIS IS WHY YOU ARE MY CHOSEN.*" Light's voice softened to the pressure of a hot summer day.

"Thank you, Light. I will do my best to repair your temple, with added gifts," his sister placated. "Why don't I have Master Gaukler come and carve your benches with etchings of the moon and stars?"

"*DO NOT SUMMON ME UNTIL YOU HAVE. OH, AND JULIA,*" the goddess added in a voice soft as a kiss, "*congratulations on your wedding.*"

And then, Light was gone.

Julian blinked rapidly, but it did nothing to stop the sunspots. He was sweating and exhausted from the small exchange, and he wasn't even the one facing the goddess directly. His sister grabbed his arm and pulled him to his feet.

"I hope you got your answer," Julia told him. "Also, your eyes should clear in ten minutes or so."

"That's good to know." Julian did *not* have an answer, but they'd tried, and that was what mattered. He wiped his forehead and pulled at the damp tunic clinging to his chest. "Gods, I need a shower."

"As your kind and loving sister, I'll guide you back to your rooms." She pulled his arm, and he readily followed.

When Julian arrived at the western garden, he was already running a bit late.

In a rush, he'd simply activated [Light Foot] to jump off his balcony, but there was no Gerda waiting for him in the garden below. Was he later than he thought? There should still be time before the official start.

"Gerda?" he called out hesitantly. No one answered. He waited five minutes more then decided he would swing by the palace entry. If she wasn't there, he'd send out a search party.

It was a short distance to the gathering point, but his heart was beating faster and faster as he went. After Julia's kidnapping, he was already fearing the worst.

All of it built up until he saw her standing there.

She was speaking with a group of younger debutants, none of whom he readily recognized. Relief washed over him, and then embarrassment, and then frustration. He'd been late, of course, but she could have waited for him . . . Julian wasn't used to letting his emotions get away from him, and he fought back against his own thoughts, trying to find his feet.

That's when she spotted him.

Unexpectedly, a bright smile pulled at her lips, and he was free from the storm of frustration that plagued him. She politely excused herself and walked his way, her eyes playful and expectant.

"You made it just in time," she greeted, taking a spot beside him.

"Did I?" Julian replied, trying to read her expression. She wasn't angry at him for being late to their agreed-upon time, just genuinely glad to see him.

Gerda glanced over her shoulder back at the group she'd just come from, explaining. "Lord Erik kept asking me who I was going with, and I didn't know how to tell him that it was you without boasting."

There was a giant staring at them with a disappointed look on his face. Another member of the group slapped Lord Erik on the back in sympathy, and Julian quickly reached out to offer Gerda his arm. "Then it's good I wasn't any later . . ."

She readily took it.

He wanted to ask if she'd forgotten they were supposed to meet in the garden. Had it slipped her mind? Or had he simply recalled incorrectly?

She squeezed his arm and leaned in a little closer. She smelled like the pine forests in the North after a fresh rain, crisp and refreshing and of the earth. "I know I'm not *technically* a part of the investigation team . . . but do you know of any assassins who escaped yesterday?"

That brought him up short. "No? Why? Did you see something?"

"Heard something, actually." Gerda sighed and dropped her hand. "But they might just be an Assassin class and not actually a problem. I'll let you know if it proves to be the latter."

"Stop me if this is rude," Julian broached, still worrying, "but is there anything *else* I should know about today?"

"No . . . Well, maybe one thing." She searched the room, found what she was looking for, and gestured with a slight head nod toward a human woman without a partner. She had chestnut brown skin and long black hair, bright pink eyes, and she wore a very exciting shade of pink that hurt to look upon. "The girl in the unfortunate pink. She's going to light her date on fire at the ball tonight. Which isn't so much the problem as what comes next . . ."

"What comes next?" he asked, dragging his eyes away.

"He ruins the toast." The troll shook her head sadly. "Knocks into a waiter while he's trying to put out the flames and shatters glasses everywhere. I was going to do something about it, but it would probably be easier if you just let the staff know ahead of time?"

"Alright," he agreed. Having a date who knew the future had its perks, the least of which was knowing the future, honestly. Gerda herself was already keeping him on his toes. A small part of him relaxed for the first time in what felt like days.

"I'm not saying that's the *only* thing that will happen," she said, immediately shattering his calm. "But that is the only thing I'm going to tell you."

She raised an eyebrow at him in challenge. Julian took a deep breath and managed an, "As is your right."

"You're right it is." She nodded, and he was taken aback by the hard edge in her voice. She softened it by slipping back into a smile. "But you can relax. Honestly, nothing else is going to affect you much, and if it does, that's only because you're escorting me. Sorry."

Julian didn't think he was going to relax again anytime soon. Maybe when he was not-so-safely back in the North, fighting off another monster surge and getting some of this nervous energy out on the battlefield.

"Welcome, everyone." Grand Duchess Calisto descended the grand staircase in the lobby, glancing around the room until her eyes rested on Julian. He caught her eyebrow twitch when she saw whom he was partnered with. "And thank you for joining me today. I've moved us to a shaded area near the goblin-lily pond."

There were a few happy whispers from the crowd of debutants. It was a hot summer's day, and no one wanted to be out under the direct sun for long. Especially in semiformal attire.

"Please follow me." His mother looked kindly at a few of those standing off to the side, alone, adding, "And if you have yet to find a partner, you may pair up now. Do not worry, we are simply making introductions. Meeting new people is all a part of the experience . . . I will partner with you, Lord Shiro."

The fox stiffened but recovered quickly and hurried over to offer the grand duchess his arm.

Calisto eyed Julian once, and from the look she gave him, he realized he'd dodged a flaming arrow—she'd planned to partner with *him* and use him as a proper etiquette demonstration.

He barely contained the shudder, unconsciously holding Gerda closer.

It was time for tea.

CHAPTER 53

Enough Emotional Maturity to Count for Two Lifetimes

Gerda

"Please find a seat; I will be with you shortly." Calisto waved at a long table set under an open-sided tent. There were beautiful lily floral arrangements in front of every fourth seat, and vines hanging from the beams of the tent.

The duchess smiled at us before leaving to go speak with one of her attendants just a little ways off.

"Your seat." Julian courteously pulled out my chair for me, and I raised my eyebrows at him. His mask of polite indifference was back in full force. I had to admit, it made me want to tease him.

"Thank you." Was all I said, taking my seat.

We were seated just down from the head of the table where his mother would be sitting. Lady Amy was seated at the far end, between Lord Erik and the arson in pink. It was too far away for me to lend a helping hand if Amy needed it, but the elf girl seemed happy, laughing at something the giant said.

There were a few things to note about Grand Duchess Calisto's afternoon tea. This was often the first "official" event for coming-of-age youngsters. That number varied from region to kingdom, with it being as low as sixteen in some and as high as twenty-five in others. That didn't mean I was surrounded by teenagers, because there were as many reasons to join high society as there were to avoid it.

If a baker leveled up to sixty, they would join the other elite on the continent and receive an invitation. If a once cursed hedgehog prince was finally freed, he might decide to join—considering if he was still single after that. The point of the afternoon tea was to help marriage-minded individuals meet other people around their level. And, of course, there were political alliances to be made, rivals to be tested, and enemies to be bested.

Tabitha and Gail, Duke Julian's cousins, had told me all about the tea party at the Spring Ball—and I noted that Duchess Calisto had started *that* event off by leaving everyone to their own devices as well . . .

"How many of these have you been to?" I asked my escort.

"Too many." His eyes met mine, and he broke into a small half smile that made my heart beat faster. Stupid heart. "This is usually only for newcomers because Mother wants everyone to be at ease, but I've been brought in to even out the numbers when there's need."

I poked him in the arm to lighten my own mood. "Why do I think that is more often than not?"

"I'm sure she'd like me to find someone, but . . ."

"But you have business in the North," I said, repeating the phrase he'd used in the game. I nodded.

Julian stared at me. I smiled at him.

After a moment, he leaned in close to whisper. "Miss Gerda . . ."

"Yes?" I replied.

"I would like to apologize," he broached, "for being late to pick you up in the garden, and I understand if you are—"

"Oh my gods." The words slipped out before I could stop myself. I felt the blush all the way up to my pointy ears, and I covered my face. "I am so sorry. I completely forgot that was where we'd planned to meet."

The half elf raised an arched brow. "This from the oracle who knows all? Am I so forgettable?"

He was playing with me, I could see it in his eyes, and so I answered accordingly. "Oh, you should be flattered that I remembered we were partnered at all."

"Noted." Julian leaned back in his chair.

"I'm sorry to interrupt, but is this a good time for introductions?" a dwarfess sitting on the other side of Julian cut in awkwardly. She had brown hair with purple streaks, and a purple beard with brown streaks. She wore matching light-purple pants and vest over a white tunic. Her buttons were large cut amethysts. "I'm Lady Betta Ameth of the Baldorin Mountains, and this is my partner, Sam Glenwood of Servalt."

Her partner was an elf with brown skin and strawberry pink hair, wearing a hood with intricately embroidered oak leaves over a sky-blue tunic and pants. Sam waved nervously.

Julian and I shared a look. His face resumed its stern neutral expression while I smiled wide, showing off my pointy troll tusks.

"It's nice to meet you. I am Miss Gerda Jones from Nilheim, and this is my partner, Duke Julian von Slyke, Border Master of the Northern Fortress, heir to the duchy of North Sumbria," I stated, purposely highlighting the duke.

Lady Betta's eyes took on a sharp gleam. "I can't imagine what it must be like, living in the Dark Enchanted Forest. I could never—"

"You are being too humble." His voice carried an edge as he interrupted the dwarfess and waved a hand at me. "May I introduce my partner, Miss Gerda Jones, an elite member of the Dark Horde—and the famous Madame Potts."

"What an honor!" Sam clapped once.

"Thank you for waiting, everyone." Calisto returned and elegantly sat in the chair at the head table. "And for joining me in a light bit of refreshment before tonight's celebration. I'm so happy that you could make it."

Her head was held high as she swept them all a friendly smile, and I didn't need my ludicrously high perception to notice that she stared at Julian and I longer than the others, her smile getting wider. I started to sweat under that look.

"For many of you, tonight will be your first debut into society." The duchess waved a hand, and servants in palace livery came forward with enchanted tea pots full of different varieties of expensive tea. The one set before Julian and I was an aromatic blend of mint and citrus with a hint of something familiar I couldn't place. "While our tea is brewing, allow me to explain a few important details.

"First, you all should have an escort for this evening. If anything changes between now and then, let me know *immediately*. We want you to feel comfortable and have someone you can trust by your side during the festivities. Everyone is going to meet in the main hall outside the ballroom. Usually, we would announce everyone as they enter, but this is a masquerade ball. Where's the fun in that?

"Instead, we will simply enter as we did today. There will be time to mingle and enjoy the open buffet for an hour's time, then there will be a toast. After that, Chloe and Julia will open the dance floor with a solo performance, after which we have an hour of dancing before the great mask reveal. You are *not* expected to keep your mask on all evening. Please take it off any time you wish."

"Your Grace!" An eager hand popped up from the end of the table belonging to a lizardkin woman with orange scales and long black hair. "I don't have a partner for this evening." The lizardkin shot a look at Julian that surprised a moment of jealousy out of me, and my fingers twitched.

If this were a cheesy romance, I might have grabbed Julian's arm or glared at the lady . . . but I was a grown woman with enough emotional maturity to count for two lifetimes—and Julian had already promised to escort *me*, so she was just out of luck.

"I'm sorry to hear that, Miss Terralith. Come see me after the tea party." The duchess smiled reassuringly at the lizardkin before addressing the group again. "Now! Let's pour some tea, and then I will go over a basic etiquette lesson for anyone interested in a refresher."

As to be expected, the tea was delicious. The smell that I couldn't discern earlier was immediately recognizable with the first sip. My mind remembered the joy of root beer in my previous life, and savored the familiar taste. It had no carbonation or foam, but it was so close to home that I closed my eyes and let the moment take me.

I wondered where they'd found the sassafras? I could make and share a root beer float recipe—No. There wouldn't really be time before I left for the North.

I placed my glass down and looked up at Julian, who was staring at me and my tea. We would be leaving tomorrow.

And that was that.

CHAPTER 54

He Didn't Want Them to Clash

Julian

After the tea, Julian escorted Gerda to the western garden. He didn't know what she was going to get up to in the two hours before the Masquerade, but he had a few tasks to complete himself before he could get changed into something more elaborate for the occasion.

"Thank you for escorting me." Gerda let go of his arm when they reached the fountain. She demonstrated a perfect curtsy—as learned from his mother only thirty minutes prior.

"The pleasure was all mine." His lips twitched as he said, "Am I to assume that *this time* you won't forget where we are meeting?"

She raised both eyebrows and smiled at him. "Only if *you* aren't late."

"You wouldn't have even known I was late," Julian pointed out, "if I hadn't told you."

"But you *did* tell me," she countered, lifting up her new purple fan and hiding her smile behind it.

A tray of fans had been presented as gifts to the tea party attendees, to keep and to practice with during his mother's lessons. Gerda had chosen one that obviously matched his own coloring. A darker purple like his hair, with silver decoration like his eyes. It was painted with a crescent moon surrounded by clouds.

"Does your fan match your outfit tonight?" he asked. He wanted her to say yes because his own outfit for the ball was already picked out and ready for him. It wasn't arcane magic to guess, since they were his household colors, but his mask had purple-and-silver accents that would go hand in hand with her fan. The costume and mask were specially designed, and he couldn't change them now . . . or at least, he never would've thought to change them until now.

Julian was considering what he would do if she said no; he didn't want them to clash.

"Yes." Her soft brown eyes caught his, and there was a touch of . . . embarrassment? She hid behind her fan and said, "The fan matches my outfit perfectly, so if you'll excuse me, I'll be going now."

She already knew what he was going to wear. She could see the future, *had* seen the future, and had deliberately chosen the fan to match with his outfit.

Julian called after her, "I'll be here."

He waited until she slipped into the western wing before he chuckled to himself. The tea had been a repeat of everything he'd done previously, with nothing new . . . excepting, of course, his partner. Gerda had been the only saving grace.

She'd perfected five types of curtsy, the head nod, and the fan snap.

She'd struggled holding the fork in her left hand, instinctively picking it up every time with the right instead.

She'd mastered recognizing when someone poisoned her glade crystal drink instantly, noting the sounds of the glass before and after he added juice.

She'd laughed when Cousin Tabitha hit herself with her fan while trying to signal that she was interested in going for a walk around the ballroom. It had been genuine, and she'd apologized to Tabby right away for the slight.

Then Gerda had scrunched up her nose in distaste when the human Baroness Hermingard had grabbed her partner by the wrist and dug her long, pointed nails into flesh. The preela adventurer, one Yeshik Amil, was a guest from the Empire of Sands, and the pair had only partnered because they'd been paired together at the end. Yeshik had used a skill to poison her drink for the demonstration, and instead of letting it happen, she'd made a show of stopping him.

The baroness was from Drendil, young and foolish. Julian agreed with the troll's quiet, long-suffering sigh at the young woman's antics.

But he needed to stop thinking of Gerda and start thinking about what he was supposed to be doing next.

Julian returned to his rooms before summoning his second-in-command and paladin.

"What do you mean I can't go to the ball!" Sir Tully yelled, shocked and appalled at the order.

"I'll make it a thousand experience points quest," Julian replied, enticing the man with his banked personal stash. His Duke title granted him a certain amount of EXP every month to hand out quests, and he'd saved up quite a bit.

Julian set his coronet on his head then delicately worked it into his dreads, adjusting it straight. From the mirror, he could see Visha standing at attention looking calm and collected, and Sir Tully rubbing his neck in frustration. Tully was in full formal royal guard wear, with a purple embroidered tabard over plate armor that had been polished until it sparkled.

"I *can't*. I'm supposed to escort my cousin Penny. I *have* to go, or mother will skin me alive and feed me to the griffins—"

"Miss Penny Bracken?" Julian turned to face his flustered paladin.

"Yes! I'm supposed to be watching out for her." Sir Tully shrugged. "She's got a bit of a temper and, well, you know how the Masquerade crowd can get."

He did know. Julian also knew Miss Penny was the young lady in pink that Gerda had warned him about. He wasn't surprised that any lady would light his human friend on fire. Sir Tully did that to people.

Julian was smiling again; he forced his face back to normal as he turned to stare at Visha. "And you? Do you have plans for the evening?"

His second-in-command looked at Tully, sighed, then met Julian's eyes. "No, Your Grace."

"She's still not drinking anything, so the whole event is a waste for her," Sir Tully said, gaining a sharp glare from Visha.

"Tully," Julian cut in before Visha stabbed the human. "Go escort your cousin."

He didn't need to be told twice. Tully thumped a fist on his chest before ducking out the door. Then he promptly stuck his head back inside the room. "Oh! And can you stop and chat with us for a few minutes tonight? I want to show my cousin that she's wrong and I'm a valued member of the team."

"Maybe," Julian got out. This was his last chance to warn his friend about the upcoming evening's events . . . and he chose to wave Tully away instead.

It wasn't the first time Tully had been set on fire. He'd be fine. Julian would worry about the furniture instead.

"Alright, Visha, here is what I need you to do . . ."

CHAPTER 55

Miss Lilywearer's Finest Wearings

Gerda

I arrived ten minutes early, just in case, finding a seat at the fountain but being careful with my long hair. I had to pull it over my shoulder so I wouldn't sit on it or risk it getting wet.

The summer sun meant everything was bright and hot, and I did not regret my choice in dress. The gown was something I'd found in a dungeon. I'd brought it to *Miss Lilywearer's Finest Wearings* in Sumbria, and they'd altered it to my desires. I'd chosen it not just for the +2 Dexterity enchantment but because it was *perfect*.

The dress was a lilac purple, soft and sensual. The corset top dipped at my cleavage and rounded out like the top of a heart. Layers of the sheer lilac-colored fabric skirt fell to various lengths, but the base layer underneath was a soft green just a shade lighter than my skin tone. It gave off the illusion that you could see right through the thin silk.

I'd had Lily sew on royal-purple delphinium fabric flowers with tiny ornate embroidered leaves starting between my breasts and going down in an arch to my left hip. Matching purple flower straps fell off my shoulders, offering absolutely no support at all.

The dress barely touched the floor because, as much as I fantasized about billowing skirts that trailed behind me in an enchanting puddle . . . I didn't want to dance in a fabric puddle.

I wore matching dark purple boots with silver leaf embroidery, and lilac fingerless gloves that came halfway up to my elbows. With my thick muscular arms and strong shoulders, there was no sense in wearing longer gloves.

Besides, showing off my arms complimented the green in my dress.

After much debate and careful consideration . . . I'd decided to let my hair down. Unraveling my braids gave it a distinct wave. I'd been tempted to let *all* of my hair down, but instead, I'd braided my bangs and woven them around the strap of my purple-and-silver half mask.

I had to wear the Ancient Gamblers Amulet around my neck. If I unequipped it, then every time someone crossed my bridge, I'd be forced to pay them in experience points instead of gold . . . and my massive treasure trove of gold was the only reason I could traipse across Valaria enjoying myself instead of doing my job. Luckily, the amulet was silver. While unimpressive on its own, it didn't clash.

My perception immediately noticed when Julian arrived. It also noticed that the half elf didn't greet me right away.

He stood there for a solid thirty seconds, unmoving, but I didn't call out to him. I liked to think he was standing there staring at me in shock.

A troll could dream.

"Miss Gerda." He cleared his throat.

I stood and offered him a smile. It was my turn to stare at him. Julian wore exactly what he'd been wearing on the cover of season two's promotional picture: a black undershirt, a long royal-purple silk vest with delphinium flower print, and black pants. His silver buttons matched his silver pendant, also unassuming in comparison to the rest of his outfit. His mask was similar to my own.

His lips were in their usual unimpressed, harsh line. I wanted to poke the half elf on the cheek and force a smile, but I didn't.

"Duke Julian." I curtsied naturally. Then, I couldn't resist the tease. "It looks like we both made it in time today."

Julian's lip twitched, and then he covered his mouth to hold back laughter.

"So it would seem," he managed, walking closer. He held out his arm to escort me, and the gentle smile on his face made my toes curl. "I have to ask . . ."

Knowing that my raised eyebrows were hidden behind my mask, I took his arm and said, "Yes?"

"Did you arrange to wear that dress *before* you knew that I was going to escort you?" He eyed me from the side, looking to the flowers trailing down to my hips and back up to my mask.

My shoulders stiffened, and I fought to keep the lighthearted smile. "What can I say?"

"You can just say that you knew all along," he replied, though I noticed a hitch in his voice that I couldn't place.

In a very dumb move on my part, I decided not to lie. "I knew what you were going to wear, but I had no idea we were going together. Promise."

It was true. My own interaction with the storyline had never come up. I was never seen by the eyes of the chosen in any scenario, or forewarned of in any perk.

Granted, I rarely interacted with the story itself.

His voice dropped ever so slightly even as he said through a smile, "If I didn't ask you, who were you planning to go with?"

"Lady Amy," I replied. I knew many people in attendance . . . but not personally. And while there had been a pile of invites delivered to my room after my identity was revealed, I couldn't have planned for that.

Julian nodded. "Her loss . . . Is she also wearing purple today?"

I pulled out my fan with my free hand and hid behind it. "She's wearing green."

"I see."

"The delphiniums were an add-on," I offered. "But you have to admit the outfit looks great."

He opened the door for me, and I stepped ahead of him, thankful for the magical equivalent of air conditioning that kept the palace cool. I needed it.

"You're right, Miss Gerda." Julian leaned down. His voice tickled my ear, sending a shiver down my spine. "You do look lovely in purple."

Magical air conditioning, you have failed me.

CHAPTER 56

A Moment of Possessiveness

Julian

Julian wasn't expecting Gerda to look so breathtaking.

And he wasn't expecting to feel a slight twist in his stomach when she'd spoken about taking someone else to the ball.

And he *was not* expecting to feel a sense of accomplishment when his compliment left her speechless and flushed before he dragged her to the hall. Her light green skin darkened all the way down to her exposed collarbone, as did the tips of her long ears.

"Ger—Greetings." Queen Henrietta was immediately on them as they walked into the hallway outside the ballroom, the Dark Lady almost slipping and using Gerda's name. It was rude to reveal someone's identity so early in the evening. Many in the room had magically changed their hair, eyes, skin, or fur color for the occasion. Some had even shapeshifted.

There was an enchantment on this room and the ballroom that helped obscure the guests to better assist in the fun of the masquerade . . . but no one was going to be fooled when Queen Henrietta was being her usual self and King Keith didn't hide his single horn.

King Keith held his wife around the shoulders. The Dark Lord looked over their outfits, and his eyebrow twitched, but he simply nodded. "How was your afternoon?"

Julian smiled. "Informative."

"Good."

"I'm impressed you got matching outfits so quickly!" Queen Henrietta exclaimed, not one to hold back like her husband. Her eyes sparkled as she looked over Gerda. "You both look *amazing*."

"Thank you." Gerda's voice choked a bit, but she recovered. "So do you."

The royals wore matching blue, each outfit having a high neck and not a single embellishment on the fabric. They chose, instead, to adorn themselves in heavy gemstone belts, brooches, and jewelry.

Probably all of them enchanted.

"I haven't seen your hair down since the bridge battle." Queen Henrietta admired the waves of dark emerald green that fell past the troll's waist. It looked luscious, with enough volume to frame her figure without being too thick to run his fingers through . . .

Not that Julian was thinking about running his fingers through Gerda's hair.

"It's a bit of a pain." The troll sighed wistfully, running a hand on a section that fell over her exposed shoulder. "But I love it."

"I can imagine. I wouldn't last through a single hairbrush before giving up." The queen leaned in closer, smiling up at Gerda. "I know it's not the right time or place, *but* I have a surprise for you!"

"What—?"

Henrietta pulled out a bag of cookies. Julian recognized them immediately.

"Stardust skirts?" Julian's jaw dropped before he reached out to cover the cookies and Gerda's hand. "Quick! Hide it before my mother sees!"

Gerda slipped them into her storage ring. "What are stardust skirts?"

"Only the most delicious baking I've ever had outside of your own!" The queen stuck both hands on her hips and nodded once.

Julian added, "They are baked *specially* for the married couple, and *only* for them."

"But . . . why did you give me these?" Gerda asked, confused.

"I wanted to thank you somehow . . . for everything," the queen explained. "I helped bake the stardust skirts for Julia and Chloe, and those were my trial cookies."

"You didn't need to—"

"I really did," Henrietta assured her.

"—but I will *gladly* accept your cookies."

"Good." Reassured that her gift was well received, Henrietta took her husband by the arm. "They're made out of concentrated star mana, pixie dust, dried markleberry powder, nettle, minos cow butter, and the zest of a pink lime."

"*There is dried markleberry powder?*" The vehemence in Gerda's voice startled everyone.

"It's very, very rare." Henrietta gave her a sad smile.

"It's time." King Keith drew their attention to the other guests as everyone started to move. He recommended, "Let's continue this after we find our place in line."

Since this was a masquerade, there was no official order of precedence and no official greetings. Instead of announcing names, the attendants were greeting everyone and offering them a dance card with the schedule on the back.

"We can go looking for some at the market tomorrow," Henrietta promised.

"She'll be leaving with me tomorrow," Julian said. "So you should plan something early. We are leaving at lunch."

"No," said a polite voice that cut in right behind him. "You are not."

"Hello, Mother." He turned, ignoring the cold chill that ran down his spine.

"My dear." Grand Duchess Calisto was standing arm in arm with Their Royal Highness Rowen. The fox had on a long tight black dress, hoop earrings, and an ornate black tiara set with rubies.

"Your Grace," King Keith and Henrietta greeted, Gerda a beat behind them.

"You *do* recall that you're speaking at tomorrow's closing ceremonies." The words were spoken through a smile, but he couldn't miss the daggers in his mother's sharp eyes as she stared him down.

"Of course, Mother."

"Which means you will be leaving, *at the earliest,* right after lunch," Grand Duchess Calisto let him know.

"Of course, Mother."

There was no way around it. Julian knew his mother would be there with knights in hand to drag him back if he tried to sneak away early.

"So I have you all tomorrow morning!" Henrietta clapped.

"You are both forgetting the council meeting, where Gerda has been summoned to speak," Their Royal Highness spoke, and Henrietta's shoulders slumped. The fox shot her a wide grin. "But in the meantime, let's all enjoy tonight."

The fox escorted Calisto into the ballroom ahead of them.

"I'm sure we'll find some time before I leave." Gerda shot Julian an apologetic side-eye that this conversation had foiled his plans.

Julian sighed. "With everything changed, you can take your time. We'll meet at the stables after you're done."

"What if I don't have a horse?" she asked quietly. Before he could reply, they were accepting their dance cards and entering the hall.

Julian immediately led her off to the side of the hall, where they were out of the way. "There are more than enough horses. I'll have one prepared."

A palace knight carrying a tray approached.

"For the toast," the knight said, presenting a variety of drinks. She was one of his mother's personal knights, a level fifty-three paladin with poison detection. She recognized Julian right away, her eyes glancing at his partner with interest.

"Thank you, Sir Rumel." He took a red cherry cider, and Gerda chose a dry pear. "Keep up the good work."

"Have a good evening, Your Grace. Miss." Sir Rumel bowed her head then left to offer drinks to the rest of the guests. The duchess wasn't leaving anything to chance.

Gerda immediately tapped the glass with a fingernail, noting the distinct crystal chime. Her dance card was hanging off her wrist by a black braided thread, and it swayed delicately.

"May I?" Julian motioned to the card. When she lifted it, he used a bit of mana to activate it and write out his name on the first line. Then, in a moment of possessiveness utterly unlike him . . . he added his name to the last spot as well.

"I'm not the best dancer," she warned, unbothered by his claiming multiple spots.

"Between your Dexterity and my expertise, I'm sure it'll be fine," he said, but she had turned away to scan the crowd.

The room was filling up fast. She was distracted, and after the second pass, he realized she was looking for someone in particular.

"If you're looking for our young lady in pink, she's standing beside Tully over there." Julian tilted his own glass toward the far side of the hall. Miss Penny Bracken was wearing a different outfit than the one she'd worn at tea . . . and this one managed to look *even more* pink than the last.

The dress was an interesting design that reminded Julian of a pincushion.

"No . . . I'm looking for someone else. Ah, there's Erik."

It was the giant whom she'd been laughing with before the tea party. He stood next to a table that was elbow high for his companions but hip high for Erik. The giant had on red tights, a long loose black tunic with a jeweled belt cinched at the waist, and a golden chain around his neck.

Julian let Gerda drag him over to the young group despite wanting more time with her alone.

"Erik! Shiro!" The troll smiled a greeting. "Have you seen Lady Amy? She disappeared after the tea party. We were supposed to talk, but all I got was this note."

A green leaf appeared in Gerda's hand, unfurling to show shining golden scrawl clearly visible to all.

I'm sorry, something came up. I'll see you at the ball.

The pair exchanged looks and stepped away from their friends: another fox, a human, and a catkin. The others tried not to appear like they were listening in and failed.

"No, we parted ways in the main hall," Erik replied.

Gerda sighed. "I have a bad feeling about this."

Julian didn't need to hear more. Tapping his foot twice, he drew Shadow John's attention as he leaned down and spoke into Gerda's ear, even knowing everyone could hear him. "I'll quietly send out a search. Just in case."

She gave him a short nod, accepting the help. "Thank you."

Julian's shadow flickered. John got his message and was off.

"Don't you already know the future?" Erik tapped the table beside his drink. "Or is that rude to ask?"

"That's a bit much Erik," Shiro chided softly.

Gerda flinched. "It's . . . complicated."

CHAPTER 57

No Poison

Gerda

"I already checked on tonight . . . but that doesn't account for something I did in the meantime unknowingly changing things," I offered the simplest response.

I didn't want to explain that my powers were at the whims of Fate. I'd woken up with the sun to check [Oracle] and seen options from Julia about tonight, and then two others: Pirate Abra, the Bringer of Chaos, and Rebecca Smith, the Herald of Void.

I'd forgone the pirate battle and checked in on Rebecca. It was rare for Rebecca to appear in my visions, since she wasn't a very active chosen, but she was following a distress signal from her sister and got caught battling a stoneskin wombat on her way out of the Dark Enchanted Forest.

The vision with Julia had only shown the Paladin of Light pulling Chloe out of the way when the lady in pink lit Tully on fire.

"I shouldn't worry, since Slake said he would keep an eye on Amy while she was here . . ." I sighed. The grimalcat was also nowhere to be seen.

Just then, I was distracted by a blinking notification.

[Passive Perk: **Sense Fate** has activated. Duke Julian von Slyke will be shot through the heart on the eve.]
[You have crossed paths with a fate that can be changed. Area of effect radius: Level 65 x Perception 43 x Foretelling 4 = 11,180 sq/ ft. Fate herself will guide you.]
["A battle rages within, but slips the weak hand to the bow. Love strives, but a heart shaken is a heart still determined to quest. Her breath a choice has delayed the point but soft spoken are empty words against action at best."]

"Gerda?" The gentle breath on my ear sent a shiver down my spine and pulled me from the perk. Julian was close enough that if it were anyone else, I might have panicked. His silver eyes were so striking, but this was not the time to be distracted from my distraction.

"A new prophecy," I said, waving at the notification only I could see. "You're going to be shot."

"When?" Julian pulled me closer and stepped away from the table. Suddenly, we were engulfed in a clear magical shield. People looked our way, but only in passing interest; backstabbing or hidden attacks were a staple of any good ball.

I shook my head. "I didn't get a vision of your imminent death, only a passive perk telling me someone is going to shoot you in the heart tonight."

Erik's friends were whispering among themselves.

"Amazing."

"Did we just get to see a prophecy firsthand?"

"Melvin is going to be *so jealous* that he missed this year."

"*He* decided his research was more important than his debut." The catkin who said this smirked.

The shield disappeared, and Julian let go of my arm. He took a step back. "Then, it would be better if we parted ways here."

"No need. I won't let you die," I said, matter of fact.

"Death is only a slight inconvenience." Julian glanced near the front of the hall, where his mother stood. "Though I would hate to ruin my sister's reception. Julia would never let me live it down if Chloe had to revive me tonight."

"True," I agreed.

"If you get the chance, would *you* revive me instead?" Julian asked.

"Of course."

"Shouldn't we, I don't know, inform the guards?" Shiro cut into our back-and-forth, concerned.

"The sooner the better," Erik agreed, picking up his drink and downing the entire glass. "I'll get to it."

"Wait." I stopped him, closing my eyes and going through my visions. I didn't see Julian in his sister's vision. Which meant that he wasn't on that side of the ballroom during the errant fireball.

He was standing on *this side* of the hall.

When I opened my eyes, everyone was staring at me—including a few masked individuals from outside the group.

"You should probably raise that shield again . . ." I told Julian.

"I'll do more than that." Putting his glass down on the table, he reached out to poke my forehead.

My mouth opened a bit in shock, snapping shut before I asked, "What did you do?"

"[Guard]," he explained, opening and downing a mana potion at the same time. "A simple defense spell."

I knew what [Guard] was. I also knew he didn't need to poke me to activate it.

"Am I or am I *not* going for help," Erik asked.

"No time," I replied, sounding like I'd foreseen it but in actuality I'd just watched Grand Duchess Calisto let go of Rowen's arm and raise her glass.

"Greetings and a warm welcome, everyone." Calisto's voice echoed across the room, amplified by magic so that all could hear her at conversational volume. The room quieted, and everyone turned to face the duchess with their glasses ready.

Erik cursed under his breath, ducking his glass below the table and refilling it with something from a flask pulled out of nowhere. Julian picked his up from the table again, making sure to tap the side with the index finger holding the glass.

No poison.

I tinked my own glass, just in case.

And just in case was right. The note was distinctly different from what I had heard earlier.

"It is with great pride that I invite you all to toast the brides, Countesses Julia and Chloe von Slyke."

The pair stepped forward, hand in hand. Both wore purple, Chloe in a smart five-piece suit with heeled knee-high boots over black pants and a long black linen tunic that fell to the thigh over a purple silk tunic embroidered in silver crescent moons. A black-and-silver corset was laced on top, and draped over one shoulder, a black mantle trimmed in purple. Julia wore a long purple gown that showed off the taller paladin's curves.

Everyone raised their glass and took a sip. I simply pretended to drink mine.

Only one person collapsed, a rabbit beastfolk wearing Peldeep-style robes. His friends cursed, and there was a minute lost while they argued over which antidote would work on the unfortunate fellow. They guessed right, and the beastman survived. He nodded apology to the room.

Calisto continued, used to these kinds of interruptions.

"Julia, you are my pride and joy. I am so pleased that you have found your other half, the woman who completes you. Let her be a companion and guide, a word of wisdom, and a lifelong friend." The duchess placed a hand on her daughter's shoulders, smiling with love. She turned to her new daughter-in-law. "And Chloe. You are my own from this day forward. I am so thankful that you are my daughter's wife, and know that we will always be here for you. We are your family."

"Thank you, Mother." Julia squeezed Chloe's hand, who was just standing there, stiff. The necromancer's face was hidden by a mask, but a slight glint betrayed tears on the small woman's face.

"I love you both, so much," Chloe whispered, even *my* perception only barely picking it up.

Julia smiled warmly at her love and lifted Chloe's hand to her lips. "May I have this dance, wife?"

Chloe's lips pulled into a flirtatious smile through the tears. "Darling, that's my line."

The crowd parted to the sides of the hall as the couple walked to the center of the dance floor. A soft note carried before the musicians played a slow song while the two began the first dance.

Julian leaned down. "Really . . . thank you."

"I only introduced them," I said, knowing exactly what he was thanking me for. "The rest was all them."

"You introduced them?"

"You didn't hear that."

Julian was about to say something when a figure rose from his shadow.

CHAPTER 58

What's a Little Kidnapping and Murder Between Neighbors?

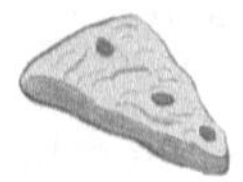

Julian

John appeared from his shadow, fully formed. "I have prevented Sir Tully from ruining the toast. No one was lit on fire."

"Excellent," Julian said, noting with amusement that his swordfighter, Jeffry, was chatting up Miss Penny opposite the hall. Jeffry was the viscount of Fell, and *never* bothered with this kind of thing. He'd completely sworn off love . . .

"What did you offer him?" he asked, curious.

"The Eye of Effeldor."

Julian kept a straight face. "Why?"

It was an impressive treasure his rogue had won during their last dungeon raid, and expensive.

"I have to admit, I'm curious too." Gerda leaned in. "That's the pin with the [Flight] perk, right?"

"It is." John's face didn't budge when he said, "The staff were prepared, but it would be best if no fire took place at all. I thought Jeffry was the best half elf for the job, and I have no need for [Flight]."

"Is that so?" Julian accepted it, but he knew better.

Jeffry hated these kinds of events with a passion—more so than Julian, even—and John wanted to see their good friend suffer because Jeffry was an insufferable know-it-all.

"Yes," John continued. "And I've confirmed that Lady Amaryllis Elm is not in attendance yet. I have issued a silent search for the saintess, and will inform you when she is found."

Gerda frowned. "Thank you, John. Could you also let Henrietta know?"

As much as the Hollow elves claimed independence, they were still a part of the Dark Enchanted Forest. Julian could only imagine the nightmare

Her Viciousness would face if something happened to Lady Amy during this event.

His rogue looked to Julian for approval, and he nodded.

"I shall. Then, if there is nothing more, I will continue guarding the event." John offered a shallow bow, but Gerda stopped him before he could leave.

"Actually, could you leave a shadow in that area of the hall to warn us of any impending homicidal archers?" Gerda pointed to a spot by the window.

"Send us," Erik offered. "We can deal with any assassins."

Gerda started to shake her head but stopped, eyeing the group of young debutants. A few held their breath, and one looked like the stars themselves were lighting up their eyes.

"Alright," she agreed. There was an exhilarated, subdued cheer. "But don't crowd the area. We want the assassin to set up and *then* get caught, not change their mind and pick a different area."

"You can trust us, Miss Gerda," Shiro replied, bowing slightly.

Gerda released Julian's arm. The bridge troll put her glass into her storage unit, and in its place, she summoned forth a potion bottle. "Here. Take a Revive and give it to anyone who might need it tonight. And keep an eye open for Lady Amy."

Shiro reached out, taking it with care. They left, just in time to join for the celebratory clap as Julia and Chloe completed their shared first dance. Julian gave John a signal, and the rogue disappeared back into his shadow.

"You just did that to give them a task, didn't you?" Julian chuckled softly; they were trying to casually walk over to the window and failing miserably.

She smiled up at him. "Yes. Though it is a perfect line of sight to where we are standing."

"What now?" He asked, "Just wait for it to happen?"

"Now, we dance," she replied, holding out her hand.

Julian took it readily, drawing her out to the dance floor. Other couples took up spots beside them.

"I'll admit, I didn't think we would actually get to dance," he said as his arm wrapped around her waist and his other hand carefully cupped her palm in a prepared stance. "What with an assassin to foil and a saintess to find."

"It's hard to use my powers here, so we might as well." Gerda's eyes met his, a light glimmer in their depths. "And you *did* sign your name for this song."

"True."

"Besides," she added, "I'm under the impression that this is the norm at North Sumbrian balls. What's a little kidnapping and murder between neighbors?"

"Also true."

The drum started a soft beat, and they both took a step into the music, which carried them up the hall with the other couples. Her body fit against his, and she followed his lead without hesitation. She smelled like the forest, a compliment to her soft green coloring. He felt a deep sense of satisfaction that they were wearing matching outfits . . . and wondered how he could add green accents for next time.

Not that there would be a next time, but as the duke, it was perfectly acceptable that he accompanied her as a representative of North Sumbria in future events.

He already knew she had an invitation to the Fall Ball and the Winter Feast.

"After the dance is over, let's slip away." He pulled her closer for a moment, and Gerda looked up at him with enquiring brown eyes. "I have a private room set aside."

"Okay." She nodded. Her movements were a bit stiff. It took a few steps for her to relax, and he dipped them into a turn at the end of the hall. They circled back the way they came, moving around the dance floor. At the other end, Julian lifted one hand to send the troll spinning out. Her long green hair lifted in an arc, and her skirts brushed against his tights. He brought her back into an embrace, then continued their dance back down the hall.

Her breath caught, and her cheeks flushed against white freckles. Despite the threat of danger, Gerda was smiling openly, clearly enjoying herself. They were able to go another turn around the floor, and by the end, he was fighting a grin as well.

When the music signaled a close, he spun her dramatically into his embrace, catching her and stopping with the final note of the song.

"That was fun." He promptly dropped his arms and took a step back. He adjusted his vest, pretending like his heart wasn't pounding wildly.

"Yes." She snapped open her fan and fluttered it for a cool breeze. "It was."

They'd stopped close enough to the exit he was aiming for, and it was a short walk to the open doorway. The hall beyond had a number of break rooms and the washrooms at the end. Julian had claimed one of the private rooms for his own as soon as he'd found out that he was going to be escorting his bridge troll.

He was thankful he did.

Pushing open the door to a small lounge with a couch and table, there was a jug of fresh water infused with mint and cranberries on a table with a few crystal glasses at the ready, and a tray of light snacks.

Julian tapped his foot on his shadow thrice, letting John know that he would go in alone.

[I'll return if I get word.]

John sent the message over [Shadow Chat], and then he was gone.

Julian closed the door and immediately went over to pour himself a glass, downing half of it while Gerda took a seat on the couch. She shook her head when he lifted up a second glass to offer her some as well, continuing to fan herself.

"Before we go on," Julian said, taking a seat next to the troll, "there's something that I'm curious about."

"What?" She stiffened but didn't pull away.

"It was the way you explained your prophecy earlier . . ." He hesitated. "You said that if you weren't my partner, then I would get shot."

"Yes?" Gerda snapped the fan shut and lowered it into her lap. "And?"

He searched her eyes. "You were already my partner when you got the notification . . . So why did you think the prophecy assumed otherwise?"

CHAPTER 59

A Very Handsome Wallflower

Gerda

One of the things I enjoyed as Madame Potts was a degree of separation between myself and the story.

I could change things; I could make a difference . . . but always from the comfort of my kitchen table.

Even when I was interacting with the main characters, Gerda the Bridge Troll wasn't a character that showed up in the storyline, and she wasn't accounted for in the scenarios. The times I'd come close to a scenario before this could be counted on one hand: the time I'd helped rescue the Dark Lord in distress, and recently, when I'd rescued Julia.

The bridge battle didn't count because it, again, had been in response to an oracle. Fate had seen fit to show me the assassination battle in the eastern woods, so I'd decided to hold off the army. I'd acted entirely on my own accord to stop the army in their tracks on my bridge, without Fate to guide me.

And I'd rocked it, if I did say so myself.

Which was why it took me a second to really think about Julian's question.

"Because I don't show up in prophecies . . . It's just never happened?" I said delicately.

He leaned toward me, and the way he was looking at me made my toes curl. Intense and curious. "Never?"

I shook my head, resisting the urge to seek the comfort of distance, but the nervousness I had wasn't fear but excitement. I held my ground. "Never."

His gaze fell to my lips at my answer, and I instinctively licked them.

Why did he have to be so pretty? It was a personal triumph that I'd gotten to dance with the half elf, but anything else would just be wild imagination. Granted, I had a pretty unhinged imagination.

I didn't know what to make of that, and reminded myself that I shouldn't be outright flirting with the duke of the North . . .

"I brought you here because you said you can't use your abilities in the ballroom, but can you use them here? Or would you like to join the search for Lady Amy yourself?" he asked.

"If John raises the alarm, then I'm gone," I told him. "But I don't want to burst in on her debutante adventure. Besides"—I lowered my voice conspiratorially—"she's found someone she likes. What if they're off having some romantic picnic in the garden and I jump on top of them? I'll wait."

"Why does it feel like you're not telling me something?"

"Well, there is one thing . . . I think Lady Amy might be having an affair with your assassin." I casually dropped my suspicion.

Julian stared at me.

"What?" I asked innocently. "I mean, I could tell you that the Herald of Void is currently leaving the Dark Enchanted Forest after narrowly escaping a stoneskin wombat? Or that Julia is going to run off with Chloe tonight and travel to the Empire of Sands on a secret honeymoon trip where no one can find and disturb them. Or maybe you're referring to the meteor—"

He stood. "Julia is *what*?"

I pulled him back down. He didn't resist. "Oh, let your sister have some fun. She deserves it."

He put a hand over mine, trapping it.

"That's everything, so you can stop with the smolder!" I told him, pulling my hand free. "You want to know more, then close your eyes."

He raised an eyebrow.

"I don't want you *staring* at me while I work," I told him, and he raised both hands in surrender before closing his eyes.

He had an annoyingly satisfied smile plastered on his face. I wanted to squeeze his cheeks. Where did my grumpy duke of the North go?

Instead, I opened my map.

[You have activated the Perk: **Map**. A mini map revealing the areas
you have explored is available . . .]

[Sooth Area] showed me where scenarios were going to happen, and it highlighted the ballroom only. I wished that Lady Amy was a chosen, as it would be so much easier to track her.

Sadly, she was the saintess of a dungeon, not a god.

[Oracle] was useless, since the only scenario I'd not watched was the pirate battle—and Pirate Abra was currently looting the south coast of Sumbria, so it wouldn't help to check on it now. Still, I decided to try rewatching what happened at the ball, in case I missed something last time. I stored my fan, clenched my fist in my lap, and leaned back to get comfortable.

"This will take five minutes." I told Julian, "Don't look at me until it's done."

Bracing myself, I activated Julia's scenario a second time.

It was four and a half minutes of Julia and Chloe greeting guests, dodging a [Fireball] and broken glass, and then Chloe's reminder that they would be gone by midnight for their honeymoon.

I came out of it with a bit less struggle than this morning. Watching the same oracle was like waking from a recurring nightmare. You still had the nightmare, but the familiarity of it made it easier to distance oneself from the grip.

"Gerda?" Julian still had his eyes closed, but his voice was laced with concern.

I took deep, ragged breaths until the shaking stopped. "We'll have to check back at midnight and see if any new scenarios are ready. Though I did see you—"

"Is it always like this?" he asked, opening his silver eyes and blinking twice before looking on me with worry.

"What can I say? Seeing the future is hard." I played it off with a light shrug, but he didn't look convinced.

"If you could see me," he asked slowly, "then what about yourself?"

"I barely caught a glimpse of the top of your head over the crowd," I explained. "So no."

"Can you only see the future once a day?"

He was prying.

"One ability is like that." Since we were going to be traveling together soon, I corrected. "I have a perk which let me know you were going to be shot, remember?"

"And now, we're back to that. Shall I go and get it over with?" Julian stood and offered me a hand. "We should at least be there for the unmasking."

I took his hand and let him pull me to my feet. "Before we go, is John's shadow with us?"

Julian frowned. "No . . . Why?"

Damn his low voice and striking eyes. If I didn't know any better, I'd swear he was trying to seduce me.

"I just want to know what kind of poison is in my drink." I held up my hand and summoned my glass from storage. "[Appraise] isn't working, so it must be hidden with a powerful perk."

He started in surprise, then his mood darkened. "Since when?"

I shrugged. "It wasn't poisoned from the start. It happened right before the toast."

He cursed and said, "Let's go back."

I decided to keep holding the glass, for show. We returned with some time to spare before the unmasking, and Julian brought us to check in with Calisto first. John was standing with the grand duchess.

"There you are!" Calisto tsked. "Henrietta wanted you to know we found Lady Amy."

Relief washed over me.

"Already?" Julian squeezed my hand and shot John a questioning look.

"Just now," he explained.

"The saintess is over there." Calisto pointed toward a couple. I wouldn't have been able to tell, since the elf had changed her skin color to gold and her hair to black. The person she was dancing with was also a mystery in green satin.

"Thank the gods." That was one less thing to worry about.

"Yes. A guard found her with a young man in a hidden alcove in the east wing." The duchess snorted. "Ah, to be young again."

"Her father is going to be furious," I said. I'd promised I wouldn't reveal her tryst . . . but Henrietta had made no such vow.

"He'll get over it." Duchess Calisto smiled. "After this dance, we're going to do the unmasking." Calisto herself was wearing an elegant dark-blue feathered mask.

"In the meantime, John, could you come tell me what this is?" Julian plucked my drink out of my hand and waved it.

The man glanced at it. "Belladonna powder."

Grand Duchess Calisto frowned. "That's a legal poison."

"The joy of being Madame Potts: my first official assassination attempt." I shrugged. "Speaking of, Julian was supposed to get shot soon, so we were thinking of moving to a harder-to-reach spot."

"Son, why haven't you put up a shield?" the grand duchess inquired.

"Because it is rude to push people aside with a magical [Barrier] they can't see?" Julian summoned a shield around both of us, and the dome stuck out at an awkward arc, pushing against Calisto's dress. "And with a personal shield, I wouldn't be able to hold Miss Gerda's hand."

He drew me closer, and I let him. I did tease him with a quick, "I could go and dance with Erik or Sir Tully and leave you to stand in the corner with your barrier up. You'd make a very handsome wallflower, Your Grace."

His mother choked.

"You flatter me, but I think I'll just enjoy a walk around the hall and another dance. *Without* the [Barrier]." His shield faded away. "It's meant for the battle-field, not the ballroom."

"Have fun, you two," Calisto told us. "Rowen has almost finished speaking with their son, and I'm going to claim a dance before the reveal."

We found a quiet spot in a corner, tucked out of the way so we could watch the unmasking without being in the thick of things. Lady Amy's date was still my number one suspect, so I positioned myself between him and the duke.

And then, the music stopped. Couples left the dance floor, the clock tower chimed the hour, and a hum of excitement arose.

"Maybe you should shield up for the unmasking?" I recommended. "You know, just in case."

"If that is your wish." He activated a shield around each of us as Grand Duchess Calisto announced we should take off our disguises. I simply unequipped my mask and put it in my storage ring.

Julian did the same.

Nothing happened.

Exhilarated from escaping another near fate, I asked, "Wanna go grab a bite to eat?"

The waiters walked around with drinks, but there was a table of finger foods in the corner that I'd been hesitating to visit, in case of poison. Luckily, John was nearby, and I felt comfortable eating things if he could verify them.

"After you, Miss Gerda." Julian dropped the shield and waved me forward.

"Maybe you should keep your shield up, and I'll grab our plates?" I told him. He hesitated only a second before accepting.

He stood beside the wall while I grabbed each of us cured meats, three different cheeses, and a roasted rosemary-and-garlic phyllo pastry square that smelled *heavenly*, adding a flower-cut strawberry as well. When I turned around to show Duke Julian my selection, I felt it: the feeling of magic in the air; the subtle electricity of power.

My [Sense Danger] activated, warning me too late as a bolt of cold iron shot directly into my heart from a human standing right beside me. He had an adorably small crossbow in hand that had let loose the offending arrow which pierced my chest . . .

Or that should have.

CHAPTER 60

Is This Your Bed?

Julian

When Julian came to, the first thing he saw was Gerda's lovely face inches from his own.

Something wasn't right. He was lying on a soft bedspread; they weren't in the ballroom anymore. There was a wooden ceiling overhead, and a window nearby let in the light of the evening sun, casting a halo around his bridge troll.

She wore a complicated expression full of worry. Unthinkingly, he reached up and tucked her hair behind one very long ear. There was blood on her hair; probably his own. Hopefully his own.

"I'm alright," he wheezed. Julian questioned whether he was, in fact, alright. His chest was on fire, and he could feel himself bleeding through his clothes, not to mention his lungs weren't working very well. He felt like he was dying. Again.

Gerda pulled back, looking him over. "You don't *look* alright. Did I use the Revive wrong? Why—Oh!" She summoned a healing potion, ripped off the stopper, and shoved it down his throat.

He coughed violently when the liquid didn't go down properly, but the pain in his chest stopped.

Gerda finally gave a relieved sigh and put the now empty bottle back in her storage. "Okay, that should do it. Sorry, I should've used a Resurrect . . . I might have panicked."

She looked down at him sheepishly.

"It's fine," he said, the first thing that came to mind. She was leaning over him again, and he couldn't sit up until she gave him space. To distract himself, he decided now would be a good time to glance at his notification logs.

[**Guard** has activated. Transferring attack.]
[You have successfully redirected damage.]
[You have been hit by a **Cold Iron Bolt**. Critical Hit 1000 points
piercing damage.]
[Warning! Vital organ failure. You are dead.]
[You have been **Revived**. Health 110/1274.]
[You have the condition **Bleed**.]
[You suffer 20 points **Bleed** damage. Health 90/1274.]
[Warning! Your Health has dropped below 7%.
Rest recommended.]
[You suffer 20 points **Bleed** damage. Health 70/1274]
[You have been healed with **Greater Health Potion**. Health 1070.
Bleed effect negated.]

"Everything happened so fast," Gerda was talking to him as he read. "I didn't know what else to do."

He glanced at her as she pulled out a spell scroll. "[Cleanse]."

The spell removed the stains, magicking away the traces of his death. Except for the giant tear in his shirt, of course.

"Where are we?" Julian closed his system window and pushed into a sitting position.

They were in a small, comfortable bedroom. The bed was lush with soft covers and copious decorative pillows. There were paintings of the Dark Enchanted Forest on the wall with a door, and another was entirely covered in bookshelves full of books, knickknacks, and plants.

The opposite wall was curved out to make space for a cushioned bench below three large windows with green and white curtains. Even more pillows adorned the bench.

"My home," Gerda replied, pulling out another scroll.

"Your—Your home? You brought me to your house?" Julian immediately felt overconscious. "Is this *your bed?*"

"I couldn't very well portal us onto the sky bridge," she said, matter-of-factly. "[Mend]."

His clothing ruffled and tugged all over his body, repairing itself. The tear disappeared as if it had never happened. Though he was still a bit ruffled, he at least looked like he'd not been dead.

Julian gently touched his chest, feeling nothing out of the ordinary but still sensing a phantom pain. It should fade quickly, as these things usually did for him.

"Why *not* the bridge?" Julian asked. It would have been easier to clean up the mess and less destructive to Gerda's bed.

It was a nice bed.

He needed to not be lying on it because that trail of thought was sudden and unexpected and too much for him right now. Julian swung his legs over the side; they tangled with Gerda's skirt, and her hair fell on his thighs. It wasn't the biggest space, and Gerda was very, very close.

She tossed her wavy tresses over her shoulder and out of the way, but since she was looking down at him, the strands slipped forward again.

"I didn't know if there were other assassins in the palace. Better safe than sorry." She gave up on her hair and put the back of her hand against his forehead, nodding in approval at his stable temperature.

She then moved to fix his collar.

"You made a strange noise before collapsing." She continued touching him, focused on setting things right and not noticing he was holding his breath. "Shame about my pastries, though; I dropped them to catch you—There we go."

She stepped back and looked him over. "Good as new. Let me know when you're ready, and I'll bring us back."

Julian couldn't help it; a short laugh escaped him.

"What?" The bridge troll crossed her arms.

"Are you sure you *want* to go back?" Julian reached out and took hold of a long section of emerald hair. It pleased him to see her blush from her neck to the tips of her ears because it proved that he wasn't the only one affected.

He lifted the lock of hair in front of her. It was wet with blood.

She cursed aloud. "One second."

She pulled out another spell scroll.

"How many of those do you have?" he asked, curious. They were expensive to make but very handy.

"A hundred? Two?" Gerda shrugged. "[Cleanse]."

"You have *two hundred* [Cleanse] spell scrolls?"

"Not all of them are spelled," she explained. "I pick them up in treasure chests all the time, and it's fun collecting cantrips—I mean, *useful*. It's *useful* having all these spells ready to go. Case in point." She waved to indicate his chest. Speaking of which . . .

"Where is the cold iron arrow?" It was nowhere to be seen.

"I took it out before I healed you. It's in my storage, but I'm not pulling it out now. I just cleaned up."

"I thought we could use it to track the assassin," Julian explained. It would be easy work for his rogue as long as they had something to connect back to the archer.

"No need. I already know who it is—and so does your mother." Gerda shook her head and sighed. "Honestly, I'm more worried about Amy."

"The saintess?"

"As I thought, the man she's seeing turned out to be the assassin . . . and, um, you weren't his target; I was." She scratched her cheek. "Sorry."

"The same one who poisoned your drink?" Julian didn't mind a little death in her place, but if she was going to be so often attacked, then he had his own apologies to make.

The bridge troll shook her head again. "I don't know. Your mother said the poison was legal . . . so I bet someone's put out a hit on my head, and every registered assassin in the duchy is out to get the experience points for killing me."

"I'm sorry. You never would've been exposed as Madame Potts if you hadn't saved my family." His hands clenched. Desire warred with his etiquette, but what was the polite thing to do when he woke up in the bed of the most beautiful troll he'd ever met?

He couldn't just kiss her.

"It's fine; I was already on the Blackfog list. And I'll be safe in the North before we know it." She smiled at him reassuringly. It sent his blood racing.

He rose to his feet.

Worried and aroused, his voice dropped low as he leaned in close enough to feel her breath on his chin when he asked, "But how long are you in the North? What about guarding your bridges?"

Gerda stared at his lips as she bit her own.

He also wanted to bite her lips. He wanted to pull her with him onto the bed behind him, straddling his lap, and kiss the bridge troll silly.

CHAPTER 61

I Don't Want to Break Your Bed

Gerda

Calm your pants, Gerda.

The room, *my room*, was a cozy space that I'd made to my taste. In the process of reviving the duke, I hadn't noticed how small it really was. Now, Julian was standing so close that I could feel my gown catching on his legs and my long hair brushing against him.

But as much as I wanted to push Julian back onto my bed and have my way with him . . . that would be a bad life choice.

Instead, I said, "For one, I only need to reach the Northern Fortress so I can connect my home to your drawbridge. Then it won't matter if I pop out a few times a day to give out riddles."

"How do you know my fortress has a drawbridge?" Julian asked, that same small smile tempting me.

I put my hands on my hips. "I'm Madame Potts, remember?"

The best excuse for all of my game lore.

"And you're still going to pop out on any bridge in the Dark Enchanted Forest with a traveler even knowing assassins are after you?" His brow furrowed.

"Yes," I replied, crossing my arms. It put an extra barrier between me and my unfairly attractive guest. "I highly doubt any normal assassin is going to get me while I'm on my own bridge. I look forward to the challenge." I hadn't needed to go all out since the Bridge Battle. It would be fun to see what tricks the assassins' guilds had up their sleeve.

Julian relaxed his stance. "Alright then, if you're sure?"

"Sure as sure." Even the fact that he accepted I could take care of myself made me like him. Gah. "I've faced entire armies. Worst case, I portal away and take the loss."

I wasn't going to tell him that in the real worst-case scenario, I had a ring full of magical items to fall back on.

So many overpowered endgame items; from my legendary set to potions to my two phoenix tail feathers. Once equipped, a phoenix tail feather replaced any death with [Reborn], bringing someone back to full power. I could only equip one at a time, so it wasn't foolproof should I get killed twice in a row—but I'd just try to portal out before anyone noticed my revival.

"Besides, I wouldn't be a bridge troll if I didn't properly toll all of my bridges," I added, ignoring the fact I'd neglected to pop out and face any of the fifty-three people who'd crossed my bridges today.

Hey, I was still on vacation.

"We will have to make a plan." Julian reached out to grab a lock of my now clean hair that was touching his arm and played with it with his fingers. "So my party members know what to expect when you suddenly disappear."

Alright, it was too much for me to handle that level of fan service.

Taking a step back, my hair gently fell from his palm. The reading-nook bench pressed up against my heel, so I couldn't back up anymore, but even this small amount of space made it easier.

"That's tomorrow Gerda's problem," I said. He laughed at the phrase, genuinely amused. Before he could speak, I continued. "For now, I think it's time we get back to the ball."

Julian flinched. "My mother is probably worried."

"Yes."

"Alright." He looked pained to say it but drew himself up and offered me his arm. "How do we get back?"

"You should reactivate your shield first," I told him.

"We'll have to stand closer," he replied. "There isn't much room in here, and I don't want to break your bed."

I bit my lip to stop myself from saying what I wanted to. It took all my willpower, but I held it in.

We came together, and as I took his offered arm, I felt the shield go up.

"Alright, hold on," I said, activating my perk as I took a small step back. "[World Bridge]."

I made my selection. There was a pull, and the room faded away as we walked onto the sky bridge in the Coral Palace.

No one shot at us, but there was a welcome waiting.

"Your Grace. Miss Gerda." Lord Johnathon stood with three knights. "The grand duchess is awaiting you."

You Are in Fate's Story

Julian

"Ah, perfect, you're back," his mother greeted them as Julian escorted Gerda, arm in arm, into another private room just off of the main ballroom. The music of the masquerade could be heard a short distance away, the dancing and merriment in full swing and undisturbed by their absence.

"Mother."

Gerda asked. "You called for us, Your Grace?"

"I did." His mother was standing in the middle of the room, all of the furniture pushed aside. She was interacting with her abilities, her hands up in the air and her eyes darting back and forth at an unseen interface while magic swirled around her. "I trust you are both well?"

"Yes, no need to worry," Julian reassured her, ignoring the fact that he had been unalive less than half an hour ago. It wasn't his first Revive potion, so it didn't faze him much.

"I always worry, son." Her simple honesty left him uncomfortable. She followed it up with, "But perhaps less so now that you have Miss Gerda at your side."

"It isn't—" Julian started.

"He doesn't—" Gerda said at the same time.

The two of them paused and then disentangled themselves.

"I'm afraid we've had a bit of trouble since you left," Calisto spoke, her eyes never leaving her notification tabs. "Our Keeper of Fate took a walk tonight."

"From your dimensional dungeon? How?" Gerda didn't seem surprised, merely intrigued.

Julian shot her a look. For the barest second, he suspected her of *knowing* this was going to happen. She'd already made it clear that she wasn't going to share all of the details of her foretellings . . . but his heart told him that the troll *wouldn't* have let the celestial escape if she could prevent it . . . and she would have told him.

"Someone let her out." Calisto pinched her thumb and index finger together then opened them wide in quick succession three times on her interface.

Julian pulled the key out of his storage.

Gerda noticed and asked, "Is there more than one key?"

"I have one," Calisto replied. "And Knight Commander Karl. He's the one who let me know that she'd escaped."

Karl was an honorable, trustworthy half elf in charge of the Coral Mare Knights, but Julian knew the full weight of Alice's powers. "Did he let her out himself?"

"No," Calisto replied simply. "An invisible mage bypassed the guard and cut a hole into the subspace with a specialized Void power. Miss Alice walked out, and the pair teleported away."

"Where?" Julian asked, knowing that the teleport restrictions were especially layered in that area of the coral palace.

"She went to the stairwell lobby, then appeared in the servants' hall, then I'm assuming into a private room, and then to the east wing sky bridge, the herb garden, the wall, and then into the city," his mother explained, unhappy. "It's the *how* that frustrates me."

"The ball is *crawling* with rogues; any one of them could have let her go," Gerda offered.

"Few are so powerful that they can break into a dimensional space—let alone *my* dimensional space," Calisto said. For the first time, her eyes flickered from her task, briefly landing on his bridge troll. "It's fortunate that you were accounted for all evening, Miss Gerda."

"It is." Gerda nodded, unintimidated.

"We have a few people we are investigating." Calisto sighed as she closed her character sheets, waving them away with a soft gesture of her hand. She looked calm and collected, but his mother's voice betrayed her aggravation. "Which is just *lovely*, as I now have until tomorrow to figure out the culprit and tell the Continental Council how I lost her."

Julian asked after his first suspect. "Did Master Thomas let her out?"

"It couldn't be Master Thomas," Gerda interjected.

"Why not? I haven't seen him all night." Which meant she couldn't have seen him either.

"Thomas is . . . um, busy. With important magical matters," Gerda sidestepped the question. This after he'd *just* convinced himself she wasn't hiding anything important.

"I'll need more than that," Julian demanded, his voice harsher than he wanted it to be. Gerda could turn on him in an instant for overstepping, and the thought twisted a knot in his stomach.

Her eyes snapped to his, and he regretted it. She looked like she was trying to hide her frustration with him and failing. To his surprise, she grumbled a response.

"If you *must* know, he's off saving Valaria. Or preparing to, at least."

"Valaria needs saving . . . and you trust *Master Thomas* to save it?" He couldn't believe that. The mage was insufferable.

"Valaria *always* needs saving." Gerda scoffed. "From pirate attacks to dungeon breaks to political uprisings . . . Why do you think I started Madame Potts's Casts? My skills let me know who's the best for the job, and I poke them—which is why I'm leaving the world-ending disasters to the mage. Unless you know a better master-elemental, high-tier magic-circle user?"

"Miss Gerda, I believed you when you told us yesterday that interfering with Master Thomas would have dire consequences for my home and my son," Calisto spoke quietly; they both turned to face her. "But you *cannot* tell us that there will be a *continental* catastrophe and expect me *not* to inform the *Continental Council.*"

The bridge troll's shoulders tensed. "That is why I didn't want to say anything."

"Why did you?" The words escaped him.

She looked at him with exasperation. "Because you asked."

That hit him hard, and he had to look away for a second to calm the warring feelings inside.

His mother spoke firmly. "I am speaking to you with all due respect and consideration when I ask you, Miss Gerda, as the grand duchess of North Sumbria and a representative of the Continental Council tasked with keeping safe and secure all of Valaria—what is your official report on Master Thomas and his current course of action?"

"*Master Thomas must be left alone to complete his current work, or a great calamity will befall Valaria,*" Gerda stated firmly, invoking her fortune-telling Madame Potts's voice. She added in her normal voice, "He *really* didn't do well with others in his space or interfering with his work—even when that interference was trying to *help.* That route had a bad ending in season one. Has your Mistborn Wand been stolen?"

Julian looked to his mother for the answer. Calisto frowned. "Was that young Master Thomas?"

"See, you've already helped him." Gerda tried to make light of the theft. "If he managed to steal Mistborn *without* Henrietta's help, he's well on his way to completing his master spell circle, and we really should just leave him alone."

"Until his task is complete, you say?" His mother smiled in such a way that made Julian want to run. He didn't, though, of course; he wasn't ten years old anymore. "And then there is nothing stopping me from having a long, polite chat with the young man?"

"Yes," Gerda confirmed.

"Someone should inform the mage about what is expected of him as a standing member of the Continental Council. Thoroughly."

"Can you chastise him after Feliwyn wakes up?" Gerda asked.

His mother considered the troll before nodding. "I can."

"Thank you." Miss Gerda smiled softly. "By then, everything *should* be complete. I haven't been paying much attention to Servalt since the rains were going strong, but that is as it should be; I *hate* walking in the rain."

Julian asked after something she'd said earlier. "Are your visions of the future *also* limited to the seasons of the year?"

"Sort of," the troll replied. "I am shown things about certain people and upcoming world-changing events. Since I'm not in the storyline myself, I can try to force a different path."

"But you *are* in Fate's story," Julian countered. Gerda looked at him as he tapped a finger to his chest. "You foretold that I would be shot—and I was, redirecting the arrow from *your* own heart."

Gerda's casual demeanor cracked, her eyes locking on his chest in uncertainty and confusion. And a touch of fear. Her hands flinched, and then she firmly fisted them in her skirts.

"I guess I went too far this time . . ."

Julian felt a twist in his stomach. She'd been outed as Madame Potts while helping his family, and that was going to change everything for the troll. It might be too late to go back now, but he would be here to assist her in any way he could.

He told himself it was because he still owed Gerda . . . but he knew it was just an excuse.

And Julian wanted any excuse.

CHAPTER 63

Ask for a Favor from the Nice Bridge Troll

Gerda

Five years ago, I had to make the most important decision I would have to face after waking up as Gerda. I'd set out to change the story—but kept myself separate from it.

I was not supposed to be here, and I was not going to draw attention to that. Aside from visiting one temple—and getting no response to my questions—I'd stayed at home in my bridge. That meant no daring adventures with my favorite characters, no fixing things by my own hand, and limited Casts. I would be an outside guiding force toward everyone else's happily ever after.

Julian and his stupidly handsome face had made me overstep further than I should have, and here we were.

"If you look at it objectively," the object of my desire said, offering a small silver lining. "You can see your own future now."

I reached up with one trembling hand and swept a stray lock of hair behind my ear. "Not unless one of the gods' chosen is going to be standing around staring at me all day."

His brow knit together as he watched me, but before he could reply, there was a knock on the door.

The grand duchess called in a familiar elf knight dressed in red and silver. "The prisoner is secure, Your Grace."

"Thank you, Karl." Calisto walked to the door and looked over her shoulder at me and her son. "Why don't you two go enjoy the rest of your evening while *I* handle Alice?"

"Have you recaptured her *already*?" I asked, shocked and impressed.

"If only," Calisto replied. "No, we've captured your assassin, and I'm going to go review his paperwork."

"Ah . . . How is Lady Amy?" I made a note to make time for the elf saintess before I left . . . A note I'd made many times already and utterly failed to follow through with.

Why was it so hard juggling the future and friendship?

"She was curled up with Slake Drakeford in a resting room last I checked." The duchess said, then bid us farewell, leaving me alone with Julian.

"So . . ." he said, suddenly shortening the distance between us. I caught my breath but stayed where I was. His voice spoke with a casual air I didn't think was *quite* right for our current situation. "Where would you like me to escort you next?"

Julian raised an eyebrow, waiting for my decision. I wondered what he would do if I grabbed him by the collar and stole a kiss—something for all the trouble he was putting me through.

Instead, I reached out and wrapped my arms around his, surprising him. Good. Against my wishes, I told the duke of the North, "Why don't you drop me off with Lady Amy and you follow the grand duchess? I might have been the target, but *you* suffered the assassin's final blow. I'm sure you have questions."

"Are you sure?" he asked, gently resting a hand on mine, holding them tight as they shook just ever so slightly.

I nodded, not trusting my voice.

It was a short walk to find Lady Amy. Duke Julian asked one of the royal guards stationed in the hall, and they pointed to three doors down, closer to the ballroom.

When we arrived, Julian reminded me, "You promised me the last dance, Miss Gerda, and I am going to hold you to it." He reached out and knocked twice on the door, opening it when a muffled sound called out. I found myself standing in a room with Lady Amy sitting on a chair with a grimalcat on her lap, Julian closing the door behind me.

Amy looked apologetic that she couldn't stand to greet me. "Miss Gerda."

Slake rolled over in the elf's lap, showing Amy his tummy while eyeing me. "Madame Potts."

Lady Amy momentarily bit her lip before tentatively resting a hand on the soft belly. She held her breath. I held my breath. She let out a sigh when he didn't immediately maul her.

"I just came to check in and see how you were handling things." I walked over to take the seat across from them.

Lady Amy moved her hand up into the tuft of fluff between Slake's front legs, scratching as he purred happily. The elf's shoulders dropped. "I'm sorry. I should have warned you, but I thought . . . I don't know what I thought."

"I mean, I'm not angry. I know life and death in this world are treated more . . . *casually* than I'm used to, but I'm an elite now." I leaned back in my chair, showing my lack of very real concern.

"Do you forgive me?" Lady Amy looked up at me with anxious eyes, but at least she was looking at me.

"Of course. Do *you* forgive *me*?" At her confused look, I added, "This is your first foray into society, and I don't think Henrietta or I were very good friends. We should have been there for you, to offer advice and keep you out of trouble."

"What—No! You've been—Ouch!" The grimalcat bit her hand hard enough to draw blood. "Slake!"

"Ask for a favor." Slake licked the blood off the elf girl's hand, his eyes glowing a soft green. "From the nice bridge troll."

As expected from an intelligent grimalcat . . . the soul-eating feline creature of darkness was an expert in the proper way of things.

"Gerda is my friend, Slake, and we are *both* apologizing. She could just as quickly ask *me* for a favor. And then, where would we be?" Lady Amy turned her hand over and scratched under his chin, seemingly unconcerned by the fact that he'd just consumed her blood.

I was concerned, but I didn't really know enough about grimalcats to say anything; maybe he'd just imparted power to the elf, or maybe he ate only a tiny piece of her soul, or maybe he was just a cat whose eyes glowed.

Grimalcat lore wasn't a focus in my *Dungeon Delves and Debutantes* playthroughs.

"You would be two powerful Nilheim elite who owe each other a favor." Slake stood up, balancing on Amy's lap perfectly. His tail flicked once before he jumped down. Looking over his shoulder at the pair of us, he licked a paw. "Think on it."

With that, the door opened for him, and Slake walked out, not looking back.

"You know," I stated, "it wouldn't be the end of the world if you asked me for a favor."

Amy's eyes snapped to mine as she straightened in her chair and rushed to say, "Really? Then, could you use the Foretell Fate perk you used on Cassandra to tell me who *my* fated mate is?"

Those bright, shining eyes stabbed at me as my own hubris proved my undoing.

CHAPTER 64

To Actually Kiss Her

Julian

"Your Grace."

Visha appeared in the hallway beside Julian. She was her usual professional self, though he noticed she looked him up and down in a not-so-subtle side-eye.

She must have heard he was attacked.

"Is it that time?" Julian looked back at the door he'd just come from and sighed. "You can finish up for the rest of the evening. I think we're done for tonight."

Visha nodded curtly. "Then, if there is nothing else, I will see you tomorrow."

She walked off down the hallway toward the ball. Julian had half expected the elf to go to bed, but instead, she marched toward the music with a purpose.

"Hm." He wondered where she was headed. After another look at the door to Lady Amy's room, Julian decided that moving wouldn't hurt as long as he was in sight of the door. He casually followed behind his second-in-command.

While she entered the hall, Julian stopped to lean against the frame of the doorway.

Visha walked straight over to the food table, where Sir Tully was eating pinpin fruit from a small plate he was holding. The fruits were pink, small, and round, and popped with a single bite. Visha slapped Sir Tully on the back, causing the human to startle and pop juice on his chin. He turned on the elf, wiping his face with his sleeve. Tully said something that made Visha chuckle, and then the elf reached out and stole one of the pinpin fruit off the paladin's plate, plopping it in her mouth.

Tully put his plate down and dragged the seemingly unwilling Visha onto the dance floor for a song.

"Hm," he hummed again, pushing off the wall and walking back up the hall-way. That was unexpected . . . or maybe it wasn't. Julian wasn't a romantic. Every member of his party could've been in love, and he wouldn't have noticed a longing glance or heated look if it had happened right in front of his face . . . until now.

Now, it was all he could think about. Every small action, kind gesture, or physical touch had him second-guessing himself. He'd even sent Visha to set up and guard the resting room tonight. He'd made *General Visha Hemsworth*, one of his most trusted allies, prepare infused water and homemade poison-free treats on the *chance* that Miss Gerda would like a break from the ball.

Something was wrong with him.

Julian returned to Lady Amy's room and waited. He didn't care about the assassin, he was more worried about his bridge troll. He'd already activated [Guard] on Gerda a second time, and Julian stopped bothering to pretend like he only did all of these things because he felt guilty.

He just wanted to do things for the troll.

"Julian?" Gerda opened the door, interrupting his thoughts. She hurried to close it behind her.

"Are you finished?" he asked, pitching his voice so only she could hear.

"I am." Gerda glanced over her shoulder at the door and sighed. "I think she'll be fine. Though I had to get a bit . . . creative."

"How so?" Julian pushed aside his inner turmoil. Listening to her was more interesting than his own indecision.

"I used one of my powers that doesn't work very well these days." She clenched her hands in her skirts, so Julian scooped one arm into his own and started walking them back toward the music.

"Oh?" he urged her to continue.

Gerda explained. "One of my abilities can be used on anyone at any time . . . but it doesn't show me what's going to happen to them next; it shows me the dif-ferent futures they might've had if I hadn't changed everything."

"Ah." He squeezed the hand resting on his arm and pulled her to a clear spot against the wall, close to the dancers but far from the others mingling on the sidelines. "Not very helpful when you've done so much?"

She followed his lead.

Lady Amy wanted to know whom she should be with to get a Happily Ever After, so I looked into what Lady Amy would've been up to if she wasn't here, now, and falling in love . . . and it wasn't pretty." Gerda's voice was full of frustra-tion, angry at a timeline that had never come to pass.

Julian waved away a servant offering them drinks, having had enough poison attempts for one evening. He could pull out his own beverage if need be. "Seeing the future doesn't mean you can guarantee a perfect partner, even if you *could* see the best future for her."

"I told Lady Amy that if she follows the path set out by her father, she will end up alone. Instead, she should follow her heart," Gerda said, looking up at the floating lights overhead. Warm light brightened her face, showing concern and care etched into her expression. "I don't know if that was the best thing to do . . . but it *felt* like the right thing to say."

"That is all you *can* do." Julian dragged his eyes away from the troll, sweeping the room to see who was still there.

King Keith and Queen Henrietta had turned in early, and so had his sister and her new wife. They might already be on their way to the Empire of Sands. The younger debutants they'd spoken with earlier, Shiro and the lot, were standing by the open doors to the patio, enjoying the cool evening air.

"Her father isn't going to like a rogue son-in-law," Julian mused. He'd met Duke Briarthorn, and the elf was as stiff as ironwood.

"Her father doesn't have a say anymore," Gerda stated firmly. "She's of age now, so he'll just have to live with her choices."

Gerda let out a long sigh before lifting her free hand, drawing Julian's attention. She was suddenly offering him a teacup. "Would you like some tea? I usually have a cup around this time; I like something warm before bed."

The image of her snuggled up in her bed, in her room, enjoying a cup of tea before turning off the light made him smile. "I'd love one." No sooner had he taken the empty cup and she was holding a pot of steaming hot tea. He let out a short breath, impressed. "Your storage keeps things hot?"

"Yes." She poured, the smell of steeped blackberry tea reaching his nose. He breathed in the warmth rising from the teacup, appreciating the scent. Her storage had to be Epic quality, at least, to keep things in perfect stasis.

He smiled and nodded when she offered him milk and honey and a tiny stir spoon. Then, she made herself a cup with just milk.

They were standing there, watching the dancing and festivities and sipping their tea, when she slowly leaned toward him, her shoulder against his arm, and said, "Thank you for escorting me tonight, Your Grace. I had a wonderful time. Assassination attempt and all."

"It wouldn't be a party without at least *one* assassination attempt," he joked, turning to face her. "And it's not over yet. You still owe me that dance."

"Do I have to wait until the last dance?"

"No," he answered, and a smile lit up her face.

"Good. Because I'm ready for bed."

She downed the last of her tea and stored it. He was holding back a laugh as he offered her his own near empty cup, which vanished. Making their way onto the floor, they enjoyed a long, slow dance. Holding Gerda in his arms was torture when he was already fighting with himself over the attraction he felt for the troll, and yet, it was even harder letting her go at the end.

It was just past sunset, the stars only beginning to light the sky, when Julian escorted her back to her room. On a whim, he lifted her hand and kissed the back of it. "Good night, Miss Gerda."

She stared at her hand and then up at him. "Good night, Duke Julian."

He wondered what it would be like to actually kiss her. Would her cute tusks get in the way? Would her freckles turn pink?

Would he be able to stop with just a kiss?

It was over all too soon. She went inside her room and closed the door, and he was left standing alone in the west wing hallway. He stuffed his hands into his pockets and walked back to his own rooms, all while his mind was a mess of one bridge troll who had turned his entire life upside down in a matter of *days*.

On another whim, Julian downed another potion and left his [Guard] up.

He didn't think he was going to get much sleep that night, anyway.

CHAPTER 65

A Menace to Society

Gerda

"Is that your official statement on the matter, Miss Gerda?" Grand Duchess Calisto asked.

I was standing in front of the Continental Council, having just explained my part in the wedding attack and the interrogation. I'd politely refused to use my powers to read the future for the council; I had a residual headache from using them this morning that made me less than charitable, and I didn't want to set a precedent.

Besides, there wasn't much to say.

Carter Watercress, the Guardian of Death, was going to hold a wake for Menlomin, king of the unicorns, later this week. If I played my cards right, I could get one of the season two's treasures during the tragedy: a unicorn's horn.

I *hated* looking in on Carter. More than anyone else, his personality and mine were the least compatible. If his scenario wasn't literally titled "The Treasure for Death," I'd have skipped. But I was an avid treasure hunter who couldn't resist completing a season without at least *trying* for a hundred percent completion.

The second one was actually the easiest. Guild Master Warren Jones, the Arbiter of Shadow, was as laid-back as they came. He was the epitome of sloth, and using [Oracle] on him just made me unnaturally chill afterward.

In Warren's, he decided to officially retire and run away while Their Royal Highness Rowen was distracted in North Sumbria. His demon contract ended on the solstice, and now that he was free, there wasn't much to stop him leaving . . . excepting, perhaps, his accidental lover, the Assistant Guild Master Gemma.

I was rooting for Gemma every step of the way.

After downing a mana potion, taking a relaxing bath, and preparing myself for the worst, I'd decided to watch a *third* oracle.

The last thing it'd revealed still left me with a grip on my heart.

It was me.

Specifically, it was me at this council meeting, and Henrietta's thoughts. The Dark Lady was standing in the far back, closest to the door. My power only allowed me to assume her future for the four and a half minutes, and it'd revealed the end to my trial.

One that I'd decided wasn't *nearly* impressive enough.

"Yes, Your Grace . . . though before I finish my statement, I have a question." I drew a deep breath and looked over the room. The official council members were the highest-level elite from each nation, but any elite was welcome to attend. And apparently, Madame Potts was interesting enough that we had a crowd.

The official council members sat, while others stood behind.

"As my hidden identity is now revealed to all and my status as an elite has been confirmed, I have been dealing with my first run of assassination attempts," I began, trying to find the right words to explain my dilemma. In the pause left for breath, Master Thomas cut in.

"As soon as you reached level sixty, you were no longer protected under the council treaty. You are as fair game a target as *any* of us here. No sense whining about it now."

Yes, *that* Master Thomas. He had shown up at council this morning as if he hadn't been one of many working behind the scenes to ruin the Summer Solstice Festival. Grand Duchess Calisto's eyebrow had twitched almost imperceptibly when he walked in . . . and I was impressed that she'd managed to keep civil.

I was not so courteous.

"Master Thomas," I retorted, deciding now would be the perfect place to finally speak my mind, on behalf of myself, Henrietta, and all. In front of our peers. "I don't know how to tell you this, but you have the social graces of an alligator dog."

The mage's mouth dropped open. Just because Thomas was integral to the plot didn't mean I had to be nice to him. My words solicited a variety of responses around the room ranging from shock to amusement.

I continued. "*Of course* I expect assassins and intrigue as befits my station. Your inability to put two nonmagical thoughts together is astonishing; I have never met another so void of humor, humility, and basic common sense."

I tried to hide the joy in my voice as I unloaded on the man. Julian, standing behind his mother, bit his lips hard enough to bleed, while Witch Agatha slapped Wizard Lorthar on the shoulder in unbridled delight.

"You *dare* speak to me this way—" Thomas slammed to his feet, knocking over his chair. There were no direct attacks allowed during council meetings, but that did not include aura. Magical pressure erupted from the mage, hitting me with the force of his rage.

"Stating the obvious will get you nowhere fast. I'm on trial, and sworn to speak the truth." Unfortunately for him, I was a few levels higher than he was, and had a handy [Mental Resistance] perk. I shrugged. "What I was *going* to say before being so *rudely* interrupted is that I don't know what to do with the bodies after each attack."

The mage stared at me like I'd grown another head.

To clarify, I added, "Do the assassin guilds have a return policy? Do I just leave them on the road? Is it my job to Revive their guild members and forward them the potion bill?"

"Sit down, Thomas." Wizard Lorthar ran a hand over his shoulder, defrosting the ice that had formed from Witch Agatha's blow. "You know that there are no challenges allowed in the council room. And I will remind you, for Miss Gerda's sake, that our laws state you must wait one rest period following the meeting before you are allowed to issue any duels."

Thomas looked like he was going to argue, but then, he was under the full weight of *Lorthar's* aura. It was brutal enough to make Thomas flinch. Even if the wizard wasn't one of the highest-level elite on the continent, Lorthar was the largest exporter of magical ingredients in Valaria, and held a treasure trove large enough to rival a dragon's. Anyone who didn't pay him respect could only live with regret.

Thomas cursed and picked up his chair. He sat and glared at me.

If looks could unalive.

Lorthar turned his attention to everyone in the room. "I think now would be an *excellent* time for everyone to review their rights and responsibilities as an elite of Valaria. As such, before the next meeting, I expect each country to send a copy of the relevant documents to *all* registered elite; *The Garen Grim Treaty, Feliwyn's Oath, Lysander's Legacy,* and *The Treaty of the Gods.*"

"Well said," Their Royal Highness broke the awkward silence that had followed Wizard Lorthar's declaration. Rowen was in the guise of an old man with black skin and gray hair pulled back at the nape of their neck. The fox turned a smile on me. "Miss Gerda, to answer your question, it is polite to return the bodies to a guild if you are able, but not necessary. Many do not."

"Thank you," I said, bowing. "Then that is all I have to say."

"Members of the Continental Council," Grand Duchess Calisto spoke at that moment. As host, she was the officiant of the meeting. "As you are aware, Miss Gerda is Madame Potts. She is standing before us today as an elite oracle, one who has dedicated her craft to preventing tragedy and giving free warnings from the shadows. She has done so by Crystal Cast without a permit, the penalty for which is fifty gold coins per infraction to each affected nation."

King Keith groaned. As an elite of the Dark Enchanted Forest, he was *technically* responsible for managing me and my misdemeanors. He'd also neglected to provide me with the appropriate paperwork after my elite registration—a point for Wizard Lorthar—and could easily be forced to pay all of my fines in the event I was unable to.

"How many times have you shared a Madame Potts's Cast?" Keith sounded like his soul was fleeing his body as he asked.

"I haven't kept track of every Cast—" I began.

Their Royal Highness cut me off. "I have."

The fox summoned a parchment that rolled over the table, across the floor, and all the way to my feet. "It wasn't consistent; sometimes once a month, and other times twice a week. I've kept a complete record of every single Cast and what was said *exactly*. There are two hundred and seven Casts so far."

"*Two hundred*—" Keith pushed up his glasses to rub the bridge of his nose.

"I would say it is unlike you to prepare this much, Rowen," Witch Agatha said dryly, knowing the fox. "But why am I not surprised?"

"You don't appreciate me," Rowen replied, snapping the roll of parchment. It rolled up again, and he passed it over to Duchess Calisto.

"Two hundred and seven Casts at fifty gold per infraction on seven countries— that is, not including Nilheim—" Calisto started, though Rowen put up a hand to stop her.

"Peldeep chooses to waive our portion of the fee," Rowen offered, "because we are not a bunch of ungrateful—"

"Now, Rowen, I was going to ask who wanted to waive their charges *after* I explained," Duchess Calisto cut them off. Which was unfortunate, because I would've *loved* to hear what insults the fox came up with. "North Sumbria is also abstaining. Anyone else?"

Calisto looked at those representing Servalt, Sumbria, Drendil, Baldorin and the Empire of Sands. When no one spoke, she continued. "Then, the fine at five countries is fifty-one thousand seven hundred and fifty gold pieces."

King Keith dropped his head into his hands. "Is that all?"

"Servalt and Sumbria have levied charges of defamation and unregistered international espionage against the troll." Calisto summoned two documents and put them on the table. "Servalt is asking for fifty gold coins and the immediate capture and restraint of Miss Gerda Jones. Sumbria is asking for five hundred gold and her execution or deliverance into their hands for just punishment."

No one spoke, though Their Royal Highness shot Master Thomas *a look*. It wasn't a nice look. I remained silent.

"All in favor of Servalt's request?"

Master Thomas and one other person put up their hands. It was an angry-looking elf sitting to the left of Thomas.

"All opposed?" Everyone else raised their hand. Calisto nodded. "All in favor of the fine?"

Everyone's hands rose again.

Master Thomas frowned. "You can't tell me the council is releasing the bridge troll? She's a menace to society!"

"We *all* are." Witch Agatha leaned back in her chair, smiling. "Why do you think this council exists?"

"The updated fine is fifty-one thousand eight hundred gold." Calisto put down one parchment and waved the second. "Now, for Sumbria. All in favor of execution?"

Only Thomas and the elf from earlier raised their hand. Everyone else opposed.

"And all in favor of five hundred gold?" Again, only the two agreed. It was an unreasonable sum.

"Madame Potts has notoriously been critical of Sumbria," Wizard Lorthar offered up a solution. He laced his hands together on the table. "Why don't we ask for two hundred gold coins? That would round up the total fine to an even fifty-two thousand."

Keith choked but held himself professional. Henrietta, seeing her husband in distress, walked over and put her hand on his shoulder. He smiled up at her, tight-lipped.

"All in favor?" Calisto asked, and everyone raised their hands. "Then, Miss Gerda, on behalf of the Valarian Continental Council, you are charged with multiple counts of treaty violation to the sum of fifty-two thousand gold coins, due by the autumn equinox. You are also expected to cease and desist all unregistered Casts until you have signed a contract with a country to use their system, and to familiarize yourself with the laws regarding your station as an elite of Valaria."

I smiled up at the duchess. "I understand."

"Your case is dismissed," Calisto declared, waving a hand at the room behind her. "You have leave to go or join us. Welcome to the Continental Council, Miss Gerda."

Thomas was furious and glowering at me now.

"Thank you, Your Grace." I smiled and added, "If it's alright, I would settle my accounts *now*."

With that, I waved a hand and dropped the entire fee amount at my feet.

CHAPTER 66

May I Introduce You to Berry-Berry

Julian

Julian spent the rest of the day fighting to keep a straight face—and losing.

The bridge troll's smug satisfaction when she'd dropped a hoard's worth of coin was *unforgettable*. Julian caught himself grinning from ear to ear every time he recalled it, and his good mood took him all the way through the rest of the council meeting and closing ceremonies. Tasks he'd otherwise have dreaded flew by in no time at all.

She had been *spectacular*. A beautiful, funny, captivating delight. One who was meeting him here at the stables any minute now, as John had informed him that Gerda's goodbyes with Henrietta and Lady Amy had finished ten minutes past.

"Wait, *who* are we waiting for?" Sir Jeffry asked, his eyebrows raised. The half-elf swordfighter was fully ready to go before everyone else and already mounted. He'd probably been here for hours reviewing their itinerary and going over their travel supplies. A sheet of paper and a quill were floating in front of him, keeping notes.

"Miss Gerda," Sir Tully replied, throwing his saddle on his horse and starting on the straps.

"But . . . *why?*"

All eyes turned to Julian, who didn't look up from his own task. "She asked for the escort."

Julian had finished his own preparations earlier and was going over Gerda's mount with a final inspection. The horse was a dapple roan, playful but steady. She would do well for the troll.

"And?" Sir Jeffry pressed.

"And our illustrious leader said yes." Visha came out of the stable with her horse on a lead, Sir Pram right behind her. She was in full armor, with her enchanted twin blades shrunk and latched at her hips. "Tully, are you not ready yet?"

"Calm your horses, I'm almost done." The paladin was lavishing pets on his mount instead of properly securing his saddlebags. To the horse, he muttered, "Nobody respects me."

"Is she bringing her own supplies?" Jeffry grabbed a sheet out of the air and signed it with his fingernail. The paper disappeared.

"I prepared her saddlebags yesterday," Visha said. Just one of the many things Julian had tasked her with.

Jeffry frowned. "On whose expense—?"

"She's here," Sir Pram interrupted. Gerda was quite a ways away, but all conversation stopped as Julian's closest allies turned to watch her saunter up the path.

The bridge troll was wearing a dark-purple tunic that hung down to her thighs and cinched with a long tan belt at the waist, brown leather tights, and calf-high boots with a small heel perfect for riding. Her hair had been rebraided, and each braid woven together into a singular larger braid.

"Miss Gerda." Julian stepped forward, leading her horse to the front. "May I introduce you to Berry-Berry."

"Hello, Berry-Berry." Gerda smiled and offered her hand to the horse, who sniffed it once then butted the hand, demanding pets. Gerda acquiesced, rubbing Berry-Berry on her nose, her neck, and all the way down to her saddle. The troll turned to him. "Do I just pull myself up?"

"First step is to make sure the horse isn't going to walk out from under you." Julian lifted the reins. "I'll hold her for you this time. Then, you make sure Berry-Berry's legs are all firmly on the ground and stable. Stand by her shoulder—Yes, like that. Now, you hook the ball of your foot in the stirrup and pull yourself up. Make sure to account for the extra height of the saddle and settle in the seat slowly once you're up. Got it?"

"Sure." After her foot was in the stirrup, she hopped awkwardly three times before getting a good grip and pulling herself up.

"Perfect," he told her. "Now, hold the reins like so."

Jeffry made a choking noise. The half elf was staring at Julian like he'd grown an extra head.

"You get used to it." Sir Tully also swung into his saddle and urged his horse forward, coming up beside Jeffry. "Just pretend you don't see anything, and Visha won't hit you."

"She only hits you, Tully," Sir Pram said, matter-of-factly.

"Line up," Visha ordered, leading her horse to stand beside Sir Jeffry. Pram and Tully were in the rear. "We're on duty here until we reach the Northern Fortress, so look alive, people!"

Julian mounted his own horse, still holding Berry-Berry's lead, and led her to the front. "Do you have your identification ready, Miss Gerda?"

"I do." She nodded, turning to Sir Jeffry. "Now, what was it you were saying about expenses?"

Julian stared at his friend. Hard.

"Nothing, Miss Gerda. It's all t-taken care of." The words pained Jeffry to say, but he managed.

"Now, now." The troll shook her head and smiled. "I'm happy to pay for my trip."

"Let's talk about this once we are free of the city," Julian cut in. He clicked his tongue twice and nudged his horse forward. Gerda's mount followed on the lead, the rest following after. "We'll have plenty of time on the road."

It was later than he'd wished to leave, but they should still make it to Borrow Grove by nightfall.

Behind him, Sir Tully whispered to Sir Pram in a clear voice, "Do you think Miss Gerda is going to give up before we reach the border, or after?"

"I don't think she'll give up at all," Sir Pram replied, not bothering to whisper. Gerda pretended not to hear, though one long ear twitched.

Sir Tully smiled. "Bet."

Before Julian could chastise the paladin, Visha turned to face Tully. Whatever he saw on the elf woman's face made him shrivel in his saddle. He exaggerated closing his lips, sucking them into a thin line, and then looked away, cowed.

They were approaching the palace gates, where the first checkpoint was, when Gerda looked around and asked, "So . . . where is Sir John?"

CHAPTER 67

I Could Listen to Julian Give Orders All Day

Gerda

It turned out John was bidding his family goodbye and would meet us on the road outside the city.

We were able to join the rogue in good time, despite how busy it was. The regular gate was crowded with festivalgoers who'd gotten in line to leave after the closing ceremonies. Traveling with Julian meant we were able to exit without waiting in line, and crossing with the duke meant that no one asked too many questions.

Not that I had anything to hide anymore.

"So," Sir Tully barely waited until we were five minutes from the front gate before he asked, "did you foresee any trouble on the road today?"

"No," I replied, not even attempting to look back, as I was still getting used to riding Berry-Berry. She was a very good horse. I added, "But that doesn't mean it won't happen."

Behind me, Sir Jeffry mumbled to Visha, "What am I missing?"

"Miss Gerda is Madame Potts," Visha explained dryly.

"*WHAT?*" The fact that he'd somehow managed to go without hearing the news already was astonishing in and of itself. "*Since when?*"

"Since she started her Cast five years ago, I imagine," Sir Pram replied. The ice mage didn't sound like he was being sarcastic. He was sincere in his reply and happy to help.

Julian told Jeffry, "Miss Gerda's identity was revealed when she stepped forward to save everyone at the wedding. Which you skipped."

"I was busy." The half-hearted excuse didn't fool anyone. This was the half elf John had had to bribe with a Rare-class treasure to attend the ball last night, and only long enough to distract Miss Penny Bracken from lighting people on fire.

"Either way," Julian continued. He pitched his voice into a firm command. "Miss Gerda is *not* to be bothered. She may or may not choose to warn us with her powers, but that is entirely at her own will, and we will respect her privacy. Is that clear?"

I couldn't help it; I replied with everyone else. "Yes, Your Grace."

He shot me a look as I covered a laugh with the back of one hand, leaning forward so I didn't tug on the reins I held to do so. I could listen to Julian give orders all day. And I would, now that we were traveling together.

"I'll let you know if my perks react to anything important," I offered. "Though most of my abilities focus on the future of Valaria itself and not what's happening to just me." While the area immediately outside the city had been bustling, the further north we rode, the less people there were. The only other group within sight was an envoy from the Empire of Sands, who were outpacing us quickly.

We were traveling down a proper stone road. It was made with large purple-gray slab rocks and some magical equivalent of binding concrete. The road wound off in the distance through gentle slopes of rolling hills with patch-work forests.

John met us in the shade of a small grove of trees that came within arm's length of the road.

"So far, the road ahead looks secure," John said, bowing in his saddle. "Your orders?"

Julian looked at the clear blue sky and patted his horse. "We will stop every hour to water the horses while it's this hot. And we'll break for dinner in Fell." Fell was the last decent-sized town between us and the border, though there were a few smaller villages tucked away here and there.

"Good," Jeffry sighed. "I have to speak to my sister about last quarter's sil-versmithing inventory log. There were three more helmets ordered for the watch than normal, but no new hires."

Jeffry was the viscount of Fell, though his entire family helped manage the region.

"How long until we're there?" I asked.

"We will reach my lands in two hours, but it'll take three to get to the city." Jeffry pulled the map out of thin air. "This is where we are now, here is my city, then north of that is Borrow Grove."

"It's already later than we planned to leave," Sir Tully piped up behind me. "Why don't we just stay in Fell tonight?"

"We must leave from Borrow Grove tomorrow if we want to make it to the border by nightfall, Tully," Sir Pram said.

"No, we—" Sir Tully started then stopped. I noted that Visha was glaring at the paladin and waving a hand at me. Tully changed on a dime. "Ah! Of course. Much too far."

Whether it was my slow pace or for another reason, I accepted the schedule as it was. No sense worrying about what I couldn't change.

"One more question," I asked. "Does Fell have a drawbridge?"

I was excited to go home.

Fell did not, in fact, have a drawbridge, but there was a river west of the town that had a nice, sturdy bridge I could use. So while everyone else went into the city to walk around and stretch their legs, Julian followed me down a short path to the bridge.

"You don't have to worry," I told him when he insisted on joining me. "I'm not going to capture any North Sumbrian bridges."

That wasn't *technically* a lie.

The duke smiled. "I understand that."

"I'm just going to use it to go home for a bit," I added, my conscience niggling at me. To make something a troll bridge, it had to be properly magicked with dimensional troll magic . . . but with [World Bridge], any bridge I crossed became a save point. I could teleport to a bridge, to my home, and between captured bridges. But telling the leader of a foreign domain that I could freely teleport around his lands without a permit or a by-your-leave probably wouldn't sit right with him.

"You should leave your spell up here," he said, surprising me. The look on my face must have given me away because he added, "If you end up in trouble, I don't want to go all the way back to the palace to fetch you."

"Don't worry, I can make my way back on my own if we get separated." I had a phoenix feather that would bring me back to life if I died and an inventory of antidotes. So in the worst case, I would just portal to the sky bridge and make my way north alone. We reached the bridge, and I stopped just short of stepping onto it. Julian walked up close behind me. Very, very close.

He leaned down, his silver eyes searching mine. "Don't say that. How could I *not* worry?"

"I could send you a Crystal Cast," I offered, pretending like I wasn't going to melt into the floor any second now. "Do you have a crystal?"

"I do." He summoned a crystal in the little space between us, and my system logged it for me. "But I still think we should keep tabs on any bridge nearby, and I'll meet you there."

"Okay," I agreed, turning away quickly so I could get some space and breathe easier.

I crossed the bridge.

With distance between us, it was less awkward to face him. He was standing there, arms crossed, watching me from the path.

"Do you want to come in for tea? Or are you going to wait here until I return?"

The warm smile that lit up Julian's face made my heart pound in my chest.

"I would love to join you, Miss Gerda." He stepped onto the bridge, and we met in the middle. With purpose, I reached out a hand to take his arm so that I could teleport us together. Instead, Julian's hand wrapped around my own, and then he deliberately laced our fingers together. I stared at our hands. Then up at him. He seemed perfectly calm.

Instead of saying anything, I walked us into my kitchen.

CHAPTER 68

Driving Him to Distraction

Julian

There was a pulling sensation and then Julian was stepping with Gerda into a wood-and-stone cottage.

Gerda stared intently at their entwined fingers. He squeezed them once before releasing her and taking a step back.

"Grab a seat, and I'll make us some tea." She pointed at the table. If he were entering from the front door, the kitchen would be on the right, the table directly ahead, and a cozy seating area with a fireplace and small library stretching off to the left.

Gerda walked into the kitchen. "Don't mind me if I pop out to deal with a bridge; now that I'm back, I should start doing my actual job again."

"I understand." Julian did as he was told, taking a seat at the table and using the opportunity to openly inspect her dwelling place.

The walls were a collection of painted flower motifs, hanging herbs, and a cascading mushroom display. Bright sun filtered in from a variety of windows in all different shapes and sizes. The largest window was above the sink, overlooking a field of wildflowers.

Each window peered out on a different place. Three small round ones stacked beside the mushrooms overlooked a trickling stream in a dark forest, while another with a warped oval shape had a clear view of the ocean with towering cliffs in the distance and seabirds flying overhead.

The kitchen had a wraparound counter with a collection of knickknacks and potted herbs all over. Gerda put on a kettle and then proceeded to water all of the plants in the kitchen before moving onto the dining area and the living room. There were plants, vines, healing herbs, and even moss growing on a plaque.

Gerda watered each diligently, speaking softly to the foliage as she did so. One didn't survive her absence, and she scooped it into a small bin.

There was only one exit or entrance, an intricately carved wooden door painted with the same flower motif as the walls.

"Is it connected to the bridge we just came from?" he asked, nodding at the door.

Gerda looked up from where she was tending to a collection of glowing mushrooms that grew in a tall, tiered cylinder tucked between her couch and the wall. "No. it's at"—she glanced at the kitchen window—"the west bridge on the Great Road in Nilheim."

They lapsed into silence while she wandered back to the kitchen to grab the water. She had an impressive collection of tea set out on top of a glass cabinet filled with different types of mugs and cups, with decorative teaspoons hanging on the wall above.

She grabbed two large mugs, a glass pitcher, and a white teapot with painted mushrooms. Into the teapot she poured hot water and some loose tea leaves. It smelled bitter. Then, she pulled out a jar of honey and drizzled two wands worth into the tea itself, stirring to mix. Unusual, but he waited.

He enjoyed watching her work.

While the tea steeped, she went into a cupboard in her kitchen and grabbed a plate, pulling out of her storage ring two each of soft gingerbread cookies, hard cinnamon biscuits, and slices of dale nut loaf. Taking a small bottle down from the tea shelf, she popped open the stopper. Even from the table, Julian could smell the scent of freshly baked cookies coming from the vial. With a flick, three drops landed in the pitcher. Next came a glass of cold milk from her storage ring and a handful of ice cubes.

She carefully strained her hot tea into the pitcher, stirring it until the milk became a light-brown brew.

"Perfect for a hot summer's day," Gerda said, bringing the tray over and placing it down in front of him. It had a small bowl of sugar and two small teaspoons. She sat kitty-corner to him, at the table's edge.

He took a sip. It was cold and just lightly sweet. "What is it?"

"As close to a London Fog as I can make in this world," she said, taking a sip for herself. "Some people like to add lavender, but I am not one of those people. You can make it sweeter, if you'd like."

Her odd choice of words struck him, but it could be a troll thing. "It's good." Julian took another sip then set his mug down on the table. "Gerda."

"Yes?" she asked, looking up from appreciating her own sip of tea.

"I have something I would like to tell you," Julian broached.

"Okay?" Her relaxed expression stiffened, and she sounded unsure.

"I . . ." Julian stared at the troll, enjoying a peaceful cup of tea in her cozy cottage in the Dark Enchanted Forest.

What could he tell her? That he liked her? That he wanted to kiss her? That he couldn't stop thinking about her night and day to the point that it was driving him to distraction?

He knew he wanted something . . . but what?

"I never heard your full escort request." Julian leaned back in his chair.

He wasn't a coward; he was just taking time to find the right words. It wasn't fair or polite to express interest in someone if he didn't know his own mind.

Gerda let out a breath. "Ah. Well, I'm on a quest to the Ice Fields. I was hoping you could bring me as far north as you're able, and then I'll take it from there."

"Alone?" Julian frowned. The Northern Ice Fields were home to untold monsters, and not the friendly kind who would invite her in for tea. "I have a quest," she replied, as if that settled it, "to find a bridge. It's about as north as you can go, so I don't expect you to escort me the whole way, just as far as you can."

He could've told her it was a fool's errand, a death wish . . . but instead, he replied, "I'll take you the whole way."

Gerda's brows knit together, and she looked like she might protest, but then, her head turned to look at a notification tab. Her eyes darted as she read. "Oh, I should probably get this. Are you alright if I leave you here for a bit or—"

"I'll wait."

"Okay. One second."

She vanished.

Suddenly, there was the long, distorted shadow of a troll on the field of wildflowers in the kitchen window.

Julian kicked himself.

CHAPTER 69

Survive Season Three

Gerda

It wasn't every day that I dropped half of my stolen dungeon wealth in a single morning, but that wasn't the only reason I was itching to properly toll my bridges again.

It was a constant nagging on the periphery of my mind. I controlled *a lot* of bridges, and they all let me know in vivid distraction when someone was crossing unimpeded. This notification, however, was special. And timely.

> "To save your king, you've gone through strife.
> What would you give me for his life?"

The unicorns rarely used the road, keeping to the deeper parts of the forest in enchanted glades by crystal river streams. All the stuff of fluffy fantasy novels.

The exception to that rule stood in front of me; Brightstar, a unicorn prince. Two other unicorns I didn't know, but recognized from Carter's oracle, stood behind the prince.

"Bridge troll," he neighed, walking forward until he was at the edge of my domain. My [World Player] ability translated his words to me. "I was told that you are Madame Potts—"

"That is not the answer to my riddle, prince," I scolded, crossing my arms in front of me.

"Of course. Thank you." He shook his head and chuffed. "I would offer this."

Another unicorn approached. She was an older mare with a black coat with four white socks on her hooves and a white star on her forehead. She bowed low, and when her spiral horn touched the road, the offering appeared.

It was a dark-blue unicorn horn with light blue tinting the ridges of the spiral. It shone faintly.

"I accept. Here." I stepped forward to meet them, bending down to pick up the horn. When it disappeared into my storage, I summoned one of my two phoenix feathers into my palm. Brightstar's horn glowed, and the feather vanished.

"You need to give it to your father *before* the sun sets, or it will be too late," I told the unicorn prince. That was when the Guardian of Death would come and lay the unicorn king to rest. "And as a favor to *me*, tell Carter that Chloe looked *amazing* in her wedding dress. His loss."

Brightstar shifted his weight from left to right, anxious. "I will do as you ask, troll."

"He won't shoot the messenger." I tried to alleviate the unicorn's concern. Many feared the chosen of Death and treated the man with the utmost respect.

I did not.

I announced ominously, "Now go, before it's too late!"

Living in a magical realm meant you embraced the dramatic sometimes.

The unicorns did not have to be told twice; they kicked off, racing back into the forest through the field of flowers that stretched out north of my bridge. With this unicorn horn, I'd almost collected every treasure from season two. And season two was at an end.

I sighed; there were three other bridge notifications.

I popped out to intercept a little lizardkin boy carrying a hurt flying pig near Kith Bog, and then a merchant caravan on their way to Drendil.

I chose the same easy riddle for both.

> "What can I see below my feet
> But also way up high?
> A single piece rough in my palm,
> Where many blot the sky?"

Surprising no one, the boy got the riddle, and the merchant just tossed me a small bag of copper. I would've accepted a few different answers: rock, stone, dirt, earth, or anything of the like. The boy said that dirt becomes a mountain, so I let him go on his merry way.

The assassins weren't going anywhere, so I decided to leave them for later. I would've felt bad for abandoning Julian for so long, but he'd invited himself, and the bridges were a welcome distraction from the duke of the North. I was hiding it well, but there was only so much I could put up with from my handsome travel companion before I started to get a bit . . . *feral.*

Calm, Gerda. You got this.

I popped back into the kitchen; he was still sitting there.

"Are you all done?" Julian asked, undisturbed that I'd left him for almost half an hour sitting alone in my tiny cottage.

"Technically, no. I'm ignoring the assassins for now," I informed him, sitting and picking up my cold tea.

"Will you leave them there?" he asked.

"No." I sighed and shook my head. "They are high enough in level that they're costing me an exorbitant sum every time they cross my bridge."

"Then why wait?"

"It might take a while to handle them all. Bridge troll etiquette means I can't just throw them into the river and walk away. I *have* to issue a riddle." I explained, adding further, "And since they're looking for trouble I'll actually have to activate my abilities—some of which can't be undone until the mana runs out or the riddle is answered."

Julian frowned, but nodded, seeing my point.

"So I thought we could finish our tea, I'll send you back to Fell, and *then* I'll go deal with the assassins." Unfortunately, I didn't capture the bridge in Fell, I simply walked across it, which meant I couldn't connect the cottage to it and let Julian leave at his leisure through the front door.

"How often do you toll bridges in a day?" he asked, leaning on the table.

"As often as I wish," I shrugged. "Which is three to four hours a day on average. I could do more, but I usually stick to the bridges on the Great Road. That keeps me busy but not annoyingly so."

"And how do you plan to keep doing that while you're in the North?"

"I'll cheat," I stated.

He looked at me. I fiddled with my stir spoon.

"I realized during the Spring Ball . . . that I can just make my own bridges." It was a system oversight, but it was true. "I can build up an ice bank, lay down a makeshift bridge, and *voilà*!"

"*Voilà*?"

"It's for emphasis."

"So you can just *make* save points"—Julian's eyes gleamed—"anywhere, any time?"

"Don't look at me like that," I said, waving my spoon at him.

"I have to admit, I'd like to take advantage of your power. But only if you agree." He lifted both hands in mock surrender before resting them on his lap. It was a very nice lap. "I'm looking for a dungeon in the Northern Ice Fields, and it's been a nightmare to locate. If we could leave a save spot to portal back to, it would save us *so much time*."

I looked out the window at the setting sun. There was less than half an hour until night fell.

"I've a proposition for you," I broached, turning back to Julian. "You won't like it, and I don't expect you to say yes . . . But if you did, it would have to be now. I wasn't going to even ask, but since you're here and we're alone and the timing is right—"

"Gerda"—he reached a hand over the table and touched mine—"what do you need?"

Quietly, knowing I was probably making a big mistake, I said, "Your locket."

He didn't withdraw his hand. "Why?"

I decided to just be honest with the duke. "I have until sunset to complete a quest that requires the scepter in your locket. When I learned how important it was to you, I gave up, but . . ." It was the last treasure I had to find . . . but the accomplishment wasn't worth risking the trust I'd built with Julian. I *knew* that. I knew it, but I said it anyway. "I don't need it forever, mind you, only until sunset. I was going to offer to help you find your hidden dungeon in exchange, but—"

"Alright," Julian agreed, letting go of my hand. He reached up to unhook the chain around his neck. Without another word, he dropped it into my palm and used his fingers to close mine around the locket.

"What do you *mean* 'alright'?" I asked, my voice catching.

He smiled. "You said you'll give it back. So alright."

"But I'll have to break the glass to retrieve the scepter!" I squeezed the locket in my palm.

"I didn't even know it *was* a scepter," Julian replied. "I'll still have the locket when you're done. I can carry around the scepter on my belt or in my storage, or ask mother to put it back inside the locket if need be. It's a small price for Madame Potts to help me find the dungeon I've literally spent my life searching for."

"I would've done it anyway. You're escorting me, and you paid for my travel supplies—"

"I don't mind."

My hands were shaking. I popped the locket open, and there was the picture of young Julian and his family. The other side was only a broken piece of crystal behind a thin pane of glass.

I swallowed and asked one last time. "If you're sure?"

"Break it." The words were firm, and I pressed the glass with a green thumb, exuding more and more pressure until the barrier splintered.

A bright light erupted from the locket, and then a large scepter appeared overtop. It had looked like crystal, but it turned out to be shimmering mithril imbued with aura.

I hurried to catch it as it dropped, and a notification let me know this was *exactly* what I'd been looking for.

[Quest: Season Two Treasures Found 10/10

Nova's Celestial Pendant: An opal pendant that glows near celestials and darkens near demons. +5 Charisma with Divine.

King Kraken's Heart: A ruby pendant that allows you to breathe underwater. +5 Charisma with sea creatures.

Menlomin's Horn: The king of the unicorn's horn that will **Purify** anything it touches.

Calisto's Personal Magical Elevator: An enchanted box that can rise ten stories into the air while carrying up to four people.

Valarian Royal Mantle: +3 to Charisma when equipped. 6/6 set pieces found.

Valarian Royal Breastplate: +3 to Strength when equipped. 6/6 set pieces found.

Valarian Royal Shield: +3 to Constitution when equipped. 6/6 set pieces found.

Valarian Royal Crown: +3 to Perception when equipped. 6/6 set pieces found.

Valarian Royal Sword: +3 to Dexterity when equipped. 6/6 set pieces found.

Valarian Royal Scepter: +3 to Intelligence when equipped. 6/6 set pieces found.]

[Congratulations! You have completed the **Valarian Royal Set.** When equipped together, bonus modifier per item is elevated to +5]

I whistled. That was a disgusting amount of points. When hit points were based on strength and constitution, and mana was a multiple of perception and intelligence, that plus five in each was broken.

To better understand the ridiculous buff that was the Valarian Royal Set . . . Every time someone leveled up, they got two points to allocate to their attributes, and the set granted thirty points. It was equivalent to fifteen levels in stats.

"On its own, the Valarian Royal Scepter grants you three points to intelligence," I told him, hefting the treasure with one hand. I handed back the locket with its collapsed glass shards. Julian snapped it shut, shards and all, and put it back around his neck.

He asked quietly, "Do you know what was in my sister's locket?"

"Ah . . . yes." I summoned the mantle from my inventory. "The Valarian Royal Mantle grants a three-point charisma bonus."

Julian's fingers twitched. "Where did you get it?"

"I pulled it from the wreckage of the Spell Script Collegium. It boosted Julia's paladin abilities just long enough to keep them alive under the rubble. She's lucky her build is strength and charisma based." I stared out the window in the kitchen. "It won't be long now."

We fell into a tense silence, both watching the night creep over the world outside, each window in the cabin reflecting the fading light from a different location.

My notification tab blinked.

[Quest Complete: Survive Season Two of Dungeon Delves and Debutantes]
[Welcome to the World of Valaria, an Open-World Battle Otome RPG for the ages.]

100% Scenarios Completed
100% Map Explored
100% Hidden Treasures Found
99% Characters Found

[In Season Two, our Heroine survived the rise of corruptions from the Dark Enchanted Forest and found a partner she could depend on to bring to the Masquerade Ball . . . but is she ready for the hardest challenge yet?]
[Come back to your favorite characters with even more Dungeons, Dragons, and Debutantes!]

I immediately read season three.

[Quest: Survive Season Three of Dungeon Delves and Debutantes]
[Welcome to the World of Valaria, an Open-World Battle Otome RPG for the ages.]
[Previously, our Heroine Henrietta worked to defeat the Dark Overlord, King Monfort, and the new Lich Queen, Chloe Watercress, who turned the minions of the Dark Enchanted Forest into a legion of undead.]
Error: **Previously, our Heroine Henrietta worked hard to win the heart of the Dark Lord, King Keith, and defended the Dark Enchanted Forest against invading Blackfog.**
[But a new challenge awakens in the dark wood. A beast of legend is stirring, and Henrietta will have to face her toughest battle yet before she can find her true Happily Ever After.]

Error: **But a new challenge arises, for the Dark Enchanted Forest is being overrun by spies, an annoyance to trade and transportation that stirs the ire of the Dark Horde and threatens her
new Happily Ever After.**

[Season Three features two new ikemen love interests,
new dungeons, access to Baldorin and the Empire of Sands,
and new crafting material!]
[Can our Heroine Henrietta complete all of the quests, or will she
have even more at stake than she bargained for?]

2% Scenarios Completed
60% Map Explored
10% Hidden Treasures Found
35% Characters Found

[Come back to your favorite characters with even more Dungeons,
Dragons, and Debutantes!]

The experience points hit me, and I leveled up.

CHAPTER 70

I Want You

Julian

While Gerda was reading her notification tabs, Julian was reading Gerda.

The world was lucky that she *wasn't* more selfish. Even just asking to borrow his locket had left the otherwise confident troll in an awkward flush. She was still holding his father's mantle and scepter. If each item granted a three-point attribute bonus alone, he couldn't imagine the set all together. People had fought wars over less powerful treasures.

But she didn't seem to care about them other than for the purposes of completing her quest.

"Finally," she breathed softly, the word a whisper. Gerda refocused on him. "Thank you."

"You're welcome." He waited for her to hand him back his scepter, and considered how much he should offer for the mantle.

Gerda didn't move. She actually pulled the articles closer to her and leveled him a very scrutinizing stare. Her eyes swept over his shoulders and chest before settling on his thighs.

It riled him up as much as it worried him.

"Your Grace—" she began.

"Julian," he cut her off.

"Julian?" She shot him a questioning look.

He raised an eyebrow in challenge. She accepted with an amused smile. "Alright, Julian, I was wondering . . ."

"Yes?" Gods, his name sounded so good on her lips. Again, he wanted to kiss her.

"How do you feel about an equipment upgrade?"

She dropped the entire set. The items were too big to fit on the table, so she summoned them beside the table leg between them. The plate armor was on its side, a shield leaning up against it, and a sword jutting from the armhole. An ornate crown circlet of woven orichalcum hung haphazardly on the sword guard.

"The set grants a plus five in all attributes," she explained, sticking out her hands with the proffered scepter and mantle.

Julian couldn't help himself. He started laughing.

"Gerda." This was the second time he'd said her name without honorifics, and he wanted to say it again. But that would sound weird, so he resisted. "You can't just *gift* me the most powerful suit set on the continent."

"*Of course* I can. *I'm Madame Potts.*" She looked down her nose at Julian haughtily, like *he* was the one being unreasonable.

"At least let me pay for it," Julian insisted, not taking the items.

"I don't want or have need for gold," she told him. "And you're going to be in charge of keeping me safe on the journey north. The scepter and mantle already belong to your family; you should have the rest."

"There's *nothing* you want?" he asked, delaying until he could think up a suitable argument to change her mind. In the council room, she'd accepted fines for literally reaching out and saving people; it hadn't sat right with him. He was angry on her behalf, and disapproved of her giving so much without expecting anything in return.

Then, her gaze dropped to his lips. "Well . . . there is *one* thing."

He froze.

Her half-lidded eyes made his heart pound in his chest, and he held his breath, his imagination running wild. His whole body tightened. After days of carefully walking a line, he couldn't believe she was going to take the first step.

"Go on." His voice dropped low in anticipation. The need to hear her say that she wanted him was so strong it nearly drove him to his knees. But he waited.

"I . . ." She blinked twice in rapid succession, and the moment was gone. Gerda looked away, drawing a haggard breath. "Actually, I . . . I'm fine. There's nothing. Take it."

Julian felt like he'd been whipped. He didn't know if his own lust was clouding his judgement or if she was *deliberately* seducing him and then running away. This was a thousand times worse than her playful teasing; he felt like he was being cut loose after walking on the edge of a cliff. And he fell hard.

He'd reached the end of his control.

"Then let me tell you what *I* want." He stood, taking the items out of her hands and tossing them onto the rest of the pile. "More than this suit, and more than my father's scepter."

She leaned back in her chair, surprised at his sudden intensity, her hands retreating. They were shaking. Julian had to fight to soften the words as he gave in to his ardent frustration and infatuation with the troll.

"I want you to admit there's something between us. That I'm not the only one feeling this way." Her beautiful brown eyes went wide. He leaned over the table's edge and scooped up her long braid of dark-green hair, lifting it to his lips. "Tell me that you want me to kiss you senseless."

"I—" Her words caught as she stared at his fingers playing with her hair.

"Tell me that you can't stop thinking about me, because I haven't stopped thinking about you since the night we met, and it's taking every last ounce of my restraint to pretend otherwise."

"But—"

"I want you." The words terrified him, but he pushed forward. Before he heard her rejection, he needed to say everything so there would be no confusion on her part. He confessed, "I won't last *one* more day without breaking under the weight of this all-consuming distraction that is *you*, Gerda Jones. I want *you*."

Gerda pushed her chair back, her braid slipping from his fingertips. He let it go and stood up straight again, giving her space.

"Are you done?" The bridge troll looked up at him, a war of emotions flitting across her face. He'd always prided himself on reading her expressions. There was frustration, excitement, and longing . . . and fear.

It was like an ocean smothering the small flame in his chest.

Her previous partner, as Julian understood, had been *a monster*. A troll, yes, but Julian wasn't speaking to his race. The casual way she'd spoken about her ex-husband's abuse made him physically ill.

"Yes. I'm done." He forced himself to take another physical step back. To will his face into a calm, unthreatening mask that covered the roiling churn in his stomach.

She stood up. The suit set vanished into her inventory as she walked around the table to face him. The bridge troll stopped only inches away, shoulders set and hands clenched into fists at her sides. Gerda lifted one trembling finger and pushed Julian. For the barest moment, he resisted, but then, he let her shove him backward.

He teleported, the room shifting around him. His leg hit her bed unexpectedly, and he fell backward onto the coverlet.

"If you want me." Gerda was standing between his legs at the edge of the bed, looking down at Julian. The finger she'd used to push him over lowered and delicately traced up his thigh. "Prove it."

CHAPTER 71

On My Knees Again

Gerda

I woke up the next day with Julian's leg sandwiched between my own, my back against his torso, and his breath on the nape of my neck.

He was warm and comforting and solid.

"Good morning," I murmured, noticing the sunlight spilling in from the window. I made to get up, but a firm arm wound around my stomach, pulling me back.

"Good morning." Julian rolled me underneath him and kissed me senseless. His morning stubble tickled my cheek.

"Wait!" I half-heartedly slapped his bare chest. It was a very nice chest.

"We can't?" The half elf leaned down and gently bit my ear, sending shivers through my whole body. He whispered, "Or do you want me on my knees again, begging for it?"

"Julian!" I did think about it, but time wasn't on our side. "Your Grace."

My safeword made Julian pause, and then he had the audacity to pout. He sat up, and the covers fell back, revealing all of him. I took a second to appreciate what I saw, all while reminding him, "We have to go let everyone know we aren't dead. And I need breakfast."

We'd spent a lot of energy the night before, and I'd only managed to drink a glass of water, use the restroom, and half-heartedly brush my teeth before passing out in his embrace.

Julian climbed out of bed, giving me space to do the same as he unabashedly walked around with nothing on, teasing me with his cute butt, which I slapped on the way to the bathroom. He spun and shot me a fiery look. I smirked at him as I ducked through the door. With it set to the bathroom, he could only wait in my bedroom or join me.

He knocked when I turned on the bathwater.

I'd taken extra care with the crafting of my bathroom. The entire place was made out of red cedar walls and decorated with hanging ivy. On one side, there was a wooden vanity with a natural-wood-framed square mirror, and a hanging net plant box full of purple-and-green-colored velia ivy. I'd chosen it because it glowed in the dark.

Beside the vanity was an enchanted toilet with three candles on the back. It was in a shape I was familiar with, and something I'd had custom made by an artisan dwarf in Frolin. It wasn't made out of porcelain but purple amethyst crystal.

I loved it.

The bathtub was also cut amethyst and was six feet long, four feet deep, and double sided. The faucet was a trough style that filled the tub with hot mineral water. The tub sat beneath a window looking out into Kith Bog, its ledge covered in jars and two lavender-scented candles. And above the bathtub, I'd installed a huge rain shower perfect for helping wash my hair, which could take over an hour.

While the tub was filling, I sat on a stool beside it with a bucket of warm water and a jar of soap. Julian walked in as I was rubbing soap on my arms.

"You look beautiful against the morning sun," he commented, kneeling down behind me. He snatched my bath sponge, relathered it, and set to scrubbing my back.

"You aren't too bad yourself," I told him, sighing with pleasure. "That feels amazing."

"Happy to help." He grinned.

I flicked suds at the half elf. "Your turn."

He obliged, and we managed to rinse off and enjoy a half-hour soak in the tub together before getting changed.

Since we'd taken longer than I'd planned, breakfast was fried floofpoof eggs on sourdough. I had some ready-made meals in my storage ring, but they were all sweet. I wanted a good helping of protein and a savory flavor. I paired it with an extra strong black tea to get us going.

"So," I said when we were almost done eating. I was trying to sound like everything was normal and I hadn't pushed the duke of the North into bed, literally, the night before. "What's the plan?"

"What do you mean?" he asked, enjoying a sip of tea.

"The plan," I repeated, emphasizing my words, "for us."

His silver eyes dipped into a half-lidded satisfactory smile as Julian gave me a look that made me want to melt into a puddle on the floor. He reached out and took one of my hands, threading our fingers together. "What do you think?"

Calm your pants, Gerda. Focus.

Tentatively, I said, "Friends with benefits?"

That made him pause, his eyes flashing with something dark and possessive. He untangled our fingers and scooped up my hand, bringing it to his lips.

"More than that." I thought he was going to kiss the back of my hand, but he flipped it over and bit the inside of my wrist, sending a shock of awareness through my whole body. "Try again."

"What more do you want?" I shot back.

He dropped my hand and stood up. One step took him past the table's edge, directly beside me. He leaned down and kissed my cheek softly. "Let's find out together. It's time to get going."

"You can't just—There needs to be rules, Julian!" I sputtered, pushing my chair back and coming to my feet. I poked him hard in the chest. "You can't just do whatever you want and apologize when you go too far. We need boundaries."

He smiled. "Like what?"

"Public displays of affection," I stated. "Don't kiss me in public."

He raised an eyebrow. "Why not?"

"Because," I replied.

"What else?" he asked, seeming to accept my request.

"You can't interfere with my work," I told him. "As a bridge troll or as Madame Potts. And, and . . ."

"And?"

"And," I said, "you should tell me what you actually want!"

"Alright." Julian reached an arm around my waist and pulled me into his embrace. I let him. His free hand reached up to cup my cheek as he leaned down and kissed me. He wasn't gentle, and I could feel one of my tusks scrape his lip when I gasped for air. His tongue slipped into my mouth to deepen the exchange. The hand around my waist pressed me tight against him, and I could feel how much he wanted me.

And then he broke the kiss.

"As I said . . . I want *you*. To be with you. To kiss you." Straightening, he licked the blood off his cut lip. "I don't want anyone else seeing you like this."

"Jealous much?" My cheeks burned hot as I glared at him. "Who else *would*?"

Julian looked like he wanted to reply but thought better of it.

"We can work the rest out later . . ." He straightened, rubbing a hand on the back of his neck. "I didn't exactly tell my people that I wasn't coming back last night."

"Fine." With that, I portaled us back to the bridge at Fell. It was still early morning, though the summer sun was already bright in the eastern sky.

"You're back!"

Before either of us could get our bearings, an almost crying Sir Tully lunged towards us. Julian, still holding me around the waist, brought up one arm to shield me. In fact, by the light shimmer of magic in the air, he'd erected an actual shield as well.

"What happened?" Julian's face was back in an angry neutral frown.

I wanted to poke his cheek but resisted.

I was strong.

"Visha made me wait for you here. All night!" The human slouched, looking worse for wear.

"Is that all?" Julian replied, heartless.

"Fell is the last comfortable bed I will see in months!" Sir Tully looked up at the sky. His propensity for the overdramatic made him endearing, but sometimes, there were places to be and things to do. I asked, "Did Visha tell you the plan, Sir Tully? Where is everyone?"

He waved back toward the large city wall that encircled Fell. "The plan was to bring you back to the inn last night or meet up for breakfast at the Piping Gorse. After that, check over the horses and ride out."

I nodded. "You both go ahead. I have a few things to take care of."

Julian's arm tightened around me for only a second before he let go and stepped back. "Assassins?"

"And we left the dishes on the table," I told him.

I loved how the realization that we'd been so distracted kissing we'd forgotten to clean up made the tip of his pointy ears darken. "Alright."

Sir Tully was looking back and forth between us, confusion written on his face.

I waved at the pair and blew Julian a kiss goodbye before activating [World Bridge] and portaling away. I didn't go back inside but straight to the young beastfolk girl running down a forest trail toward my bridge. It wasn't on the main road, and she was obviously panicked and afraid, looking over her shoulder instead of at the path ahead.

She stumbled on a tree root and fell hard enough that I flinched at the impact, her fluffy tail pointing up in the air. She was so close, just ten paces from the edge of my bridge. Still, I couldn't help her up.

I could only do my job.

> "I beat without a heart.
> I carry without hands.
> I travel with the wind.
> Tell me what I am."

"AH!" She had only started to rise when my words startled her into a scream. She scrambled backward, her knee was bloody, and I sighed at seeing her terror. She was probably twelve if she was a day.

"I beat without a heart.
I carry without hands.
I travel with the wind.
Tell me what I am."

I repeated my riddle, this time with emphasis.

"W-What?" She finally realized I wasn't attacking her and calmed a bit.

"It's a riddle," I explained. "If you can answer my riddle, you can pass my bridge. If you can't, then you will have to pay the toll."

"But . . . I have nothing to give." Tears filled the girl's eyes now, despite her holding strong through the pain of her previous injuries.

"Start with the riddle," I urged, repeating it a third time, very slowly.

"A . . . bird?" she asked.

"Try again." I put up my hand beside my lips and leaned toward her as if sharing a secret. "You're very close."

"Alright. Um." She closed her eyes and scrunched up her nose in thought. One of her fluffy animal ears twitched. I had no idea what animal she was, but she was adorable. "Wings?"

"You got it!" I smiled reassuringly. It was an easier riddle because there were other answers I would accept, like music.

There wasn't much room on the bridge; it was just three planks roped together for hunters to cross the small creek. Usually, I'd poof away at this point and let her pass . . . but I couldn't just leave. "I have some ointment for that knee; would you like it?"

She nodded, though I could tell she wasn't fully convinced by her hands clenched together at her chest. There was a moment of anxiety as I stepped off the bridge, but only just.

"Here you go." I crouched down and handed over a small jar. She took it, and then her fearful expression turned into a sneer.

"Got you—"

I dodged the arrow her friend shot at me from deeper in the woods.

"Almost." I booped her nose with my finger and vanished.

CHAPTER 72

My Favorite Part of the Courtship Ritual

Julian

Tully's mouth dropped. "Did Miss Gerda just blow you a kiss—"

"Yes." Julian patted his paladin on the shoulder. "Don't worry; you'll get used to it."

Then he left Sir Tully standing there in shock as he marched off toward Fell. Sir Tully hurried to catch up, before going into a full-volume interrogation that Julian mostly ignored. His party members—Visha, John, Pram, and Jeffry—were all sitting in the Piping Gorse, each drinking their morning beverage of choice.

Visha stood when she saw them. "Your Grace!"

The relief in her voice made him feel a pang of guilt. "Visha. I hope everything was fine in my absence?"

She nodded. "Yes—"

"It was not!" Jeffry cut in. There were bags under the half elf's eyes. He looked like he'd been run over by a stoneskin wombat and hung out to dry for three days with no food or water.

"What happened?" Julian waved at Visha to sit and pulled up a chair himself. Pram handed him a menu.

"My sister," he stressed, "was *very* put out that you didn't have dinner with us last night."

"She's gonna be even more upset when she finds out His Grace and Miss Gerda are dating." Sir Tully dropped the news without a thought as he waved at a waitress across the room. The waitress smiled and headed their way as John held out his hand to Jeffry. The viscount had a pained expression as he dropped a small coin purse into the rogue's open palm.

Julian said nothing to refute the claim, only addressing the waitress. "I'll have a glass of water, please."

"Flying pork and potatoes for me, with rye," Sir Tully added, handing over his menu.

"I'll have the deep-fried shrimp and wild rice omelet." Pram smiled at the girl, showing off slightly pointed teeth. She blushed and accepted his menu, giving the selkie an obvious look over.

Julian wondered how he could have missed seeing these kinds of things before now.

"I'll have the cinnamon stone oats parfait," Visha said.

Jeffry simply asked for a refill on his tea. The half elf had probably eaten at home already. The waitress dropped off their orders with the kitchen and came to refill all of their drinks.

"So, you and Miss Gerda?" Pram asked Julian, curious. "Does that mean the plans have changed?"

"Of course the plans have changed!" Jeffry groaned. "We aren't even supposed to *be* here. We should've made it to Borrow Grove last night and set up camp there—"

"I, for one, *enjoyed* sleeping in a real bed last night," Visha said, sipping her tea.

Sir Tully slumped. "I wish."

"Our new plan," Julian told them, "is to reach Borrow Grove this evening."

"Wait, why this evening?" Jeffry turned on John. "Is there something in the way?"

John shook his head, his emotionless face betraying nothing.

"Then why don't we ride hard for the Northern Fortress? We should get there only a little bit after midnight if we push," Jeffry argued.

"We'll take the extra day and use it as an opportunity to practice traveling with Miss Gerda *without* monster attacks." Julian sat back in his chair.

The people sitting around this table had been fighting beside him on and off for years. They were his party members. They were his friends. He knew that adding someone like Gerda—who could both slow them down and send them further than ever—would take getting used to.

Two days of practice wasn't much, but it would have to do. He wanted everyone to have a good understanding of each other's abilities *before* they were in the heart of the Ice Fields, being overrun by frost goliaths or tula yetis.

"I thought this was going to be a simple escort mission . . . What am I missing?" Jeffry asked.

"Miss Gerda has offered to help us locate the dungeon in the North," he told them.

"How? Does she have a scouting ability? Can she fight?" Visha asked. While Jeffry was in charge of their logistics, Visha would be responsible for keeping everyone safe. Her orders were second only to his own.

"No. She will accompany us as a noncombatant." Julian returned Visha's dubious look with a slow smile. "She has the ability to create temporary portals with her bridges, so we'll be able to go back and forth between the Ice Fields and the fortress."

"Gods." Jeffry nodded. "If *that's* why you agreed to date the troll, then marry her."

"That's not including the fact that she has oracle powers and might just *see* where the dungeon's at," Sir Tully added.

John shook his head at the paladin even as Julian chastised him.

"Miss Gerda is under no obligation to use her Madame Potts's powers to aid us unless she chooses to do so of her own free will."

"So we'll be practicing defense formations around Miss Gerda while she's setting up her bridge points?" Pram asked.

"Yes."

Visha frowned. "I think we could manage a full defense for three minutes as we currently are. That's without any of us taking an injury." She looked around the table. "If we need more time than that, we'll have to keep back one more of John's shadows and leave Pram with enough mana to cast [Ice Wall]. I could double my attack radius if John let me borrow his Eye of Effeldor—"

"You mean *MY* Eye of Effeldor brooch!" Jeffry declared, smug. He lifted his cloak to reveal the thing pinned to his tunic. It was an obnoxiously gaudy piece of jewelry as big around as Julian's fist, made of gold and set with rubies and emeralds and sapphires and three other colored semiprecious stones that Julian couldn't name. A large tiger's eye stone was affixed in the center. "And I'm not giving it up for anything!"

Visha turned on John. "You gave it to *him*?"

The human shrugged.

"Food's here," Sir Tully noted. He'd been watching the kitchen and drew their attention to the waitress heading their way with three platters of food—one in her right hand, one in her left, and one balanced on her left arm.

Everyone paused long enough to welcome the arrival of their meal before the waitress left to get Visha's oat parfait.

Sir Tully stabbed a potato and ate it, not waiting for anyone. He stabbed another then waved his potato-skewered fork at Julian. "You know, if Your Grace used Theo's Amulet, that would raise your perception to twenty-seven and grant you plus-forty mana, which is an extra four durability to Miss Gerda's [Barrier]. After your strength modifier that would defend against—"

"Enough, Tully." Visha's voice was cold and hard as it cut off the paladin.

He shrugged and stuffed the potato in his mouth. "I was just pointing it out."

The waitress arrived with the elf woman's parfait.

Julian thought about it.

Reaching up, he fiddled with his locket. It granted him no combat bonus to equip it. Even so, he'd never taken it off or replaced it with anything else because it was a keepsake from his late father that he was told might protect him in his needed hour.

Julian unclipped the chain, holding out the locket to stare at it. After a second, he sent it to his storage ring and said, "Alright."

His party members, *his friends*, all looked at him with varying states of surprise.

Sir Tully choked on his flying pork sausage. "Wait, really?"

"Sure. Pass it." Julian held out his hand to the paladin, who scrambled to do as he was asked. As Julian equipped the amulet, he considered the other changes to his equipment and smirked. "This'll go well with my new armor set."

"*What* new armor set?" Visha asked sharply.

"Is Miss Gerda already giving you presents?" Pram asked with a knowing look. "That is my favorite part of the courtship ritual."

"I think that's only a selkie thing," Sir Tully pointed out; Pram's excitement visibly faded.

"She did, in fact, gift me my new armor set," Julian said, and Pram regained a bit of his vigor. Julian was sad he'd have to wait until Gerda returned to show off.

"Well," Visha said sternly, "I don't care if it was a lover's gift; it should be a better grade than your current set, or I'm not going to let it pass the safety inspection—even for *you*, Your Grace."

"Oh, that won't be a problem."

CHAPTER 73

Illegal Use of the Crystal Cast

Gerda

Two Days Later

"Julian, when we cross that drawbridge, I'm going back home, and I'm not bringing you with me," I told the handsome fiend riding beside me. Berry-Berry's gentle pace was the only thing keeping me on her back after two solid days of riding.

I sent a silent apology to fiends everywhere for cursing him in their name, but I needed *something* to grumble about when I felt this sore.

The sun was setting on the Northern Fortress in the distance, our not-so-final destination. And since it was the height of summer, that meant we'd gotten up at six in the morning and traveled with an unreasonable number of stops for fifteen hours *not* straight.

Every hour for two days, give or take three minutes, Julian would sound the alert, and everyone would fly into action. To get us used to working as a team yesterday, Julian had taken it upon himself to act as our attacker, his new armor making him an outright menace. The battle ended when I successfully escaped, or when Julian reached me.

The first time he'd slipped through our defenses, he'd flicked me in the forehead. The second time, he'd kissed my cheek. The third time, he'd wrapped his arms around me from behind and whispered, "Got you," so low and seductive that I'd wanted to melt.

All before lunch.

Then that evening, my companions had realized we could teleport everyone back to Fell in time for meals and a warm bed.

Sir Tully had almost cried.

After an entire day of being chased and teased, I'd dropped everyone else off in Fell then dragged Julian back to my cottage to have a turn driving *him* wild.

Today, we'd added extra hurdles. Pram would create icy terrain that we had to navigate, while John lent Julian two shadows so he could attack in groups.

The whole time, my job was to jump off Berry-Berry, pull out my makeshift bridge, and find somewhere the system would allow me to put it down as a functioning bridge. And I had to fully capture the bridge *every time*, because I couldn't just teleport that many people and horses with my own personal [World Bridge] power unless I was *touching* all of them and wanted to chance mana burn.

Too risky.

Even now, it took about four minutes to set up the bridge transport and get everyone *onto* it before Julian reached me.

His smug smile was starting to get to me, and I had already given into my desire and tugged his cheeks once.

"How long?" he asked innocently.

"I'm not coming back until tomorrow," I told him.

"Alright." There was the barest hint of a pout from my impressively outfitted half elf. Gods, that Valarian Royal Set looked spectacular. It was a dusky silver orichalcum finish with moon and sun engravings on the chest plate, and dragon-head pauldrons on the shoulders. The matching ornate dragon's face helm was straight-up stunning, and the deep-purple mantle looked obnoxiously regal.

Julian glanced at the fortress. "I'll be busy settling in and checking over things as it is."

"Have fun," I said dryly.

We were ten minutes from the fortress when the sun finally set. Usually, the night sky was awash with familiar stars; a connection to my old world, since we shared the same constellations.

Tonight was different for two reasons. A beautiful aurora borealis stretched across the sky, and I held my breath while admiring the natural phenomenon. There were ribbons of green light blocking out the stars. It was like someone had hung curtains of light over the night sky; gently wafting curtains.

"What is that?" Sir Tully pointed at the eastern horizon, where the second thing had captured everyone's attention. A too-large star shone unnaturally bright in the dark. With my perception, I could even make out the beginnings of a comet tail.

"Nothing for us to worry about, though I should probably let everyone know anyway." I juggled my reins so that I had a free hand to summon the Master Crystal out of my storage ring. To my travel companions, I said, "Give me a second."

Everyone stared at the large, awkward crystal I was holding. "If we are stopping, let's clear the road," Visha ordered, guiding her own horse off the path. There was a scramble to follow her.

"Didn't you *just* get fined for illegal use of the Crystal Cast Network?" Julian asked, sounding concerned but intrigued.

"Yes, which is why I'm only telling North Sumbria, Peldeep, and Nilheim. Everyone else can hear it the old-fashioned way." I closed my eyes, not because I needed to in order to activate the crystal but because I was thinking about all the things I might want to add to this particular Cast.

My first since being discovered.

CHAPTER 74

Every Reason He Adored Her

Julian

Julian didn't like the look of the mysterious ball of fire three times as large as any star that shone overhead, but seeing Gerda nonplussed alleviated some of his worries.

"I can't believe we actually get to watch Madame Potts make a Cast," Sir Tully exclaimed.

Visha shushed the human.

The troll bit her lip while she thought.

"Alright," Gerda said, opening her eyes as the crystal in her hands lit up with a sharp white light that warred with the soft yellow magic lights they were using to see by. She smiled and pitched her voice *just* so.

"Hello, everyone, this is your friendly neighborhood Madame Potts.

My apologies for the late-night Cast, but as you can all see, we have an impending magical disaster approaching from the eastern sky. Luckily, it is being handled with care by a professional. You can go about your nights simply appreciating the cosmic phenomenon.

Peldeep is looking for a new assistant guild master for their adventuring guild. Congratulations, Gemma, on your promotion. And I wish you and your new househusband a fine Happily Ever After.

In exciting news, the identity of the mysterious and enigmatic Madame Potts has finally been discovered. That's right, folks, my secret identity has been revealed to the public. If

your assassins could please schedule attacks between four and
seven p.m. on Monday evenings, and Thursdays from eleven
to noon, it would be much appreciated. Thank you.
The Continental Council has ruled I may only Cast
portents in realms that give me leave, which is currently Nilheim, Peldeep, and North Sumbria. So please tell your family
and friends who live abroad that Servalt is going to have a
drought next year, and they should start preparing now.
There's going to be a rockslide where the Baldorin
Mountain Range meets the Galer Plain. And later this week,
Drendil will have the chance to see a pod of rainbow whales
off the western coast.
Should anything happen to the whales, it will go very,
very poorly. I'm talking to you, Pirate Abra. Don't do it.
Have a good rest of your evening, all,
Madame Potts, signing off."

The entire time Gerda spoke into the crystal, she had this sassy smile that melted Julian's heart. She was funny and brilliant and beautiful. Her voice carried her personality through the Cast, but watching her tease the entire continent with a straightforward ruthlessness brought back every reason he adored her.

"So, who is dealing with the star?" Sir Tully thrust a thumb over his shoulder at the comet.

"A very powerful if irksome mage," Gerda told the human, putting away her crystal. "He's been preparing all year, and I think he's pretty much ready to go. Honestly, the comet was a side quest I rushed through to unlock other routes because it committed the greatest fantasy sin."

"What?" Julian asked, not entirely sure what she meant but wanting to hear more anyway. From her hints, he'd already figured out who the mage was.

"*Math.*"

There was a pause.

"Math?" Jeffry asked, affronted. "But math is the foundation for our magical system, the basic underlying principle of our reality and our place within it. It cannot be a sin. *Math is life itself.*"

"So says the party strategist. *Of course* you like math." Gerda shook her head. "I respect the art. I am even good at it. I love baking, and I understand the importance of managing mana costs. I have even gamed the tax system . . . but when a handsome mage is trying to tell me about the ratio of an angle of a line for a world-saving arcane magical weapon, it is going in one ear and out the other."

"You think Thomas is handsome?" Julian raised an eyebrow at that.

"Skinny nerds aren't my type," Gerda replied. She looked Julian up and down before meeting his eyes. "I prefer someone with more muscle. And trauma."

Visha, his prim and proper second-in-command, snorted loudly; she covered her mouth with the back of her hand and coughed to hide it. Jeffry still looked taken aback that the troll didn't like math, while Sir Tully was enjoying the back and forth between them. Pram frowned.

John had shadowed ahead and was preparing for their arrival at the fortress. Speaking of which.

"Laugh all you like," Julian told Visha, flicking his reins and leading his horse back onto the path. "But do so in your own time. Let's continue home."

"Only you would call a cold stone guardhouse *home*," Sir Tully told the duke, joining the line as everyone followed after Julian.

He smiled. "Home is where you hang your hat."

"You don't wear a hat," Sir Tully pointed out.

"Miss Gerda, a question, if you will?" Pram pulled up beside the troll and spoke softly.

"Go ahead."

"What will happen if a rainbow whale is hurt?" Pram asked. The selkie had lived his whole life in North Sumbria, and loved learning facts about the sea.

"Rainbow whales maintain the balance of the ocean's natural mana reserves by filtering it from the water and releasing it from their spout. They can grow as large as a dragon and will release giant mana laser beams if threatened," the troll explained. "They are the reason we don't have many undersea dungeons."

"How often do they migrate close to Valaria?" Sir Pram asked, intrigued.

"Every three years or so," she told the selkie.

He nodded. "Perhaps we will have found the dungeon by then, and I can travel to see it."

Gerda stared at Pram for a long moment. "Why wait?"

"I am loyal to my lord." The selkie sat straighter on his horse. "And I am dedicated to this quest. No matter how long it takes."

Julian stiffened in his seat.

He knew that every member of his party was here willingly . . . but they had sacrificed much to follow him to the North. John had less time with his family, and Jeffry was leaving his work as viscount to his sister, while Sir Pram rarely saw his cousins near the shoreline anymore.

Granted, John made enough money to buy a palace, and Jeffry had outright told Julian he wanted an adventure before settling down . . . And Pram . . . Well, Pram's family was exiled from the Underdark. He wanted purpose and had sworn to follow Julian for life.

Everyone was here for a different reason.

On a side note, Sir Tully was here on forced community service after insulting a foreign dignitary, and Visha was a spy sent by his mother.

Gerda cut into Julian's thoughts with a simple, "No need to wait, Sir Pram. I can take us all to see the whales this weekend."

Sir Pram waved a hand in rejection. "I couldn't; not while on duty."

"It'll be fine." Gerda leaned in closer, speaking quietly but still within hearing of everyone present. "I was going to take Julian there on a date anyway."

"Were you now?" Julian asked, butting into their conversation.

"I was," Gerda told him. "I've been thinking about visiting to see how Drendil is adapting to a less xenophobic leadership."

"I'm looking forward to it," Julian told her.

"Is that . . . ?" Gerda asked, peering into the darkness ahead.

"Yes." Julian nodded. A group on horseback was headed their way.

John had come out to greet them.

CHAPTER 75

Fighting Before Breakfast Was the Worst

Gerda

True to my word, I abandoned Julian at the Northern Fortress after crossing his drawbridge.

As it was well after dark, there were promises of a celebratory welcome tomorrow before everyone disbanded for the evening. Julian slipped me a note before I portaled back home, and I wondered when he'd had the time to write it.

It simply read, *I hope you sleep well. Goodnight, beautiful.*

I *did* sleep well, and woke up early enough to enjoy a solid three-hour salt bath, which washed away the stress on my body.

We weren't scheduled to go into the Ice Fields today. Instead, I was set to explore the fortress and meet the members of the border patrol. As such, I dressed in leather pants and a long-sleeved blouse; light enough to survive the summer sun, yet sturdy enough to cut the icy northern wind.

Usually, at this point, I would wander into my kitchen, make breakfast and a cup of tea, then enjoy checking in on my notifications for the day. But my notifications went off just before I tried to connect my door to the living area, and the connection failed. [Sense Danger] was practically screaming at me, and my [Domain] skill tab was overwhelmed with updates.

One glance at the log revealed all.

[Your **Domain** has taken 130 points of Void damage . . .]
[Your **Domain** has taken 97 points of Void damage . . .]
[Your **Domain** has fallen to an enemy skill . . .]

I didn't bother reading the full reports but got straight to work while considering my options. I was safe in this subspace, since my attacker had already destroyed the only door in.

[You have activated **Bridge Repair**. Cost to repair adjusted for
Pocket Dimension status, 410 Mana. Time until completion
00:27:85]

I popped a potion to recover my mana, then activated [Oracle]. Sure enough, a certain Keeper of Fate was an available option, and I was immediately treated to a future view of the two of us doing battle in my kitchen. I winced as she launched a Void spell that shattered some of my favorite teacups.

Rude.

When I came out of it, I quickened my recovery by climbing off the bathroom floor and sticking my head under the bathtub faucet, running cold water on my face to help me center myself.

It was strange and unnerving, watching our battle from her perspective.

I hated being a part of Fate's plan. Hypocritical, but seeing Fate include me in her oracles made me feel like I was being watched, and it was an unpleasant twist in my gut.

I rubbed the shoulder I'd seen take a Void attack, thankful it was still there.

For a second, I thought about going and grabbing Julian to help me deal with the problem . . . but the oracle predicted my successful escape for a simple cost. And it was high time I had a cup of tea with my new archenemy.

I prepared a few items then appeared beside my kitchen table.

"You could've just knocked," I said nonchalantly, dodging a ball of pitch-black Void energy that sailed past my shoulder. I heard it hit my kitchen window and rip a hole into the Void. That was going to cost more mana to repair.

I summoned two teacups and placed them on the table before bringing out a teapot full of hot tea. Personally, I preferred fresh tea in the morning; something about the time-stop placebo taste that was all in my mind but also very real.

"Would you like a cup of tea?"

Guild Mistress Alice readied another spell; pink magic threads dangled from her fingers, and her aura covered her entire body, playing with her shoulder-length blonde hair and reflecting in her eyes.

She looked ready to kill.

My front door had been blown off its hinges; it lay crumpled at the celestial's feet, a portion of my dining room table voided from existence as well. I was impressed it was still standing in its current *U* shape.

"I would like you dead," she snapped. "By the Will of the Eternal Rest, [Void Arrow]."

"[World Bridge]," I said at the same time, portaling to my tea cabinet and storing the entire area in my storage ring. My cast was shorter than hers, and so made it easier to dodge.

Her attack hit the already gapping dimensional space that had been my window. I had no idea where the damage went from there, but I hoped it wasn't being flung willy-nilly into the meadow outside.

I liked that meadow.

She threw a knife at my head, but I just moved my head out of the way. I waved at the table. "Why don't we sit and chat?"

"I hate you." She lunged at me, a short sword appearing in her grip. I didn't need [Appraise] to tell me that the blade was poisoned. It was Alice's blade—of course it was poisoned.

"I don't see *why*." My perception tracked the trajectory of her assault perfectly, and I dodged again as the celestial let out a frustrated scream. Someone so beautiful and lovely suffering right in front of me made my heart hurt. But that was probably the charisma modifier at work. I brushed it off.

[Mental Resistance] for the win.

"Seriously, Alice," I said, a hand on my hip. "Why are we fighting? You follow Fate, and I—"

"*Do not* speak her name." Alice stamped her foot and lifted her short sword to prepare for another attack. "You are an abomination who goes against my Fate."

"Did Fate tell you that?" I asked, confused that Alice was still attached to the idea. I'd assumed she would have confronted Fate as soon as she was free and had a heart-to-heart.

Alice thrust her sword again, and I dodged, again.

"My Lady hasn't spoken to me since I failed my mission to kill you." Alice lifted a fist to her lips, opened her palm, and blew, sending sparkling, poisonous dust all over my dining area and the tea service. I reacted with, "[World Bridge]."

But I portaled away too late.

> [You have been poisoned by **Dandyvine**. You have taken 34 points
> of **Bleed** damage to all senses. Perk **Stronghold** negates 50% dam-
> age received while defending your **Domain**. You have taken 17
> points of damage.]

"Hey, not at the table!" I chastised, grabbing the towel by my kitchen sink to wipe my face and summoning Menlomin's Horn with the other. It immediately purified the poison.

"Also, gross." I threw my towel in the sink.

The celestial had used my momentary distraction to down a mana potion.

"By the Will of the Eternal Rest, [Void Arrow]." Alice hurled another attack, this one actually hitting my left shoulder.

[You have taken 116 points of Void damage. Perk **Stronghold** negates 50% damage received while defending your **Domain**. You have taken 58 points of damage.]
[You will not be able to use your left arm until healed.]

"Ugh," I hissed. Shoot, I'd hoped to avoid that. "Have you considered Fate could be angry at you for another reason? The same reason I'm not running away now when I *could've* just portaled out?" I asked, sidestepping a poisoned dagger as I unsummoned the unicorn horn in place of a health potion.

A second dagger flew, hitting the potion before I could take a drink, shattering the glass in my hand.

[You have taken 1 point of Cutting Damage. Perk **Stronghold** negates 50% damage received while defending your **Domain**. You take no damage.]

The potion that landed on my fingers actually did heal me a little. I sighed, concluding, "Because she wants us to talk?"

"You know *nothing* of her will," Alice spoke with unadulterated loathing. "You have *ruined* my life and my life's work. Even if you ran, I would hunt you to the ends of Valaria. *I swear by Fate that I will end you and stop at nothing to right destiny if it takes my whole life to do so.*" The Keeper of Fate glowed pink, her blonde hair lifting from the subtle mana that reacted to her vow.

While she monologued, I popped *another* potion and poured it directly onto my missing shoulder. It hurt more this way, but [Mental Resistance] didn't fail me.

With a grimace, I replied, "Well, what if some of us don't *want* what was fated for us?"

"Of course *you* would say that! *You* weren't even supposed to be here! You were meant to die in some misbegotten troll village!"

"I did, actually," I told her. "Well, *Gerda* did."

Alice had raised a hand with three more poison daggers sandwiched between her fingers but froze.

"What do you mean?" She didn't relax her hold on her weapons, but she did pause long enough for me to explain myself.

"I'm not Gerda." I wasn't ready for the wave of relief that hit when I finally said it. Aloud. "Listen, Alice." I waved at the two cups on the table. "I really do think we should talk. About why I'm here. About *everything.*"

"This is a trick," she said, her fists clenching around her daggers. Behind her, I noted with satisfaction that my door frame was no longer splintered and had started repairing itself.

"It's true. I'm *not* the *real* Gerda," I told her, pulling out a chair and sitting down. I waved again, urging her to take a seat across the table to join me, knowing she would.

There was a slight hesitation before Alice lowered her arm. The knives vanished. She didn't look like she trusted me, but she wasn't trying to void me from existence anymore, so that was a plus.

While she cautiously moved to take a seat, I brought out new and not-covered-in-poison tea. Despite my better judgement, I summoned us both some homemade biscotti from my inventory. It wasn't perfect, but it was close. I dunked mine in my tea and took a bite.

Ah. Perfect. Fighting before breakfast was the worst.

"I'll give you this one chance to speak . . ." she stated.

"I'm not from this world." I told her straight up. This wasn't something I'd told anyone before . . . but the Keeper of Fate wasn't just anyone. Alice was, to put it simply, the only person who might actually understand.

"In my life before, I was able to watch Valaria and its fate," I continued. "I've watched this world and every fate it could have taken; I've worked my way through every possible ending. Good . . . and bad."

"I am the Keeper of Fate; you will gain no sympathy from me," she snapped.

"I know you've also seen the other fates; that's why I'm telling you—because this world doesn't have any path that isn't full of heartache and *trauma*." I took an appreciative sip of tea.

"Then why did you watch it?" Alice stared at her own teacup with suspicion and didn't drink.

I blushed. "Reasons."

Her eyes narrowed, and I rushed to change the subject. "Five years ago, I died in my world and woke up in Gerda's body, with all of my old memories intact."

"And why do you think that Fate welcomed your presence?" Alice demanded. She tucked a straight lock of blonde hair behind her ear and glared at me with her strikingly big blue eyes. They were as clear as a summer sky. I looked away, reminding myself that she could trap my mind if I let myself go.

"Because I could change the story," I told her. "Guide things to an actual Happily Ever After. For everyone."

"All who see the future can change it," she refuted. "That's why Fate only grants her powers to those who won't abuse them. You've abused them more than any other being in history."

"But she must've *known* that I was going to change things," I countered.

"And that I'd stop you. [Watcher of Fate]."

[You have been affected by the Skill: **Watcher of Fate**. Your fate has been sealed for sixty-three seconds or until you are no longer being watched. Character Sheet sealed. Abilities sealed. Movement sealed. Health Points sealed. Mana Points sealed. Immune to all Damage.]
[You have been affected by the Skill: **Watcher of Fate**. Time until effect wears off 00:00:62]

Though it happened differently and I managed to actually have a conversation with Alice before she hit me with her ability, this was all still according to the original oracle. Now it was up to me to properly see it through to an end where I walked away from this encounter. Fighting Alice wasn't in my skill set. I wasn't a Combat class; I was a Defense class . . . and the Arcane Magesplitter Axe would probably do more damage to my domicile than the mage . . .

Besides, who wanted celestial all over my cottage? Not me. The thought made me sick.

[You have been affected by the Skill: **Watcher of Fate**. Time until effect wears off 00:00:61]

"Finally!" Alice stood up and walked over to my side of the table. She popped a mana potion and downed it, replenishing her reserves. Then, she wiped her mouth and stored her potion bottle. "You have no idea how much I've dreamed of this day." She pushed the table over, shattering everything on it on the floor, all so she could stand in front of me.

"You've been a thorn in my side from your first Crystal Cast." She swept her hair over her shoulder dramatically, looking down at me.

[You have been affected by the Skill: **Watcher of Fate**. Time until effect wears off 00:00:52]

She paced back and forth in front of me. "You've undone *years* of planning and hard work, toppled future governments, and destroyed the fate of *countless* innocents."

That wasn't really fair; it should be that I'd *saved* countless innocents.

"*You* are the reason I'm an international criminal, forced into hiding. I can't even go to my favorite bakery anymore!" she ground out. Again, not fair; she was the leader of the Blackfog spies, and from what I knew, already an international criminal. I'd just told everyone what she looked like, and she'd turned around and exposed me, so I'd actually call us even.

[You have been affected by the Skill: **Watcher of Fate**. Time until
effect wears off 00:00:41]

"Fate has stopped answering my prayers *because of you!*" Alice yelled. "And I
can't even enjoy the simplicity of your demise because it's going to take me *years*
to undo your meddling. The very idea of it makes me want to take every extra
second to really savor this moment!"

[You have been affected by the Skill: **Watcher of Fate**. Time until
effect wears off 00:00:28]

"I'm going to void your heart, and then I'm going to use [Sever Fate] on your
body, so even *if* you've hidden a piece of it somewhere, no one will be able to
revive it." She laughed with pure and utter malice. "And when I'm *sure* you are
dead, I'll use *this*."

She summoned a small vial, wagging it in my face. "You thought I'd used
my last one in the church, didn't you? But no. I've been saving this one for *you*,
Madame Potts."

Her plan was a bit overkill, to be honest.

Not that it was going to work.

"And when I'm done"—she lifted one hand and pressed it firmly against my
heart—"I'm going to collect your ashes and scatter them on the floor of Fate's
temple as an offering."

[You have been affected by the Skill: **Watcher of Fate**. Time until
effect wears off 00:00:09]

"Goodbye, Madame Potts." Her smile was so breathtakingly beautiful. The
seconds ticked down until, "By the Will of the Eternal Rest, [Void Arrow]."

The attack was already piercing my chest when her skill ended . . . and taking
half damage meant nothing for an instant-kill hit that ripped a hole through my
heart. As I slumped to my knees, too many things happened all at once.

Alice touched my head and followed up her previous attack with, "[Sever
Fate]," before promptly dumping the vial of molten ash vane on me. A bunch of
notifications told me what was happening while I palmed Menlomin's Horn to
purify the poison.

[You have been affected by **Sever Fate**. For twenty-four hours, you
are immune to **Raise**, **Resurrect**, **Revive**, or **Respawn**.]
[Single-use item **Phoenix Feather** activated. When you would otherwise die, you are **Reborn** instead. Health Points 777/777. Mana

Points 1215/1215. All status effects nullified. All curses undone.
All equipped items at max durability.]
[You have been hit by **Molten Ash Vane**. Do you wish to **Purify**
the **Molten Ash Vane** with **Menlomin's Horn**. Yes/No.]

Alice realized something was wrong when I didn't just dissolve into a pile of ash. "WHY WON'T YOU JUST DIE?"

"[World Bridge]."

To activate the spell, I had to be in motion, so I pushed myself away from her to stand.

Both of us appeared on the bridge I had set up in view of Her Eminence Feliwyn sleeping by the shores of Lake Loria. Previously, my battle with Alice had ended on the Coral Palace sky bridge . . . and that had been a disaster.

Maybe here she'd wake up Feliwyn early, and the dragon would eat her.

Stumbling from the forced transport, Alice snarled, "*You b—*"

"WHY DO ROGUES WEAR LEATHER?" I yelled at her. It was the first riddle I could think of, and it threw her off-balance long enough for me to get off another spell.

"Enter by the Channels, [Troll Magic]!"

Alice shrilled, "You can't trap me here with your stupid riddles! [Portal]!"

She appeared not ten feet away on the other side of the bridge, turning toward me in triumph.

Of course she did; I hadn't cast any bridge spells to keep her. My purpose in bringing her here had been to get her out of my house long enough to move it, preferably somewhere she wouldn't think to look for it.

"It's because they like Hide," I answered the riddle for her.

"That's it—I am going to void you until there's nothing left," she hissed, lifting one hand.

"You'll have to find me first. [World Bridge]." I stepped backward and portaled away.

CHAPTER 76

Pompolin's Café

Julian

Visha summoned Julian to the front gate, where he found a very focused Gerda rapidly magicking sigils into the wooden frame of his drawbridge.

"What happened?" he demanded, seeing the bloody state she was in. Her dress was full of holes from attacks that she'd healed but not cleaned; one on her sleeve, the other over her heart.

"She's tried casting this same spell four times." Sir Dimmund, the current guard on duty, told him.

Julian called out to her, "Gerda?"

"No time!" she yelled back, rushing to the last unmarked section.

Then she started cursing. The entire magical array faltered and faded as she released the spell and activated another instead. "Enter by the Channels, [Troll Magic]."

She downed a mana potion and started her magical array all over again.

Julian waited patiently for her to finish. Behind him, many of the border guards were lined up, watching. They hadn't tried to stop Gerda, which he was happy to note.

This time, she successfully completed her spell.

"A Bridge Is Home, and Home Is a Bridge, [Troll Magic]," she declared, and the sigils disappeared into the wood. Gerda collapsed onto her knees, breathing heavily. "*Finally!*"

There was a murmuring from the crowd of onlookers, but Julian waved them back to their posts. Visha remained, standing quietly at attention.

"Is now a good time?" Julian asked, offering Gerda a hand.

"Yes." She took it and let him pull her to her feet. "Alice found me. I wanted to move my home bridge here, but she kept finding my door while I was casting the spell."

Julian gave the troll a once-over. She looked absolutely breathtaking and unhurt, except for the damage to her clothing. He wanted to take her somewhere and do a more . . . *thorough* check, but decided that could wait. "And you succeeded?"

"I did—but not before she completely destroyed my house. I think she thought that I'd come out if she did enough damage to my pocket space." Her face fell. "My poor plants are a mess."

"I'm sorry," Julian told her, not knowing what else to say. He'd never kept a plant before. He rubbed the back of her hand soothingly with his thumb. It equally calmed his own building rage that someone had dared to attack her—and the frustration that he hadn't been there to help her when it happened.

"No, I'm sorry." She glanced at the fortress and back at him. "It wasn't my plan to take over a North Sumbrian bridge, but I figured this was a better place to hide my door than in the Dark Enchanted Forest."

"I'm happy you did. And that you are safe," he told her.

Gerda lifted a sleeve to wipe her brow but stopped midway and stared. There was blood on it. "Wow. I need a shower."

"You do," he agreed. Preferably with him.

"Can I have one here?" she asked. "I don't want to *look* at my house right now."

"You can use mine."

He brought her inside, and after a wash and change of clothes, Julian took her to his office. If he had to work, he wanted her where he could see her and be sure she was safe. Jeffry and Visha were already there, tackling a mountain of documents that needed to be reviewed and signed. They barely registered when Julian escorted Gerda over to a chair.

She must have been running on survival and adrenaline because the second Gerda sat down, she started shaking.

"Visha—" Julian turned to order his general to go and find the fort healer, but he was cut off by Gerda's trembling hand gripping the sleeve of his shirt.

"Julian," Gerda said softly.

"Yes?"

"I want breakfast," she declared. "A real one."

"Alright."

"I want fresh bimbleberry breakfast cakes from Pompolin's Café."

Julian froze. "I don't—"

"Please?" she said, her voice also shaking. It was a request, made in a moment of vulnerability. "Come with me?"

Movement caught his eye. Visha waved at him to leave even as she continued filing. Jeffry looked less than pleased but nodded. Julian would have to bring them both something for the trouble.

"Alright."

Gerda stood, and suddenly, they were portaling to the capital of Peldeep. They appeared on a bridge in an empty park near the merchant's district. He'd honestly thought they'd portal to one of the major bridges crossing the river, but then realized the problem with doing so.

He didn't want to appear inside another living creature. That would be a disaster.

They didn't head off right away. Instead, Gerda threw her arms around him, and Julian held her until her tremors settled.

"Thank you." When Gerda pulled back, she looked a little bit more like her usual self: calm, confident, and hiding something. Her hand found his, and she forced a pleasant, "I'm better now. And I'll have you back in the North in an hour, promise."

"Alright," he said again, adding a light tease, "By that point, I'm sure Jeffry will have the appropriate forms you need to sign to register a proper troll bridge in North Sumbria."

"Ugh, don't remind me," Gerda groaned. "I pay enough taxes."

Julian quipped, "You can afford it."

"True."

Pompolin's Café served homemade pompolins, a figure-eight-shaped cake pocket stuffed with fruit and whipped cream. The usual varieties were too sweet for Julian's palate, so he picked out one with nut and seed butter, while Gerda ordered a triple berry with cream. Julian waited until they had ordered and were settled before broaching his thoughts.

"This might be a bad time to ask, but what do you think about traveling into the Ice Fields right away?"

It was something to distract her. And it worked.

"I'm fine with that . . . Actually, that would be even better." She took a bite of her pompolin and left a bit of cream on her lip. Julian was distracted watching her tongue lick it clean and almost missed her next sentence. "It'll cost more mana, but if I make bridges in the North and move my door there, I can keep ahead of our Blackfog mistress."

"What happens if your bridge is destroyed while the door is attached?" he asked, dragging his attention back to his own breakfast.

"Nothing good." She sighed. "Without the anchor, the pocket dimension drifts in the Void and takes damage. If I don't fix it quickly, it'll start to destabilize and could even collapse."

"So we'll have to be careful where we put them."

"And I'll need to make a second traveling bridge," she reasoned, "so I can leave one with the door while creating a new one at our next rest stop. Or just move the door back to the Northern Fortress every time?"

"That's a lot of extra mana and time. We can build you a second bridge if you have the space to carry it. If not, I'll send a request to my mother to make a storage ring for that size. It'll take a week, but—"

"I have the storage." She waved away his concern.

Julian eyed her ring, which already professed to contain two hundred scrolls, a Master Crystal, and had originally housed his Legendary-class armor set. "Gerda, my dearest . . ." She paused midbite of berries and cream, eyes going wide at his term of endearment. He enjoyed watching her blush. ". . . Should I ask after your equipped items and travel supplies? Or is it better not to know?"

Gerda swallowed her bite of pompolin as she eyed him, sizing him up to determine if he was trustworthy or not. He was glad to see that he passed. "I guess I could show you my inventory. Hells, I haven't planned what to do with it after, so let me know if you want anything—"

"After what?" Julian interrupted, a sense of unease gripping his gut.

"After the, well, after I'm done in the North. That'll be my last big quest, and then we'll see what Fate decides. Either way, I probably won't need all of this." She held up her hand, showing off the ring. "As much as I like the idea of pretending to be a dragon hoarding treasure . . . there are people who could actually use this stuff. I figured I'd just, I don't know, do like the Lady of the Lake and hand out rare magic swords to would-be heroes." Her voice caught, and she pretended to smile.

"You can auction treasures you aren't using and use that to recover the fines you just paid. Or just keep them for when you need them," he countered, frustrated that she kept giving so much away for free. From the life-saving Crystal Casts to the Valarian Royal Set . . . but he didn't want her to see his anger, so he shot her a smile and asked, "How many rare magical swords do you have to give away?"

"Thirty-seven."

Julian choked. "Thirty-seven?"

"Thirty-seven," she repeated. "And twelve magical spears, nine daggers, six bows, five axes, three shields, two war hammers, and a partridge in a pear tree."

The list made him reel; the last confused him. "A partridge?"

"There is a song where I come from, and we sing it for winter solstice. It ends with that line after a long countdown list. I know it's dumb to say it here, but sometimes, I need to say these things to remember where I'm from." She smiled thinly. "Maybe I'll sing it for you if I'm still—if *we* are still together by darkest day."

Julian reached out and grabbed her hand. "We will be, unless you're planning to abandon me already."

"No." The look on her face told him she wasn't sure. It hurt . . . but he didn't push the issue.

"Alright, then." He knew *exactly* how her last relationship had ended, and he could wait until she felt more certain of his affections. He would just have to win her over until she stopped hesitating every time they spoke about the future.

She recovered and said, "Speaking of heading north right away, I was thinking about our travel schedule."

It was a deliberate change of topic, but Julian didn't stop her. She had things to work through . . . and he would be there until she was ready to let him in.

CHAPTER 77

The Rainbow Whales

Gerda

Three Days into the North

"ANYTHING?" Julian yelled at me from behind his Valarian Royal Shield.

Poor timing was forcing us to retreat. After fighting a pair of level forty-seven glacial serpents, our party had been immediately set upon by four snow leopardans; they were like snow leopards, if snow leopards were the size of a school bus and spat venom.

"Do you know how hard it is to put a bridge down in a *flat field of ice?*" I yelled over the sounds of battle, searching for any spot that my [Bridge Sense] skill told me would work. Usually, I used this skill to *find* bridges, but it was proving perfect for finding apt places to lay new ones down as well.

"[Sword Slash]," Jeffry said. He didn't use his ability to attack the beasts but instead hit the icy floor and cut a line in the terrain. "How about now?!"

"By Battle's Grace, [Bludgeoning Kiss]." Tully's war hammer knocked one leopardan into another, sending them both sliding on the ice.

"Not yet!" I couldn't duck while holding up a half-moon bridge as long as I was tall, so Julian's [Barrier] took the blow when the fourth leopardan broke their defenses and hit me. Visha jumped onto its back, and it bucked against her hold, rolling while trying to get the elf to let go.

"[Piercing Blade]." Jeffry's blade sunk straight down into the ice, and there was a great shudder. Everyone, including the leopardans, paused midbattle.

A crack formed in the ice, running between the swordfighter's legs and splitting into a terrifying crevice. I was a safe distance away, but Jeffry and Pram, as well as the leopardan Julian was battling, all desperately scrambled to not fall in. After an uncomfortable twenty seconds, the rumbling stopped.

"Got it!" I dropped the bridge down where I instinctively knew a bridge could go. And by instinctively, I meant it was my passive skill.

[**Bridge Sense** has found a usable bridge.]

I ran across. "Alright, everyone, to me!"

There was a mad dash to get to the bridge, with Julian as the last member fighting his way toward me.

I portaled us out.

"Daddy!" A little girl with honey-brown hair in two long pigtails ran up to us and threw her arms around John's leg. He swooped down to kiss her on the cheek.

"Let me go clean up, and then we can play," John told his daughter, Phoebe. She took his offered hand, and they headed for the manor. He wandered off with only a wave over his shoulder goodbye, Phoebe already talking his ear off about the magical bubble maker she wanted to show him.

Lord Johnathon Thomas had decided to install a pond with a bridge on his property so he could go home for meals, and I'd portaled us all here, since it was nearing dinner.

I was shouldering off my winter coat when Pram came up behind me.

"Miss Gerda?" The selkie positively glowed with excitement when he asked, "Do you think the rainbow whales are going to come today?"

I nodded, "But I only know they're passing by the coast; it'll be Luck if we find them."

"I want to try," Pram said.

Julian reached out and took my hand. "Know any good places to eat in Drendil?"

"Benny's Fish Shack," I answered, remembering Henrietta's date with Sir Phineas at the seafood restaurant during the knights' route. "But only if Tully orders everything alone and brings it down to the beach for us."

"Hey!" Sir Tully wore his normal full-plate paladin armor but took off a pair of fuzzy mittens he used while in the North. "Why do I have to buy lunch?"

"You're human?" I shot back. My free hand pointed at my tusks and then at Julian's ears for emphasis.

"Oh, yeah. Fair."

"[Troll Magic]." The second jump dropped us at the top of a hill. A wide river stretched down to the ocean below, with a cute seaside town on their right. Off in the distance, far out on the waves, swam a pod of rainbow whales. I focused my perception until I could see them as clearly as if they were right in front of me.

They were swimming in the opposite direction.

"They are so beautiful," Pram breathed, leaning on the small ledge of the stone bridge we were all still standing on. "I'll meet you all here in an hour!"

With that, Pram leapt over the ledge and dropped straight into the river below. His clothing faded away, and where once there was Pram, now there was a blue sheen seal.

"Think he'll actually be back in an hour?" Visha asked Jeffry.

Jeffry scoffed. "Unlikely."

"Bet?"

"You're on."

The two shook hands.

"If you're done." Julian placed my hand on his arm. "Let's go."

Tully went into town to get us something to eat, and the rest of us followed a foot-worn path down to the ocean. I wasn't partial to sand, so I set up a picnic blanket on the grassy hill overlooking the surf. Julian and I sat on the blanket and enjoyed a cold ice tea while Jeffry summoned a chair, a wide-brimmed hat, and a book. Below, Visha went for a walk along the beach.

The food ended up tasting great, and Pram was only half an hour late.

CHAPTER 78

I Do Love Gossip

Julian

One Week into the North

To say that travelling with Gerda was wonderful would've been an understatement. Instead of pushing through until they were forced to give up and go back to the fortress, they were making steady progress, and spirits were high.

The days were spent leisurely exploring, and the nights were spent in a warm bed.

"Good morning." Julian bit Gerda's neck playfully then sat up before she could swat him.

Fresh ocean air drifted in from the open window. Gerda had moved it to a small bridge she had at the southern tip of Sumbria. It made the summer nights bearable.

"Morning." Gerda stretched languidly, and he wished they had more time together. He craved it . . . But work called, and so did the bathroom.

They'd developed a routine in the days they'd spent together; they would bathe, get changed, tidy up the bedroom, and then have breakfast. That morning, he'd snuck a note under her pillow before they left. He enjoyed writing his thoughts to Gerda, and this one said simply, *I can't stop thinking about your smile.*

Breakfast was overnight oats with cinnamon sugar and freshly picked peaches. Gerda had gone out and picked the peaches while he poured over reports from the Northern Fortress at the table.

"Corporal Saunders sent word," he told her when she brought over the food. "There's been elevated monster activity in the area."

"Alright." Gerda put down their plates before pouring him a glass of his new favorite drink.

"We'll have to prepare for a surge." Julian enjoyed the smell of fresh cranderberry iced tea. His glass had slices of candied citron stirred with the ice, and a tart bite. Just like his bridge troll.

"Just leave Tully behind to defend the fort; he could use the experience points."

"He's dodged a month of disciplinary punishment already, with us coming to the North. I bet Visha would approve." He chuckled, setting aside work to eat.

"Oh?" she asked.

"He was tasked with training the knights in the afternoons for a month, which means we could abandon him at the border with due cause."

"Is he enough to hold back a surge?" Gerda asked, dubious.

"Tully can handle the first wave of monsters just fine, and we could come back for the actual battle." Julian picked up their dishes and carried them into the kitchen. While he washed all of the breakfast dishes and set them to dry on the rack, he told her, "The hidden dungeon has been sending out monster surges every few months. We're all used to it by now."

Gerda came up behind him and wrapped her arms around his back. "Let's go tell him."

Two Weeks into the North

"How do you get used to *this*?" Gerda wondered aloud, looking at the chaos below. They'd received a summons from Tully that afternoon and had come back to help.

"Aerial team, hold off the frost goliath. Vanguard, attack the snow craigies." Julian stood beside her on the fortress wall. He'd already activated his [Battle Call] to direct the soldiers. To Gerda, he joked, "You just throw away rationality or hope for peace." After a pause, he let himself give a more honest answer, adding, "Or think about those you are defending."

Visha took down two snow craigies, fluffy beasts that looked like snowballs with long ratlike noses, sharp teeth and claws, and long, hairy tails. The remaining three were surrounded by his knights and defeated.

Tully hit the frost goliath with his war hammer, sending the monster back a step. It shook itself and swung a fist at the paladin. Behind them, Julian counted twelve holly treants and forty-seven armored trouters. The fish monsters only came up to his knee, but they had a vicious bite.

Gerda turned on a dime, lifting her hand to shield her eyes against the sun. "There are more monsters circling around the east side. None Shall Pass by, [Bridge Barrier]." She set the same riddle that everyone had already agreed upon, "What do dragons use to measure things correctly?"

The answer was their scales.

The drawbridge remained lowered during the battle to let the knights retreat in case of an emergency. Any monster would have to circle to the south side of the fortress to access it. And answer the riddle to cross.

"Eyes to the east, Jeffry. Flankers incoming." He gave the order without hesitation.

Jeffry left off distracting the frost goliath to scout the area Gerda pointed to.

"Five rocksoc; what are your orders?" Jeffry yelled down at us from the sky. The creatures were burrowing rodents the size of a cat. Usually, they cut through the frozen mountainside and made their homes inside the dark caves.

"Corporal Saunders, fall back. I need your party to circle around the fort and set up a subterrain defense line," Julian instructed. "Pram, you're with them."

The selkie moved with the group.

"Dearest"—Julian grabbed Gerda's hand and pulled her closer, dropping a kiss on her cheek—"I think it's time I head down. Can you hold the fort?"

"Of course." She waved him on. "Just make sure everything is cleaned before dinner—I had a surprise planned for us tonight, remember?"

"I remember." He leapt off the wall, over the moat, and straight into a row of trouters.

He wouldn't risk their date or his alone time with Gerda.

It was time to wrap this up.

"We're having dinner here?" he asked, watching Gerda set down a picnic blanket on the grassy field beside Lake Loria. He knew she'd deliberately been avoiding Nilheim until now.

They were in the shade of a tree at the forest's edge. Nearby, a family of sprites were on vacation, sunbathing on a patch of sand. A ways away, three mermaids frolicked on a rocky bank, singing a lilting harmony. Plittsmouth, the underwater city in Lake Loria, couldn't be seen from the shore, but on a beautiful day like today, there were countless denizens of the deep enjoying a swim to the surface and a spot of sun.

There was also a fire-breathing dragon napping about fifty paces away. Her Eminence Feliwyn was curled up on a dragon-sized blanket much like the one Gerda was using now.

"Yes, now come help," Gerda told him, sitting down and pulling out an actual picnic basket full of food. She was perfectly able to store everything in her ring, so the basket was purely for aesthetics.

Julian unequipped his Valarian Royal Set. He also stored his socks and shoes, wearing only a simple tunic tucked into his britches before he dropped onto his knees and helped. There were potato wedges, roasted fowl, honey butter buns, smoked cheese, fig jam, pickled cabbage, and a bowl of fresh fruit.

Gerda pulled out a bottle of wine, and he accepted a glass.

Tinking their drinks together, the vintage that met his lips tasted like the sun itself, bright and acidic. It was lovely, with the smell of forged iron and a tang that settled on his tongue long after he pulled away to look at the glass and scrutinize its delicious contents.

"What is this?" he asked, savoring the taste.

It was one of the best wines he'd ever had.

"I got it from the Dark Queen Roselia's hidden treasure trove," she said, shooting him a grin over her own glass. "That's King Keith's great-great-grandmother, I think?"

"I have so many questions," he said. Instead of asking any, he simply took another sip and enjoyed the flavor.

"I'll be happy to answer them later, but for now . . ." Gerda turned toward the giant green-and-purple dragon who'd just shifted in her sleep.

"You knew?" Julian froze, wondering if he should reequip his set.

She didn't answer, simply shuffling across the blanket to lean against him. Since she was unconcerned, so was he. Julian wrapped an arm around her waist and waited.

Her Eminence Feliwyn stretched like a dragon would: arched back, forearms sliding forward until they brushed the grass at the edge of her blanket. She flexed her talons in the earth and yawned wide, showing off teeth the length of a kitchen knife.

Golden eyes opened with a hint of sleepiness, the irises like thin black diamonds.

The entire forest was silent as everyone held their breaths.

Feliwyn turned her gaze on all: the mermaids, the sprites, and the pair of them. One eyebrow rose delicately at the sight of Duke Julian of the North cuddling a troll woman on the banks of Lake Loria.

It was important to show proper courtesy to a dragon, or they might eat you, so Julian tried to stand and greet the dragon.

Gerda stopped him, grabbing his hand and pulling him back down to the blanket.

"Your Eminence." The troll waved a hand at their picnic spread. "Would you like to break your fast with us? It's been eight years, and I promise you, I have *all* the best gossip."

The dragon eyed them for a moment longer before her face split into a wide, toothy smile, and she spoke with a deep, effeminate voice, like warm honey cake.

"I *do* love gossip."

CHAPTER 79

Not the Only Love Story

Gerda

I'd popped by the lake to watch Feliwyn before—who *wouldn't* go and look at a real-life, fire-breathing dragon a stone's throw away from their front door?

And in all that time, I'd thought that I'd built some immunity to the dragon.

That was not so; in fact, it was only my [Mental Resistance] which kept me from melting into a terrified puddle of fear at the immense aura pressing down on me as Feliwyn dragged her picnic blanket over to ours.

Her body was the size of a truck. Her head was the size of a recliner leather chair, and despite the terrible size-comparison analogies, she was anything but clunky or plush. Her scales were sleek and lovely, and she moved with grace.

"I didn't know what you'd like," I said, bringing out everything I had prepared for this day. "But I hope something catches your fancy?"

I started with four loaves of bread, sliced lengthwise and toasted: cheesy garlic, cranderberry, honey nut, and plain rye. Besides that, I served four whole-roasted floofpoof birds, seven pounds of flying pig bacon, eight floofpoof bird eggs scrambled and topped with a drizzle of maple smoke barbecue sauce, a serving bowl with ten cups of warm rice, an open barrel of black coffee, and a bucket of cherries jubilee.

I also brought out a tray of twelve warm cinnamon buns and put them off to the side to cool. I'd stored them right out of the oven.

"This looks delicious, troll." Feliwyn reached out with her claws and daintily picked up the bowl of plain rice. After smelling the dish, the dragon gave a pleased smile and then ate the entire thing, bowl and all. "I'm *famished.*"

"May I introduce you, Your Eminence, to Gerda the Bridge Troll?" Julian said. He reached out and placed a hand on mine. "She is an oracle who has been helping Valaria prevent disaster while you were in slumber."

"I see." Feliwyn's eyes dropped to where our hands were linked.

"I've only been here for five, but I'm happy to tell you everything I've learned since." I leaned in close to the dragon, jumping right into it. "Princess Penelope eloped with a bear beastman who runs an inn and tavern in Gren's Keep! All of the royals are as they were except for Drendil, but Regent Havork is holding down the fort. Their Royal Highness Rowen is thinking of abdicating—and Guild Master Warren Jones finally retired. Now, his assistant has captured his heart. Literally."

"Really?" Feliwyn smiled slowly. "Do you know where he kept it hidden?"

"The Temple of Justice," I explained, knowing this bit of lore from my playthrough of Bastian's route combined with the oracle of Warren's freedom. "She had to wait for the *exact* moment his contract broke, then she could steal his heart and summon Warren for herself. That's not the only love story either . . . King Keith got married in this very field."

Feliwyn froze. "Keith is wed?"

I'd deliberately waited a bit to tell her, to help ease the news. "And Chloe."

I knew from the slitted eyes and intense look that Feliwyn was deciding how to feel about that. I pressed on, adding a helpful, "Rufus is only engaged."

"Any children?"

"No plans yet."

The feeling of a knife on the back of my throat subsided as the dragon withdrew a bit of her intent. "Good." Then she stuffed the entire tray of cinnamon buns into her mouth, threw back the coffee, and shook herself. Wings spread wide enough to block out the sky in front of us.

"I will remember you, Miss Gerda." The dragon nodded at my date. "Julian, give my regards to your mother."

With that, the dragon launched herself into the sky.

Julian lifted my hand and kissed the back of it. "Don't do it."

"What?" I stopped, my other hand already outstretched toward the dragon's picnic blanket, a season-three treasure if ever I saw one. "She won't even remember it's gone."

Three Weeks into the North

"You never said there would be stairs."

There were an endless number of steps stretching ahead, and while I had super troll abilities, it didn't stop the stairs from being an annoyance.

Julian smiled at my grumbling. "You could ask Jeffry to borrow the amulet—"

"Not happening!" Jeffry declared, swooping past them. Great eagle wings carried him on the winds as he scouted ahead.

"—or not."

"It's a four-day walk to the end of the canyon, and four days back," John told me. He was cheating, sending a shadow along while he remained behind and then shadow walking over whenever it reached the perk's distance limitation. "Or cross it this way."

"Who even made these stairs?" I asked, dejected.

"The stairs were first constructed during Duchess Emelan's rule." Jeffry flew down and landed at the front of the party, his wings folded in. Never one to resist educating someone, he launched into it. "Her wife, Duchess Yulia, created the canyon during one of their battles. The pair were considered as passionate in hate as in love, and took to the Ice Fields whenever they needed to settle a quarrel."

"How—" I began, but Julian answered, "They were both level eighty by the time they retired."

Jeffry cleared his throat at their interruptions and continued. "It took four years to complete the project, and legend says they never even stepped foot on the path themselves."

"Incoming!" John pointed at a glint of light further up the stairs.

Jeffry launched himself back in the air while Julian brought up a [Barrier]. Visha ran sideways on the wall up and over our party in some gravity-defying perk, while pulling out curved twin blades.

Tully stood with me. He wasn't allowed to use his war hammer on the stairs.

"Ice spiders," Jeffry called out from the sky. "Three ahead, two behind, and one above."

"I'm never letting you take over scouting again, Jeffry," John said. "It's an ambush."

"They're literally see-through, John!" Jeffry defended, pulling out his sword and immediately swiping it. "[Sword Slash]." There was an angry hiss as the attack hit a spider like iced-over glass the size of a Great Dane that had tried to jump on top of us.

It stumbled over the edge.

"Okay, that's going to give me nightmares," I said, more casually than I thought my racing heart would've allowed. Up ahead, Julian and Visha were battling three spiders, Jeffry was attacking one from the rear, John was cutting the spurs, and Pram was concentrating on the overhead.

Tully just mumbled a dejected, "This sucks."

"I know, it's not fun waiting it out." I patted him on the pauldron. "Do you have any buffs?"

He shook his head. "Nothing. I can't do anything but fight. I'm a paladin of Justice, total damage dealer."

"He's also good with sewing," Pram commented. He had a bow with a large magical ice arrow set on it, aiming for the spider above. "You made that plushie for Phoebe for her birthday."

"That's not helpful, Pram," Tully said.

Frozen spurs latched onto the side of the stairs, piercing and anchoring into the ground at my feet. Two more followed as one long leg climbed up over the edge.

"Mine!" Tully pushed me up the stairs and out of the way as he swung his war hammer. It hit the spider and sent it flying out into the ravine. Unfortunately, the spurs were still connected to the spider, and it ripped the stairwell apart beneath us. Despite knowing I could portal to safety, I still screamed as I fell into open air.

"I've got you!" Julian was suddenly there, grabbing my hand. Far below me, Jeffry had caught Tully and was cursing loudly as he flew the paladin back up to safety.

"Don't let go!" I told Julian.

"Of course." He pulled me up with one hand, the other using his Valarian Royal Shield to defend against a web spur shot. When my feet were on solid ground, he took the extra second to kiss me on the cheek. "I would never let you go."

"Feliwyn swooped in and lifted me clean out of the garden! Can you believe it?" Henrietta was beaming at me over a mug of ale.

"I can," I said, remembering the sheer ferocity of the dragon.

We were on a girls' night at a tavern in Peldeep. As soon as she had returned from her trip with her dragon mother-in-law, I'd abandoned Julian at the Northern Fortress and dragged Henrietta out for an evening of fun.

"Her Eminence flew us straight to the Depths of Despair Dungeon to test me. It was amazing!" Henrietta regaled. "She took over the entire dungeon so she could watch my battle technique. And she was so nice! She told me that I cleared it faster than Keith did when *he* was my level. And she told me I was doing a great job as Dark Lady." The smile on my Henrietta's face softened. "She's more than I could've hoped for in a mother-in-law."

"I'm glad."

"I do feel bad for my husband, though." Henrietta set her chin on the palm of her hand and leaned on the table. "She's thrown everything into chaos since coming home, and he was very worried when she kidnapped me without notice."

"He'll be okay," I assured her. "It's always hard when family comes to visit— let alone when they are a dragon."

"She wasn't even going to stay with us, but someone ransacked her cave in Thistlecrick, so we are just waiting for her while she picks out a new lair. How is living with Julian?" Henrietta's eyes lit up with curiosity.

"Good." Unbidden, I thought about exactly how wonderful it was living with Julian. "He leaves me notes."

"Notes?"

I showed her one that I'd found under my plate the last time he'd made breakfast and had to duck out early for work.

I hope you enjoy breakfast.

"That's so sweet—" Henrietta paused when the lights dimmed overhead. The show was about to start.

Minstrel Brownie came out on stage, and we enjoyed an evening of good food, music, and friends.

CHAPTER 80

Wisdom Isn't an Attribute

Julian

Four Weeks into the North

August was almost over.

"Are you sure you don't want to head in?" Julian asked. They were alone, lying on the Ice Fields under the full moon.

"Five more minutes." Gerda snuggled closer to him, running her hands up his chest and playing with the string of his tunic. They were on top of a pile of enchanted blankets. The bottom layer had a cooling feature that prevented the heated upper layer from melting the icy ground below. "It was hard today—there were fourteen assassins clogging up the roads, and I'm starting to get complaints."

She showed him a letter with the most politely worded chastisement.

> *To Miss Gerda Jones,*
> *Due to an increase in traffic disruption on your controlled bridges, the Dark Horde is experiencing delays in all areas of transportation. We would like to inform you that all complaints will henceforth be liable to affect your unit domain registration.*
> *Please deal with any future disturbances in a timelier manner.*
> *Signed,*
> *Keith Monfort of Nilheim, King of the Dark Enchanted Forest*

Julian wondered if she wouldn't let the entire party face Alice head-on for her . . . and why she hadn't asked yet.

She breathed slowly, the tension leaving her shoulders. "I love it out here. It's beautiful."

"It is." Julian covered her hand on his chest.

They would start climbing the mountain range tomorrow, but tonight was a date under the northern lights. And while many of the stars weren't visible through the aurora, one comet shone clear and bright.

"I wonder if Master Thomas is ready yet?" Gerda mused, though she didn't sound concerned.

Julian grumbled a soft, "He'd better be."

Five Weeks into the North

They reached a bridge of ice that connected one mountain to the next.

"Once we cross here, we *should* be clear through the mountain pass," he told Gerda as he pointed to a peak further south along the mountain range. "That was the path we took last time, and it showed this bridge leading to a staircase that will take us straight down."

They rarely took the same path twice while searching the mountains because they were always searching new areas for the hidden dungeon, and this trip was no exception.

So far, Julian had barely had the opportunity to search the grounds on the northern tip of the Ice Fields. Aside from searching the fields, canyons, and the hundreds of caves throughout the mountain range itself, they'd also had to return to deal with monster surges and his mother's seasonal balls. There was a five-month stretch between the Winter Feast and the Spring Ball because the winter solstice ushered in larger and more aggressive monster surges than the rest of the year.

The entirety of North Sumbria's military came out in full force to guard the border. As such, the vassal families and North Sumbria's elite weren't free until late spring, so that was when the Spring Ball heralded in the matchmaking season.

"The bridge is secure." John came back from his inspection and added, "But there are some weak spots. Just don't—" The sound of cracking split the air. They all turned around to see Sir Tully, one foot lifting from a spot of splintered ice. "—step on the white lines," the rogue finished, his teeth clenched. "Tully!"

"In my defense," the paladin said, watching the cracks creep forward along the bridge until the entire structure began to crumble and fall. "I didn't use the war hammer this time."

"Do you think he has a curse?" Gerda asked. "We should have Chloe check him, just in case."

He shook his head. "Oh, she's checked."

"Wisdom debuff?" Gerda asked in all seriousness.

"Gerda, love"—he paused—"wisdom isn't an attribute."

She paused. "Ah, of course. Intelligence? Perception?"

This wasn't the first time something like that had happened. His troll had strange mannerisms, created foreign foods, and sometimes used incomplete or even false logic. He didn't know how different the trolls were . . . but he had long suspected it wasn't just because she was a troll.

He was thinking she might not even be from Valaria. His suspicions had started when she'd told Feliwyn that she'd only been here for five years, and he'd only found more clues in the weeks since.

There were two other continents . . . a year's sail away. Through monster-infested waters.

Maybe her husband had been so terrible that she'd literally chosen to make the journey to get away from him—or sent a bridge in her place. As many scenarios as he could imagine, he hadn't brought it up; if she wanted to tell him, she would have.

"Chloe has checked for *everything*," Julian told his troll. "The only thing we can't check is if he annoyed Luck somehow and she's doing it to him on purpose."

"I can hear you." Sir Tully sighed. "You know that, right?"

Eagle wings sprouted from Jeffry's back as he looked between John and Gerda. "Who am I flying to the other side?"

John stepped forward. "I'll go."

"I might be able to make a new one," Pram said. The ice mage considered the area. "I just need to remember the right spell."

"Don't tell me you could have been making bridges with ice magic all along!" Gerda accused.

"Alright." Pram nodded. "I won't."

The selkie eyed the expanse before lifting his hands.

"By the Frost Fae right in . . . No," Pram started then shook his head. "By the Fae Frost, Strike Fast out of Sight, [Ice Arch]." On the last word, ice magic burst forth from the mage's hands in an arc and hit the other side of the divide. He carefully dropped the arch on this side to the ground and then used another spell to freeze it fast.

He looked up at them with a smile. "I did it!"

Julian walked over and put a foot on the ice bridge. It was as wide as he was, and didn't shift under his foot.

"Here, let me." Gerda placed a hand on his shoulder. "I'm the bridge master, after all."

He nodded and stepped back. Gerda bent down and touched the bridge. "My abilities say it's a bridge, but it's not stable. Once I capture it, I can fix that."

She closed her eyes, and a bluish teal aura settled onto one corner of the structure. She reached out and touched the other corner to set another bridge point before standing. She made her way across slowly, the distance from here to there about forty feet.

When she was just over halfway across, the other side of the bridge shifted and promptly slipped off the mountain's edge.

Gerda let out an annoyed curse as she dropped. "Oh cr—"

"Jeffry," Julian instructed, the half elf already in motion. He flew after the troll.

The ice bridge hit a jagged peak jutting from the mountainside, broke into various pieces, and ricocheted into Jeffry, who barely managed to dodge in time.

Gerda didn't notice their rescue attempt—or didn't trust them, and portaled away.

Pram looked crestfallen. "I'm sorry; I thought—"

"It's fine, Pram. These things happen," Julian said, pretending that his heart wasn't racing in a terrified panic. "Let's head back to the save point."

CHAPTER 81

Queen's Seal and Master Crystal

Gerda

Six Weeks into the North

It was my usual Thursday morning bridge battle.

> "If you have it,
> you want to share it.
> If you share it,
> you don't have it."

I didn't bother activating any particular ability as I dodged the arrow. "You could at least *try* to solve it. That would save us so much—"

I ducked an axe.

"You know what, *fine*." I whipped out both arms and shouted, "Bridge Blast!"

Instead of activating a real perk, I summoned a ball of paralysis fog from my storage. The poison would knock out anyone who inhaled it, freezing them for a solid two minutes.

The assassins braced to defend against my bridge ability as the ball rolled between their feet, erupting in a plume of blue smoke.

"What—" The catkin holding the bow keeled over right away, his companion not too far behind. While they were momentarily indisposed, I grabbed the two of them and portaled us to a bridge on the eastern tip of Servalt.

"The answer is 'a secret,'" I told the unconscious pair, then left them there.

This was getting ridiculous . . . so I scheduled a meeting with my king.

* * *

"What is *this*?" Keith pushed up his glasses to read my proposal.

"An answer to *both* our problems," I told the Dark Lord.

Henrietta stood behind him, looking over my request. "Oh, that would work. But do we have the personnel?"

Keith pointed to one part. "Why are you asking for six teams and not four?"

"There are four major bridges, yes, but what about the bridge near Gren's Keep?" I pointed out the next highest-traffic path after the main road. There were *two* dungeons beside Gren's Keep, and the beastman village saw a lot of foot traffic. "All of the other bridges move around, and I'll need a team to manage them."

"That's reasonable," Henrietta said, smiling. Keith's brow pinched together.

"If I lead a division of the Dark Horde to manage bridges, then we can better defend against all of these pests who are getting through your barrier," I added.

"And yet," Keith pointed out, "if you just gave up the bridges you aren't able to properly manage, that would also solve my problem."

I knew he was going to fight this, if for no other reason than revenge for all the trouble I'd caused. He *could've* been thankful—he wouldn't even be alive right now if it wasn't for me—but telling him that wouldn't get me anywhere.

Instead, I listed off all the reasons I was right.

"With a properly run bridge brigade, there will be better security against assassins and spies. We could establish a proper merchant checkpoint system to oversee goods and wares transported through the woods. And there would be less traffic stops because I won't be managing the entire kingdom's bridges *by myself*. And!" I stressed the last, "you will continue to receive my *generous* tax payments. All while *I* continue to maintain our roads and highway infrastructure *free of charge*."

"You have to admit, love"—Henrietta wrapped her arms around Keith's neck—"it's a good plan."

Keith turned around in his chair to face his wife. "If you think so . . . "

"I do."

"Then I'll leave it to you." Keith shot his wife a wide, vicious grin. The Dark Lord handed over the paperwork to a surprised Henrietta, instructing, "Now that Her Eminence is back, she can find you the queen's seal *and* the Master Crystal. Let me know if you need any help hiring the personnel—"

"You just don't want to ask her yourself!" Henrietta chided but took the paperwork and dropped a kiss on his cheek.

His smile got wider. "Me?"

Henrietta also smiled. "You're lucky I love you."

"I am."

Ever since I'd taken over the drawbridge at the Northern Fortress, I'd also had to pay for it.

Every day, I handed Julian a purse of coin for the cost of the scout team that came and left from the fort. And every day, he passed it right back. By the end of August, I was used to the comings and goings of his people, and I immediately noticed when there was a change to the schedule.

"Wait," I called out, stopping in my tracks. Technically, stopping in Julian's tracks, since he was in the front, and we were marching single file through the snow.

The lands north of the mountain ridge were harsher than the Ice Fields near the border. Cutting winds blew up snow sideways into sweeping storms that came out of nowhere and lasted for hours. The sun was lower in the sky, its warm beams fighting the icy chill and losing. Even on the hottest days, I had to wear a thick cloak to block the cold wind.

Everyone halted, looking back at me.

"Someone is approaching the Northern Fortress," I told them. "Someone powerful."

Julian looked at Visha, who shook her head. "I didn't get word of a visitor."

Julian frowned and grumbled a bit. "It's probably my invitation to next month's ball."

The autumn equinox was in late September, when Grand Duchess Calisto would be hosting her Fall Ball.

I'd already acquired my invite.

"This isn't the best place for a bridge," Tully piped up. "Should we dig a trench?"

Jeffry pulled out his sword as Visha summoned her blades. At this point, we were all deft hands at preparing a makeshift bridge for me. It only took three minutes to cut a long hole in the snowy field and lay down a bridge.

I portaled us back to the Northern Fortress and immediately had to dodge a blast of Void energy. It hit Tully in the arm, and the human grunted from the damage. Julian lifted a [Barrier] between us and the attacker.

It was Alice.

"I found you!" she exclaimed, her face a mix of exhilaration and bloodthirst.

"I see that."

I was actually surprised that my [Oracle] ability hadn't shown me that she'd found me, but I'd had no Alice prophecies since the last time we'd faced each other.

"Guild Mistress Alice," Julian cut in, stepping forward and resting one hand on my shoulder. The other hand lifted his Valarian Royal Shield. "On behalf of the Continental Council, you are hereby under arrest for the unlawful assassination of citizens under level sixty, three counts of unregistered international espionage, and the harassment of one bridge troll. Come quietly."

Alice stared at Julian and then at me. "You *didn't* . . ."

"I did." I shrugged. Why hide it. Behind us, Visha was giving Tully a health potion, John had vanished, and Pram stood ready to attack.

"Don't you feel guilty for ruining his chance at Happily Ever After?" she asked. "Or is that why you're helping—because he would've already found his dungeon if you hadn't interfered?"

"What's it to you? Shouldn't you be organizing a coup somewhere?" I said before activating, "[Force]."

Since she was standing on the edge of my drawbridge, I could force her off. The blast sent Alice flying, but she landed on her feet.

Julian released my shoulder and said, "John."

The rogue burst out of Alice's shadow with a set of Veralyn's Enchanted Restraint Manacles. Unlike last time, however, Alice was prepared. She grabbed John's wrist and struck a dagger in his chest. John made a gurgling sound as he fell to the ground. Even Julian's [Divine Heal] didn't save his friend.

We would need to retrieve the body and resurrect it, and soon.

"Break," Visha said. Jeffry activated his flight powers, launching himself into an aerial attack. Pram tried to cast an attack that froze its target for thirty seconds, but Alice dodged. Her racial trait as a celestial gave her angel wings, and she'd used them to fly just out of reach.

Her voice fell over us. "*Lay down your weapons. I'm your friend.*"

The charisma-driven command hit me like a brick.

Julian shook himself, but Jeffry dropped to the ground and Visha lowered her blades. Tully looked like he was struggling with himself.

Pram just pointed at Alice and shot her with a, "By Sleek Blades of Frost, [Ice Javelin]."

The long icicle cut Alice's cheek as she tried to dodge. Angry eyes met mine.

"Your friends won't always be there to guard you," she said, then portaled away.

"Yes, we will—" Julian tried to tell me something poignant, but there was no time. I grabbed Julian's hand and ran with him to John.

The dagger I pulled out of his heart was coated in belladonna poison, so I summoned my unicorn horn and dumped a Resurrect potion down his throat. Julian helped the man to stand and told him he had the rest of the day off.

Then he gave *everyone* the day off.

Except for me.

"Gerda, we have to talk."

CHAPTER 82

You Don't Know What I Think

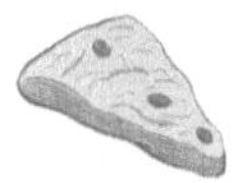

Julian

Gerda portaled them into her cottage.

As usual, they divested themselves of their winter gear first. Traveling north meant heavier layers and ice-caked boots. She'd put out a thick mat at the door that caught the worst of it. His bridge troll shed layers fast, and immediately after, wandered into the kitchen.

Julian followed her.

The window over the sink looked out into the gray rock and snow of the Northern Ice Fields; there was a bit of cold air from the frost on the pane of glass. He waited until she'd lit the stove and put the kettle on to boil before wrapping his arms around her from behind and burying his face in her neck.

"That was frustrating." Julian's muffled voice carried a hint of annoyance. "And you face her once a week?"

"It's not so bad," Gerda said. "Since I moved my bridge door where she can't find it, I just portal away."

"I know there are a hundred reasons why you're facing Alice alone. Least of all because the duke of North Sumbria shouldn't be crossing the border unannounced to hunt down international criminals. I *know*, and I respect that. But I have to ask . . ." He stopped, searching for less accusatory words. None came. She turned to face him, and he stared into defensive brown eyes. "Are you doing this on your own because you're worried about what the celestial will say to me?"

Gerda tensed. "It's not what you think."

Alice had outright told them that Julian would've already found the dungeon by now if Gerda wasn't here. From one future seer to another, there were probably *many* things Alice could tell him that Gerda didn't want him to know.

"You don't know *what* I think," Julian replied.

She wasn't expecting the kiss and gasped. He slipped his tongue into her mouth between her tusks.

"I know you aren't telling me everything." He lifted her onto the clean counter across from the stove. "And I don't care."

He kissed her again, this time soft and sweet. Her hands were in his shirt when the kettle whistled and Julian cursed. They broke apart and he said, "I'll set the table."

"Are you sure?" Gerda asked; there was a light tease in her voice. She straightened her dress from where his roaming hands had left things askew before addressing the loud kettle.

"We are sitting with a table between us so I can think straight," he told her.

Julian moved to the tea cabinet and grabbed her favorite nettle brew, cups, honey, and a teapot. He grabbed two tiny spoons decorated with painted mushrooms and plopped one in each cup before putting everything onto the table.

"Alice was right." Gerda brought over the hot water and filled the teapot, then stored the kettle. "There is a timeline where Henrietta would've been sent here as a potential political match. You would've grown close and fallen in love . . . and she would've helped you find the dungeon already."

"But why bring it up when Her Viciousness is already in love with King Keith?" Julian asked. He couldn't imagine falling for the sweet Dark Lady. Her naivety and joy would've made it hard to connect with her, and she was too *young*.

Honestly, he couldn't think of falling for anyone other than Gerda. His troll was strong—inside and out. She had a wicked sense of humor and enjoyed her peace and quiet. Her sense of justice was just as strong as the Heroine of Justice, but Gerda used her cunning to direct armies and guide nations. She was brilliant.

Gerda explained, "Because I interfered, *you* never went exploring with Henrietta, and *she* never found a secret passageway into the heart of the underground caverns and the abandoned ancient home of the dragons. The same caves that opened up into the far side of the mountain range . . . and to the dungeon you've been searching for."

"So you already knew where the hidden dungeon was?" he asked.

She looked away.

"But we are headed there now?"

"Yes," she whispered. "But even without Henrietta . . . you would've found the hidden dungeon. I've just been slowing you down." She took a ragged breath. "Actually . . . I've been delaying you."

"Why?"

Her deep brown eyes found him. They were full of pain and uncertainty . . . and something else.

"I like you, Julian. A lot."

"That's good," he said. "Because the feeling is mutual."

"And I don't want this to end." She waved a hand between them. "So I'm dragging you on dates and taking time away from searching."

He didn't understand. "This doesn't need to end when I reach the dungeon. Unless I'm going to die?"

"No." She shook her head. "No, you should be fine. You're even stronger in this timeline, with your armor set."

A small worry fell from his shoulders; it was reassuring to have the most powerful oracle on the continent tell him that he was going to find the dungeon he'd been searching for *and* defeat it without suffering permanent death in the process.

It was less reassuring that she was hinting at the end of their relationship.

"So what's the problem?" he demanded.

Gerda didn't answer right away; she was warring with herself. Her pale freckles scrunched up with indecision and worry.

At last, she said, "I can see your future, Julian . . . and there is a timeline where I'm not in it."

CHAPTER 83

I'm Not the Real Gerda Jones

Gerda

I didn't know how else to say it.

How could I tell the half elf I was sleeping with that I might complete a secret bridge quest that could let me travel through the Void and return to my old world?

I wasn't even certain I wanted to go back, but I felt driven to try. When I'd been dropped into Gerda five years ago, it'd seemed like the right course of action. There were wonderful things about living in a fantasy world . . . but waking up as a beaten-to-death troll housewife hadn't exactly been the *ideal isekai*.

Not that I'd want to be Henrietta. No. I did *not* dungeon delve or enjoy battle or want to travel the world fixing everyone else's problems. No, thank you. I was happy to do that from the comfort of my kitchen table with a Crystal Cast.

Being a troll got some getting used to, but five years was a long time to *get used to it*. And if I portaled back to Earth, I'd be doing so as a troll . . . which also wasn't ideal. At this point, I had an amazing lover, a beautiful home, a fulfilling job, and a healthy body with epic muscles and no back pain.

So I was probably an idiot for pursuing my original goal.

Julian's expression darkened when he heard what I'd said. "Which timeline?"

I answered as honestly as I could. "After we reach the dungeon, there is a split. One where I'm here, and one where I'm not."

"Then we don't need to go to the dungeon." Julian stood up and came around the table, kneeling at my feet. He grabbed my hand and pressed it to his cheek. "If Henrietta defeated the dungeon before, she can do it again. I'll contact Nilheim—"

I hurried to say, "Julian. You can't just give up like that—"

"Can't I?" he argued, still on one knee. "Can't you?"

I shoved my chair back and stood, pulling my hand from his grasp. "I need to complete this quest . . . I have to."

"Is it your quest or mine that is going to separate us?" he asked, bracing a hand on the table to stand. Julian didn't grant me any space, chasing me as I tried to put distance between us.

He could see the answer on my face.

"Gerda." He reached out and grabbed my arm. Not hard but not kind either. "What aren't you telling me? What does Alice know that you're so afraid I'll find out?"

"I—" The words caught in my throat, and I closed my mouth. I stared at where he held me, knowing for a fact I'd messed up.

Julian never let anyone in. He was a hurt, angry man who'd watched his father die in a civil war and then spent his entire life trying to fill his father's shoes. For every two steps forward, Henrietta had been forced to take one back while she was trying to win over the dark, brooding duke of the North.

But he'd melted in my hands like butter. *And I'd let it happen.*

Whatever he saw in me, Julian suddenly dropped my arm. He looked away and rubbed his face with the palm of his hand, drawing in a sharp breath.

When he looked at me again, there was a sad smile on his lips.

"I'm sorry," he said, taking a step back. "I didn't mean—I wanted you to tell me when you were ready."

"I'm sorry," I whispered, angry that I couldn't even tell him *why*. I crossed my arms and held myself.

"No," Julian said, stern. "I knew what I was getting into when I fell for you."

"Did you?" I countered, though it wasn't fair to lash out at him with my own secrets.

"Gerda, I'm dating *Madame Potts*." He choked on a laugh. "Even *before* I learned the truth, I could see that you were a walking ball of secrets—the *least* of which was your identity as Madame Potts."

I remembered our first official meeting, when I'd handed him a locket and then run away.

Julian continued. "And being together with you means that there will *always* be secrets between us. You know everyone's business from here to the Empire of Sands, every possible timeline for anyone you set your sights on, and everybody's secrets . . . including my own."

"I can't see *everyone's* future," I mumbled.

"But you can see *mine*."

". . . Technically, no," I replied. "I get notifications from Fate telling me things about you with an ability. My *sight* ability only works on the champions for each god."

"And?" he pressed, knowing I had other powers.

"And Foresight lets me see what my target would be doing in a timeline where I didn't exist," I added. "So yes, I *could* learn things about you that you don't want me to . . . but I've changed fate so much that it's almost moot at this point."

"And yet, there is still something you aren't telling me." His silver eyes met mine, and I felt a twist in my stomach.

Was there any reason *not* to tell him?

Would he even believe me?

"Alright," I said, lowering my hands to my sides. "After everything, *you*, at least, deserve to know . . ." I paused, closing my eyes. Bracing myself. When I opened my eyes, I looked at the half elf in front of me.

He was standing in my home, wearing a tunic with rolled-up sleeves tucked into his pants. His dreads were pulled back into a ponytail, and his locket hung about his neck. Julian looked at me with a gentleness unimaginable to how he was in the video game or any other timeline.

I met his eyes and said, "I'm not the real Gerda Jones."

CHAPTER 84

We Can Let Fate Decide

Julian

Julian had been expecting any number of secrets.

The troll was powerful enough to establish portals in *every single* kingdom from here to the Southern Sea. The window beside her couch overlooked that very ocean. She could have admitted to any ability or skill, and he wouldn't have been surprised.

But he wasn't expecting this. Anxiety twisted his heart and crept into his voice. "*How long?*"

"Five years," she replied, standing straight and holding her ground. His worst fears dissipated as fast as they'd come.

"Five years?" Julian approached her.

She nodded as he lifted both hands and gripped her arms, leaning down and burying his face in her neck. "Then that's fine. Gods, Gerda, don't scare me like that."

She stiffened. "I literally woke up in this body, Julian. What do you mean *it's fine?*"

"You are still the troll I met and fell for." He kissed her shoulder before pulling back, looking her in the eyes. "If Life and Death mixed up your soul in revival, then you might have come back in the wrong body. It's the stuff of legends, but it's not unheard of with inexperienced necromancy—"

"I'm not from Valaria," she cut him off. "I'm not even from this *world.*"

He kissed her nose. "Which explains your strange manner of speech."

"I'm being *serious,* Julian." Gerda put out both hands to push against his chest, forcing him back.

"So am I," he replied. His hands slid down her arms until he scooped up both of hers in his and squeezed them reassuringly.

"You don't *sound* like it," she accused.

"Gerda—" He stopped. "Is that how you want to be called?"

". . . Yes."

"Gerda," he restarted, "*I'm not a fool.* I've been with you night and day for *weeks.* Do you think I haven't noticed you make food that I've never even heard of before and talk about things that don't exist? For a while, I thought you might've journeyed here through the Sea of Monsters or found some lost bridge portal—" Julian stopped, his blood going cold. "The bridge in the North," he said softly. "Our paths don't split at the dungeon—they split at the bridge you're looking for."

She held his gaze. "I have a chance to go home."

Julian dropped her hands and took a step back. She was so sure. *So ready to leave.*

"What is waiting for you there?" he asked, all emotion leaving his voice. It was hard to even speak, and his words were harsher than he'd intended. "A family? Your ex-husband?"

Despite his earlier claims, he *felt* like a fool.

"Actually, that was something Gerda and I both had in common." She smiled tightly. "But no, he isn't waiting for me. No one is."

"Then *why?*"

"Because I don't belong here," she said.

"You don't believe that,"

"Julian, I have to at least *try.*" She waved around them. "I arrived here with nothing and knowing no one. It was all I had to keep me going for a long time . . . and it's *so close.*"

The words were a mirror to his own soul, and he hated it. How long had he spent—against the wishes of his loved ones—throwing himself into leveling up? Into searching the North? Into a single-minded task that was his reason for living? When he'd sought strength enough to protect his family, he'd forced his family at a distance to do it.

And Gerda had been trying to keep that same distance with him from the first day.

"Alright," he said, emptiness settling into his heart. He forced a smile. "I'll escort you to your bridge. As promised."

"Julian—"

"And you'll show me to my dungeon," he spoke over her, not sure he could make this choice again if he didn't say it *now.* He couldn't even look at her, turning to face the kitchen window and the icy blizzard outside. "And we can let Fate decide."

Green arms wrapped around his stomach. Julian's black hands hesitated only a second before settling over hers. She pressed her face into his back. "I'm sorry . . . and thank you."

They stood there for a while, quietly.

The tea on the table had long grown cold.

CHAPTER 85

Why Was He So Stupidly Hot

Gerda

I woke up in Julian's arms, sore and tired, with a notification blinking at me.

[Prerequisite Achieved. Would you like to have a child with Julian von Slyke? Yes/No]

I flushed and mentally selected *No*. That's what I got for exhausting myself and falling asleep right away.

If I'd thought that telling the half elf my secret was going to push him away . . . then I'd failed spectacularly. After a tense silence that had stretched on forever, he'd turned, swept me into his arms, and told me to bring us here, where he'd shown me *exactly* what I was giving up in my quest. No dinner. Not much sleep. Just a break for water.

My stomach told me how it felt with a loud rumble and Julian's arms tightened around me. He took a deep breath. "Good morning."

"Good morning," I replied, surprised by the lighthearted greeting.

He'd been everything *but* sweet last night.

Julian let go and slipped out of bed to go to the washroom. When he came out a few minutes later, he was drying his body with a towel.

"I'm ravenous," he said, smiling at me. "What say I make breakfast today?"

"Alright," I replied, sitting up nervously with my blanket up to my chin. Not because I thought he'd jump me again. No. I just wasn't expecting the casual return to routine. Like last night hadn't even happened.

He leaned down and kissed me on the cheek. "Let me into the kitchen, and I'll have it done by the time you're out."

I nodded, connecting the bedroom door to the front entry. Julian threw on fresh clothing from his storage ring and slipped out.

I was left alone.

For some reason, I didn't want to get out of bed. I didn't want to do anything. I wasn't ready. When was the last time I'd slept in?

The sun shone outside on a bright field of flowers. A white stag was grazing at the banks of the river, and butterflies flitted about. I lay back down and covered my head with the blankets but couldn't go back to sleep. I was too hungry and too on edge.

Fifteen minutes later, I gave up and went to the bathroom. I felt like one of Keith's golems, going through the motions: washing, dressing, and tidying up.

For a second, I wondered if I was actually dreaming, but a pinch on the cheek proved otherwise.

"Perfect timing," Julian called over his shoulder when I came in. He had his sleeves rolled up and was wearing an apron covered in unicorns. The tea service from last night had been washed and was sitting in the dish rack, and Julian was washing the breakfast pan. I stopped and stared.

Why was he so stupidly hot?

"I made London Fogs," he said, drying his hands on a cloth then pointing at the table.

There were place settings, with two hot drinks and plates piled high with scrambled eggs, bacon, ham, cheese, hash browns, and toast. Julian was terrible at making hollandaise sauce, but he'd whipped up a sweet and tangy barbecue sauce to drizzle on top.

I didn't take my seat. I stood there staring at the breakfast and the clean dishes and Julian. He took off his apron and came around the kitchen counter. I thought he was leaning down to press a kiss to my forehead, but he tilted to the side and *bit my ear*.

"Ack!" I jumped back. "Julian!"

"You looked lost." A half smile pulled at his lips.

"You didn't need to *bite* me," I retorted.

"You liked it." Julian pulled out my chair and waved.

"That's beside the point," I grumbled, taking my seat. I took a sip of tea to calm my nerves. It was lovely, with just the right amount of bitter star fruit juice to give it a rich vanilla flavor. "Thank you, this looks lovely."

"*You* look lovely," he replied, biting into his toast. He'd always been playful, but for some reason, his flirting today felt . . . different. Or maybe I just thought that everything was different.

I gave in to hunger and speared a slice of ham with my fork. We ate in relative silence for a few minutes.

I broke first. "Why haven't you asked about it?"

"About what?"

"About me! My past. Who I am." I put down my fork. "About last night."

"Gerda." His smile was as gentle as his good mood, and as fake. "Are you ready to talk about it? Or would it just make you worry and push me away? If I asked about your old life, would you long for it even more?" I made to reply, but he continued. "Don't get me wrong, I want to know *everything*. But you forget—I've only ever known you as you are. Your past is your past . . . I only regret forcing the issue."

"I think Alice forced the issue," I grumbled. That celestial was going to be the death of me. Again.

"No." He shook his head. "I lost my temper. I'm sorry."

"There is one more thing I haven't told you . . ." I said. "I was just trying to find a way to explain it."

Julian reached out and put his hand on mine. "I'm all pointy ears."

I pulled away and wrapped my fingers around my warm mug; Julian hesitated before grabbing his own mug as well.

"In my world—"

"In your *old* world," Julian corrected. I shot him a glare for interrupting, but he returned it with an encouraging look.

"In my *old* world," I repeated, "I could read about and watch this world."

"In a book or crystal ball?"

"Both." I tapped the mug. "Imagine a crystal plate that showed what was happening but also had written notes on the bottom. And mine had the ability to follow Henrietta around for this year, showing me all of the different futures she *could've* had—including one with you."

"So even without your [Oracle] abilities, you had a good picture of the future." He said, nodding. "Which is how you amassed wealth, found the Master Crystal, and became Madame Potts."

"Yes," I confirmed. "But now, I've pushed the story so far off from the original that I'm just relying on my powers."

There was a moment of silence as I sipped my London Fog, Julian appearing contemplative.

Suddenly, he downed the last of his drink and *thunked* it on the table. "I have a question."

I raised an eyebrow.

"What have the gods said?" Julian asked. "About you coming to this world or going home? What did Fate say?"

One of my ears twitched. "Well . . . Fate often sends me helpful tips and prophecies that I can use to change the future."

"But when you went to her temple and asked for guidance, what did Fate actually *say*?"

I shook my head. "She said nothing."

CHAPTER 86

A Wayward World-Jumping Soul

Julian

Julian's eyebrows rose of their own accord. "Nothing?"

"She never answered. And I haven't—Wait." Gerda scrunched up her nose. "Does the sanctuary count as a temple?"

"Yes."

"Ah, then I've only been to Fate and Light's temples."

"Just that?" he asked.

Gerda shrugged. "Yes?"

"You found yourself in another world and *didn't* immediately go to *every* god and ask for guidance?" He asked, incredulous. He would be storming every temple in the kingdom if something like that had happened to him. His own family had long followed Light, so much so they'd built the sanctuary in her honor, but different gods held different domains. If one didn't answer, it could be because there was another god more apt for the task.

Still, he was surprised that Gerda's prayers had been left entirely unanswered. The gods didn't speak to *everyone* who prayed on their sacred grounds, but they did offer guidance on important matters or exceptional circumstances.

And a wayward, world-jumping soul seemed exceptional to *him*.

"Why bother? I had system and quest notifications that told me where I was and what I needed to do." She shrugged. "And it wasn't like I was in a position to just go on an adventure to hunt down every temple—I was thrown into things pretty quickly."

"Did Gerda's village not have a temple for every god?" he asked, tripping a bit as he referred to the previous Gerda, but *his* Gerda knew and didn't seem to mind.

There were only ten gods; it was rare for a town *not* to have a small shrine for each, even if they had only one temple.

She shook her head. "It wouldn't matter if there was. When I woke up, I was trying to process Gerda's memories and figure out what happened. It wasn't pretty, and I ended up throwing Gerda's ex-husband off the mountain . . . Unfortunately, he was the mayor of Yoka Village, and pretty well liked for an abusive piece of garbage . . . So I didn't stick around for long."

Julian recalled her previous retelling, and the twisted knot of anger that grew in the pit of his stomach was just as strong hearing this story the second time.

"That's when I ran away to the Dark Enchanted Forest." She looked off in the distance, reminiscing.

"I met Larry, this ancient bridge troll who took me in while I was still figuring things out. He was looking for an apprentice, and I needed a place to stay . . . I ended up living in the spare cot under his sewing table for a month. I wasn't okay." She reached out an unsteady hand to grip her mug, though she didn't drink from it. "It took a while to get used to having a troll body."

"What were you before?" he asked.

"Human," she replied.

"Hm." Julian tried to see her as a human, like his mother. Softer, with the same bright brown eyes but no tusks.

He would miss the tusks.

"There are ways—" he started. She shook her head.

"I know what you're going to say, but I *like* who I've become. I'm built like a brick house, and I feel amazing." Gerda smiled; the first sincere smile he'd seen since yesterday. "It just took some getting used to. Besides, I've already found a treasure that lets me pretend to be human for a while, if I want to."

"I'm glad."

"Me too." She took a sip of her tea, then continued, "So it took a while before I went to Saren Sanctum in the Black Fortress. I tried to speak to Fate, but she didn't answer."

Fate was Keith's patron deity, and the largest temple in Nilheim. Fate was also the driving force behind Gerda's [Oracle] abilities.

Again, he couldn't understand *why*.

"It wasn't until months later, when I leveled up to forty and got oracle powers and started getting actual direct messages from Fate that I thought I should go visit her again . . . But I've never been in the habit of going to church, and why start when Fate was *literally* up in my notifications telling me things."

"Still . . ." Julian considered then stood, holding out his hand. "Want to try going now?"

Gerda choked. "Now?!"

"You wanted to find a way back . . . We can ask now." The words came out normal, but inside, he felt like he was trying to swim up a raging waterfall just to hold a half smile. "The other gods might have a way. Life and Death might know, or Dream."

"Why Dream?" She raised an eyebrow.

"They are in charge of the soul." He added, "Memories are the embroidery to the fabric of the soul, and if you'd merely taken Gerda's body, I don't think you should have her memories as well. It's something to ask about."

"I don't want to," Gerda stated, rejecting his offer.

Julian withdrew his hand and stared down at his troll. For all that she was different, this was the first time he'd thought he couldn't understand her. Everyone knew that the gods were there. They were in the system messages; their power flowed through each person who wielded an ability, and their voice came readily in times of need.

It was just the natural thing to do.

"But—"

"What if I'm really *not* supposed to be here? What if the gods shunt me back to my world without a by-your-leave? Or worse, Carter shows up to put me to rest?"

Her reasoning was a cold reality he hadn't considered. "Who's Carter?"

"The chosen of Death. I hate that guy—he's *impossible* to reason with." Gerda's brows knit and her jaw clenched. "So why draw attention to myself? I'd rather have the chance to make my own decisions, and I don't regret any of the ones I've made so far . . . except maybe one."

Gerda's eyes met his. "I wasn't expecting to fall in love with you."

CHAPTER 87

I Don't Think That Umbrella Is Going to Protect You from Meteorites

Gerda

I said the words because I was a cruel idiot.

Sitting here, telling Julian I was looking for a way to leave, but then telling him I loved him.

My resolve was breaking but not broken. I'd set out on my search to the ends of Valaria, and things were finally coming to a close.

Julian's eyes glinted with some powerful emotion before he closed them, drew breath, and opened them again. He was still standing, and took the single step needed to bring him closer. From the tension that cut the air and his earlier frustrations, a half-forgotten fear crept into my throat. Years of survival instinct made me flinch as he leaned down and placed a hand on the table, trapping me in my chair. Anyone would've started shaking under the intensity, I'm sure.

"Good," he said softly, dropping a kiss on my forehead.

Straightening, he turned away, summoning his heavy winter jacket and equipping it. "Then let's go get this over with."

Alice wasn't there when we portaled onto the drawbridge at the Northern Fortress. Just to be sure, I was holding Nova's Celestial Pendant, the treasure from season two that glowed in the presence of other celestials.

Its yellow gemstone remained constant.

"You're back!" Sir Tully waved from on top of the parapets. The paladin jumped down and landed in front of us with a gentle clang of armor. "We haven't seen any sign of Guild Mistress Alice since you left. Orders, Your Grace?"

Julian was back in action. "Tell Jeffry to pack for a longer trip. We are setting out as soon as everyone is ready."

"Back to the grind it is!" The paladin saluted and turned to do as he was told.

Julian added, "We'll be pushing harder than before, so plan accordingly."

The paladin flinched and looked back at us over his shoulder. "Does that mean . . . ?"

"Two weeks," the duke told him. "And a dungeon delve."

"Really?" Sir Tully shot me a look.

"Do I look like I'm joking?" Julian frowned, his usual dark countenance in full force.

"Wow, alright." Sir Tully was unfazed, scratching his head once before his face split into a wide grin. "I'll go tell the party."

I told the paladin, "Don't forget to pack a spare war hammer."

"Good idea!" He waved and ran off.

Julian sighed. We walked after the excited paladin, not hand in hand. After last night, it felt like I was closer to Julian than before, but with a deeper pit between us.

"Was that a helpful reminder, or a warning?" he asked.

"A warning," I told him. "He's going to break his in the next battle. Or that's what I've gathered from [Sense Fate]."

[Passive Perk: **Sense Fate** has activated. Sir Tully Grey will break his beloved War Hammer in his next fight.]
[You have crossed paths with a fate that can be changed. Area of effect radius: Level 66 x Perception 45 x Foretelling 4 = 11,880 sq/ ft. Fate herself will guide you.]
["Strike fast when elemental form, brace but harder than the hand, face foes succumbed in storm, and shatter where they stand."]

"Anything else we should be wary of?" he asked, offhand.

I glanced at my notifications. "There's only an oracle about Henrietta . . . but I've stopped looking in on her unless I have to." It seemed like an invasion of privacy. [Foretelling] what was supposed to happen was next to useless, since Feliwyn wasn't fighting Henrietta in this life—she was doting on the Dark Lady. Though I did use it to follow a few side plots.

Without planning Madame Potts's Casts, it wasn't as necessary to check in on every little oracle. At this point, the only one I'd be interested in watching would be Alice, if for no other reason than to prepare *against* her.

I wasn't as interested in season three of *Dungeon Delves and Debutantes*; I just wanted to survive long enough to reach Julian's dungeon and my bridge and make peace with my life.

"Your Grace, Miss Gerda." John appeared out of the shadows beside us. "Visha says we can be ready to depart within the hour."

"Good." Julian crossed his arms.

Seven Weeks into the North

We were approaching the shores of the Northern Sea and the area where my [Map] showed we might find Julian's dungeon.

"We should stop here!" I stuck my head out around Visha and called up to Julian at the front. We were speed-walking north single file through the snow, and had been doing so for hours.

Julian spoke over his shoulder, not slowing down. "At the top of the next ridge."

There was a hill in the distance with a few trees.

"We should *really* stop now!" I said, and the group slowed. It wasn't ideal, as we were ankle deep in a snow drift, but gauging the timing, I thought now should be about right.

"Do we need to put down a bridge?" Visha asked, one hand on each of her weapons.

"No." I pointed up.

Overhead, the meteor could now be seen in broad daylight. It had become bigger by day and brighter by night, until it was a concerning celestial body taking up a permanent spot in the summer sky.

"I'm just saying, for a ball of rock crashing toward us, it's very pretty." Sir Tully shaded his eyes from the sun, squinting as the light reflected on the snow all around us. It hurt from the glare of the snow.

The paladin was right. Whatever the meteor was, it was magical in nature and shimmered beautifully. The tail was a glittering arch, and with my high-level perception, I could focus until it was as clear as looking through a telescope. The comet's magic pulsed in different colors, while the tail that trailed behind it looked like golden glitter from a child's art table.

Julian trudged through the snow to stand beside me. "What did you see?"

"I think they're going to deal with the meteor soon. If we wanted to prepare," I told him.

I had my [Map] open, and Servalt, specifically the Mages Tower, was suddenly highlighted yellow from [Sooth Area]. A game scenario was playing out there, and I knew which one.

"What would *we* need to prepare?" Jeffry asked; he was right behind me in the line.

"Umbrellas," I said, pulling out my own. "Healing potions, and a shield in case there's debris from the explosion?" As I spoke, there was a sudden *pop* from the south that echoed across the hills. High above, glowing magical writing in intricately crafted mana circles appeared one after the other, all in a line toward the meteor. Each ring was a hundred steps across, at least.

The mana to power the spells was enough to mana burn a dozen elite mages, and it was only possible because Master Thomas had been draining his own min-max mana supply into crystals every day for months.

I opened my umbrella as a bullet of water half as wide as the spell rings burst through the magic circles, hitting the meteor. It exploded in an eruption of mana that lit up the sky like a second sun. I let out a painful grunt and covered my face.

[Divine Heal] hit me with Julian's shield, repairing the damage to my eyes.

"I don't think that umbrella is going to protect you from the meteorites," Sir Pram pointed out.

"I thought that six months of rain harvested from Servalt would evaporate into mist like cloud seeding and cause rain clouds to form overhead, then I'd look smart with my umbrella all ready to go," I told the selkie, still holding my umbrella in case I was right.

"It doesn't *feel* like it's going to rain," Sir Tully noted, rubbing one eye from his own healing experience.

"Everyone's a critic," I said, one hand on my hip. "Why don't *you* try being the oracle for a change?"

"Don't encourage him," Visha said, poking the paladin.

"I'd rather hit things," Sir Tully replied, hefting his new war hammer onto his shoulders.

It made sense that the comet fell three weeks before the Fall Ball—Henrietta would need time to go and collect the fragments before the celebration. I could only imagine Master Thomas doing something completely wasteful and making it into a dress made out of starlight or fashioning it to a symbolic ring.

If I found one, I'd take it to Grand Duchess Calisto; that woman would know *exactly* what to do with a potent mana rock.

I said that, but I still owed her a pile of Master Crystal research that I'd told myself I'd give her months ago.

"We'll wait until the debris falls," Julian said, "and then it's back to hiking."

"I don't think it will land anytime soon," Jeffry told the duke. "It if takes a few days to walk across North Sumbria, it should take a few days, *at least*, to fall from the Void space."

Between my dislike for math and this being a magical world with unknown physics or gravity, I was willing to believe almost anything. And Jeffry sounded sure of himself.

I put away my umbrella.

Julian nodded. "Then we can keep walking. Jeffry, fly ahead and make sure there isn't anything unpleasant waiting for us."

"Yes, Your Grace." Jeffry smiled, happy for any excuse to use his flight ability. "Right away, Your Grace."

"Alright, everyone," Julian addressed us. "March."

Jeffry flew back in a hurry.

"Julian!" he exclaimed, slipping into an informal address in his excitement. "You can see the dungeon from the hill! We've found it!"

CHAPTER 88

You Break into Dungeons and Loot Them?

Julian

Julian's breath hitched as he looked down on the dungeon gate he'd been searching for.

At the bottom of the hill was a pit the size of his mother's Coral Palace. In the middle, there was a large magical platform, and in each cardinal direction, there were giant ice bridges as wide as a frost goliath that connected to the central platform. As they watched, the platform started to glow with a blue light, and four rocksoc appeared on the platform.

The beast rodents immediately headed west, crossing the bridge and disappearing into the snow.

"Well," Gerda said, coming up to stand beside him. She laid her hand on his arm. "It looks like we *both* found what we were looking for."

The words brought him out of his reverie. "So it would seem . . ." Julian stared between Gerda and the ice bridge. A cold, hard feeling settled in his stomach.

This week, they'd pushed harder than he'd done even before Gerda joined his party. They'd slept in shorter stints and relied more on potions to keep up their stamina and speed. They'd returned to the Northern Fortress only once, to check if Alice had shown up in their absence.

She hadn't.

"There's one more thing I haven't told you about . . ." Gerda squeezed his arm as they trudged through powdery turf. "I have a *unique* [Dungeoneering] ability."

Julian stiffened. "Do you want to enter the dungeon with us?"

"I was thinking of it," she replied.

"What ability?" They both knew she wasn't a combat build.

"Dungeons are built of manipulated dimension magic, and I can cut rifts into the levels," she admitted.

To be sure he understood correctly, Julian asked, "And what does that look like in practice?"

"It means that I go around dungeons, breaking in the back door, looting all of the treasure, and then sneaking out again," she explained.

"You break into dungeons," he repeated, "and loot them."

"Yes," Gerda said. "I'm assuming you want to actually *defeat* the dungeon, but I'm pretty handy to have around if we don't want to waste time looking for a floor boss or unlocking doors. I have about twenty Juliper petals left in my inventory, so I can hang out in the back, invisible, for most of the battles . . . And I want to be there," she spoke the last quietly, "when you defeat the dungeon core and complete your quest."

"Alright," he said. As if there was any other answer. If his choice was to watch her leave before or watch her leave after, he would take every second with her he could get.

They reached the southern ice bridge.

"Did you hear that?" he asked over his shoulder to the rest of the party. "Gerda is joining us in the dungeon."

"But Your Grace—" Visha started, immediately rejecting the idea.

"It'll be alright, General Visha," Gerda reassured the elf. "I might not be the best, but I'm still an adventurer, and I've made my way through most of the dungeons in Valaria."

"How?" Visha demanded to know.

"She's got a level-jumping power," Julian told everyone. Pram and Tully looked interested, but John was smiling.

The rogue *never* smiled.

"What's up with you?" Jeffry asked, unnerved at the human's change in demeanor.

"I'm retiring," the rogue declared, sending a wave of shock throughout the group. "This is going to be my last run, and if Miss Gerda's coming, then it'll go by so much smoother—assuming you can keep up?"

"I have a few Haste potions I've been saving just for this," Gerda told the rogue.

Sir Tully put a hand on John's shoulder and squeezed. "No surprise you wanna get back home to your wife and kid, but don't just abandon us with no warning! You should step down after the celebration."

John said, "I'll think about it."

"What celebration?" Sir Pram asked, confused.

"The one Grand Duchess Calisto is going to throw as soon as her prodigal son returns victorious!" Sir Tully explained.

That sent a shiver down Julian's spine. More evening events, and no convenient excuse to escape. He shook off the feeling and addressed the rogue. "Thank you for staying with us to the end."

John pushed Tully's hand off his shoulder. "Of course."

"Alright, everyone. Let's get ready," Julian told the group. "Gerda, can you set up your makeshift bridge here just in case? Jeffry, cross the dungeon bridge first to make sure it's stable. If anything happens, be ready to fly. John, call back your shadows."

Everyone jumped to get to it. When they were ready and the bridge was deemed safe, everyone crossed together.

The platform lit up when Julian took a step on top, activating the portal dungeon gate.

[Activate portal to Forgotten Frost Dungeon? Yes/No]

He was surprised; he thought the notification would say they were the first to find it . . .

Someone had beaten them to it. Since there were still monster surges, that meant no one had managed to reach the dungeon core yet, so whoever had been here before had either perished or given up and left.

Julian waited until everyone was on the platform before selecting *Yes*.

CHAPTER 89

An Uncanny Number of Treants

Gerda

If the Northern Ice Fields were cold, the Forgotten Frost Dungeon was *freezing*.

The temperature dropped so suddenly and so fast that my nose started burning from the chill. The first floor looked much like the outside, with patches of forest in the distance and rocky slopes. A stark straight-cut mountain rose up behind the platform and wrapped around to either side in a gentle arc. The ground was so cold that the earth was frozen with black ice.

As if to juxtapose the sheer inhospitality of the environs, there was a blue, sunny sky overhead.

I was so wrapped up in looking around that I nearly jumped when Jeffry initiated the party request.

[Jeffry has invited you to his party. Do you wish to join? Yes/No]

I selected *Yes*. As I glanced through the party interface, I noted that everyone present was in it. By default, parties were locked to groups of four, but high-level [Dungeoneering] perks could allow for larger groups.

Parties were a part of dungeon delving, and they came with chat logs. Simply thinking out the sentence wrote it down, and then I had to *will* it to send. I sent a quick message to Jeffry to ensure everything was working.

[Six party members, huh? Is it a perk?]

"Yes," Jeffry said aloud after reading my message. "I also have the ability to control how much experience points everyone gets, and a stat monitor that lets me see everyone's health and mana totals. So don't think I won't notice if you do something dumb, Tully."

"It was *one time*," Tully protested.

"You charged a drake with only twenty hit points left. While screaming *Tulllly Greeeey.*"

"I survived."

"Is that the time Visha threw a health potion on your head?" Sir Pram asked.

"I was picking glass out of my beard for a week," Tully grumbled.

"Health potions cost less than a Revive," Jeffry noted, matter-of-factly.

Beside me, Julian said, "John."

The rogue nodded. "I see them. Three wargle wolverines on the tree line heading toward us, and one para-para snake hiding in that rocky outcrop."

"Visha, you and Pram handle the wolverines. Jeffry, stay here with Gerda. Tully and I will take on the snake," Julian directed as everyone jumped into action.

Except me, who stood beside Jeffry.

"Do you normally split the party?" I asked, this time aloud. Our vantage point gave me a good view of Julian tanking a snake twice as long as he was. It spat paralysis venom, hence the imaginative name.

"Yes?" Jeffry replied, surprised at the question.

"I thought it was bad luck." I shrugged, recalling that it was a sure way of getting killed on tabletop quests.

"First I've heard; is that a troll thing?" He wasn't really interested, I could tell. His eyes were tracking the fight and flitting to his notification logs.

Combat was neatly wrapped up within five minutes.

"Are we going to fight all of the monsters on each floor?" I asked Julian when he returned from his one-sided bout.

"Only the ones we come across," he replied, signaling to Visha at a distance to stay where they were. We started walking toward the forest. "It helps finance the trip."

Noted.

[*I don't wanna fight those.*]

Sir Tully posted over the chat logs. He was peeking over the edge of a cliff on the dungeon's third floor. He'd wanted a better look and had crawled over himself. In plate.

Below, there was a valley *full* of pine-tree treants.

Or was it a valley full of pine trees, and *some* of them were treants? Judging from the wiggling branches and shifting foliage, either option was bad.

[We could burn it all down?]

That was Pram, asking hopefully.

The group, as I discovered, rarely used the chat. They liked anything that drew in more monsters to fight . . .that didn't apply now. Everyone was being extremely careful.

John shook his head as Jeffry pointed out,

[It would take hours to set up the flare traps, and they might just turn around and smother the flames with ice magic. Treants are one of the more intelligent monster classes, even if they suffer from dungeon madness.]
[We could skip this level?]

I made the offer. I didn't see the platform to the next level anywhere in the valley below, so we could probably just skirt the fight completely. I hadn't had a chance to do it yet, but now seemed like a good time to offer.

Jeffry replied,

[That's an uncanny number of treants. At this rate, they might cause a stampede . . . Either way, we should clear some of them out.]

Visha added,

[What if we set up traps to divide them long enough to pick them off? We can have John's shadows light four or five fires around the edges of the forest but focus our ambush on one.]

Julian considered for a moment, then,

[It's still risky. Let's try this instead . . .]

After reading the plan, we all left to get into place.

An explosion rang out on the far edge of the forest from where I was sitting. While I wouldn't be fighting any treants myself, I did have one important task.

"That's the signal," John told me, and I concentrated as hard as I could on the forest below.

Perception forty-five was no joke; I could make out every movement below, every ruffling branch, every swaying tree. Though it was difficult to divide my attention over the entire forest.

"Twelve . . . twenty . . . thirty-three . . . thirty-seven treants, but I can't be sure that's all of them," I said, adding it to the chat log.

[37 so far. I'm counting 154 trees and 37 treants.]

Julian wrote back.

[Alright, everyone, prepare to back up Tully and Pram.]

After the explosion had gone off, the treants had rushed toward the sound, their branches snapping back and forth like whips. It would take them a while to reach the hidden party, which gave me plenty of time to observe them and inform the group.

[The treants are averaging four feet per second. With a ten-foot reach if you include the vines.]

When the monsters arrived at the location of the explosion, they found nothing but some blackened rocks. With nothing to attack, they searched the area for ten minutes then settled down.

I sent another message.

[Two treants fifteen feet from Visha. The next closest is thirty feet back.]

Jeffry came in.

[Perfect. Visha, you'll have seven seconds to deal damage before John ports you out and Tully arrives. Ready?]
[Ready.]

While Tully traveled toward her, Visha waited for the treants to come directly below her location before jumping from the top of the ledge. As she fell, she sent two aerial attacks at one treant. She wasn't level sixty yet, and so couldn't manipulate her aura, but she made up for it with perks and sheer brute force.

Both attacks landed right before she alighted on a tree branch nearby, strategically placing herself between the two monsters. For seven seconds, she used a swirling blade attack and trimmed the attacking vines. Her goal wasn't to actually *defeat* the treants, but to control their reach by reducing their longer branches.

At exactly seven and a half seconds, Tully jumped off the same ledge.

He did *not* arrive delicately, plowing his hammer straight into the treant on Visha's left. Its slightly reduced health plummeted further, and it stumbled back into the other treant, tangling it up and preventing it from getting closer.

"Ready," Visha said aloud. The time it took to write and read the messages didn't make up for a simple spoken word. The elf was swallowed in a shadow and vanished.

"Alright, come at me!" Tully yelled, in part to enrage the treants further but also to get the attention of others nearby.

[Two more on your left. Incoming twenty seconds.]

Jeffry sent the message, though I wondered if the paladin saw it. He was taunting the two treants in front of him even as he defeated the weakened of the two. Suddenly, a blast of icy leaves smashed against the [Barrier] Julian had on Tully, almost breaking the defensive shield.

The first of the treant's reinforcements had arrived.

"Again!" Tully yelled, swinging his war hammer. The excitement of battle riled him up, it would seem, because he was grinning like a fool and laughing wildly.

[Should John pull him out? The next wave is almost there.]

Jeffry asked, but Julian replied,

[No. Let him have his fun. I'll just reinforce the barrier.]

Later, we had to revive Sir Tully, but not before he took down nine treants by himself.

Put This Under Your Tongue to Avoid Detection

Julian

Julian let himself fall into directing the party instead of addressing the metaphorical jagged knife threatening to cut into his chest at the end of the dungeon.

He almost regretted tackling the dungeon right away. At least if they'd addressed her leaving first, he could've used the dungeon as an outlet for the storm inside.

But here they were.

The party was strong enough that they progressed through the dungeon levels at a reasonable rate, and besides the treants, there weren't any other large monster groups overpopulating their respective areas on the fourth or fifth floors. With a few hours to spare until their designated resting time, Julian called for a halt; they could clear one more floor or set up here for an early break.

Everyone agreed to hit one more floor before sleeping. At this rate, they could clear the dungeon in two or three days.

They arrived on the sixth floor to an unexpected sight: destroyed terrain from a recent battle. The platform was in the middle of an icy lake, and a storm was rolling in from the left. That side was all gray mist and black, dense cloud cover. A chill wind whipped at their clothing, carried over the frozen waters.

To the right, off in the distance, there was an outline of trees.

A few of them were on fire.

Gouges and shattered ice littered the frozen lake, a testament to a violent battle. There weren't any bodies, just the littered remnants of arrows, but that was to be expected since defeated monsters dissolved into shiny experience points.

Only monsters that escaped the dungeon took on permanent form.

"There's someone else here." Julian spoke the words quietly, lifting his hand and making a symbol to scout ahead. "That's why we didn't get the achievement."

John disappeared. Jeffry had his wings ready, but before he could take off, Gerda tugged on the half elf's arm and handed him something. "Put this under your tongue to avoid detection."

It was one thing to get attacked by monsters; it was another entirely to face off against unknown adventurers in an unexplored dungeon.

Jeffry nodded, doing as instructed. He vanished, but Julian could feel the rush of air as the half elf took off.

Julian wrote in the chat logs.

[We're heading for the fires.]

I walked with him and Pram while Tully and Visha spread out to search the shoreline ahead.

[Jeffry, fly ahead and set up base. I want us braced and ready for the storm.]
[Right away, Your Grace.]

John added,

[I've found signs of a battle further out on the lake. Unfortunately, it looks like it broke the direct route across the ice. We're going to have to take the long way around. Or wait for the dungeon to reset.]
[Do you think they're still here?]

Jeffry was the one who replied.

[No. I'm at the fire now, and based on the embers, it's been at least a few hours. The trees still on fire are all tarnel yules and can burn for days.]

Visha added,

[I found blood in the snow on the far bank, and tracks leading toward the fire.]

They reached the rendezvous point and found Jeffry already setting up a shelter, one of the reinforced round canvas tents with a cap at the top to let out smoke or bring in fresh air while protecting them from the rain. With the summer weather so agreeable outside, they'd only had to use it a few times on this trip.

The wind turned from forceful to painful as shards of ice and sleet plummeted against Julian, and he quickly ushered Gerda inside before following in himself.

[I'm calling everyone in. Now. John, go get Tully.]

Not three seconds later, John's shadow deposited Tully in the doorway. The paladin stumbled from the teleport. "Hey! I can *read*, you know!"

Gerda, who'd otherwise remained passive to the party banter, asked innocently, "But will you? It remains to be seen."

"Not you too, Miss Gerda!" Tully lamented, pushing aside one of the slumped tent flaps to join them.

"Look what I found!" Pram wandered in with a chunk of burning yule log. It was giving off a pleasant heat. He put it down in the middle of the tent.

Gerda pulled out her enchanted blanket and put it down beside the fire. The ice and snow from her boots and cloak muddied the edge, but she looked comfortable.

Pram sat on the ice directly, Jeffry summoned a three-pronged leather stool, and Visha stood beside Julian. Tully leaned on his war hammer.

[John, report.]
[My shadows are following a clear path of destruction around the lake, and I've found no signs of monsters. I would bet money they've already moved to the next floor.]
[Three gold they're still here!]

That last one was Tully.

[That's what you reply to?]

Visha added. Aloud, she sighed. "I'm not even surprised anymore."

"Change of plans." Julian told the group. "Since someone cleared the floor before us, the monster spawn time has been moved forward. If we stay here, we might not get a proper resting period, but if we push ahead, we might not get one at all. We've no idea if the other adventurers are friendly. We also don't know how familiar they are with this dungeon.

"Even *if* they haven't previously conquered the dungeon core, they could've been grinding levels here for any number of days, months, or years. Which means we should assume they could be hostile *and* have the advantage."

"The storm doesn't seem like it's going to let up anytime soon." Jeffry reached for the two tent flaps, dropping one but leaving the other open. There were small, tasseled ropes hanging on each flap, and he tied them together. Doing so activated an enchanted barrier against the elements; rain, snow, wind, and heat were repelled, allowing everyone to see outside without worry.

"I say we push ahead," Sir Tully stated.

"John will find out if they're still here even if we don't." Visha eyed the human with exasperation.

"What's the loss of one rest period?" he said. "A few mana potions, and we'll all be good to go."

Pram mused, "I like sleep, but I'm happy to continue on without."

Julian asked,

> *[John, how is the storm?]*
> *[It's bad, but it doesn't look like it'll let up anytime soon, and I could shadow jump everyone when I find the next platform.]*

That would leave John without mana and his ability on cooldown when they crossed into the next floor. He only had so many shadow jumps per hour.

> *[Then we'll move ahead.]*

Julian made the decision. To everyone in the tent, he said, "We'll stay here until John finds the entry to level seven. Enjoy the warmth while you can."

CHAPTER 91

There's Someone Else Here

Gerda

"I've never actually used [Dimension Rift] on another person before," I told my party members. "But the ability allows it."

We'd arrived at the portal platform for the next level, but it was deactivated. That meant monsters were already respawning and the level was repairing itself.

And that meant I could finally show off my dungeon-breaking-and-entering skills.

"We are ready," Julian told me, even though they weren't ready at all.

"I'll need everyone holding hands," I said. "And could you hold on to me while I activate the ability?"

There was a shuffle as everyone took off their winter gloves. John took Pram's hand, who took Tully's, who took Visha's, who took Jeffry's, who took Julian's, who in turn took mine. I didn't know why it was so important that I see exactly who was holding whom, but watching Visha stare daggers at Tully's hand was priceless.

Good job, me. My shipping powers were still in full force.

"In Between the Light Unseen,
Void and Space All Mixed in Place,
By Portal's Gift, [Dimension Rift]."

[You have activated the Perk: **Dimension Rift**. Bridge point detected: **Forgotten Frost Dungeon Level Six Portal Access Gate** to **Forgotten Frost Dungeon Level Seven Portal Arrival Gate**.]
[You are attempting to open a bridge in a Dimension Barrier:

Forgotten Frost Dungeon Level Seven Portal Arrival Gate. You
have succeeded.]
[Transport to Level Seven? Yes/No]
[Transport Party to Level Seven? Yes/No]
[Transport Julian von Slyke to Level Seven? Yes/No]

And on it listed options. I selected the second, teleporting all of us to the next area platform.

[Dimension Rift] was a perk I'd gotten from my [+Troll Magic], the + meaning I'd evolved the skill by getting it to level ten. Once that happened, the perks offered were more powerful. My previous abilities were on the level of [Bridge Repair] or [Bridge Sense], and now I was ripping holes through dimensions to make my own bridges.

As one does.

"Well, that's unexpected." Tully let go of Pram and lifted his free hand to shade his eyes. The seventh floor looked like regular farmland. It was hot and sunny, with a gentle breeze playing in the leaves. Apple blossoms fell delicately across a field of flowers from an orchard that stretched out behind us to the left.

Tully continued to hold Visha's hand, and the elf noticed. She wrenched it away as fast as she could and took a step to put distance between them.

"Permission to reequip, Your Grace?" Jeffry asked, and I realized that sweat was pooling between my shoulder blades and at my temples. The winter gear wasn't heavy, but it was becoming torturous against the heat.

"There aren't any signs of life for thirty feet," John informed us.

Julian nodded. "Alright."

The duke himself didn't change his clothing. After stripping down to a simple tunic, tights, and boots, I eyed Julian. He was still wearing the Valarian Royal Set, with the mantle folded and pinned with a hood; he hadn't added much except a scarf and gloves, which he put back into his storage ring.

With a smile, he lifted his free hand and revealed a bracelet on his wrist.

"Ice Elemental Resistance. Takes the edge off so I can still wear the armor set as is," he confided. "More advanced than a normal Cold Resistance charm. Mother made it for me when I started spending more time here."

"And you didn't secure one for your eternally loyal party members?" Jeffry drawled, having overheard.

"You have *three* Cold Resistance charms," Julian shot back, unfazed. "You'll be fine."

"So." Sir Tully leaned back and scratched his head, looking out across the clear fields that stretched in all directions.

Something caught my eye, and I focused as hard as I could directly ahead of us. There were a few trees along the horizon, but otherwise, it was rolling hills into the distance. There was movement in one of the trees.

"Something's coming," I told everyone; the group immediately settled into formation as a [Barrier] popped up, covering everyone on the platform.

"Jeffry, scout from the sky," Julian ordered. The half elf didn't need to be told twice. "John, keep an eye behind us."

The rogue disappeared. Far off, one of the trees started to shimmer. And then another. Jeffry flew until he was a third of the distance between us and the trees.

"It looks like . . . magic?" I thought aloud.

By then, it was more than just the trees; the entire horizon moved with a long line of silver. Above us, Jeffry spun midair and sent us a panicked, all-capital message over the chat log.

[RUN!]

No one questioned it, immediately activating their various fast-travel abilities. A Haste potion was good enough for me. I quaffed one and booked it after the rest of them.

[What is it?]

Julian asked, to which Jeffry sent back,

[The dungeon level is a terrain challenge. We have to outrun the Flash Frost. If it touches you, then you're as good as dead.]

Visha sent,

[Terrain floors reset as soon as there are no more living challengers, so we can pop back and pick up anyone who isn't fast enough. Right, Tully?]

The paladin didn't reply, and I couldn't help laughing. Even in this situation, he wasn't checking his chat log. Luckily, John piped in with the location of the portal before anybody got too tired. It was a madcap sprint to the finish, but everyone made it through.

Even Tully.

CHAPTER 92

Burrowing, Biting, and Paw Bashing

Julian

They took a moment to catch their breath after they made it through the portal.

"You were cutting it a little close there, weren't you?" Tully slapped Jeffry on the shoulder, hard.

"I made it, and that's what counts." The half elf stood straighter and placed a hand on his sword. Julian drew his own blade.

They were standing in a dark, cold cavern. Stalagmites rose from the floor haphazardly. The walls were stone, with white ice that crept up to about Julian's knee height at the base. A few feet forward, the cavern exited into two tunnels. Icy wind blew from the one on the right, and everyone re-equipped their winter wear.

"I say we go left." Tully said, motioning in that direction.

"Well, I say we go right," Visha snapped, an edge in her voice.

It was unlike the elf, who usually maintained a stricter level of indifference. Tully stopped and stared at Visha, then hesitatingly said, "Uh, alright?"

"I like walking with the wind," Pram reasoned. The selkie smiled, missing the tension.

"We'll have John scout both and make an informed decision after," Julian stated.

The rogue vanished as instructed. A short while later, John's chat arrived.

[There are no monsters to either side. Or signs of battle. Should I go further?]

Julian usually restricted how far any one person should scout, as there could still be monsters further along. There was also the chance that the other party had cleared things ahead of them without leaving a trace . . . or they'd already left the dungeon.

"We'll start on the right," Julian announced, reaching a decision. "And follow the wind."

"Did we want to rest first?" Jeffry broached. "Let half the party get a full recovery?"

Due to the unknown adventurers already here, there was a driving sense of urgency that made Julian want to push forward . . . but he wasn't in this alone. "Okay. I'll stand guard while everyone rests."

He might as well, since he wasn't going to get much sleep as it was. There was a shuffle as sleeping bags came out. They hesitated between sleeping *on* the platform, which was warmer, or the frozen cavern floor. But there was a chance, however slim, that another group might portal in and land *right on top* of them while they were sleeping.

They chose the cavern floor.

Julian sat down on the edge of the platform while everyone else slept. Waiting. And thinking.

At the three-hour mark, he pulled out parchment to write a letter to his sister. Sometimes, writing to her helped everything make sense—and it was a habit he'd developed long ago.

He ate some of his rations after that. His storage ring couldn't keep things in stasis like Gerda's, so he went with cheese and smoked boar, and sourdough with butter and bimbleberry jam. He was used to trail rations while out on expedition, and he had to shake his head at the sheer wonder of eating hot meals in a dungeon. His eyes drifted away from the tunnels and down to the bridge troll, still asleep.

He pulled out more parchment and set to writing a new letter.

Julian felt a presence approaching through a tunnel at hour seven. It was coming from the left passage.

Instead of waking anyone, he set up a [Barrier] and walked over to meet whatever was coming down the tunnel. It was a star vole, an underground-dwelling rodent monster known for the star-shaped white fur around its eyes. Sitting hunched over a bit, the star vole was as tall as Julian's shoulder. It was known for burrowing, biting, and paw bashing.

Julian activated [Charge], barreling toward the beast. The star vole, noticing his approach, tried to lash out with its long front claws, each the size of a pocket dagger. The sword sliced into one of the claws as the star vole hissed, but dungeon madness pushed it forward through the pain. Julian ducked and struck again. Even if it *could've* landed a hit past his Valarian Royal Shield, it wasn't too much of a threat on its own.

[You have defeated a **Star Vole (Level 26)**. +13 EXP]

If monsters were suddenly appearing now . . . that meant the previous party had cleared them out roughly eight hours ago and it was respawn time. Unfortunately, everyone had been pushing through on potions to get here, and Julian didn't want to disturb them early.

He could hold off a few monsters for an hour.

CHAPTER 93

Just One More Star Vole

Gerda

I woke up well rested and with a fresh day of foretellings.

Before addressing my notification tabs, I gave a yawn, sat up, and stretched. Everyone else was stirring as well.

There was nothing as rewarding as a good night's sleep in Valaria. If only my previous life had had regenerating health bars and a rest system. Granted, the notifications tab was equal to if not worse than a phone addiction. I could throw my phone out a window, but I couldn't turn off my system interface.

Ignoring it momentarily would have to do, because I realized a problem at roughly the same instant as everyone else.

Julian wasn't here.

[Julian?]

I sent the message over the chat logs. There was a familiar [Barrier] guarding us, but the half elf himself was nowhere to be seen.

[One second.]

He sent a message back, and we all shared a look.

Except Tully, who had jumped to his feet. "Where's—Ah."

"Let's pack up and be ready to move out," Visha ordered, already rolling up her bedroll and slipping it into her storage. Tully just waved at his, and it vanished. He smiled. "Ready."

I folded mine before storing it in my storage ring. I preferred summoning a blanket that didn't immediately flop all over the floor. Jeffry was the slowest, looking like he'd been hit by a train.

"Here," I offered, handing him a hot cup of extra strong, steeped red tea.

"Mm, thank you." He ran a hand through his scraggly bed hair before accepting the cup. I then sat down on the edge of the platform and checked my logs.

[Passive Perk: **Sense Fate** has activated. Duke Julian von Slyke will fall into a pit trap.]

[You have crossed paths with a fate that can be changed. Area of effect radius: Level 67 x Perception 45 x Foretelling 4 = 12,060sq/ft. Fate herself will guide you.]

["The eyes of Fate are on the chosen of her company, and by the end of grace might hear the sound. That moment when the third crosses the fingers reach, the earth herself will hold and drag him down."]

Alright, that sounded . . . not good.

[Julian, watch for floor traps!]

I posted it as soon as I was finished reading the warning.

[Too late for that.]

When he *didn't* immediately follow it up with more, I held off yelling at him in all caps, calmly asking,

[And!!?!]
[It's fine.]

Still no real explanation.

"John," I called out to the rogue, who was reading his own notifications. His eyes glanced my way, and I said, "Go get Julian."

"Alright." The shadow man disappeared into his own shadow.

"Wow," Tully laughed. "John listened to you."

"Of course he did. She's Madame Potts," Pram explained.

Jeffry added cheekily, "And she's sl—dating the duke."

John and Julian appeared back in the cavern, the duke slung over John's shoulder. He looked the worse for wear. One shoulder was gouged pretty badly, there was a cut on his cheek, and one of his legs was clean missing. From the blood dripping through his clothes, there were other unseen injuries as well.

Julian was deposited on the platform while John wordlessly handed over mana and healing potions.

Tully made an impressed whistle, but no one else spoke.

"Fine, huh?" I marched up to Julian and poked him on the side of the chest that wasn't torn up. As much as I knew this world didn't work the same way mine did . . . seeing him in this state made me *angry*. "I was almost done," he replied. His face was clammy, and his eyes unfocused. "Just one more star vole, and then I would've healed myself."

"You're a wreck!" I told him, poking again. He flinched. John was already opening another potion and handing it over as he came to Julian's defense. "It's true, Miss Gerda. *Usually*, His Grace could tackle twenty star voles unscathed." John gave Julian a *deliberate* look. "Though I've never seen you come back *this* injured before."

"He fell into a pit trap."

Julian grunted.

John nodded. "Ah, that would do it."

Between the potions and Julian's [Divine Heal], his leg came back before our eyes—barefoot and without a pant leg, of course. I handed him a [Mend] scroll, and he swapped out a new pair of boots.

"Enough fuss," Julian said, handing back the empty potion bottles and standing up. "It's time we head out. I suspect the other party is still in the dungeon, and since the dungeon status hasn't updated, they haven't reached the core. Everyone needs to be on high alert."

"How far did you go into the tunnels?" Jeffry asked. He'd changed his wings for a pair of glasses that let him see in the dark. And instead of his usual standard-size sword, he had equipped a half-sword that was easier to maneuver in tight spaces.

"Not far. The star voles came from the left side, and there's been nothing from the right."

"So, are we still going left?" Visha asked. Everyone was standing, ready to head out.

"That will be difficult." John had on a slight smile. "Since most of it has collapsed."

" . . . "

Something in my eyes made Julian crack. His rough leader demeanor faltered, and he rushed to explain, "Everything *was* fine. I was simply going to heal up *before* calling John over for a teleport."

" . . . "

"And despite the way I looked, I still had a quarter of my health. Gerda—"

"Okay," I cut him off. Something about his panic and desperate explanation was cute enough that it distracted me from my worry and upset. He looked relieved, so I poked him in the chest another time. "But don't lie to me like that again. Explain things properly, or I'll get really angry next time."

His gaze suddenly softened in a way that made me feel guilty. "Next time . . . I will."

My ear twitched as I looked away.

With that, the team set off down the right tunnel.

CHAPTER 94

Very, Very Lucky

Julian

If the left tunnel was full of giant star voles hell-bent on eating them, the right tunnel posed a unique and equally difficult challenge.

Or it would have, if Gerda wasn't in their party.

"The answer is that blue triangular stone," she said, pointing at the one Visha needed to press.

They were all standing in front of a dead end with a colorful mosaic floor. Visha, as the most dexterous of the group, was following Gerda's directions to bypass the puzzle. The elf's left leg was on a red circular stone, her right leg was in an almost-full wide split to access the green square tile opposite, her right hand was pressed on a yellow swirl directly underneath her torso—propping up her body—and her left arm reached up to touch the blue triangle.

Nothing happened.

"What next?" Visha asked. She wasn't uncomfortable; this would be nothing for someone with a thirty-eight Dexterity.

"You need to release your mana into each stone," Gerda explained. "It's why one person has to do it: the mana signature has to be the same across all four points."

"Alright." Visha did as she was instructed, and the four tiles lit up with the soft green color of her magic.

"Now you need to release the pressure on the tiles in a new sequence. First, your right hand . . ." Gerda trailed off, noting that was the hand she was using to hold up her entire body.

"Of course." Visha sighed. She clenched her core muscles and tilted forward so that her body was balanced on the sole of one foot and the toes of the other.

The problem, of course, was that now she was starfished with one hand in the air.

"Next, lift your left leg," Gerda said, forcing Visha to balance on the toes of her right foot and her outstretched left hand. She tilted her body sideways to the floor to do so, but looked concerned.

The tiles that she'd released continued to glow with a faint green magic.

"Now, the right leg," Gerda said.

Visha braced her fingers then pushed into a handstand. "Now what?"

"Can you jump back over here?" Gerda asked.

"Only if you all move out of the way," Visha replied; the group moved back to give her room. "Somebody catch me if I slip up."

Tully put down his war hammer and held out both hands.

"*Not you*," Visha ordered while the paladin just smiled. She bent her elbow, flung herself in an elegant arch, and landed perfectly on the other side of the mosaic.

"It's still not working." Pram drew their attention back to the floor.

"One last thing," Gerda said, pointing at a hole on the opposite side. "Visha has to hit that with an attack infused with her mana."

Without preamble, Visha threw a dagger across the room, landing it square inside the hole. The entire wall shuddered then dropped into the floor, opening the path.

"Good job!" Sir Tully hefted his war hammer back onto his back and made to walk onto the mosaic. Gerda caught him before he put down his first step.

"Ah, no. Don't you remember the floor spikes last time?" She shook her head and pointed at the red circular stone. "To jump across, we have to go in order of tiles. The first person needs to step on the red circle, the second on the green square, the third on the yellow swirl, and the last on the blue triangle."

"But there aren't four of us," Pram noted. "There are seven."

"I'll take Tully across," John said, disappearing into the shadows with the paladin even as Tully tried to protest that he should take someone else.

"Gerda?" Julian unequipped his shield and sword, storing them temporarily so they would be out of the way.

Gerda lifted her arms and wrapped them around Julian's neck, her smooth, muscular body holding on tight. He scooped her legs out from under her and hooked an arm behind her shoulders in a princess carry.

"Good job getting us through." He pitched his voice low and spoke into his troll's ear. Julian smiled when she shivered.

"You're lucky I was here." She poked his cheek.

"Very lucky," he agreed.

"Especially when *someone* blocked the other tunnel." She poked him on the cheek a second time.

Julian turned at the last second and kissed her finger.

"Very, very lucky then."

Visha had crossed first, then Pram, then Jeffry. Lastly, Julian crossed without incident.

Feeling playful, Julian didn't let Gerda down, holding her as they continued down the tunnel. After his earlier battle, his body might have been repaired, but he was starting to feel a deep sense of wariness sinking in.

Holding Gerda made him feel like he could go another twenty-four hours without rest no problem.

CHAPTER 95

Giant Pink-Tinted Void Bubble

Gerda

"I've found another." John held up one hand, blocking the group from progressing.

John discovered most of the traps on his own, while I was called on for the puzzles and riddles: from moving wall parts that slotted together to open hidden doors, to discovering that the only way across a spike pit was to send Jeffry up to the ceiling and pull a disguised lever that raised ice pillars in the pit to walk across.

One time, the answer had been simply yelling, "Albus Rolling Yarn."

This was the eighth so far, and I was still in Julian's arms. He'd used the excuse that I was the only one without a fast-travel skill . . . but we both knew he just liked carrying me around.

I liked it too, so I didn't fight all that hard.

Currently, we were stopped at a sharp bend in the tunnel where it veered left and out of sight. On the wall ten feet ahead, words were faintly carved into the dirt.

> *How can the sun rise in the deep?*
> *Where the old and ancient sleep,*
> *Onward into darkness fight*
> *Or safely walk where light is right?*

I shifted and Julian put me down. I patted him once on the arm then walked to the front of the group. After scanning the other walls to see if I was missing anything, I turned back to the riddle and read the words over carefully while unconsciously tapping my chin.

Then I checked my [Map] function and smiled. "That's fun."

"What's the answer?" Julian asked.

"The tunnel turns west, but the sun rises in the east. It's saying that if we follow the path, it will set off a trap, but if we go east, then we will reach the end," I explained. "By the old and ancient verse, I'm going to assume level ten is the boss battle and the final floor of the dungeon."

Originally, that would have been cause to celebrate, but instead, it put everyone on edge. We still hadn't caught up to the other party in the dungeon or received a notification that they had captured the dungeon ahead of us. That meant we were potentially going to drop into the middle of someone else's boss battle, or we were walking into a trap.

Or both.

"Let's push forward." Julian decided. He turned to me, "I want you to stay in the back. If this is an ambush, I might not be able to protect you."

"Okay," I agreed.

In order to bypass the puzzle, I told him to walk up to the writing, close his eyes, and turn right facing the tunnel wall. He didn't hesitate when I told him to walk straight into the wall, and then he was gone, having passed straight through.

It was an illusion.

We followed him cautiously, but there was no attack waiting on the other side. Instead, we were in another wide cavern open to the sky above. Sunlight shone down, playing off the rocks. In the middle was a large portal platform that would take us to the next level.

And blocking the platform was a giant pink-tinted Void bubble.

I cursed aloud.

"It's Alice," I explained, waving a frustrated hand at the bubble. "*She's* the one who's found the dungeon ahead of us and is waiting for us on the other side."

"But . . . why? Doesn't it *help us* if she clears the dungeon and stops the monster surges?" Jeffry unequipped his see-in-the-dark glasses and reequipped his Eye of Effeldor broach.

"She *hasn't* stopped the monster surges. The dungeon is still undefeated," Julian noted.

"Maybe she was hunting Miss Gerda all the way to this dungeon and reached the end only to realize we hadn't been there yet, so she set up this barrier that'll inform her when we break it, letting her set up an ambush on the other side to kill us all and finally have her revenge?" Pram pointed out.

"But *how*? How did she get here before us?" Visha asked, stepping forward to examine the bubble. Black flecks gleamed in the pink barrier.

Previously, when King Keith had been trapped inside a similar-looking bubble, anything that touched the surface would take Void damage. The celestial so far had displayed Fate, Void, Light, Rogue, Charm, and Portal-based abilities. I'd assumed she was level sixty, but if she was level seventy, then she might have Barrier abilities as well.

But based on my previous battle with the celestial, I couldn't see her as that powerful yet.

"She and I have similar powers; we can see the future, and we have portal abilities." I clenched my fist at my side, looking around the party until I met Julian's eyes.

"She knew where I was going, helping you find this dungeon. Who knows how quickly she could've gotten here. Hells, she could have portaled here *right* after our battle at the Northern Fortress, or gathered a party and arrived minutes before we did. Either way, she's here now, and we will have to deal with her."

"Do we really?" Tully asked, drawing our attention.

"What does that mean?" Visha eyed the paladin.

Tully shrugged.

"Can't we just let Guild Mistress Alice defeat the dungeon and go home? You have your special bridge powers now. We could just leave.." The paladin waved a hand at the bubble blocking their path. "I don't think Alice can hole up in the dungeon for a whole *week*. Fighting the same boss monster again and again and never claiming the prize? *I couldn't.* I'd get bored after a day and then go home."

I didn't know what to say . . . because I might not be here in a week.

We all turned to Julian to see what he would decide.

CHAPTER 96

King Kraken's Heart

Julian

Gerda caught his eye, and Julian knew what she was thinking.

The reminder hurt, but he also knew she was determined to cross her bridge after the dungeon was complete. He could understand . . . but he wasn't happy about it.

"No," he told the party. "Guild Mistress Alice is an international criminal who should be detained at all costs. Leaving her when she's here waiting for us and potentially at lessened strength from fighting the dungeon boss would be foolish. As foolish as walking into an ambush we were already expecting and could prepare for."

"So then, how are we going to prepare for the ambush?" Jeffry asked, concerned. He knew their inventory better than anyone and didn't seem keen on continuing to the next level with their current resources.

"I can help with that!" Gerda lifted her hand. "Ah, let's see. Tully, you should take this."

Gerda summoned an Epic-tier war hammer called Dawn of the Last Dragon Hammer, granting a +3 strength buff. It also lit its opponent on fire on a crit success, dealing burn damage. Sir Tully's hands were shaking when she handed it over, and he looked like he was going to cry when he read the stats for himself.

For Jeffry, she pulled out the Legendary grade sword told about in ballad and song, Badgerclaw Best Blade. It had a +5 strength buff and a fifty percent chance to crit against dragons. The half-elf whispered, "By the gods, *it's real?*"

For Visha, she pulled out Epic-tier twin blades, one that dealt paralyzing electric damage on a crit, and the other that shot out water blades when infused with mana. Visha had one Epic-tier blade already, an heirloom in her family that had been passed down for generations. She held her new weapons in outright awe.

When Gerda reached Pram . . . something unexpected happened.

She had just pulled out the King Kraken's Heart, saying, "Here, Pram, you should have this," when Pram hit the floor on his knees. She hesitated by his sudden action but placed the pendant around the selkie's neck.

She'd handed over Telv Kingdom's greatest treasure, the lost king's pendant . . . and the reason for Pram's family being exiled twenty years ago.

Pram's parents had been the diplomatic emissaries to Sumbria when the civil war broke out.

The war had started on the elven queen's coronation day. Her family had been cruel and unjust to the citizens of Sumbria, but the new queen had decided it wasn't enough. On the day she'd stepped up, Terra Glade had issued a new rule: elves were no longer allowed to marry non-elves, and all previous unions were dissolved. All half breeds, who were already second-class citizens, were to be stripped of their rights and demoted to third-class citizens with the rest of the non-elf cast.

The Telv queen's consort, Prince Tori, had been a guest of honor at the coronation dinner that evening. Pram's parents had not been able to save Prince Tori *or* his regalia, which had been stolen in the chaos of battle.

In her grief, the selkie queen had banished Pram's family from the Underdark until they could return her husband's treasure, the King Kraken's Heart. Only a few merfamilies lived in the waters around Valaria, most resided in the Underdark—a long deep sea canyon off the eastern coastline. Telv was the only kingdom in the Underdark, and Julian knew that being able to right his family's honor and return to the depths had been Pram's dream since they were young. Pram was crying. Whatever bonus the pendant gave was nothing to its meaning.

Gerda stepped back, looking obviously confused. Knowing Pram wasn't able to, Julian placed a hand on her shoulder and asked, "You just had that lying around?"

"It's one of the treasures that Henrietta found in another timeline. Since she's with King Keith, I went around collecting all of the artifacts and legendary items she wouldn't be needing anymore," Gerda explained. "They're world-quest items, like the scepter in your locket."

"And, uh, *where* did you find King Kraken's Heart?" he asked.

"I stole it off Crown Prince Deryl Glade at the Spring Ball," she said, casually bringing about the destruction of Sumbria's ocean trade. "using *these*."

She pulled out a pair of gloves that looked like cat paws while Julian went over to help Pram to his feet.

"Here." Gerda handed the treasure over to John.

When he saw what they did, the rogue's eyes went wide. "Interesting."

It was surprisingly funny, seeing the otherwise solemn, quiet, human wearing cute cat gloves. John flexed his hands once, and then a wide grin spread across his face.

At that look, Gerda joked, "Don't make me regret giving you that."

John looked up at the troll, made to say something, and stopped. His eyes opened even wider.

"And you aren't allowed to steal my ring!" she exclaimed, covering the ring with her other hand.

"It's actually saying your most valuable item is the Trickster's Scarf," he said, amused.

"Really? I didn't realize it changed to suit the wearer's needs." Gerda smiled. "Oh, did you need another Veralyn's Enchanted Restraint Manacles?"

"I'm fine," John replied.

With that, Gerda dropped a variety of specialty potions, two for each of the party members to carry. She also handed over a few sleep and paralysis poisons.

"Isn't this a bit much?" Jeffry asked, holding up an advanced, high-level health potion that would heal a thousand hit points instantly.

"No," Gerda replied, reminding him, "This is the woman who has prepared *specifically* to fight us. We only just discovered she's here."

"This is also a reminder that no one is to directly face Alice," Julian ordered. "Leave her to me."

"Or me," Gerda added, and there was suddenly an ax in her hands. She walked up to the Void bubble and poked it with the weapon. The bubble popped easily.

Julian assumed the barrier wasn't actually blocking passage; dungeons responded to blocked gates poorly. The mana inside built up quickly and exploded everything in the area to reopen the path.

Gerda turned to face them. "One last thing."

Julian raised an eyebrow. He couldn't think what else they would need on top of everything else.

"Activate these before we go." Gerda summoned spell scrolls. Seven. She handed them out, one each and two for Tully.

[Spell Scroll: **Mental Resistance**]

Ah.

CHAPTER 97

A Suitable Final Boss

Gerda

The first thing I saw when we arrived on level ten was a colossal cavern. Ice stalactites larger than I was had fallen from the ceiling, splitting the floor in places.

In the center of the room, an icy wyvern only slightly smaller than Her Eminence Feliwyn lay dead, curled up on the cavern floor. Guild Mistress Alice sat on the wyvern, looking down at us. Around her were three others: her dungeon delving party members.

She looked like a suitable final boss.

"At last, you're here," Alice said, jumping down from the boss monster. Her white feather celestial wings spread out behind her, delicately controlling her fall.

"Is that dungeon monster dead?" Pram asked from somewhere behind me. "And still here?"

"Looks like it," John replied.

"It's time to *end* this, Gerda." Alice took a fighting stance.

One of the celestial's party members, a lizardkin wearing wizard robes, turned to their seven-foot-tall giant tank holding a broadsword. "She never told us it would be four versus seven?"

"Worth the money," the giant said, holding up his sword and getting into a fighting stance. The lizardkin looked unconvinced but started chanting.

"Were you just sitting up there waiting for us this whole time?" Sir Tully asked Alice, sounding confused.

"You have to admit, it looked spectacular," I told the paladin.

He pulled out his extra [Mental Resistance] scroll. "Did you need this?"

"I'm going to kill you," Alice said, lifting one hand. "By the Will of the Eternal Rest, [Void Arrow]."

Her mage also cast, "By the Great Sun, [Fire Spear]," as her tank swung his sword in an arch. "[Bludgeoning Cut]."

Both hits landed on Julian's [Barrier], but it held. The last member of Alice's party was a beastfolk in folk form, and she didn't attack because John had grabbed her by the ankle, dragging her down into a shadow.

She appeared a moment later, falling from the ceiling. Pram attempted to hit her with an ice spear but missed.

The last member of Alice's party didn't attack because John had dragged him into a shadow by the ankles, dropping him from the ceiling near Pram.

"The place is trapped!" I told the group. "Stay clear of the left side of the platform, that rock face, that ground icicle—Antidotes, now!"

The adventurer that Pram had tried to skewer with his ice attack jumped to her feet with eight bottles of poisons, one squished between each finger ninja-knife-wielding style. She threw them at us and they exploded in a large cloud of poison.

I'd handed everyone a bunch of potions for this very reason. Spies, assassins . . . I'd assumed this place was as dangerous as the sanctuary wedding before I got to it.

There was a split second where every person in the room except Alice and John stopped to drink a high grade antidote. It was kinda silly, but it worked.

John used the opportunity to pop out of the shadows and cut the legs out from under the lizardkin mage while he was drinking his antidote. The mage surprised the rogue by pointing down and silent casting [Fireball]. He'd deliberately cast aloud earlier to catch us off guard now. Both attacks landed. Pram was ready to help put out the fire when John appeared back on the platform.

"I'll clear an opening!" their tank said. "[Charge]."

Holding his broadsword, the giant barreled through the plumes of poison smoke. Before he reached the [Barrier], Julian jumped down from the platform and met the broadsword with his Valarian Royal Sword. The weapons clashed, sliding down to the handguard, and then Julian's blade was swung wide until it hit the ground. At that point, the half elf silently activated [Crushing Blow] and hit the giant with his shield.

The giant grunted under the blow.

While John healed up, Pram was back to firing another [Ice Spear] as the cooldown came off. One hit a trap, and an explosion rang out across the room. The ice stalactites still hanging from the ceiling shivered from the blast, but only one fell. It landed six feet from where Julian and the giant were engaged in battle.

Visha decided that the quickest way to join the fray without risking setting off more traps was going up and over. She crossed the cavern by jumping from the top of the ice stalactites that had fallen and pierced the ground. Her twin blades were drawn, and she lashed out with one, shooting a water blade at the beastfolk poisoner.

Jeffry stood beside me, his epic blade drawn and his wings activated so that he could leap into flight at any second.

Alice smiled. Surprisingly, she stood back, waiting.

I didn't like that.

Julian clashed swords with the giant three times in quick succession while Pram attempted to hit him with a [Freeze] spell, but it was repelled. Visha locked down the beastman as John, healed, vanished into shadow again.

Sir Tully had earlier jumped off the right side of the platform and was walking very, very carefully, almost on tiptoe, across the cavern floor and between the fallen ice. At this point, he activated his first trap. A blast of Void damage hit the column of ice behind him, and it vanished.

"I'm alright!" he reassured us, taking another step and falling into a pit trap.

Julian had the upper hand on his opponent, and whittled down the giant's hit points as Pram finally ran out of mana and retreated to stand beside me. Jeffry traded off and flew to go help Visha. The elf wasn't faring well against the beast-kin, who was agile enough to dodge her attacks and had ranged [Claw Blades] that had already dealt Visha some damage.

"This is going well," Pram told me with a smile, pulling out his mana potion.

A soft voice whispered from across the cavern, "Now."

Julian was bringing up his shield to block another strike when the giant shifted midswing, spun in place, and threw his sword. It landed against the [Barrier], shattering it.

"[Sever Fate]." Alice appeared behind me, her palm on my back.

> [You have been affected by [**Sever Fate**]. For twenty-four hours, you are immune to **Raise**, **Resurrect**, **Revive**, or **Respawn**.]

Pram stabbed the celestial with a pocket dagger before she managed to portal away again.

I cursed.

Across the cavern, the wyvern disintegrated into sparkling experience points.

CHAPTER 98

Tully Lost His Temper

Julian

Julian could feel the shift in battle as things turned for the worse.

His own fight was rounding down, and he felt like he could best the giant with one or two more blows. His opponent had already taken a few hits from his shield and one from his sword, so he was flagging. On the last pass, one of John's shadow men popped out and stabbed the giant while Julian had him locked sword to sword.

"Hey!" the giant glared.

Not the most honorable, but neither was ambushing with intent to permanently wipe out his party.

"Give up now, and I will show mercy."

"Sorry." The giant adjusted his grip. "Contract work. Doesn't look good if you betray your boss."

Julian stabbed at the giant. "It also doesn't look good if you PVP."

Party versus party was taboo in the adventuring guilds and dungeon delving community, and anyone caught party killing would have their guild membership revoked or even get banned from certain dungeons.

"I'm not an adventurer; I'm an assassin." The giant pulled back. He raised his sword and fainted a sweeping blow. When Julian set his shield to block, the giant turned and threw his sword at the [Barrier] defending the platform.

The [Barrier] fell.

Julian activated [Multi-Target Shield], but not before watching Alice appear behind Gerda and touch the troll's back. As the shield came up, Alice portaled away.

Julian's heart stopped—until he realized that Gerda was otherwise fine. "[Piercing Thrust]." The giant had summoned a new sword from somewhere, and Julian barely managed to lift his shield in time to take the blow at an angle.

[You have been dealt 350 **Force** damage. Valarian Royal Shield blocks 200 damage. You have taken 150 **Force** damage. Health: 964/1274]

Julian cursed under his breath. He needed to finish this *now*. At his direction, John's shadow moved to intercept the giant, but his opponent noticed and jumped back.

There was a flash in the corner of Julian's vision. Visha had taken a blow to the stomach that sent her clean through two giant icicles . . . where she hit the left side wall of the cave. The trap that Gerda had warned them about activated, pulling the entire wall down on top of the elf, crushing her beneath the rubble. By some miracle or skill, no more stalactites fell from the impact.

Jeffry sent over the party interface,

[We've lost Visha.]

And that was when Tully lost his temper.

The human exploded in a burst of red light, charging across the cave at the beastfolk who'd hit Visha. His war hammer hit the ground instead of the transformed leopard who had been standing there previously.

Two things happened simultaneously. The leopard jumped on top of Tully, large claws attacking his back as the paladin stumbled from the impact. His strength was higher than anyone else's in the party, however, and he did manage to throw the beastfolk off him.

At the same time, the force of his hammer sent shock waves throughout the entire cave, and the remaining stalactites fell all at once.

The giant in front of him vanished.

Julian braced his shield and sank most of his mana into defending his party members as a ceiling of varying-sized ice spears crashed down on top of them.

[You have been dealt 980 points damage. Valarian Royal Shield blocks 200 damage. You have taken 780 points damage.]
[Warning! Your Health has dropped below 15%]
[Warning! Your Mana has dropped below 10%. Rest is recommended or you may suffer **Nausea**, **Heartburn**, **Indigestion**, **Upset Stomach**, or **Death**.]
[Current Health: 184/1274]
[Current Mana: 23/500]

But that wasn't all.

[You have been poisoned by **Dandyvine**. You have taken 40 points
of **Bleed** damage to all senses.]

In preparation for the ambush, Alice had poisoned some of the ice spears, so the debris and snow and dust that had kicked up from the impact had poison effects.

Julian cursed, but since he was protected under the pile of ice braced overhead by his shield, he took a moment to pop an antidote and a health potion. He'd barely opened the top of a mana potion when he heard the muffled sounds of talking.

"A little earlier than planned, but it'll do."

"Julian!" Gerda's voice was laced with panic, and Julian dropped the empty mana bottle to thrust aside the ice spear that had been trapping him.

Alice was downing a potion, unharmed, with the rest of her party members, standing where the wyvern had been. The boss monster was gone, and in its place was a blue spire pedestal with a glowing orb on top. The dungeon core.

He turned to see the wreckage that was his party.

Jeffry was nowhere to be seen, trapped somewhere under the rubble. Tully cursed as he downed an antidote, but otherwise looked unscathed. Pram was standing with Gerda under an ice wall that wrapped around them for protection . . . and John was at their feet, semicrushed by a pile of large ice spears. The man was unconscious.

Julian immediately cast [Multi-Target Shield] again and sunk his newly refilled mana into healing his party members with [Divine Heal].

If Alice reached out to touch the dungeon core, she would open the exit. She could escape, having claimed her prize. But then Gerda might escape as well, and Julian didn't think the celestial would allow that.

It was two steps with [Light Foot] to land on the platform beside his panicked troll.

"It'll be alright," he told her.

"No, it won't. You need to focus on fighting and not defending me," Gerda argued.

Julian lifted the ice off John as Pram pulled the human free.

Gerda suddenly pulled Julian's shirt, bending him forward toward her shoulder. A blast of [Void Arrow] whizzed where his head had been.

"Thanks," he said, straightening. "John."

The newly healed rogue groaned. "One second." He was still lying at their feet, with Pram crouched beside him checking his recovery.

"One," Julian said.

"Alright, alright." The rogue sank into a pool of shadow that disappeared into the field of ice spears and slunk into the stalactite graveyard.

Alice lifted a hand in some unknown signal and ordered, "Defend the dungeon core but don't touch it."

Tully, who was closest to Alice's party, pulled out a small hand ax and hurled it at the beastfolk. The leopard ducked, and the ax hit the lizardkin blunt side to the nose.

She toppled over.

"Ah, ah, ah." Alice pointed at Tully. "Wrapped in Empty Embrace, [Void Cage]."

Tully tried to leap out of the way, but since he was hemmed in by ice, Alice guessed his next move perfectly. A pink Void bubble trapped the paladin.

"By Battle Movement Be Undone, [Prisoner Exchange]." Tully activated one of his rarer paladin abilities. Tully and the giant traded places, bringing Tully within range of the dungeon core . . . but before he could touch it, Alice's hand grabbed his wrist.

And Tully was suddenly portaled away, dropping from the ceiling upside down toward a particularly jagged collection of ice and stone.

He barely managed to catch himself.

Alice waved a hand at the Void bubble and it popped, releasing the giant . . . just in time for John to reach out of the shadows and lock a familiar set of manacles around the giant's wrists.

"Not *you* again," Alice cursed, attempting to throw a poison dagger at John, but he'd slipped back into the shadows.

"Alice! " Gerda shouted. "Why are you even here? You're the Keeper of Fate. You *know* it was Julian's fate to conquer this dungeon, and yet here you are, standing in the way of his destiny."

"You're one to talk," Alice shot back.

"But I thought this was what you cared about?" Gerda waved a hand around them. "Isn't that why you were so angry at my intervention? Because I was changing things?"

"I'm *angry* because everything is *wrong* now." Alice snapped. "And if I can't right it, I can at least go after the person responsible."

Julian stood in front of Gerda. "Over my dead body."

"As you wish."

CHAPTER 99

A Vow Given. A Vow Broken

Gerda

A Few Minutes Ago

Julian wasn't reading the chat logs, or he would've seen my messages.

I tried again anyway.

[Julian, we need to get to the dungeon core.]

Tully lifted his head from where he was draped over a bunch of ice. He didn't look comfortable. The paladin sent,

[I tried. Distract her again; see if you can get her to attack you.]

John added his own,

[Still looking.]

"Alice!" I shouted. The celestial whipped around to face me, and I asked what was already on my mind. "Why are you even *here*? You're the Keeper of Fate. You *know* it was Julian's fate to conquer this dungeon, and yet here you are, standing in the way of his destiny."

"You're one to talk," Alice shot back. She signaled to the giant, who climbed onto the ice spears and started running toward us. From the corner of my eye, I saw Tully rise up to meet him—war hammer versus sword.

"But I thought this was what you cared about?" I waved a hand around us. "Isn't that why you were so angry at my intervention? Because I was changing things?"

"I'm *angry* because everything is *wrong* now," Alice snapped. "And if I can't right it, I can at least go after the person responsible."

Julian stood in front of me. "Over my dead body."

"As you wish." Alice flew up into the air and pointed at Julian. "By the Will of the Eternal Rest, [Void Arrow]."

Not wanting to damage his new shield, Julian stepped aside. The [Void Arrow] struck the platform and vanished.

"Julian." I stopped bothering to conceal our conversation. Pram helped by shooting an [Ice Arrow] at Alice, forcing the airborne celestial to duck. He quickly followed it up with the larger [Ice Spear].

"Go capture the dungeon," I told my duke of the North.

He obviously disagreed with my decision. "But then she could escape—"

"You forget, we aren't actually here to fight Alice," I reminded him. "You're here to touch that dungeon core; she's just a bonus prize."

"You can't be serious? She's literally out to get you," Julian asked quietly.

John's shadow moved out of the ice rubble and stopped beside us. Jeffry appeared, unalive, and I bent down to give the half elf a much needed Resurrect potion.

"Did we win?" Jeffry coughed, clearing gunk from his throat.

"No," Julian replied, offering his hand. Meanwhile, Tully was neck and neck with the giant, and Alice was swooping in to attack him as well.

Considering, I pulled out a vial of belladonna poison and threw it at the beastfolk standing beside the dungeon core. It sailed through the air but was shot down by a claw strike from the same beastfolk.

"Jeffry. Give Julian the Eye of Effeldor," I ordered.

Jeffry clutched at his pendant for dear life.

"He'll give it back," I said, feeling a little absurd that I had to make the reassurance, but apparently I did, because Jeffry struggled with himself to take it off even then.

Julian took the brooch. "Are you sure?"

"Yep." I shooed him away. "You focus on the dungeon core, and we'll focus on finding Visha."

[Still looking.]

One of John's shadows must have overheard us.

Julian leaned forward and kissed me. We broke apart as a poison-tipped dagger sailed between us.

Alice was standing on an ice spear. She stared at Jeffry. "Why won't you all just *stay dead*? Must I [Sever Fate] all of you?!"

"I'll be right back. Don't die in the meantime," Julian told me, activating his new wings and leaping into the air. He spared no time, darting straight for the dungeon core as fast as he could.

"Wait!" Alice shouted.

The beastfolk stepped forward to intercept Julian, changing into a half-leopard, half-folk warrior, claws out.

Their roles weren't evenly matched. Julian was a high-defense, sword-and-board tank, and the beastfolk was a melee fighter. Julian put all his strength behind his shield and *pushed*, taking a claw to the face but managing to throw the beastfolk woman. She blew through the terrain and landed against the cavern wall to the far right of the dungeon core.

He dropped his sword and reached for the orb.

A trap went off, exploding shards of poison-tipped mithril. Julian took the attack head-on, sliding back three feet and dropping to one knee. He could've probably defended against one or two shards of poison attacks . . . but not the ten that blasted into him.

At the same instant, Alice portaled on top of him, a beautiful smile on her face. "Got you."

Julian slumped forward, asleep and dying.

When he was beside me, it seemed like there was no way we could lose. A certainty that with Julian, everything would turn out fine. I knew his dedication, how hard he'd trained to be here. I knew that despite everything I'd done to alter the course of his fate . . . it was still his fate.

But I was wrong.

And even though we outnumbered Alice, watching her stand over the love of my life finally broke me.

"Alice!" I shrieked, jumping down from the platform and sprinting toward them. Jeffry tried to grab me, but I evaded. The precariously icy terrain made it difficult, but my Dexterity kept me going. At the very least, I could offer to trade myself; I was the one she actually wanted. "Wait! I surrender!"

"You think I *trust* you?" The celestial pulled out her short sword and stabbed it downward . . . into the shadow *beneath* Julian. Right between his arm and his chest.

John let out a strangled cry, appearing against the left wall where Visha was still buried. He had a gaping hole in his side and was fumbling for a potion. Alice let go of the hilt of the sword, which stayed upright.

"You can't kill him, Alice!" I yelled, now halfway across the cavern. I was trying to reason with the celestial even as I knew that she didn't care. "He has to defeat this dungeon. You know he does! Fate—"

"No. He doesn't," the celestial said. She shifted her head to dodge a sword-aura strike from Jeffry. Alice laughed. "You have the audacity to say that *I'm* not allowed to change fate? When she's already *abandoned me?*"

I was almost there.

"He will *never* defeat this dungeon," Alice decided, a soft smile lighting up her face. "And if I take him with me, *you'll* be the one chasing *me* for a change." She reached up for the dungeon core, hesitated for the barest second, and then touched it.

Divine magic swirled around her. Unlike a mortal's colored mana, the motes of shifting rainbow light looked like experience points; it overwhelmed the celestial. She screamed and sank to her knees at the foot of the pedestal.

A divine voice resounded in the cavern, burning into the soul of everyone who heard it. My own knees gave out only a few steps from reaching Julian.

"*A vow given. A vow broken,*" Fate spoke into the air. It was nostalgic: familiar and yet unknown. It filled my body with purpose, and it promised the future. Like hope, but there was no uncertainty.

There was only Fate.

"*I swear by Fate that I will end you . . .*" A ghost of Alice's own voice echoed around the chamber beneath the goddess's words. "*I will end you and stop at nothing to right destiny . . .*"

A circle of that shimmering crystal light wrapped around the celestial, lifting her a few feet off the ground.

"*Alice Smith, Keeper of Fate, Chosen of Mine.*" Fate's voice hitched with the slightest emotion; something deeper than her accusations and stern punishment.

It was sadness. Regret. A deep, unending sorrow.

"*You have sworn by my name, and you have betrayed that vow,*" Fate continued. A firm resolve shook reality around us. I fought the pressure, but my body was weak against the force even as my mind kept some clarity.

[Mental Resistance] for the win. Again.

"*By the Rule of the Gods, I hereby strip you of my touch. You are forever banned of My Temple, and you are never to know the weave again. Be glad of my mercy, daughter of my heart.*"

Alice slowly lowered to the floor as the goddess withdrew her presence from the room.

But before she was entirely gone, I felt a kiss brush against my cheek, and a small secret whisper in my ear. "*Thank you . . . and I am sorry.*"

[Status ailment: **Sever Fate** has been undone.]

"Fate!" The celestial was crying and shouting at the ceiling. "Come back! You can't do this!"

Which was when Julian, sword in hand, lunged up from the floor and stabbed Alice through the heart.

CHAPTER 100

You Have Defeated Forgotten Frost Dungeon

Julian

Something brushed Julian's cheek, and he was suddenly wide awake, a surge of adrenaline rushing through him. His body was on fire, his injuries burning, and he was barely alive.

Alice stood over him, saying something. There was a ringing in his ear, and everything moved in slow motion.

With the last of his strength, Julian grabbed the sword beside him and lunged forward.

[You have **Died.**]
[You have been **Resurrected.** Health 1274/1274. Mana 500/500.]

The next time Julian opened his eyes, he saw the most beautiful troll in the world looking down at him; she was brushing his hair out of his face. He reached up, putting his hand over hers and turning it to kiss her wrist.

The relaxed atmosphere around him let him guess, "We won."

"Yes." Gerda nodded and smiled. "Jeffry manacled everyone, and John's looking for Visha. Everyone else is ready to go."

Julian grunted and sat up to assess the situation. Jeffry and Tully had the three other adventurers tied together and manacled. Two were still unalive, yet manacled anyway. Pram stood to the side with Alice, who had a bag over her head. It was a cloth grocer bag printed with a familiar unicorn pattern.

"Why—"

Gerda knew what Julian was asking before he said it. "She's unalive. But I don't have extra [Mental Resistance] scrolls, so we're being *extra* cautious."

He nodded. "The dungeon core?"

"It's still waiting." She pointed over her shoulder, where the orb was floating over the pedestal with its threatening red swirls. She smiled at him. "It looks like you get to fulfill your fate, after all: you defeated a dungeon boss *and* get to conquer the dungeon core."

Julian choked at her outrageous joke at Alice's expense, replying, "I don't know, a dungeon boss usually comes with more experience points."

[Found her!]

John's message arrived as his shadow brought Visha out. Tully looked like he was at war with himself, looking at the elf and back three times in quick succession. John poured a Resurrect potion on Visha as Tully dragged a hand down his face in frustration before handing his enchanted rope over to Jeffry and walking forward to be there when she woke up.

The rogue wasn't a fool; he stepped back for Tully.

Visha was the most dexterous and fast recovering of the group. She was on her feet in an instant, battle stance ready.

"We won," Tully told her. Simple and straightforward. "It's over."

Visha looked up at the paladin in frustration and anger. "I missed everything?!"

"Not *everything*." Tully smiled softly at the elf, thrusting a thumb toward Julian.

That was his cue. Julian waved a hand to store his sword and shield, then stood with his troll.

It was only a step to the dungeon core.

Gerda's hand found his, and he squeezed it once before he reached up and touched the orb.

[You have defeated **Forgotten Frost Dungeon**. Would you like to **Conquer** the **Dungeon Core**? Yes/No]

Julian selected *Yes*. The pedestal sank into the floor, turning into an exit platform beneath their feet.

[You have received the Unique Title option: **Dungeon Conqueror**.]

Jeffry made a choking sound when he saw the overflowing treasure chest appear, and was already pulling out a scroll to write down the contents so it could be divided later.

"Congrats," Gerda whispered. Julian couldn't describe how he felt. It should have been fulfilling or been a cause for celebration . . .

After his father's death, he'd felt like his own life had ended. Like he couldn't be himself anymore, he had to be something more. Something stronger. Someone powerful enough to take over his father's shoes. While throwing himself into leveling up, the North had grown more and more dangerous until he'd turned his drive and purpose to defeating it. He didn't need to reach level ninety . . . he just needed to protect his home. A goal he could actually touch and taste.

A goal that he'd finally realized.

And it only felt like his life was ending all over again.

It was nearing lunch hour when they popped out onto the dungeon entry platform.

"I can't *wait* to get home." Tully turned his face to the sun and stretched.

"You still have two months of community service left," Visha pointed out.

"Don't remind me." The paladin groaned.

Gerda was standing there, staring at the northern bridge, her hands clenched at her side.

"We ready to go?" Jeffry asked, a bright smile on the half elf's face.

"Actually," Julian stated, "I'm sending you ahead. Gerda and I . . . we have some things to settle first." He had a portal scroll ready to get himself back home . . . and Gerda knew that.

She wasn't going to leave before he finished his dungeon . . . and he wasn't going to leave until she'd crossed her bridge.

Pram walked over and put a hand on Julian's shoulder. "Good luck, my friend. I hope she says yes."

Julian stiffened as Gerda coughed.

"*Goodbye,* everyone." She waved once then portaled them all to the Coral Palace in North Sumbria.

Julian walked up behind his troll and wrapped his arms around her. He pressed his face into her hair and squeezed once.

They stood there for a long time.

"Do you really need to go?" he eventually whispered in her ear.

She caressed his cheek, and a single tear rolled down hers. She whispered, "I need to *know*."

"And you can't come back?"

Gerda hesitated, "I don't know . . ."

He handed her a folded-up note. "Here."

She took it, then pulled off her storage ring and handed it over. Taking a step back, Julian let her go.

Gerda drew a steadying breath. She looked back at him with a tight smile that didn't reach her eyes. "I'm ready."

And then, his bridge troll crossed the bridge and disappeared.

CHAPTER 101

Do I Have to Leave?

Gerda

Five years.

Five years of living alone in a world of magic and monsters, not knowing why I was here, *how* I was here . . .

Five years of being *green*.

It wasn't all bad. Being green.

In fact, I kind of loved it. I *loved* being Gerda. I loved my life and my home and my new world.

But a burning question ate at me. *Could* I go back?

Would I go back?

If only for a day.

[Perk: **World Bridge**. Establish a permanent link to any bridge you cross, even those not under your control. You may travel to that bridge as if it were under your control. All previous **+Troll Magic [Dimension]** bridges under your control are included in **World Bridge**.

Bonus Abilities Available:

1: If you control all bridges in a Domain, gain double experience for bridges in that Domain. Current Domains Unlocked: Dark Enchanted Forest.

2: If you control a bridge in all Domains, mana cost to travel between Domains is halved. Current Domains Unlocked: Dark Enchanted Forest, Drendil, Peldeep, Servalt, North Sumbria, Sumbria.

3: If you control the furthest bridges at the four corners of Valaria, unlock the ability to travel between any bridge you

have ever crossed, even before obtaining **World Bridge**. This power can pass through the Void into alternate and subspaces for additional mana cost. Current Bridges: South: Faren's Arch in Sumbria; West: Daffolyn Bridge in Peldeep; East: Sea-to-Sky Bridge in Servalt; North: Forgotten Frost Bridge in Northern Ice Fields.
4: If you control all bridges in Valaria, unlock Hidden Domain: Valarian Royal Palace. **World Bridge** Perk upgrade: Empress of All Bridges. Unlock Title: Empress of Valaria.]

[You have unlocked **World Bridge** bonus ability. You may now travel to any bridge you have ever crossed.]

I closed my eyes for a second, not trusting what I would see, but when I searched the list of available bridges I could teleport to . . . there they were.

Bridges remembered from another life. Another time.

A time before I was Gerda the Bridge Troll . . . And I noticed with a sad smile that there was also a bridge from Gerda's old village.

I hesitated, wanting to look back at least once, but I knew that if I saw Julian standing there, I would lose the nerve.

[You have selected **Lions Gate Bridge**. Mana Cost 1000.]

Suddenly, I was walking through portal space . . . but not as I was familiar with it. Crossing a dimensional bridge in Valaria was over in the time it took to blink: one step, a rush, and then it was over.

Traveling between worlds wasn't fast; it was harrowing. Each step felt like my feet were going to fall out from underneath me. There was a lurch in my stomach, my mind reeling against a momentum that threatened to make me vomit. I could feel the "bridge" beneath my feet, but I couldn't see it.

I took ten steps that lasted an eternity. All in Void space.

Then suddenly, there was a barrier, a translucent film where this bridge ended and *another* began, and I *knew* with absolute certainty that I'd reached the edge of this world and was going to cross into another.

I opened my eyes, only knowing they were open because I was met with another prompt.

[Thank you for playing ***Dungeon Delves and Debutantes***. Would you like to exit the game? Yes/No]

I stared at it. I couldn't answer.

Julian's note was still in my hands. I couldn't even read it in the darkness of the Void.

"*Why are you crying?*" a familiar voice whispered into my ear. It passed through me like a gentle gong. The sound lingered, like a hum in my bones.

"Fate?" I asked.

"*I opened this path for you; I thought you would be happy?*" the goddess said.

The world shifted, and I could *see*. I was standing on her mana: hundreds of thousands of small motes of divine magic that stretched behind and in front of me. The goddess was made of pure mana, the outline of a tall figure, effeminate and ethereal.

"Why did you bring me here?" I asked, knowing it was rude to answer a question with a question but doing so anyway. "*Was it you?*"

"*I asked Luck to find me a soul who could change this world for me. Someone who knew what would happen here and would have the will to change it.*" Fate bent down and her gentle hand wiped away one of my tears. "*She found you.*"

"Then why did you ignore me? *I went to your temple!* You could have—" I was yelling at a goddess, but she simply shook her head.

"*I could not appear and risk drawing attention to you,*" she explained. "*You needed to be truly a part of this world before my siblings noticed you . . . or they might have removed you.*"

"So I get dragged here, do all the work fixing the weave, save everyone—and then what? I get kicked out?" My heart pounded against my chest as anger laced my words. "Did I even *need* to unlock this stupid bonus ability? Or were you just going to send me back anyway?"

"*I did nothing. You chose to come here,*" Fate reminded me gently.

"Does choice even matter when there is Fate?" I challenged.

"*Do not let Luck catch you speaking this way,*" Fate chided. "*And who are you to say that, Madame Potts!*"

She was being awfully forgiving for an all-powerful goddess. The rage inside me dimmed into fear, resentment . . . and grief.

"Do I have to leave?" The words escaped me, even though I didn't want to hear the answer.

"*No, my sweet soul.*" Fate held my shoulders and directed me back to the system prompt. "*It is your choice. You may, of course, choose to stay in Valaria. But—*" I looked up at the goddess. "*I cannot leave a gate between worlds open.*" Fate let go and took a step back. "*Whatever you choose, I must close the way.*"

"I understand," I said. I knew what I was going to choose.

"*Then I will leave you to decide on your own. But first—*" Her divine mana wrapped around my hands, and the words in Julian's letter were made clear to me.

I love you, Miss Gerda Jones

Fate's divine energy fell back into the Void. As it did, I thought I saw the shifting outline of others in the endless expanse.

I glanced at the prompt.

And made my choice.

CHAPTER 102

He Waited

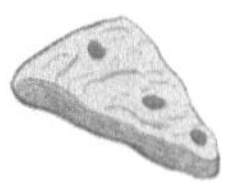

Julian

Julian walked to the end of the bridge, following Gerda's footsteps exactly with his [Tracking] skill.

He stopped where she'd disappeared. There was a faint smell of pine trees. Or maybe it was his imagination clinging to the last time he'd held her.

Knowing it would be the last time made it hard to breathe, so he turned his mind elsewhere.

He sat down on the bridge and waited.

He waited as the sun crossed the western horizon.

He waited while the cold sea wind cut at his face and pulled at his hair.

He waited until the first star appeared overhead. The North Star.

He waited . . . and still, she was gone.

When she'd walked away, he hadn't had the heart to say goodbye. He didn't want to hear it, and he didn't want to say it. He couldn't even write it in a letter. The greatest gift she could have left behind was her last, "I'm ready."

Because he wasn't ready to live without her . . . not yet. But knowing that *she* was ready made it almost bearable.

He waited and he closed his eyes and he lied to himself.

He wasn't waiting for her. He was just waiting for this feeling to pass.

"Julian?" Arms wrapped around him from behind, and he broke.

"You came back." He reached up and pulled her around and into his lap, burying his face into her hair so she couldn't see his eyes.

"I did."

Her hands were warm..

"Julian?"

"Hm?"

"I love you too."

"I know." He smiled.

"Your armor is poking me, and you're freezing cold," she stated matter-of-factly.

"Sorry." He pulled back and kissed her cheek. "Shall we?"

She smiled and portaled them away.

"I don't know how I feel about this . . ." Julian held Gerda's hand as Their Royal Highness positively vibrated in excitement at the gift of a certain Guild Mistress.

The second word had traveled that Alice had been defeated and the Blackfog spies were no more, a very strong but polite request had come from Peldeep regarding the celestial's capture. And since Calisto was busy planning an even *bigger* Fall Ball to celebrate the return of her prodigal son, she'd been all too willing to move the celestial elsewhere.

Which Gerda had kindly volunteered to arrange.

It had taken the better part of ten minutes between landing in Peldeep, meeting Knight Commander Bastian, and being escorted to the Emerald Palace. Their other party members were being met with a lavish welcome in a palace room with the best food, drink, and a pile of gold each. The reward for taking down Alice was generous, and that was the only reason John was here instead of already enjoying his early retirement.

Julian and Gerda were the only ones permitted to go into Rowen's inner palace to hand over the celestial herself.

"She already escaped *your* underground security," the troll pointed out. "And you have to admit, Rowen has probably suffered the most by her hands. They should have the right to her sentence."

He would've argued, but she was correct. They were still repairing sections of the burnt down palace from the celestial's attack at the Apple Blossom Festival—though it looked like it was almost done.

"Thank you, both of you." Rowen swept over to take up Gerda's hands. "I can finally sleep in peace again, knowing this is finally over."

"You're welcome," Gerda said.

"As long as it *is* over," Julian grumbled.

"Oh, *it is*." The fox smiled, showing all of their teeth. They released Gerda's hands and snapped a finger. Knight Commander Bastian stepped forward with a medium-size wooden box in hand. It was short but wide enough to fit in the drakin's arms. "And now, my friends, since you've brought me what I most desired, I've prepared a few thank you gifts!"

"Oh?" Gerda's excitement was palpable, though Julian hesitated, uncertain what the fox had up their sleeves.

Bastian offered the box to Gerda.

"Open it!" Rowen urged.

She unhooked the latch and peeked inside. And then she gasped.

"Is that GoldLeaf Grand? And nettle from Moondew Meadow? Wait! *Powdered Markleberry!*" His troll was beside herself, beaming up at the fox with shining eyes over a case of the rarest teas on the continent. "Your Highness, this is . . . I don't know what to say!"

"Say you like it," Rowen instructed.

Gerda closed the box with care then took it into her arms lovingly. "I *love* it."

"Good." The fox nodded before raising an eyebrow at Julian. "Now, *am I* to assume that you will finally be stepping up as the grand duke of North Sumbria and letting your mother retire?"

"That is the plan," Julian admitted. His mother was officially announcing it at the Fall Ball, which was only three weeks away.

"Then I think it's time I gave you this."

Bastian brought forward a silver tray with a white silk cloth draped over the gift. Julian's hands were shaking when he lifted his father's ducal coronet, one he'd only seen in portraits.

It was fashioned into bimbleberry leaves shaped from burnished orichalcum, and in the center of each leaf was a mithril snowflake that shone from the small moonstones imbedded on each point.

"How . . . ?"

"I visited your father before the last stand . . . Before he passed," Rowen explained softly. The fox reached out and put a hand on his shoulder. "And I want you to know, he would be proud of you, Julian."

The slip of formal title only made the words hit harder.

"Does my mother know you had this?" Julian asked, ignoring the ache in his chest that threatened to bring back all of his long-forgotten grief.

"She knows I've kept safe *many* things for you father." Rowen smiled. "Things he gave me before his final confrontation with Sumbria."

"Like what?"

Rowen listed on their fingers.

"Treasure enough to cover North Sumbria's budget for a year in the case of financial troubles, anniversary presents for your mother—he had *a hundred* years of presents prepared, can you imagine?" Rowen shook their head, amused. Then continued, "He gave me the amulet you are wearing now, for your coming of age. I also have wedding presents—Julia already has hers—and presents for your children, should you have them."

"But . . . *why?*" He didn't understand why his father hadn't just left everything to him from the get-go; why he'd needed to leave it with someone from another kingdom altogether.

"It was a terrible battle, but he was fighting for you and your future . . ." Their smile slipped. "A future he didn't know if he was going to get to see. So he wanted *someone* to remind his family that he loved them—that he loved *you*. That he wanted to be there for you, all throughout your life . . . even if he never came home."

The words brought Julian to tears more than the gifts. Gerda put a hand on his arm, reassuring. It steadied him.

Rowen eyed the pair of them. "There is one more thing."

Julian shot the fox a look; he didn't think he could handle any more surprises today. "Oh?"

Another tray appeared in Rowen's hand.

"Forgive me, I know I *shouldn't* have. But—" They pulled off the cover and revealed a smaller matching circlet to Julian's, but with nettle frame leaves to mount the snowflakes and moonstones. "I've had a matching coronet prepared specially for *you*, Miss Gerda."

CHAPTER 103

Keeper of Fate

Gerda

A Week Later

The weather was turning, and the trees of the Dark Enchanted Forest were starting to change into their autumn colors. The first few leaves had fallen that morning, floating in the moat below my door.

My kitchen window looked out over the moat of the Black Fortress. I'd moved it here when I invited my Dark Lady, Queen Henrietta of Nilheim, over for lunch.

Henrietta gasped. "Is that . . . ?"

"Mm-hmm." I brought over two cups of warm unigoat milk mixed with the powdered markleberry mix. "Hot chocolate."

She eyed the drink with fervor, her excitement palpable. "You mentioned it in your cookbook."

"If you can figure out a way to make markleberry powder without pixie magic, I expect you to share," I informed the woman.

Henrietta laughed and solemnly swore to do so.

"Now!" I said, pushing a cup toward the queen. "Before I add the toppings, you should taste it as it is."

She took a sip and made an appreciative hum. "It's so rich! And so different from the tea. I love it."

As much as markleberry had a chocolaty flavor, the berry was commonly processed into jams and jellies and added to hot water. It made a weaker, watery chocolate jelly tea that was nothing like the creamy delicacy I was currently holding in my hand.

I lifted my own cup and breathed deeply, smelling the familiar scent. The nostalgia alone almost made me cry.

"Wait until you try it with whipped cream and sprinkles."

I pulled out a bowl of each, homemade.

The next morning was still dark on the horizon when my eyes shot open; I was wide awake, with a restless energy that wouldn't settle.

I checked my character sheet.

My domain was safe, and my [Sense Danger] was silent.

I was just *awake*.

There was no chance of falling back asleep, so I decided to treat myself to a long, luxurious bubble bath. Julian mumbled unhappy noises when I lifted the blankets to escape, but he went back to sleep.

The half elf had practically moved in, and I would pick him up from the palace every day after work. True to his word, Julian was taking over for his mother. It was all-consuming work, learning the ins and outs of ruling North Sumbria, but he was managing well.

For me, my job had only gotten *easier* after hiring a bridge brigade. I came out for important travelers or elite making their way through the Dark Enchanted Forest, but otherwise passed along new riddles for my bridge minions to use every week.

I had *no idea* how things were going to work if I decided to accept the coronet and rule North Sumbria with Julian. Keith would never allow me to continue to control all of his major highways as the ruler of a foreign nation, and I wouldn't expect him to.

Maybe it was time I considered conquering all the bridges in North Sumbria?

The bubble bath was heavenly, and Julian even managed to join me for a bit before it was time to get ready and grab breakfast. I'd made a fresh citrus loaf with a drizzled sugar glaze the night before, and I couldn't wait to enjoy a bite.

"Do you have any exciting plans for today?" I asked when we sat down at the kitchen table. It had become a habit to check each other's schedule so I knew when I should come get him. We were planning a bridge in the west garden that I could move my front door to for future use, but in the meantime this was working for us.

"The same old," he let me know. "Though Lord Johnathon just bought a new manor, and I think we should send over a gift. Do you want to visit the market with me tonight?"

It took me a second to process that he was talking about John the rogue. "Absolutely. Actually, let me check to make sure we don't have any surprises."

This had also become a habit. Julian would stay with me while I checked on my daily notifications, and then we would discuss.

There was an unexpected prompt waiting for me.

[**Oracle:** You are witness to the strings of Fate and her weave. The story unfolds, and the Chosen of each deity mark the way.
You have found 12/12 Chosen.
Impending Scenarios: 1/12 Chosen.
Keeper of Fate - A New Beginning
Timeline access granted.
All Scenarios within Valaria available.
Oracle timeline: 4 mins 30 seconds.
Please select Chosen.]

My oracle restrictions had been lifted. I would have to ask Fate what that meant, but that could wait until later. I was more interested in whomever had taken over for Alice as Fate's new chosen.

My mana flared as swirls of teal light flooded my vision.

"It is an honor that Nilheim should welcome you, Keeper of Fate. I am Lady Moira." *An elf priestess smiled warmly as she welcomed me into the Saren Sanctum. "The Dark Lord has always been a follower of Fate, and I'm sure he'll be so pleased to hear the goddess has announced that you are her new chosen. Please, come this way."*

I decided to hold my tongue and simply nod, knowing that King Keith was going to be anything but pleased by my new title . . . and I wasn't too thrilled myself. It would have been polite of Fate to at least ask me before she announced her prophecy in every temple across Valaria. Instead, she'd done it before I had breakfast.

The Saren Sanctum was as beautiful as I remembered it. Tall silver pillars lined both sides, and Fate's statue stood twenty feet tall at the front of the room. There were two other priests standing at the goddess's feet, waiting for us, but the place was otherwise empty.

"Welcome, Keeper of Fate." The older priest, a lizardkin, bowed. "We are so happy you are here. I am Monk Monlith."

"Welcome, Keeper of Fate. I am Novice Venlith." The younger priest, a lizardkin barely twenty, also gave a courtesy bow. His eyes were shining when he said, "And may I say, it is such an honor to meet you, Madame Potts."

CHAPTER 104

Happily Ever After

Julian

The Fall Ball was in full swing, and Julian's mother had outdone herself, as usual.

The entire ceiling had been converted into an autumn forest canopy, and floating lights drifted like fireflies in the foliage.

There had been a grand to-do announcing Julian's position at the start of the evening before he'd opened the floor by dancing with Gerda. Then they'd stood around for a great many congratulations.

Now, the more relaxed part of the evening was starting. A giant fountain that spouted apple cider had been brought out, along with tables of finger food. Golden leaves made out of real gold littered every table.

"Grand Duke Julian." The Dark Lord tilted his glass of cider in welcome when Julian joined him near a standing table.

"King Keith," Julian replied, tilting his own glass.

"I see your wife is distracting my wife." The Dark Lord looked over at where Gerda and Henrietta were laughing and pretending to drink.

After a prophecy from that morning, Gerda had let him know that they shouldn't eat the floofpoof pie or drink the cider. She couldn't be sure if it was their glass or the fountain itself that was poisoned, so his troll would routinely walk over and stick her unicorn horn into the party cider, just in case.

Henrietta thought it was great fun, and was now going with her to act as an accomplice.

Julian grinned. "She's not my wife."

Yet.

It was too soon to ask, but he was already having the rings forged for the day he was ready. They weren't in a rush.

"Well, let me know when you have the good news." King Keith downed his own cider, not caring if it was poisoned or not. "I've got the paperwork all drawn up for her to retire from the Dark Horde, release her bridges, and emigrate far, far away."

"We share a border; it's not that far," Julian pointed out. "Ah, here they come."

"Keith!" Henrietta grabbed the Dark Lord by the hand and pointed to the opposite end of the hall. "Chloe's back!"

"Then we should go and see her." Keith's face softened into a warm smile for his wife, and he let her drag him away.

Gerda grinned after them. "Ah, young love. Oh, speaking of . . ." His troll stuck out her foot and tripped a man with a pencil mustache as he was walking by. The man made a strange noise as he fell right into the awaiting arms of a surprised elf woman.

Gerda turned her back on the couple as if she weren't responsible and took a fake sip of her cider. "How was your talk with King Keith?"

"Informative." Julian kept an eye on the man with the pencil mustache as he found his feet and looked around for the cause of his tumble. His eyes lingered half a second on Gerda's back, but then he ran a hand through his sideswept hair and set about apologizing to the woman who had caught him; the elf, for her part, told the man that he could make amends with a dance.

He hesitated, Julian could tell, but he let the elf pull him onto the dance floor.

"Oh?" Gerda asked, drawing Julian's attention back to her.

"King Keith wanted to know when you were moving to North Sumbria," Julian told her, and she froze. Then, her white freckles flushed a little pink as she looked away, her eyes following the man and the elf as they swirled together up the hall.

"Soon, I imagine."

"I guess that's good for me to know as well," Julian teased. He nodded at the dancing pair. "They look like they're having fun."

"I thought so too," she agreed. "They make an excellent couple."

"Ah." He reached his arm around her waist and pulled her close. "Is that why you tripped him?"

"That, and he poisoned the cider," Gerda whispered.

"Help!" A shrill voice resounded across the hall. "Oh, help! My love has been poisoned!"

Julian looked over to see a beastfolk frothing at the mouth, his wife crying as she held him. It was Lord Jarl of Canters and his wife, Josephine.

"Should we—" Julian started when General Visha swooped in and offered the couple the appropriate antidote.

"It's fine." Gerda waited until Visha had finished helping the guests before waving her over.

"Your Grace, Miss Gerda." Visha gave a proper salute. "I hope your evening is going well."

"The man with the pencil mustache poisoned the cider. If you wait by the door to the restrooms, you can catch him," Gerda informed the general.

Visha didn't look to Julian for confirmation, trusting the troll completely. "Thank you. I'll handle it."

Then the general was off.

"Now that that's done," Julian leaned down and whispered into her ear, "what do you say we slip away?"

"Leave the ball *before* midnight?" Gerda asked in mock horror that turned into an endearing smile. "You know me so well."

And so, Gerda the Bridge Troll portaled away with the grand duke of the North, back to her home under the bridge, where they shared a loving kiss and went to bed early, and they lived Happily Ever After.

Epilogue

The notification was from a long, long time ago.

[Quest Complete: Survive Season Three of Dungeon Delves and Debutantes]

Welcome to the World of Valaria, an Open World Battle Otome RPG for the ages.
79% Scenarios Complete
67% Map Explored
40% Hidden Treasures Found
51% Characters Found

[Our Heroine has survived the trials and tribulations that threatened the Dark Enchanted Forest, and found her own Happily Ever After.]

[We hope you enjoyed, Dungeon Delves and Debutantes]

"But Mama!" A small green hand squeezed her mother's. "That's not the end of the story. *I'm* not there yet."

"Tilly, you goose—*none* of us were born yet." Princess Azalea poked the troll on the arm.

Nealan sat quietly in the back, tapping his finger in a steady beat against his fur. His younger sister Tamora was beaming down at everyone with delight. The giantess declared, "We can just make our own stories!"

"And Nealan can turn them into songs!" Tilly jumped up, ready to start on her adventure right away.

Tilly's mother cut them off, "That will have to wait until *after* lunch."

There was a collective, "Awww."

The sentiment changed when they found out that the Dark Lady was cooking.

Yes, the next adventure could wait until after a snack.

About the Author

Mystic Neptune was born and raised on an island surrounded by temperate rainforests, lakes, mountains, and endless ocean. She started writing books when she was twelve, and by the age of fourteen she'd written her first novel. It was about an elven space princess whose evil stepmother messed up her trans-dimensional portal trip to university and sent her to a war-torn restricted universe instead. It was very cheesy, and the ultimately-nine-book series was lost forever on the family PC (Windows 95, anyone?) that died a very final death the summer she was sixteen.

By then, Mystic was living with her very sick single mother and her little brother, and working nights to help pay the bills. There was a little time to read during her school breaks, but not for much else—and no money to replace the home computer. So she filled notebooks with the beginnings of stories and eventually got a laptop in college. Around that time, she also met the love of her life, who read just as much as she did, and they got married shortly after a terrible accident befell her . . .

One day when Mystic was walking to the mall, an iron fence from a construction site fell on her. She suffered from amnesia so bad that she had to relearn English and re-meet all her friends and family. She even walked past her mother in the street and didn't recognize her. But it's OK! She got better!

Once she could read again, Mystic got into isekai because she was tired of picking up books only to remember she'd already finished them. Isekai was new at the time, so she didn't need to worry that her silly memory would come back halfway through a story and spoil the ending. Mystic enjoys reading light novels, webnovels, LitRPG, gamelit, and fantasy. She also loves middle grade and YA books. Her favorite authors/heroes are Patricia C. Wrede, Tamora Pierce, and Diana Wynne Jones.

In Mystic's spare time, she writes and does edit-swap date nights with her husband, Jolly Jupiter. O he of famed dwarven comedy! She also runs after her daughter, Phoebe Vaara. Phoebe is named after Saturn's moon, and Vaara means Danger in Finnish and Stranger in Greek. Phoebe is a rockstar social diva toddler who hikes mountains and has more friends than both her parents combined, so it fits.

Mystic is probably writing right now.

RESPAWN YOUR CURIOSITY

follow us on our socials

podiumentertainment.com

@podiumentertainment

/podiumentertainment

@podium_ent

@podiumentertainment

www.ingramcontent.com/pod-product-compliance
Lightning Source LLC
Chambersburg PA
CBHW030922120726
47906CB00002B/441